By Fortitude and Prudence

ALICE BONTHRON

DEDICATION

To Drew

Forever Is As Far As I'll Go

ACKNOWLEDGMENTS

This book would never have come to life without the critiques, advice and encouragement of some very talented writers. Thank you to my good friend Julie Rief and my Workshop Group – Mary Blain, Annette Morgan, Laurie Claypool, Sara Thorn and Bernie.

Special thanks to Barbara Rogan, author of *A Dangerous Fiction* and one of my favorite mystery writers, who also happens to be a fantastic teacher. Without her, the Workshop Group would never have come into being.

Finally, a very special thanks to Nikki Coffman for the punctuation and spelling edits.

CHAPTER 1

Baltimore, Maryland – 1874

"Daniel, I just received a note from Uncle Frank asking me if…" Midway across her husband's study, Rasheen Langston dropped the hand that had been waving the letter to her side. Her fingers curled tightly around the paper, crinkling it. "I'm sorry. I didn't realize you had a visitor."

A spasm of irritation crossed her husband's face as he slid his chair back from the large mahogany desk, stood and motioned toward her with a long-fingered hand.

"Mr. Hilliard, allow me to introduce my wife."

The portly visitor grasped his chair arms as he struggled to push himself into a standing position, and then gave an exaggerated bow that almost sent his backside falling onto Daniel's desk.

Rasheen bit her lower lip to keep from smiling and was about to politely excuse herself when she noticed the gift box sitting on the edge of Daniel's desk with the paper weight in the shape of a steam engine that rested next to it.

Mr. Hilliard must be a representative of the railroad come to seek Daniel as an investor. "Is that a replica of the Lafayette?" The Lafayette was one of the first steam engines with a horizontal boiler that the Baltimore and Ohio railroad had purchased back in the late 1830s. Her grandfather had spoken of it during his lifetime.

Speaking as if she weren't even in the room, Mr. Hilliard turned away from her toward her husband. "Bless their hearts, the dear little things. Isn't it wonderful how they try to please us by showing an interest in things of which they have no understanding?"

Her face burned in anger. "But it is the Lafayette; is it not?"

"Mr. Hilliard doesn't have time for explanations right now." Daniel gestured toward the door, and gave her a thin-lipped smile that set her teeth on edge.

She held her tongue; but slammed the door behind her as she exited the room.

*****

Rasheen stared at the small silver-framed wedding picture on the parlor mantle. Though it was shaded in brown and black, she knew the coloring of the happy couple. The groom's eyes were hazel hued, with ash blond hair and fair skin that bordered on pale. The bride's eyes were dark, as was her hair. The groom wore a happy smile, as did his bride.

Rasheen couldn't remember the last time they had smiled at one another like that – genuinely happy just to be together. She looked at the man in the picture with the premature receding hairline, and thought she knew no more of his hopes and dreams now than she did then. Oh, she knew what shades and styles he preferred her to wear, how he expected her to behave in his presence and in his absence. She knew he was a stickler for punctuality, and that he considered her a social necessity, but not a particularly valuable asset to his life. Other than those sobering realizations, she knew nothing of the man whose life she supposedly shared.

She reached for the picture and knocked a crystal figurine from its perch. In a panic she lunged forward and grabbed at the ornament in an unsuccessful attempt to prevent it from falling to the floor. "Sweet St. Brigid," she muttered as she bent down and picked up the small giraffe's body and looked about for the rest of the figurine. The head and neck had fallen nearby and lay neatly broken into two pieces. She placed them in the palm of her hand along with its body and straightened. With a sigh she let them drop from her hand onto the mantle.

It was then that she looked up at the portrait of Daniel's mother which loomed above the mantle. The woman's mouth turned down in a frown of disapproval. Cold gray eyes assessed her just as they had done from the moment she had set foot in the Langston mansion as Daniel's new bride. How she wished to rid herself of those judgmental eyes, but he would never agree to the removal of his dear mother's portrait.

Everything in the Langston mansion was held to the standards set by the woman. Even the smallest details in their lives seemed to be controlled by her, as though she were a third person in their marriage, though she had died before Rasheen met him.

She turned away from the portrait and saw the butler standing in the doorway. "Excuse me ma'am, but Mr. Langston would like to see you in his study."

****

Rasheen let out a sigh, gave a knock on the door and waited for permission to enter. Upon obtaining it, she crossed the room and seated herself in the chair facing Daniel. Hands folded in her lap, she waited for the admonishment that was to come.

He studied her silently, lips drawn in as if in deep thought. Finally, he leaned his slight form back in his chair and folded his arms across his chest. "What was so urgent that you found it necessary to completely disregard my privacy?"

She clenched her folded hands tighter. "I was so excited I forgot how upset you get about being disturbed when your door is closed. Uncle Frank sent a note asking if I might help out at St. Peters. It seems one of the nuns took ill and will be out for the rest of the year. They need someone to teach in her place."

Daniel raised his brows in amazement. "And you actually gave it serious thought?"

"It would only be for two weeks. Please, Daniel, it would mean so much to me to be able to use my education."

"You would seriously consider doing the work of a common laborer?"

She felt her temper rising, but tried to keep her voice calm. "Teaching is an honorable profession and more than a bit above the common laborer."

He shook his head. "I forbid it. There will be no more talk of such foolishness."

Tears began to blur her vision. "At least I'd be doing something useful with my abilities." She looked down at the paper weight. "I was right about the Lafayette. Why couldn't you have told Mr. Hilliard that? My grandfather spent a good part of his life in the employ of the Baltimore and Ohio Railroad. You let that man treat me like I hadn't a measure of sense." She gave up trying to hold back the tears and let them drift down her cheeks.

He came around to where she sat, stood over her and brushed the droplets with his thumbs. "Now, now, tears aren't becoming to such a beautiful face."

She heaved a sigh. "You said you admired my intelligence when we married."

"True, but I expected you to use it as is proper for a woman. I certainly didn't envision you disrupting my business meetings and insulting my visitors."

"That gentleman was not the injured party," she argued to no avail.

"Not only did you insult Mr. Hilliard with your head strong behavior, but me as well. Must I once more remind you of your responsibilities as my wife?"

She had to fight against the notion that he wasn't interested in sharing himself with her or knowing her beyond the exterior surface. That he only wanted someone who would make his life comfortable; someone he could indulge and pamper like a small pet to be rewarded with his affection when it suited him. She couldn't have made the mistake of marrying such a man.

"But I want to be more than just someone to see that your household is run smoothly."

He kissed her fingertips and then placed a kiss on her forehead. "A woman's place is to provide comfort and refuge for her husband, to be a worthy companion, a competent domestic manager, and a suitable teacher for their children. If you want to share something with me, buy yourself a pretty dress and wear it for me. Better yet, buy yourself a tempting negligee, and then you'll have something more suitable for a woman to share with her husband."

CHAPTER 2

Baltimore, June, 1876

Rasheen turned the ring over and stared at the wisp of blond hair resting behind its jet stone. The trouble with living up to the expectations set by others, was that it only met with disappointment for all concerned. Daniel's past reprimands still rang in her ears even though his image was fading from her mind as a dream dissipates upon wakefulness. She closed her fingers around the mourning ring digging the seed pearl rim into her fingertips. He would certainly be displeased to see her sitting alone on a public park bench with her gloves tossed in her lap. Such behavior was simply unacceptable.

Her lips formed a rueful smile. Now she knew why her wedding ring had always felt so weighty. Along with the ostentatious yellow diamond had come the revered Langston name and all the responsibilities of keeping up the social facade that a life studded with wealth and privilege entailed.

Weary from her memories she leaned her head against the top of the bench. Dappled sunlight from a nearby elm tree found its way through the black veil covering her face and warmed her skin. The whisper of human voices carried by the summer breeze, mixed in the with the muffled clip clop of horseshoes hitting the street surrounding the park, were a soothing melody to her ears. In the midst of such a tranquil atmosphere she tried to forget the past and contemplate her uncle's recent offer. Though it was tempting, she should tell Uncle Frank to find someone else for the position.

She couldn't manage a teaching position and her responsibilities as the widow Langston. It was time for her to return to the Langston mansion. She had been away far too long. At her mother's insistence, she had come to stay with her family after Daniel's funeral for a few weeks, but the weeks stretched into months and now an entire year had gone by. She had to return. After all, she was Daniel Langston's widow. There were expectations to be met. She sat up and squared her shoulders. Back on her finger went the mourning ring. Back on her hand went the glove to cover it. Somewhere up in the branches a Blue Jay squawked in protest.

She started to rise to leave, but dropped back onto the bench when she saw a young woman pushing a pram down the pathway. As she stared after the disappearing figure, a familiar emptiness engulfed her, but not for long. A persistent presence nudging her hand interrupted her gloomy reminiscences. Startled, she looked down at a large brown dog. The animal gave one last determined thump before placing a muddy paw in her lap. "Well, hello there fellow." The dog put his other paw in her lap, raised himself up so that he was eye level and then proceeded to push his nose under her veil and lick her face, knocking her bonnet askew in the process. Struggling to move his paws back to the ground, she laughed. "Now see here, that's not very mannerly."

"Down," commanded a firm male voice before she could get the dog under control. The dog jumped down and scurried off into some nearby Azalea bushes.

Rasheen looked up at a deeply tanned face, crowned by

thick ebony hair. The breath left her body, and for several long moments she couldn't speak a coherent word. She recognized those handsome features, those cobalt eyes which had once offered encouragement, and the slightest bit of indulgence. Her heart thumped erratically at the memory of a young girl's secret infatuation. Even now, the intensity with which he looked at her beneath those dark lashes completely unnerved her.

"Are you all right, Mrs. Langston?"

She sucked in as much air as she could and tried to focus on the present. He might very well be the most handsome man in all Christendom, but the arbitrary attitude of command he had just displayed irritated her.

"I'm fine, thank you just the same." She twisted her head toward the direction where the dog had run. The sudden movement caused her loosened bonnet to plummet from her head with the veil slipping through her fingers as she tried to prevent it from falling to the ground.

"Now look what you've done!"

Before she could lean forward to retrieve the errant bonnet, he scooped it up and held it just out of her reach for several long seconds during which his eyes caught and held hers. It was as if he was taking her measure, and she wasn't sure if she passed the test. Well, she was familiar with not measuring up, so he could take those mesmerizing eyes and go the devil as far she was concerned.

"Mr. Reilly, are you going to give me my bonnet or stand there holding it all day?" She asked in the most aristocratic tone she could muster.

"I'm not the one responsible for your mishap." He presented the errant bonnet to her, and brushed her gloved hand with his fingers, whether by accident or design, she wasn't certain. The warmth of his touch through the fabric of her gloves and his overwhelming masculinity provoked a wealth of familiar sensations.

"Oh bother it all!" she shouted as she threw the hat

beside her on the bench after a futile attempt at returning it to her head. "I'm perfectly capable of handling a friendly dog without a gentleman's assistance."

His dark eyebrows arched in disbelief. "I didn't realize the animal was yours. I'm sorry to have disturbed you." Before she could reply, he tipped his hat, turned on his heel, and strode off muttering something about ejit blue bloods.

She regretted being so nasty, and if she were to be honest, it wasn't him she was angry with, but herself. Guilt welled up to remind her that she was still in mourning and had no business letting such improper thoughts creep into her mind. Although one could hardly use the word creep when it came to Connor Reilly. Flash or speed would be a more accurate description.

"Can't even mourn properly. Just add it to the long list of failures," she whispered to the ghost of Daniel's memory. "But is it my fault that I still remember the physical intimacies of our union? Wasn't that the one time we were in perfect harmony?"

She looked down at her dirty lap and decided she'd at least brush the mud from her skirt. After only one quick swipe with her hand, the dog came out of hiding and repeated his affectionate assault. She wrinkled her nose when the dog's wet fur came close. "Good heavens, where have you been swimming lad?"

Rasheen looked about to see if anyone was searching for a lost dog. Finding no one, she decided to walk home. Her dress was badly soiled, and she didn't even try to put her hat on, but carried it at her side. To make matters worse, she now smelled like the dog, which trotted alongside of her.

Quite a few heads turned to look at the dirty pair as they made their way out of the park. Hopefully, she wouldn't encounter any of her late husband's acquaintances. It would not sit well with the Langston peers for his widow to be found in such a state of disrepair.

"Well, my good man, it looks as if you're coming home with me. You need someone to take care of you. What do you say to that?" The dog sat in front of her and gave her his paw. "It's settled then. You'll have to be charming to my mother, but I think you're up to the challenge. I wonder if she is."

When they reached the back door of the Thornton home, Rasheen peeked inside to make sure her mother wasn't in sight, and then took him to the basement where she and the maid pushed, shoved and lifted him into a round metal wash tub.

"Miss Rasheen, your mother is never going to allow you to keep this monster in the house." Mary took the bucket and plunged it in the little space between the dog and the tub to fill it with water.

Before she could rinse him, the dog broke loose from Rasheen's hold, and jumped out of the tub. He shook his body, slinging sudsy water all over the two women. Just as he was about to bolt toward the stairs, Rasheen dove on top of him, keeping her arms tightly wrapped about his neck. Together she and Mary shoved him toward the tub and lifted his front section over the side.

"Miss Rasheen, this isn't exactly a lap dog." Mary huffed as she somehow managed to place his back end in the tub while Rasheen held onto his neck keeping the front end in place. Once he was rinsed, they let him jump out again and dried him with some old towels.

"Now, you have to stay down here until you're completely dry. Mother's going to be more difficult to charm than I was." Rasheen patted the dog's head. "You'd better let me see if I can soften her up a bit before we introduce you.

"Be a good boy and I'll see what I can find for you to eat." She bent down and threw her arms around the dog's neck.

"Would you please give him some water?" Rasheen

asked Mary over the top of his head.

"Yes ma'am. He surely is the biggest dog I've ever seen."

"You aren't offering any encouragement, you know."

"I've none to offer. I know your mother. I don't think you'll win this battle, no matter how much you wheedle."

"Aw, Mary, have a little faith."

"Faith, I have plenty, but it will take more than a miracle to sway Mrs. Thornton."

"You're forgetting Granny."

"Even your Granny can't help with this one."

*****

"Good morning, Mr. Reilly, Father Hughes is expecting you." The housekeeper stepped aside, allowing Connor to enter and led him down the rectory hallway to the familiar room. Frank Hughes sat in his favorite chair with the worn side arms. He kept his head bent over the text before him, but raised his hand and motioned Connor to step through the doorway.

"Good book?" Connor asked.

Fr. Hughes repositioned his book marker and snapped the book shut. "Good enough."

Connor settled himself in the opposite chair, and got right to the point of his visit. "Have you found someone for my school?"

The priest pulled the wire framed spectacles from his face, dropped them on the closed book lying in his lap, and rubbed his forehead with the palm of his hand. "I have someone in mind. She has the proper credentials, though she has never used them. Still, I think she is an excellent choice."

Connor took a long breath and let it out slowly. "Jaysus, Frank."

"Can we dispense with the blasphemy?"

"Sorry, but you do realize the teacher is going to live at Sara's Glen."

"I believe you mentioned that."

"Then you know it wouldn't be proper for a woman to be living in my house."

"And why not? You have Martha and John there as chaperones." Martha was his Aunt Elaine's cousin. She was in charge of the household affairs while her husband, John, helped Connor run the farm.

"What about one of the Jesuit novices?" Connor persisted.

"They're needed at Loyola. Father Leo can't spare anyone."

"You could have talked him out of a teacher if you tried." Frank could talk the Pope out of the Vatican if he had a mind to.

"All right, all right, now. The woman is my niece, Rasheen Langston."

Connor eyed the priest in disbelief. "Why would Mrs. Langston want such a position? She certainly has no need of funds. Her husband left her a fortune."

"Teaching would give her a chance to use her education to improve the lives of others. She needs more in her life than trying to live up to the Langston legacy of one society event after another."

"I doubt that." Connor remembered being introduced to her at one such event shortly after her marriage to Langston and was astonished at how she had changed. It was as if all the warmth had been drained from her, and she had become an ice queen. She appeared to be in her element as she stood next to her king and made no mention of their childhood friendship. Her movements had been mechanical, her speech lifeless. "I think she rather enjoys her status in society."

Father Hughes waved a dismissive hand. "If she remains in Baltimore," he insisted, "when she comes out of mourning, my sister will be pushing her to find another husband."

Ah, so there it was, and no doubt his Uncle Patrick's

hands were in the cookie jar too. Connor folded his arms and glared at the priest. "And you, Father Hughes?"

Frank met the glare with a steady gaze of his own. "I'd like to see Rasheen have the opportunity to use her education. I trust you to treat her not as some silly female, but with the utmost professional respect." His voice was calm and even, as if he were teaching a lesson in his former assignment as a teacher at a boys' school.

But Frank was a parish priest now; and Connor was no longer his student. "There are patients in hospitals she could read to, orphans she could teach or take on outings, and a number of other charitable endeavors she could pursue. With the Langston name, her assistance would be welcome anywhere. Why does it have to be my school?"

"The Langston name means nothing to you. She could stand on her own merits; something she would be unable to do elsewhere."

"Even if all you say is true, I doubt your niece would want to take this particular position. She doesn't seem to have a favorable opinion of me." Connor related his encounter in the park with Mrs. Langston to the priest.

Father Hughes merely smiled and said, "Why don't we let her decide?"

Confident that Mrs. Langston would refuse the offer, Connor decided to play along. "Looks like I have no choice in the matter if I'm to have a teacher."

"If you find it doesn't work, you can notify me and I'll try to find a replacement, but at least give her the opportunity to prove herself."

"If she refuses the position, you'll honor my original request, with no more delay." Connor banged his hand on the chair arm for emphasis.

"Fair enough then, but she won't refuse. Would you like for me to arrange a meeting with her to discuss your requirements?"

"I've no desire to meet with Mrs. Langston again until the day she is due at Sara's Glen." And he hoped that day never came. The young Rasheen Thornton would have fit in at Sara's Glen, but the widowed Rasheen Langston belonged to High Society. Still, Frank wouldn't saddle him with someone who wasn't capable. He would just have to let it rest for now. One thing was for sure, they would have an understanding from the start that he was in charge and she wouldn't be playing the role of snooty aristocrat.

He didn't wish to debate the matter any further so he took the conversation in a new direction. "What about the other matter you wrote about?"

"Would you take a court case for one of my parishioners?

Connor settled back in the chair. This subject matter was more to his liking. "Give me the details."

"Kiernan McPhail's a mechanic for the railroad and was injured when a section of the roof on the building where he was working fell in. I'm not sure if it will be necessary for him to seek legal recourse, but I wanted to discuss it with you just in case."

"Has the company claimed responsibility for the injury?"

"They haven't admitted to anything. As the months go by, they'll stop paying his wages and claim he was let go because he couldn't perform his duties. By that time, the matter will have been swept aside. They neglected to make needed repairs to the roof, in order to cut expenses. I'd wager next week's collection on it, if I were a gambling man."

"I'll have someone investigate the matter discretely so that I have the needed evidence should it become necessary."

"Kiernan has no funds to pay you."

Connor shrugged his shoulders. "Let's see if we can help Mr. McPhail and his family."

"I would imagine you'll want to speak to Kiernan at some point." Frank went to his desk and wrote McPhail's address on a sheet of paper and handed it to Connor.

Connor read the address and then folded the paper and tucked it in his coat pocket. "I'll wait until we see what the railroad's going to do before I see him. If they let him go, I'll be in touch. You can tell him you spoke to me and that I'll take his case should it become necessary. Ask him not to speak to anyone about the possibility of me taking the case. I don't want the railroad to know I'm involved until my man does some digging. Otherwise, they'll do some burying."

"You were always the clever lad; must be your Irish heritage."

"Well now, you and I would say that, but others might have a different opinion. I'll have my man start the investigation in the McPhail matter before I return to Sara's Glen."

"Look at you - lawyer, businessman, and horse breeder," Frank said. "The horse trainer's son is a long way from Ireland."

"I prefer the last of those titles, but it keeps Uncle Patrick happy that my education is put to use helping him in his business affairs."

The two men left the rectory office and walked down the hallway. At the open doorway Frank asked, "Where's your carriage?"

"I hate sitting at a desk all day. These last few days attending to Uncle Patrick's affairs have been torture. My legs need a good stretch."

Halfway down the steps, Connor looked over his shoulder. "I'll expect your niece at Sara's Glen by the end of August. You can write me with the details as to her arrival."

"I'll handle everything. You won't have to be bothered," Frank said and turned to go inside.

"Oh, to be sure," Connor muttered to himself.

CHAPTER 3

Rasheen's mother waved the back of her hand toward the door. "Kindly remove that filthy beast from the parlor."

Ignoring the request, Rasheen patted the dog's head. "Just look at his lovely coat now that he has been bathed. I think I shall call him Finn because he is so large, just like the giant. What do you think?"

"No such person ever existed. It's only a Celtic tale, like all the others your grandmother likes to tell. As for what I think, what I think is that I want that dog out of my home. You have more important things to be concerned with than a mangy cur."

Rasheen knelt next to the dog and leaned her head against his neck. "He deserves better than to be referred to in such a manner. After all, did the Good Lord not make him?"

"Are you listening to me at all? We cannot keep that dog. The servants have enough work keeping this household in order without the added burden of an animal to care for. And for the love of the Blessed Mother, please don't bring God into this." Her mother sat in the blue needlepoint side chair, back straight, hands now neatly folded as they rested in her lap.

Rasheen wasn't the least intimidated. "Your difficulty is that you only see God's face on your little holy card pictures."

Finn squirmed away from Rasheen's hold and walked over to put his head in her mother's lap, but his big brown eyes and soulful expression failed to soften the older woman. She pushed him away. "Shoo, shoo, go away."

"You're a priest, try and talk some sense into this child," she said to Rasheen's Uncle Frank who was seated in the gentlemen's chair on the opposite side of the small rosewood table.

A smile curved his mouth as he returned his tea cup to its saucer on the table. "Moira, first of all, she isn't a child, and second, she is right. St. Francis of Assisi was very fond of animals. Legend has it that he used to converse with them, but since you seem to have no such inclination, why don't Rasheen and I get Finn out from underfoot for a bit? I could use a nice walk."

"Perhaps you can see that your niece returns in a more dignified manner than she did the last time she visited the park. You wouldn't have recognized her. Her skirts were wet and soiled, dirt smudged on her face, and her hair disheveled like some street urchin."

Rasheen swung her head around toward the hallway where Mary had just passed after retrieving the morning's mail. She couldn't believe that Mary had told on her.

Following her glance, her mother shook her head. "No one told on you, I saw you going up the stairs. I was too shocked at the time to say anything."

"I am a wretched creature." Rasheen hung her head in mock shame. She had to do something to lighten the situation. Her mother's scolding made her feel like a wayward child, and she was far too familiar with that feeling from the many rebukes she had received from Daniel for what he deemed improper behavior.

As if reading her mind, her mother's voice softened. "I give up. Go on, off with the two of you."

"You know I didn't mean to upset you. I *am* sorry." Rasheen kissed her mother's cheek.

"I know, but we're going to have to do something about that beast." Her mother gestured toward Finn.

"We can talk about it when Uncle Frank and I return from our walk," Rasheen said, knowing that she could persuade her uncle to help her plead Finn's case. She put the dog's leash on and took Frank's arm. In spite of the animal's mammoth size, he gave her no trouble.

A short while after they had left the Thornton home, they reached the entrance to Mount Vernon Park. Though it wasn't large like Druid Hill, an abundance of trees rendered welcome shade, and a small formal garden provided benches where visitors could sit and rest a spell. Frank directed her to take a seat on one of them and dropped down beside her. Finn pulled on the lease to continue the walk, but sat reluctantly alongside the bench when Rasheen gave him the command to sit. She stroked his head as consolation for the interrupted walk.

"I thought it would be nice if you and I got out and had a chat away from prying ears. You know your mother isn't going to allow Finn to stay in her house." Frank reached down to pet the dog that had now moved next to him and rested its head on the priest's knee. "Have you been to the Langston residence recently?"

Her stomach churned with anxiety and frustration. "I went back the day after I found Finn for a few hours, but there were so many memories."

Uncle Frank put his arm around her shoulders and gave her a gentle hug. "Sometimes memories can be comforting."

"Not for me. Everything in the Langston mansion had been held to the standards set by Daniel's mother. Her ghost dominated even the smallest details of our lives. Her portrait loomed over the mantle in the parlor condemning my every move. How can I justify myself to a dead woman I never even met? I wasn't very successful in my representation of the Langston name when Daniel was alive, and the thought of resuming that role frightens me –

the monotony of the same boring conversations, and never being able to express my true opinions on any matter less it be unworthy of my position in society."

Rasheen gave a resigned shrug. "I don't seem to have any choice. If I stay with mother, she will begin to push me about my future when I am out of mourning, and no doubt feel it her responsibility to see that I am occupied, which will mean endless Ladies Sodality meetings and teas to benefit your parish." She squeezed her uncle's arm on the last words. "Not that I mind doing things to help your parishioners, it's just that I would like to be in charge of my own life for once."

Frank sat quietly for a few minutes and then finally asked, "Have you given any thought to our conversation about using your teaching qualifications?"

Rasheen had given it serious consideration, but how could she accept? Her life had ceased to be her own the day she married Daniel, and now the burden of the Langston name would be hers for the rest of her life unless she remarried, and that was one thing she would never do. "You are the one person who always had faith in my capabilities. Do you remember when you asked me to fill in for one of the nuns at St. Peter's when she became ill?"

"You told me you had too many social obligations, but if the choice were yours, you would have gladly helped."

Rasheen gave a weary sigh. "I could have canceled those engagements. Daniel forbade me to enter a classroom. He couldn't believe I would even entertain such an idea. He felt that teaching was little more than common labor." She left out the part of how she had shed tears of frustration; of how Daniel gently brushed the droplets away as if he was handling a small child.

Frank tilted her chin and looked into her eyes. "The choice is yours now."

She took a deep breath and let it out. "I would welcome the opportunity, but the school year is over, and you have more than enough time to replace any of the nuns at St. Peters if someone is ill.

"There are other places besides St. Peters. Would you be willing to take a position on an estate in Northern Baltimore County?"

If she were out of the city, she would not have to answer to the Langston peers. Excitement began to build, but she tapered it with caution. "How do you know of such a position?"

"The owner is a friend. He has a small school house on the property and wants to provide an education for the children of the area. You would live on the estate so that would get you away from your obligations as a Langston, though I'm sure a few society matrons will frown at such a course of action. Since they will be the very ones you seek to escape, that will be of no concern to you. As for the position, you may come home on holidays and during the summer if you like. I'm sure you would be happy there. It's a lovely area."

Rasheen twisted Finn's leash in her hand as she considered the offer. "Tell me more about the owner."

"He is a fine young man, a former student of mine from my days at Loyola."

"And what of his wife?"

Uncle Frank didn't answer, but sat with his hands folded loosely in his lap, rapidly tapping his thumbs together.

She raised an eyebrow and inquired, "His wife?"

"Connor is not married."

"Oh?" She waited for an explanation.

He gave her a knowing smile. "The estate originally belonged to his uncle, Patrick Reilly. Connor became its owner a few years ago. He needs a teacher, and you would make an excellent teacher."

Her spirits fell. "Connor Reilly is not going to want me for the position."

Frank's forest green eyes crinkled at the edges. "I've already recommended you for the position. It's yours if you want it."

"I can't believe he agreed to give me the position." She placed her forefinger to her lips, in a thoughtful gesture, wondering what her uncle had said to the man. Obviously, Mr. Reilly had told him what had transpired in the park.

As if reading her thoughts, he said, "It'll be fine, just fine. Connor took no offense from your actions. He realizes you are still not yourself."

"Perhaps I should meet with him and apologize."

And would it be sincere now?" He tapped the tip of her nose with his forefinger.

She had to be truthful. "For the most part it would be. I was wrong in the way I spoke to Mr. Reilly, but I'm so tired of concerned people. After the way I behaved toward him, I don't think Connor Reilly has a very good opinion of me."

"He'll come round."

"Uncle Frank, you seem to be forgetting something. Mr. Reilly isn't married, and even though I am a widow, it would hardly be proper for me to reside at his estate, even with servants in attendance." Though the position offered promise, she still wasn't comfortable with the idea of living under Connor Reilly's roof.

"Martha and John Schmidt help manage the place. They are more than servants. She is his aunt's cousin. There would be no impropriety."

"It does sound like something I would like," she mused. "What about Finn?"

"Finn may have gotten off to a bad start with Connor in the park, but I doubt he would hold it against the animal."

She scratched behind the dog's ear producing a delighted moan. "How would you like to live in the country, lad?"

"So does this mean you'll take the position?"

Rasheen decided if she was ever to take charge of her own life, it had to be now. "Yes, if he has agreed." Yet, there was still an uneasy feeling in the pit of her stomach when she remembered her reaction to his hand brushing hers. Nerves, she told herself, that's all it was, just nerves. After all, she was about to change her entire life.

"Good, good. Now you leave everything to me and don't concern yourself with anything except what a wonderful teacher you're going to be." He gave her a smile that chased away her fears. No one had ever had faith in her like Uncle Frank.

"We better start for home or we'll be late for dinner. I don't want to find myself in your mother's bad graces." He took her arm and guided her toward the path leading out of the park, but she sensed that there was something weighing on his mind.

"Is there something you haven't told me about the position?"

"I think we covered all that there is on that subject, but there is another matter I would like to discuss. Please don't think I am of the same mind as your mother concerning your future, but I don't think you should shut yourself off to the possibility of another marriage someday. I know you're still in a great deal of pain, but you're a young woman."

"Uncle Frank, I love you, but there are things you could never understand. You are a priest and have no experience in the matters of a marriage."

"You may be correct in that my dear, but I still think you should be open to the consideration if the right person comes along. I don't think the Good Lord intended for you to be alone for the remainder of your life. No matter what opinion you may have of yourself, you were a good wife and would have been a wonderful mother."

"I don't think it was intended for me to have children. Daniel and I were married for two years and I don't have a child to remember him with now, do I? Was I a good wife? I doubt that Daniel would agree with you. Aren't wives supposed to be submissive to their husbands? Be assured, he found me lacking in that virtue."

"Just keep your heart open. Sometimes it's just a matter of someone coming into your life to help you get beyond all that has come before – someone to help you recognize the rainbows in your soul created by all those tears shed in unhappiness. You'll understand what I'm saying when the time is right."

Before she could answer him, a squirrel ran across the path and the temptation was too great for Finn. He broke away from Rasheen and tore after the small animal, which scuttled up the nearest tree in a streak of gray fur. Finn pawed at the bottom of the tree's trunk, barking loudly while the angry squirrel stood on the branch above him chattering and twitching its tail furiously. From the safety of his newfound position, he reprimanded the bothersome dog. The humans laughed at the pair as Frank retrieved the leash from the ground and began walking once again. "It's a good thing your mother isn't here to witness this performance."

"Holy Mother of God help us." Rasheen raised her eyes heavenward.

"Mary and Joseph, Brigid and Patrick, all the saints and a few ancient Celtic gods and goddesses," Frank added.

"Amen to that." She tucked her arm in his and quickened her pace to keep up with his long strides.

*****

Rasheen put Finn in the basement to avoid further problems with her mother, and then slid into her seat next to Granny at the dining room table. Uncle Father Frank, as Rasheen's brothers laughingly called him, had waited for her before saying the blessing which was followed by plates and bowls being passed among the diners.

23

"I don't know how they expect those poor men to take care of their families," Granny said in reference to an article in the morning paper stating that the railroad had cut salaries again.

Richard Thornton gave his mother-in-law a weary look. "The country has been in a depression for almost four years now, businesses are suffering. They have to do what they can to keep going."

"That may be true, but they aren't cutting the stockholder's dividends or management's salaries. I've seen what this is doing to the families in my parish," Frank said.

"It's unfortunate, but the railroad is facing a great deal of competition. When Garrett took over as President, he turned the company around in the space of a year and built it into a thriving enterprise that provided good paying jobs. The railroads aren't the only ones cutting salaries or letting men go. Millions are out of work," Rasheen's father replied.

"Well, Richard Thornton, we haven't seen you dismiss any of your employees or lower their wages, now have we? If you can afford to treat your workers fairly why can't the others?" Granny pointed her empty fork at him, and gave it a few shakes before spearing a piece of meat.

"It isn't that simple. We have no investors to please; nor do we have any competition, and we still weren't able to give our workers an increase in wages last year. This year doesn't hold much promise either."

"Aye, that may be true, but you treat your employees fairly. They've cut the working man's salary to the bone, while ever increasing profits for themselves," Granny argued.

Frank heaved a weary sigh. "She's right. Greed is an insidious vice, always hungry and never satisfied. This thing is going to get ugly if changes don't come soon, but it is not for us to settle this evening."

Rasheen pushed the food around the edges of her plate. The lull in conversation afforded her an opportunity to announce her decision. She struggled to form the right words in her mind to gently break the news to her family.

Uncle Frank looked at her from across the table and winked as if so say, "It's time, lass."

She took a sip of water, swallowed it quickly and cast her eyes in Uncle Frank's direction for support and spilled out the words, "I've decided to take a teaching position in North County." There – she had done it.

The food on her mother's fork slid off and onto the tablecloth next to the dinner plate. Rasheen almost laughed at the picture, since her mother was never caught off guard.

"Why in heaven's name would you do that? Where will you live? It isn't proper for a young woman to live alone in a strange area." Her stunned mother was firing the questions as fast as she could speak. "Have you given this any thought at all? Why haven't you mentioned it?"

Granny reached over and patted Rasheen's arm. "Sure and now, hasn't she thought this through? She would never do anything foolish."

Rasheen felt an ache in her chest at the thought of being apart from her family. While it was true they could be meddlesome, it was also a fact that they loved her fiercely. "I'll be back to visit. It is not as if I'll be gone forever. I'll live on the estate where I'll be teaching, so I won't be alone."

Her father asked more questions. Whose estate was it? What was the size of the estate, how old were the children she would be teaching, how many?

"I don't know that much about it yet. Uncle Frank is a friend of the owner."

"So you're behind this?" The raised chin and glare in Uncle Frank's direction were reminiscent of the indictments Rasheen and her brothers received when her mother was displeased with them.

The priest coughed a few times, and then reached for his wine glass, taking a large gulp for fortification.

Her mother delicately maneuvered the errant food onto her fork and returned it to her plate.

Rasheen sucked her lips in to keep from smiling. This was an evening of firsts – her mother's faux pas and now the esteemed Father Hughes acting like a school boy caught pulling the girls' braids.

Uncle Frank looked at her when he spoke, avoiding her mother's steady gaze. "The name of the estate is Sara's Glen. Patrick Reilly was the original owner, but he has turned the place over to his nephew, Connor. Martha Schmidt and her husband reside at Sara's Glen. I believe you are acquainted with the Reilly's and the Schmidt's."

Granny chimed in, "Your brother would never suggest anything twas not in the child's best interest, now don't you know?"

Her mother's tone softened as the frown lines around her mouth morphed into a Mona Lisa smile. "The Reilly's are lovely people. Perhaps you're right. A change of scenery might benefit Rasheen, and as you noted, it will give her the opportunity to put her education to use."

After dinner, the family retired to the parlor where the men played chess, while her brothers watched and questioned their elders after each move. The two older women sat near the window making use of the last light of day as one read and the other worked her embroidery needle in the intricate pattern on the fabric pulled tight through the circular frame.

Rasheen sat at the small table where the kaleidoscope rested. She touched the hand-finished wood body and ran her fingers down along the brass pedestal and rim. Speaking to no one in particular, she commented, "These things have been around for a long time, but they only became popular this last decade. I wonder why that is."

Her uncle looked up from the move he was contemplating, "Modern manufacturing makes them more affordable."

"I guess my generation takes many things for granted."

"Things are changing quickly as we continue to enter into the age of machinery. I would imagine you will see a great many new inventions during your lifetime," her father added to the conversation.

She peered into the end of the scope and turned the crank. The beveled glass jewels revolved on the leaded mirror panel in a vivid burst of pink, burgundy, and teal coming together to form an eight-point star, then disbursing out into various shades and mixtures until they rearranged themselves into a majestic cathedral window. A few more turns of the crank and the pieces broke away disassembling the beautiful image into scattered fragments of pretty glass. Scattered fragments, she thought, that's what her life with Daniel had been – beautiful pieces that didn't fit together. It was time to find different pieces and see what kind of a pattern developed. She detached the object case and reached for another one from a wooden box that rested nearby.

CHAPTER 4

Connor handed the maid his card and watched her walk down the hall where she stopped to tap on a closed door before disappearing behind it. This was his second call of the morning, the first being to the Langston residence. Frank hadn't bothered to mention that Rasheen Langston had taken up residence in her parents' home. It had been over a year since her husband's death. How was the woman supposed to manage at Sara's Glen, when she wasn't even managing her own home?

His stomach was a jumble of knots, tighter than the ones the men tied to hold goods in the wagons on their way to the freight train. Images of the warrior goddess, Scathack, skewering him with Gae Blog, the magic spear that shot lightening, flickered in the recesses of his mind. The goddess's features were those of Rasheen Langston.

He pushed that picture from his mind, replacing it with one of Mrs. Langston standing quietly next to her husband at a dinner party. Rather than engaging in any conversation, she had looked to her husband to speak for her. Though she had grown to be a beautiful woman, the spark in her eyes was missing. With a tinge of regret, he assured himself that was the woman he would see in the next few moments. The girl he had once nicknamed

Scathack was long gone.

Perhaps, but for a brief moment he had seen the flicker in her eyes, the one that used to come just before one of their verbal combats when she was an adolescent. If she still had that energy, she just might be able to handle a school room full of students. Sweet Jaysus, why was he even entertaining such a thought? He had decided that the best thing for all concerned would be to terminate this arrangement. If he could only convince her to do the sensible thing, then she would be the one to deal with Frank. Guilt tugged hard at his conscience when he thought of his promise to his old friend.

In an effort to loosen its hold, he took in his surroundings. There was a large parlor on one side of the entryway and a small crimson sitting room on the other. A vase of peacock feathers rested on an ornately carved table over which hung a gilded mirror.

Peacocks strutting about fanning their tail feathers to gain attention – that is what women like Mrs. Langston did. No, that was wrong, wasn't it? The male peacock had the beautiful plumage. Besides, the woman with the dirty skirts and smudged face, whose only concern was for an oversized mongrel, didn't fit the image. Nothing about Rasheen Langston made sense to him anymore. Damn Frank Hughes for putting him in this situation.

Before he could curse Frank further, he heard footsteps coming down the hall behind him. When he turned around the maid said, "Mrs. Langston will see you in the study, sir."

"Thank you," Connor stammered as if she had somehow read his last thoughts regarding the good priest. He handed her his hat and followed her to the room at the end of the hallway. The door was open now and the maid stepped aside for him to enter.

The petite Mrs. Langston was seated behind a large oak desk, head bowed, as she intently studied something before her. When he approached the desk, he noticed the papers on its surface. Bills, receipts, and investment documents sat before her arranged in neat stacks. She looked up from a leather bound ledger in which she was making entries and motioned for him to be seated in a chair across from the desk. Another man might be annoyed at such behavior from a woman, but Connor was fascinated by her concentration on the ledger before her.

He took advantage of her preoccupation with her papers to study her as he took his seat. The widow's black made her cream colored complexion look almost ivory. It reminded him of fine porcelain china, but he doubted there was anything fragile about Rasheen Langston. Her sable hair was fixed in a tight braid that framed her head much like a halo. What would it be like to undo that halo and let all that glorious hair cascade down around her bare shoulders? Without warning, his imagination began a lustful detour. He was all the way to the part where the rest of her was about to be as bare as the shoulders when she looked up from the ledger.

"My apologies, Mr. Reilly, I thought I was finished, but I caught something that needed attention just as you walked through the door."

He mentally shook himself. What was wrong with him? The last thing he needed was to entertain any thought of attraction to Rasheen Langston. Time to get to the point.

"Mrs. Langston, I wanted to talk to you about the position at Sara's Glen." He tugged at his collar. The stupid thing was choking him. Once more, he damned Frank Hughes for putting him in this predicament.

She held her hand in front of her. "Before you say anything further, please allow me to apologize for my rudeness in the park the other day."

"No need to apologize. I should have asked if you needed assistance before plowing in."

"I don't want there to be any unpleasantness between us, because this teaching position is important to me."

Sincerity shone in her dark eyes.

He rubbed the palm of his hand across his forehead and let out an uncomfortable breath. This was going to be more difficult than he had anticipated. "I don't think you realize the nature of the position. This is a rural school. It's not like the schools to which you are accustomed." He paused for a second in order for her to grasp the meaning of his words and then plunged in. "Perhaps you'd be happier teaching in one of Baltimore's finishing schools. Since I was unable to reason with your uncle, I was hoping I might persuade you to change your mind." He sat back and waited for her agreement.

She carefully closed the ledger, and leaned over the desk, supporting herself with her palms. "Am I to understand that you're dismissing me before giving me a chance to prove myself? Such action hardly agrees with the Connor Reilly I once knew."

Her reference to the past caught him off guard. He would never have guessed that she still possessed the obstinate nature he had once admired, but there it was. She kept it well hidden beneath the spiritless exterior she presented. "I gave my word to your uncle that the position was yours if you wanted it, but I was hoping you would reconsider and save us both an inconvenience. What is to happen when you decide that it doesn't suit you? Then I'll have to find another teacher, and the students will be disrupted."

She dropped back down into the chair and studied him in silence. Back on track now, he refused to squirm but steadily returned her look as the silence lengthened between them. Here was the Scathack he remembered, except now she had grown into a more worthy opponent. The spark flickered in her eyes and then flamed until he could almost feel it singe his cheeks.

It was difficult to justify his recent opinion of her after he had seen the papers and neatly scripted columns entered in the ledger. They chipped away at his image of an empty headed, spoiled rich woman, but then he had known Frank would never saddle him with such a teacher for his students. So what was his problem with her?

While he dwelled on the question, she folded her hands over the closed ledger and stared down at them for several seconds. Finally, she spoke in a firm, quiet voice. "Let me stay for one year and at the end of that time if you're displeased with me, I'll save you the trouble of dismissing me. You have my word that I will not leave before the school year is completed no matter what happens."

Connor could see there was no use in taking the discussion any further. He had given his word. There was no escape. "I warn you – expect that you'll work hard. This is a teaching position and not some woman's charity event," he said as he stood to take his leave.

"I assure you, Mr. Reilly, I am not a member of the idle rich. Don't be so quick to judge me." By now she had come around the desk and stood before him, arms folded across her chest. Though she had to be a good foot smaller than his six feet, two inches, she was a determined force.

Her last remark stung because though he was loath to admit it, she was telling the truth. However, he would not concede that to Mrs. Langston. Let her prove herself first, and then he would reconsider his opinion.

"Very well then, I will expect you to be at Sara's Glen in late August," he tried to make his voice sound businesslike, but a hint of frustration colored the words.

She offered him her hand. "I'll be there in time to set up the classroom before the school year starts."

He hesitated for a second before taking her hand and clasping it in agreement. The second his fingers wrapped around hers, his blood seemed to race faster through his veins. Confounded and frustrated by the sensation, he dropped her hand and left the room, not waiting for the maid to return to show him out. As he opened the door to the outside world, he heard rapid footsteps behind him, but didn't look back. He bounded down the front steps, two at a time and strode with no particular destination in mind, just escape.

The maid called after him, "Sir, your hat."

He turned sharply, walked back to the steps, and reached up to retrieve it from the maid. The smile on her face denoted a touch of amusement. Well, he certainly wasn't amused. Every time he was in Rasheen Langston's company, he felt the need to flee. What would he do when she came to Sara's Glen? He sure as hell wasn't going to be running from his own home. The woman was going to be trouble.

CHAPTER 5

With Mary trailing behind her, Rasheen gathered her skirts up and walked up the marble steps of the Langston residence. Bright red geraniums spilled over the window boxes, the same window boxes where she had once wanted to plant pink petunias. Nothing had changed. Geraniums always adorned the Langston home and there were no exceptions, not even for a new bride's desires. She released her skirts from her tightly fisted hands and reached in her purse for the house key.

The key was never turned in the lock as the door was promptly opened by a Langston footman. She motioned to Mary to take a seat in one of the chairs that rested on either side of a turtle-topped center table. As they took off their gloves and bonnets, she dispatched the young man to retrieve her trunks from the attic. Once that was accomplished, she steeled herself for the task ahead and proceeded toward the second floor.

When they reached the landing, the Langston maid appeared at the top of the stairs. "Would you like me to help you, Mrs. Langston?"

"Mary and I can manage." Somehow, she felt more confident with Mary by her side. "I'll ring if I need you." The young woman curtsied and left them.

Mary looked down over the railing and said, "I thought your family's home was grand, but this one is a palace."

"Maybe, but I was never the queen," Rasheen whispered in a fragile voice.

"What did you say?"

"Nothing of importance."

Rasheen opened the door to the bedroom and motioned for Mary to follow her inside. The room was dark and dreary and smelled of wilting roses.

Mary walked over to the windows and pulled open the tightly closed drapes and then threw open the windows. "No wonder it's so stuffy in here. Guess they don't bother with this room since you aren't in residence here." Her gaze traveled to the table where the white roses rested. "That's what I smelled. Why on earth would someone put roses in a closed up room?"

"Because it was a Langston tradition that roses, white ones, were always placed in this room. Daniel's father started the practice when he brought his new bride here."

"And your husband continued the practice for you. That's real nice, Miss Rasheen. Don't be upset with me, but I wouldn't have thought he was that romantic."

"He wasn't. The roses were ordered on a weekly basis and he continued the practice in his father's place for his mother. These were sent more for his mother's memory than anything else. If he'd wanted to send me roses, he would have ordered red ones." *But he never bothered to ask my preference.* Rasheen walked over to the roses and knocked the petals off of one of them with the back of her hand. "I'll have to remember to have the deliveries discontinued."

She went to the large mahogany wardrobe and opened it to inspect her clothes. There were a few things in subdued shades of grey, purple, and mauve that she could wear during her six month half-mourning period which would soon begin. Next, she pulled out a walking suit and some dark skirts and shirtwaists. The maid had stored her winter clothes and placed the lighter summer garments in the wardrobe, which made no sense to Rasheen since she wouldn't be able to wear them this year. Routines were kept in the Langston residence with no exceptions, not even death. Just looking at the summer clothes made her feel like her body was in a well stoked furnace. She wiped the perspiration off her forehead with the black-edged handkerchief. Her perspiration soaked clothes clung to her. The afternoon sun blazed upon the front of the house rendering the open windows powerless to relieve the stifling heat.

She took Mary by the arm and led her out of the room. "Let's go downstairs and have something cold to drink, and then we can finish here."

Once downstairs, she rang for the butler and informed him that they would be having refreshments in the parlor. The man bowed politely, but looked upon Mary as one would a cockroach needing to be stepped on.

Mary settled herself on the royal blue velvet sofa. "I shouldn't be sitting here like this. Your butler obviously doesn't approve of my being here."

"I don't think he ever really approved of my being here either."

"Why wouldn't he?"

"He was hired by Daniel's mother. Old loyalties die hard."

"But the woman's been dead for years."

"Her ghost remains."

Pamela Langston's presence dominated the room. The woman in the portrait, whom Rasheen had never met in life, looked down on her with the same disapproving grey eyes that had always made her uneasy. A chill reached deep down into her bones, yet gave her no relief from the unrelenting feeling of suffocation. Her vision took in the room - the priceless vases, paintings, carved walnut tables and chair limbs, until it finally rested on her wedding picture sitting on the mantle dwarfed by the magnificent painting of Daniel's mother.

Following her gaze, Mary said, "You made a beautiful couple, so happy."

"Don't be fooled by a paper image."

"What do you mean?"

"Appearances are often deceiving." Rasheen rose from her seat, walked over and picked up the small silver-framed picture. She was still fighting against the notion that her husband had wanted a wife who would mirror his mother's image, an image that was never satisfied, but constantly demanding more and more of her spirit. Why had he always tried to change her, reminding her of her imperfections? She threw the picture at the imperious Mrs. Langston's likeness.

"You were the reason. You controlled our lives even from the grave. Well, you have him now, and you can have your damn house and all its priceless treasures," she shouted as the cold black pain she had borne for so long suddenly burned in white hot rage.

Mary jumped up from the chair where she had been sitting. "Miss Rasheen, maybe this is all too much for you right now."

Before the concerned maid could reach her, Rasheen rushed over to a table behind the sofa, picked up an antique vase, and threw it at the mantle. It hit the corner and crashed to the black marble below in a burst of blue and white pieces. The sound of priceless porcelain shattering reverberated throughout the room, unleashing a destructive force within her. She picked up a china figurine and hurled it at the painting. It made a thud against the canvas, before it, too, crashed to the floor and broke into several sharp slivers. She was about to grab a crystal bowl, when the horrified Langston maid came running into the room.

"Is everything all right ma'am?" she asked.

By this time Mary had reached her and had her in a fierce embrace. "Miss Rasheen, Miss Rasheen, please stop."

Shaking in Mary's arms, Rasheen screamed, "Everything is fine, just perfect. I'm leaving this mausoleum."

The maid looked at her uncertainly. "I beg your pardon, ma'am, I don't understand."

"It no longer matters." Rasheen said in a quieter tone, as she struggled to be free of Mary's arms. Her composure now regained, she faced the older woman and said, "I have something I must do before I return home. I want you to pack all of my clothes – everything."

Then to the butler who had suddenly appeared, she ordered, "Have the Langston carriage brought around and load as many of my packed trunks on the carriage as it will hold. Instruct the driver to take Mary home and then have him return for the remainder of my things."

The butler gave a silent nod, bowed, and backed out of the room.

"I don't think you should be alone just now," Mary said.

Rasheen took Mary by the hand and led her out of the parlor. "I'll see you at home this evening. Make sure that all of my clothes are there when I arrive. Tell mother I'll be using her vehicle and driver for a bit longer."

The butler and the maid were in the hallway whispering. Their conversation stopped abruptly as soon as they noted her presence. Ignoring them, she directed Mary towards the stairs and walked out the front door. For the first time she realized that the house was not empty and barren because of Daniel's absence; it had always been that way. She had never noticed it before because she loved him.

*****

The solicitor's clerk looked up from the paper on which he was scribbling and cleared his throat. "May I be of assistance?"

"I'd like to see Mr. Anderson, please."

The man opened a book to the side of the desk and checked its page carefully. "He's very busy today. Perhaps we could schedule an appointment for late in the week," the man apologized.

"I would very much like to have this matter settled. Would you please ask him if he could see Mrs. Langston?"

With the mention of the Langston name, the man jumped up from his desk and offered her a seat. Seconds later, he was knocking on the door of the adjoining office, and, once given permission, hurried inside, closing it behind him.

If I had been any other poor woman, he would have dismissed me, but not a woman bearing the royal name of Langston, Rasheen mused to herself.

In less than a minute, the clerk returned and ushered her into the solicitor's office. The older man stood until she was seated and then motioned for the clerk to close the door. "Mrs. Langston, you didn't have to come into the office. I have met with your father several times over the last few months, and it has been no trouble at all dealing with him." Not waiting for her to state her business he continued, "I assume you need more money in your monthly allotment. That will be no problem, no problem at all."

"No, I have more than enough. There is something else I want you to do for me. I wish to sell the Langston house," she said.

The surprised man coughed and sputtered several times before he was able to speak. "Have you talked this over with someone? That property has been in the Langston family for three generations. I really think you should have someone with you before you direct me to make such a move."

"Do I need anyone's approval or permission to sell my own property?" She sat rigid in the chair determined not to appear weak or indecisive. It may not have ever felt like her home, but legally it was her property to do with as she pleased.

"Well, no, you are the only heir and it is yours, but this is such a drastic move to make. I really think you should talk it over with someone; have someone with you." He leaned his bulky form forward to rest his arms on the desk and heaved a labored breath. "Why not have your father advise you on the matter? I've found him to be quite knowledgeable regarding your financial affairs. I am certain he would agree with me that this would be an unwise decision."

"My father has merely acted as my messenger. He has left the decision making in my hands. I seek his advice only when I feel it necessary. He has confidence in my judgment, I assure you. I am moving from the city, and I want the matter settled. Start the necessary paperwork at once. The house is to be sold with all its contents. If that is not possible, have them auctioned off."

"Mrs. Langston, are you certain about this?" he asked. "Don't you want to keep the family heirlooms?"

"Just take care of the matter quickly. Also, I would like whoever buys the house to keep the staff. If that cannot be arranged, then I want their wages covered until positions can be found for them.

"You don't need to worry about the staff. That isn't your responsibility."

"I realize that, but it's my choice. Now, is there anything else you need from me?"

The man shook his head and stood to see her out the door. "I'll carry out your wishes, but I'd feel much better if you would consult someone," he pleaded nervously.

"Mr. Anderson, I am fully aware that by someone you mean a man. I find that insulting, but if it will ease your mind I'll have my father stop by tomorrow to see to the papers and bring them to me for signature."

He pulled a handkerchief from his breast pocket and mopped his brow with it. "Thank you, Mrs. Langston."

He walked her to her carriage and helped her inside.

Just before he closed the door, she said, "Oh, there is one more thing. A portrait of Mrs. Langston is hung above the mantle. Remove the frame to be sold, and donate the canvas to an art school for reuse." Those cold eyes would no longer judge anyone.

*****

By the time Rasheen arrived home from the solicitor's office, her mother and Mary were unpacking the trunks brought from the Langston residence. Several garments were strewn about the bed.

"You won't need these until next summer." Her mother began gathering up the brighter colored items. "You've sent so many boxes already. We can send these to you later."

"I'm not wearing black anymore and I'm not wearing dark colors until the winter comes. I'm tired of being miserable. As of this moment, I'm finished mourning Daniel Langston." Rasheen peeled herself out of the heavy garment she was wearing and threw it across the room.

"I'm going to have a nice cool bath, and then Mary can lay out one of my summer dresses for dinner, something with a nice light color and fabric." She waited for an argument from her mother and was shocked when none came. Her mother merely blinked once or twice and then nodded mutely.

Mary grinned at Rasheen, but quickly changed her expression when Rasheen's mother turned to her and said, "There's a box of old clothes up in the attic that the boys used to wear when they visited my brother's farm. Please see that it's sent along with the other things. Perhaps some of Rasheen's new students may find them useful. The trousers are good strong material and will wear well."

Rasheen hugged her and kissed her cheek. "Thank you for not chastising me."

Her mother's voice caught as she said, "I don't want to see you unhappy anymore." She turned quickly and left the room.

"Never liked you in black anyway," Mary whispered as she squeezed Rasheen's hand. "If you ask me, this whole business of what one wears as a show of grief, is ridiculous. One year in black, nine months in trimmed black and then six months in dark grays and mauve isn't a measure of a person's grief. How can anyone judge what's in another person's heart?"

Rasheen felt the pressure of her mourning ring against her finger when Mary was holding her hand. Once the maid released her hand, she stared down at the ring. "I wonder if we know our own hearts sometimes." She pulled the ring off and carefully put it in the small drawer of her dresser. Her bare finger reminded her of the Langston jewels. She had forgotten to tell Mr. Anderson to dispose of them, and she didn't wish to upset him again. They were in a bank vault anyway, so she could deal with that problem at a later date.

CHAPTER 6

Fear, excitement, and sadness at leaving her family all whirled inside Rasheen as the carriage neared the train station. She looked over at Finn who was on the opposite seat with his head out the carriage window. "I think he's more excited than I am." Her father nodded and then took her hand and held it securely in his own, just as he had done when she was a little girl.

Uncle Frank was standing at the station's entrance when they arrived. "I have an early meeting with the bishop, but I didn't want to miss saying goodbye," he said as he hugged her. "Everything all right?"

"I'm just now realizing how different it's going to be without the family close by." She blinked back the tears that were starting to well up in her eyes.

"It'll be fine, wait and see," Uncle Frank said.

Her father returned from speaking with the conductor. "You're all set, my girl." He leaned down and kissed her forehead. "No tears now."

"I'm ready." She squeezed her eyes shut and then opened them as she took a deep breath.

Uncle Frank winked at her and said, "Good lass. I wish I could wait for the train with you, but I have to be going or I'll be late for my meeting. Have a safe trip, and don't forget to write to your favorite uncle." He gave her a hug and then bent down and patted Finn on the head. "Take care of her, lad." Then he straightened, gave her another hug before turning quickly and walking away. Her gaze followed him until he disappeared.

Rasheen frowned as she noticed a gentleman approaching them from the same direction where her uncle had just gone. It was Mr. Hilliard, the representative from the Baltimore & Ohio Railroad who had called her a dear little thing when he had come seeking her husband's business. Even now, she fumed at the memory of that afternoon.

Nothing would delight her more than to show the portentous man how wrong he had been in his remark. Instead, when he approached them, good manners forced her to introduce him to her father as a business associate of Daniel's. After learning that the man was a former acquaintance, her father invited Mr. Hilliard to join her in the Langston private car. He had done it out of paternal concern to ease his mind knowing that she would have a male escort. While she appreciated her father's concern, she saw no need for an escort. The car was richly furnished, with a sleeping area, tiny kitchen, and a parlor, not that she needed any of that. It wasn't a long trip to North County and she wouldn't be leaving the car until their arrival. In fact, she wouldn't even be using the private car were it not for Finn. She couldn't stand the thought of him riding in a cage in the baggage car. Now it seemed she and Finn would be forced to endure this unwanted guest.

Reginald Hilliard eagerly granted her father's request, not bothering to address her. "It would be my pleasure, Mr. Thornton, let me assure you. It will be a rare treat to have such lovely company on the ride home."

There was no escape; she was trapped. To seal her fate, the train arrived letting out a sssshhhhhhhh as the steam escaped the boiler. Once the arriving passengers disembarked, the conductor shouted out for all others to come aboard. They walked down the platform to the spot where the private car waited, and the conductor put a step down for them. Hilliard held out his arm. "Allow me to assist you, my dear."

She kissed her father, and reluctantly gave Hilliard her free arm, holding Finn's leash tightly with the other hand. Her skirt train dragged behind her when she ascended the step into the car. She prayed that it did not catch and cause her to trip. The last thing she wanted was to fall into the man's arms.

*****

"Though my position with the railroad is of such importance that it keeps me in the city for long periods of time, I try to slip away to my country home as much as possible, but one still doesn't escape the many social obligations. There's always one or another function, and duty implores me to attend them all. But no one would understand that better than you." In emphasis he reached over to pat her hand, but a low growl made him drop his hand before it reached hers.

She let her hand fall on top of Finn's head and rest there. Too bad he couldn't make the babbler be quiet as effectively as had dispatched the man's unwanted attentions. Besides his endless prattle, Mr. Hilliard had an annoying habit of giggling at his own perceived witticisms. She never heard a man giggle before; laugh loud and hearty maybe, but not the high pitched tittering that this one produced.

Eventually, she was able to shut out his voice and daydream. He was too engrossed in his own conversation to realize that she wasn't listening. She gazed out the window and from time to time looked at him to mindlessly nod. This was all that was needed to satisfy him.

Once the train departed the city limits, they passed small rural communities and corn-filled fields where spiked tassels looked like russet tipped flames as the train's passing stirred a breeze which waved them about. She tried to settle her nerves by concentrating on the scenery. This position would be a completely new experience for her. There may be reasons to be afraid, but so many more to celebrate. Uncle Frank had given her a choice, and in doing so had forced her to make the decision to take the upper hand with regard to her future. With a satisfied sigh, she patted Finn's head and rested her head against the seat. Sara's Glen was a place where she could start afresh.

*****

Conner pulled the wagon under a large maple tree near the station's pick up area. The simmering heat and soaking humidity were signs that Maryland was slogging through August. He jumped down from his seat, grabbed a bucket from the back of the wagon, and went to the well pump to get some water.

Sweat dripped from the hair that fell into his face and around his ears when he removed his hat, reminding him that he was sorely in need of a haircut. The salty liquid trickled into his eyes and down his cheeks before it ended on his already drenched shirt. He filled the bucket and splashed the water on his face before taking it over to the horses.

Once more, he damned Frank Hughes for getting him into this situation. He scowled at the train tracks, remembering his previous encounter with Mrs. Langston. There had been no contact between them since his failed attempt at discouraging her from coming to Sara's Glen, other than the multitude of boxes she had sent ahead. To his surprise, they had been books and things for the classroom and not the latest fashions.

Perhaps it would not be as bad as he imagined, after all, she had not always been a member of High Society. He tried to remember the young girl he had once teased, but only the memory of the aloof Mrs. Langston came to mind. And the plain truth was that she hadn't begun life as he had. She may not have been born into the High Society into which she had married, but her parents weren't members of the lower class either.

Well, she may carry the Langston name and be entitled to all that entailed in Baltimore Society, but things were different here. He was going to have an understanding with Mrs. Langston that Martha was not her maid. Not only that, but he just might tell her that she had to help with the household chores when she wasn't teaching, even though that had not been his original intention. That might just hasten her departure.

The thought of Mrs. Langston trying to light a stove almost made him smile. She would probably burn the house to the ground. More than likely she had never been inside a kitchen long enough to know where the oven was located. Amelia certainly wouldn't go near a kitchen, but then Amelia would never take a teaching position or anything else of that sort. Her sole purpose in life was to secure a position in the highest places of society. Rasheen Langston had such a position, yet was determined to leave it. In that respect, she was unlike his former fiancée. Once more he wondered if Mrs. Langston realized what she was doing

The shrill whistle of the approaching train warned him that it was time to head over to the station. "Hello Mack, how are things going today?" he asked one of the workers waiting on the platform.

"They're good, Mr. Reilly. Are you shipping anything? Freight train's not due in for another hour."

"Nothing going out today. I'm here for the passenger train coming in now."

"Mr. & Mrs. Reilly coming for a visit? "

Connor rolled his shoulders back to relieve some of the soreness he was feeling from the morning's efforts to train a horse. "My aunt and uncle won't be visiting again until Christmas; they're busy in the city these days. I'm here to meet the new teacher."

"I heard about that. It's about time we had someone to teach the youngsters. I would expect that this is your doing."

Connor shrugged. "It's nothing my uncle wouldn't have done if he saw the need."

Mack looked toward the tracks as another blast of the whistle announced the train's arrival. "I better be gittin over there. Good day to you, Mr. Reilly."

The train hissed as it slowly pulled into the station and stopped alongside the platform. He looked toward the passenger cars for Mrs. Langston, but no one was disembarking from them. Connor exclaimed a string of profanities in Gaelic before he saw the blue railroad car with the Langston name painted on the side. A private car, the woman couldn't even make a short trip without the luxuries to which she was accustomed. Once more, he wondered how this arrangement was going to work.

The conductor opened the car's door and out stepped Reginald Hilliard, followed by Mrs. Langston. Hilliard gave the man a dismissive gesture and extended his hand to the lady in a gentlemanly fashion. Her face wore the same unapproachable expression Connor remembered from when she stood by her husband's side at the few social gatherings he had attended where they had been present. So which Mrs. Langston was he going to have deal with – the aloof one, or the hostile one? Not much of a choice.

Misgivings began to chew at him once more, until he recognized the large dog at the end of the leash which she held in her other hand. It was the same one who had run off in the park. The animal was obviously of questionable parentage, not the type of canine he would have expected such a lady to own. Women like her had small lap dogs with the purest pedigree.

He reminded himself that he was doing this for Frank, let out a long breath, and headed in her direction. Hilliard held onto the woman's arm, as if she were some sort of grand prize as he introduced her.

She wore a wide brimmed straw bonnet with a green ribbon tied beneath her chin. There was a large hat pin holding the headpiece in place and Connor couldn't suppress a grin. At least he wouldn't have to retrieve any errant bonnets on the ride home.

She looked up from giving the dog a reassuring pat and extended her hand and gave him a warm smile in greeting. "It's good to see you again, Mr. Reilly."

Her dark eyes reminded him of chocolate for some silly reason. He had a sudden craving for something sweet and delectable. Where was this coming from? Steady, lad, steady, he thought as he extended his hand.

"Welcome to North County, Mrs. Langston. Did you have a pleasant trip from the city?" The last thing he wanted right now was to waste time with idle chit chat, but if he didn't display his best manners, he would have Martha to deal with later.

"It was a most delightful ride, delightful indeed." Hilliard answered the question as if it were directed at him, and continued to clutch her arm. She smiled politely, but Connor thought he detected a hint of annoyance in her expression.

He was tempted to tell Hilliard that he had not addressed the question to the latter, but bit back the remark, instead, excusing himself to retrieve Mrs. Langston's bags. A few minutes later, he was back with several bags balanced under his arm and holding the straps of two larger ones. "If you'll wait here, I'll bring the wagon around."

Hilliard waved a dismissal. "There's no need for that. I'm sure Mrs. Langston would be more comfortable riding in my carriage. You can take the dog along with her things."

Connor watched the supercilious little man and tried his best to keep his face clear of what Martha called his mocking amusement look, but knew he was failing, which was usually the case every time he came in contact with Reginald Hilliard.

Mrs. Langston broke free of Hilliard's hold on her arm and held the dog's leash with both hands. "That's most gracious of you, Mr. Hilliard, but I don't want to leave Finn."

"My dear, I insist." Hilliard tried to take one of her hands in an effort to move her toward his carriage. He jumped back when the dog rewarded him for his efforts with a nasty snarl.

Mrs. Langston seemed to be stifling a grin. "It's quite all right. I don't mind riding in the wagon and I don't want Finn to be separated from me until we get settled. He seems to be a little upset."

Anyone with a lick of sense would have heard the resolve in her voice, but Hilliard was reluctant to hand over his prize. "Mrs. Langston, really, you would be more comfortable riding in the carriage."

Connor could see that such insistence was beginning to annoy her, and he made a valiant effort not to grin. It would be amusing to see how she handled Hilliard, but a wiser choice would be to avoid any conflict. "I think the lady has her mind set. She needs to get used to country travel anyway and now is as good as time as any."

Hilliard finally accepted defeat and made a disgruntled departure to his nearby carriage where his driver waited. The man was tall and thin with long stringy hair and had a mean air about him. A young boy hurriedly jumped down from his seat next to the driver and went to retrieve Hilliard's baggage from the platform. It was more than the lad could handle, but the driver offered no assistance. Instead, he angrily shouted at the youth to get a move on.

In his rush to obey, the boy tripped and dropped one of the bags. The driver cursed at him as the boy scrambled to retrieve it, falling in the process. Neither Hilliard, nor the driver came to the child's aid. Connor dropped the things he was carrying and walked over to the boy.

"Here, lad, let me help you." He put his arm out to help the child who kept his eyes downcast and whispered, "Thank you, sir."

They loaded the carriage in silence, and then the freckled faced youth jumped up next to the driver. He barely made it into the seat when the vehicle left the station at an unnecessary speed.

Mrs. Langston looked after the departing carriage holding the dog's leash so tightly that her knuckles were turning white. He could hear traces of temper in her voice when she turned back toward him and said, "Thank you for helping that poor child."

Connor gave a nod, but decided not to say anything more, and bent down to pet the dog which promptly licked his face. His own anger was bubbling just below the calm exterior he was trying to present.

"Finn, stop that. Bad dog! She pulled hard on the leash, but was no match for the dog's strength.

"That's all right, I like dogs, even ones that run away into bushes in parks."

"I hope you won't hold it against him. He really is a good dog." Gone was the aloof smile that had been frozen in place just a few minutes earlier. In its place was the young girl's smile she had once bestowed upon him. Though he preferred the latter, he decided the former would be safer.

"I'm sure he is." He took the leash from her and patted the wagon's dropped gate. "Up you go. There's a good lad." The dog jumped up and found an empty space among the wagon's contents where he settled himself for the ride ahead. Connor put the gate up and secured it. Then he brought his attention to Mrs. Langston, putting his hand to her waist and taking her hand to boost her up. Such an action should have meant no more than if he had helped Martha or his aunt, and yet it took him by surprise when it triggered that familiar tightening in his gut, the kind that he had not felt for a long time. He reluctantly let her hand go once she was in her seat. Steady, he reminded himself once again.

It was no better once they were on their way. He was uncomfortably aware of her body next to his. Her skirt draped her body so that he could clearly see the outline of her legs, the curve of her hip beside him. Before she had always seemed so prim and proper, but now she was provoking the most sensual thoughts in him. Sweet Jaysus, he had been too long without a woman, if he was entertaining such ideas. It wasn't like the woman was wearing a silk negligee.

He swallowed hard and took a stab at conversation. "When did you acquire the dog?"

Amusement flickered in her eyes when she looked back at the dog. "Finn acquired him, the day you chanced upon us in the park."

"He does seem a rather large animal for someone as small as you."

"I suppose you would rather see someone of my stature with a smaller creature such as a cat or perhaps a lap dog with a pedigree."

"There's no trace as to this one's breed, that's for certain. He seems to be a good animal, though." Connor reached around over the back of the seat and patted the dog on the head with his free hand while keeping a secure hold on the reins with the other.

She gave him that long ago remembered smile again. The one that made her eyes sparkle, and set him off balance. "He's a wonderful dog, and I do want to thank you for letting me bring him along. I couldn't leave him behind. My mother wasn't happy with him."

"Sara's Glen is a farm and there's plenty of room for him to run about. How did you come by the name of Finn?"

"He reminds one of the giant, Finn McCool. Don't you agree?"

"He does at that." Connor felt himself returning her smile.

During the rest of the ride to Sara's Glen, they talked about the town, her students, and the farm. He grudgingly admitted to himself that he was enjoying her company, but she was still a member of the Beau Monde. He would have to keep his guard up. But how could he fault a woman who rescued a stray and named them after a Celtic legend?

She interrupted his mental arguments with her next question. "Were you one of Uncle Frank's students?"

"Frank is a close friend of my aunt and uncle, and they made sure I was placed in his classes when he was teaching at Loyola. I believe you're acquainted with my aunt, Elaine Reilly."

"I visited her a few times with my mother when I was a young girl. Actually, I was there a few times when you were home from school, but it was so long ago you probably don't remember."

He was pleased by the fact that she had acknowledged the past. "How could I forget those conversations? You were very bright as I recall. I enjoyed our debates." He was about to remind her of the nickname he had bestowed upon her when she sidetracked him with her next remark.

"It's nice to know that someone other than Uncle Frank approved of my intelligence."

"Why would anyone disapprove?" He suspected her reference was to her late husband.

"It matters little now." She heaved a sigh and then changed the subject. "So you have remained close with Uncle Frank?"

"Your uncle has always been someone I've admired.

"What did you do when you finished school?" She seemed genuinely interested and not just making polite conversation

"Practiced law, worked for my uncle, but mostly I'm developing Sara's Glen to be a prosperous horse farm some day."

Her dark eyes widened at the last. She seemed surprised that he would choose horse breeding over a legal career. He saw no need to defend his choice to her. He had enough of such discussions with Amelia.

Thankfully, she didn't pursue the course of the conversation, but instead asked, "Do you think the boy with Mr. Hilliard's man will be one of my students?"

"I don't know anything about him, but I could speak to Hilliard and say you requested the boy's attendance, or perhaps it might be better if you spoke to him yourself since he seems to hold you in high regard."

"Mr. Reilly, I would prefer that you do whatever you can to get that child in my classroom. If your efforts prove unsuccessful, then I'll try and persuade Mr. Hilliard."

It seemed that Scathack had returned and Connor was none the sorry for it.

CHAPTER 7

Wild honeysuckle and leaf-covered soil thickened the air with their perfumed and pungent scents, as the wagon wheels bumped over the rutted road. Rasheen took a slow breath to savor them. The woods lining the road were filled with pine, oak, and dogwoods which had long since lost their white blossoms. Birds rustling in the tree branches trilled their songs above the wheels' rhythmic clacking. In the midst of her excitement, she felt a peacefulness she hadn't felt in a long time.

When they came to the sign marking Sara's Glen, Mr. Reilly stopped the wagon and jumped down to open the black wrought iron gate which was ornately designed like those leading to some of the mansions on the outskirts of the city. A double row of White Pines bordered the curved driveway that led to a large house. Clematis climbed from pink and cream roses and wreathed the surrounding porch. She could just imagine sitting in the swing to enjoy the panorama of nearby woods and pastures.

They went around to the back where he hitched the horses to a fence rail and helped her from the wagon. Such a simple thing to do, putting his hands about her waist to support her as she climbed down from her seat, and yet she felt his touch so acutely. She wondered if he sensed it. If so, he gave no outward sign.

He released her as soon as her feet touched the ground, and asked, "Why don't you unleash Finn and let him explore his new surroundings?"

"Are you sure it would be all right?" Mentally, she thanked him for breaking the awkwardness she felt.

"And why would it not?" He directed her towards the steps, took her bags, and followed her. Finn ran a short distance, stopped to sniff, and then trotted on ahead of them to plop himself on the porch. When they reached the door, he jumped up to follow them inside.

She bent down and stroked his head. "No, my lad, you stay outside."

The dog didn't try to push past, but stood close to her wagging his tail.

Connor set her bags on the porch, opened the screen door, and stepped aside so she could enter first. "Martha won't mind if he comes inside. She has a soft spot for dogs. Isn't that right, Martha?" He said through the doorway.

After Rasheen had gone inside, he continued to hold the door open for Finn, not waiting for an answer.

A woman with silver streaked sandy hair pulled back in a bun, looked up from the table where she was capping string beans. "Sure do. Bring him on in."

Martha, who Rasheen judged to be somewhere near her mother's age, rose from the table. "Welcome to Sara's Glen. It's going to be nice to have another woman around here. We aren't strangers, you know."

Rasheen searched her memory trying to recall where she had met the small ample figured woman. "Mrs. Schmidt, I must apologize for I am at a loss as to when we might have met."

"You were very young, no more than two or three years old. We had come down from our place in Frederick to visit my cousin Elaine in Baltimore and your mother came to call with you. You were the prettiest little girl, but then I am partial to little girls, since I never had one." Martha put her arm over Rasheen's shoulder and gave her a gentle squeeze. "And if you don't object we'll dispense with the formalities. You'll call me Martha like everyone else does." She waved her hand towards the kitchen table. "Now the two of you just sit down for a spell and let me get you something cool to drink. I made a few pies this morning with the peaches John brought up from the orchard. Would you like a slice?"

"Martha makes the best pies in the in the world. One piece isn't enough though." Mr. Reilly pulled a chair out from under the wide oak table and waited for Rasheen to be seated.

"That boy is never filled. If I don't watch him, he'll eat an entire pie." Martha clucked, but the pleasure from the compliment was evident in the smile she gave him.

"That's what you get for being such a good cook and I'm hardly a boy anymore." He kissed her cheek before taking his own seat.

She briefly rested her hand on his shoulder before taking her seat. "You may be a grown man, but you'll always be one of my boys."

"How many sons do you have?" Rasheen asked.

"Three sons by birth, and then we added Connor to the brood."

Connor finished his pie and then gulped the last of his drink. "I'll leave you two ladies to get acquainted. I want to get out to the orchard and see how the picking is progressing. If we want to ship those peaches to Baltimore tomorrow, they have to be on the wagon, crated, and ready to go by this evening." The words trailed behind him through the screen door.

Martha shook her head and laughed. "Do you suppose he'll remember to bring your things in?"

"I can manage if you'll point me in the direction of my room," Rasheen said.

"When you're finished eating, I'll help you. If you don't mind, there is probably no sense in waiting for him to get back."

Rasheen looked about the large kitchen. One of the walls was made of stone and contained an alcove for the over-sized nickel-plated range that resembled the one in her parent's home. She noted this to Martha who gave her a surprised look that she would be familiar with the things in a kitchen.

"My grandmother still bakes the brown bread at home. She said it didn't matter if my mother had a dozen cooks, her grand-daughter had to learn to bake the bread the same as she did. Mine isn't quite as good as Granny's, but it is passable and I can make a meal when necessary."

Rasheen saw no need to mention that she hadn't been allowed near the kitchen in the Langston house, or that she had to instruct the cook on the week's menus from the small ladies writing desk in the sitting room, just as Daniel's mother had done during her lifetime. How she hated that floral painted desk with its narrow space and three dainty drawers that weren't even large enough to hold paper.

This room pushed such thoughts aside; it was cozy and functional with lots of shelves and cabinets built-in around the walls. Blue curtains in a pretty floral print framed the window over the large sink. She could envision herself spending a lot time in here talking to Martha over a cup of tea. Somehow she felt at home here already. The realization both surprised and comforted her.

Martha removed the dirty dishes from the table and walked to the screen door. "Let's get your things up to your room."

Bags in hand, she followed Martha up the stairs to a room that was a lovely shade of lavender with two windows overlooking the back of the property. Though cold weather was difficult to remember in the current heat, she was happy to see a small black cast iron Four O'clock stove setting in the room's corner. It meant she would have a nice toasty room to which she could retire, provided someone heated the coals by four o'clock as the stove's name suggested.

Pointing towards the two bags they had just sat on the bed, Martha remarked, "You must have more bags than just these."

Rasheen laughed. "Oh my, yes. I guess Mr. Reilly left my trunks in the wagon. He did seem rather in a hurry to get out to his orchards. I should have sent them on ahead with my other things, but the books were more important. Have you received them yet?"

"Connor didn't mention any books, but the men may have picked them up on one of their trips to the station and taken them directly to the school, if they were marked."

Martha didn't bother to show her the other rooms, but proceeded down the hall and led the way downstairs. "Don't worry about your trunks, he'll either bring them up himself or send up one of the men do it."

Once they were back in the kitchen, she motioned for Rasheen to sit and then proceeded to pull out pots and pans from the cupboards in preparation for dinner.

"Please, let me do something to help," Rasheen said. "No, no, this is your first day here, just sit and talk to me while I work." Martha gently pushed her into the chair.

"Please, it would make me feel more at home." Rasheen twisted her hands in her skirt folds and fought back the same useless feelings she had experienced at the Langston mansion.

"Welcome home then." Martha grinned and set a big pot in front of her along with a bowl of potatoes to be peeled.

Once the potatoes were peeled, Rasheen got up to rinse them and put them on the range to cook. Sensing movement, Finn jumped up from his spot near the door and walked over toward her. When he realized he wasn't going to get a handout, he decided to explore and left the room.

"Get back here, Finn," she called, but the dog ignored her.

She followed him into the parlor where he had plopped down in front of a large rosewood piano. Its carved limbs and mother-of-pearl in-lays were more elaborate than any she had ever seen. She couldn't resist running her fingers over the lid.

Martha stood in the doorway. "It was custom made by the Steiff Company. My cousin said that if she was going to spend her summers here, she would at least have her music."

"I can't imagine wanting to live in the city after spending time here," Rasheen looked about her.

"Elaine doesn't care for the country, but she endured it for Connor's sake. Patrick always said he bought this place as an investment, but I think the true reason was to make things easier for the boy so he wouldn't be so homesick. He was but fifteen years old when his father died, leaving him an orphan, and a horse farm in Ireland and Baltimore City are about as different as salt and sugar."

Martha removed one of several framed pictures that sat on the piano and handed it to Rasheen. "This is my youngest son, Peter, and that's Connor next to him. They were sixteen when that was taken, and already closer than most brothers. They were always together, and got into quite a bit of mischief."

Rasheen swept her glance over the other pictures. "What of your other sons?"

"Peter came here with us when Patrick and Elaine asked for our help in running the place. Our oldest son was about to be married, so we left our farm in his care, with the second one to help him."

"It must have been difficult, leaving your home."

"It worked out well for all of us. Elaine is as a sister

to me, and the boys had not one, but two mothers. She and Patrick would take Peter back to the city during the school year so that he could attend Loyola with Connor. Peter wanted to study to be a doctor, so Patrick sent him to medical school. John and I could never have done that."

Rasheen leaned down and tugged on the dog's collar, pulling him to his feet. "Finn, you go right back out into that kitchen this minute." The canine reluctantly rose and padded into the other room.

"Was he a big pup?" Martha patted Finn on the head as he walked past her.

"I have no idea. I only became his owner a few months ago." Rasheen then went on to tell how Finn had found her in the park and about her unfortunate encounter with Mr. Reilly.

Martha drew in her lips and frowned. "When Connor returned from that trip, he was in a sour mood for a time because of what he termed a mishap with an ejit woman and her wild dog. He didn't bother telling us the ejit's name."

"I was very rude to him that day. He had a right to be upset with me. It's just that I was so tired of people telling me how to handle my affairs, and when he tried to help with Finn, I took out my frustrations on him. I would have apologized if he hadn't left so quickly."

Martha burst into laughter. "That devil! Thought you would be a nuisance, "a spoiled and self-centered rich young widow," I believe were his words. But don't you bother about it. You'll do just fine."

"I'll just have to prove him wrong," Rasheen spoke with quiet, desperate firmness. "I'll prove them both wrong."

"Them?"

"Mr. Reilly isn't the first man to doubt my abilities," Rasheen answered.

She offered no further explanation, and Martha didn't

press her, but simply took her hand and gave it a reassuring squeeze.

*****

Connor grabbed a biscuit as Martha passed him with a tray fresh from the oven. "Ouch!" He tossed it back onto the tray; spilling coffee from the cup he held in his other hand.

"Serves you right, you should have waited until they were on the table. Now you can march over there and get a rag to clean up the mess you've made," Martha scolded.

"Would you deny a starving man nourishment?"

"You know better than to get in her way when she is trying to set breakfast out." Careful to use a potholder, John took the biscuit tray from Martha and set it in the center of the table.

"Aye, and now I have sore fingers to show for it." Connor sat his cup on the table and placed his injured digits under cold water, before wetting an old rag and cleaning up the spilled coffee.

He noted Mrs. Langston's struggle to keep her mouth from turning upward as she set out the breakfast plates. Though it twitched somewhat, she showed remarkable control and refrained from grinning. Instead, she asked, "I sent some books and things ahead. Did you receive them?"

"They're over in the school house."

"Wonderful, I want get started on unpacking and setting up the classroom."

She flashed him an appreciative smile that threatened his defenses. Trouble, yes, she was going to be trouble. Talk about anything, he told himself, anything to keep from looking into her eyes and being mesmerized by the way they sparkled at the mention of her classroom.

"If you need any additional supplies, they're to be charged to my account at Becker's General Store in town."

"Oh my yes, you will find that our young Mr. Reilly is very generous and I might add fair minded too." Martha raised her brows and looked directly at Connor.

He was aware of the sarcastic emphasis placed on her last words, making it clear to him that she disagreed with his original assessment of the ejit woman with the dog. He gave her a sheepish grin. Mrs. Langston may not realize it, but she was now under the protection of a mother hen. The way the two women kept up a steady stream of conversation throughout the meal, one would think they had known one another all their lives.

When breakfast was finished, Connor asked Mrs. Langston if she was ready to go see her new classroom. She checked with Martha first to see if she needed help with the dishes, but the older woman motioned toward the door. "Your job is to teach, mine is to keep this house running."

Connor watched her pleased expression when they stepped inside the school house. "Martha made the curtains. She wanted the room to be nice for you and the children."

Mrs. Langston began pulling the bright red curtains back to open the windows. "They're perfect for adding some cheerfulness to the room."

"The boxes over in the corner contain slate boards for the students. The two in the back have spelling books. I didn't have them put in the bookcases because I figured you'd have things of your own and would want to place them accordingly."

Her eyebrows rose in amazement. "How did you know to order the *NOAH WEBSTER'S BLUE-BLACK SPELLING* books?"

"I made some inquires when I decided to open the school. If you need any other books, order them and have the bill sent to me."

Pointing to the wood burning stove in the corner of the front of the room, he said, "When the weather changes, someone will start a fire for you in the morning before school, but you'll need to have one of the boys keep it stoked. There's plenty of wood outside in the back for your use, but make sure you let the fire burn out toward the end of the day."

He set her things on the desk and took his leave, but walked only a short distance before turning to study her through the open door. Unaware of his observance, she reverently touched the desk and ran her hand across the globe resting on a small table.

Just before he turned to go, she gave that disarming smile so reminiscent of the past. He had thought the young girl sweet, but the grown woman was far too much temptation. Perhaps it would have been better to have the more aloof Mrs. Langston working for him. This friendlier woman was taking his thoughts to places he wasn't ready to go. It would be so much easier to dislike her if she were more like the other female members of Polite Society. But she wasn't. Under other circumstances, he would enjoy discovering the true Rasheen Langston.

As things stood, he was grateful to be leaving on business for his uncle in the next few days. A visit with Kiernan McPhail would also be necessary since it now looked like the case was going to trial. Normally, he would be unhappy about such a trip, but not this time. He needed some distance between himself and his alluring new employee. A few weeks' absence on his part would be beneficial to both of them.

When he returned from Baltimore, she would have had enough time to decide if she was up to the task of teaching the community's children, and it would be best if he weren't around while she was settling in. Before, he had been certain he wanted to be rid of her. Now he wasn't so sure and that bothered him.

There was much more to her than the image burned in his mind of the silent woman with the frozen smile, standing regally next to her husband. He felt a twinge of guilt when he recalled how Martha had looked at him when she made her remark about his fair mindedness. She knew he was unhappy about being saddled with Rasheen Langston. Hopefully, he had heard the last of her remarks and she wouldn't chastise him when he got back to the house.

Why was he feeling guilty? He was the one viewing things with reason. How could someone who had been married to a member of High Society teach in a rural school? Still, Martha had confidence in her. Well, maybe Martha was right, maybe she might work out after all.

"Right," he grumbled to himself as he walked away, "And pigs can and fly - Damn Frank Hughes, and damn him again!"

CHAPTER 8

"Hallo in there, you must be Mrs. Langston."

Rasheen looked up to see a young woman standing just outside the schoolroom's open door.

"I was just at the Reilly home and Mrs. Schmidt informed me you would be here." The young woman laughed. "Oh dear, you must think me completely lacking in the social graces. I'm Bernice Peterson." She fumbled through her purse to retrieve a silver case and then let it drop back inside. "It seems rather silly to hand you a calling card, now that I've already introduced myself."

Rasheen stepped around the box of books she had been unpacking, and extended her hand. "No need for a calling card, and please, just call me Rasheen." She guessed that Bernice Peterson was near her age. The similarities ended there, since her visitor was tall and willowy, whereas she was small and curvaceous. A tight bun pulled golden hair from the young woman's face presenting an austere appearance that contrasted with the soft, friendly voice and celestial blue eyes.

"All right, Rasheen - you seem to be rather busy, could you use some help?"

"As you can see, there is much to be done." Rasheen walked around the desk to a cupboard in the back and pulled out two aprons, handing one to Bernice.

"I hope you don't mind a little dust."

"I'm just happy to be of some use," Bernice said as she unpinned her hat and set it down on a nearby desk so that she could get the top of the apron over her head. Next, she struggled to tie the bottom half of the apron over her bustled skirt in the back.

"Let me help." Rasheen pulled the strings up over the bustle and tied them securely in a nice bow. "I've decided that there's going to be no bustles or high fashion for me here, just plain dresses, skirts, and blouses."

"I wish I could have that freedom, but mother would never allow it." Bernice looked longingly at Rasheen's simple dress.

"I'm fortunate to no longer be under anyone's watchful eyes." Rasheen gave Bernice a sheepish smile. No need to mention that she wasn't referring to her mother.

The two women set about cleaning and dusting the room. As they worked, they talked about their families and backgrounds, and the afternoon passed quickly.

Bernice put the last book on the bottom shelf and then stood and stretched. "Oh my, I almost forgot the reason for my visit. Mother wanted me to invite you to luncheon tomorrow, but I must apologize in advance because it's more about prestige than hospitality."

"Oh, I doubt the Langston name is well known in these parts by most folks. Your mother has ties to Baltimore Society, and that's why it means something to her."

Bernice shook her head. "The Langston family is written about in the Society Section of the newspaper almost as much as the Ridgley's of Hampton. You are always at the head of some charity event."

"I worked at events with my mother and grandmother. They're concerned about the welfare of the poorer citizens of Baltimore. Of course, my mother enjoys the pomp and circumstance more so than Granny, but her heart is still at the center of the matter. Most of their efforts are primarily to help my uncle's parishioners, and I offered whatever influence I had with the Langston name to assist them."

"Your uncle is a minister, how wonderful."

"He's a Jesuit priest who was a teacher before the bishop asked him to take charge of one of the city's predominantly Irish parishes. Uncle Frank is more in tune with their needs, since he's the son of Irish immigrants. He is quite content as a pastor, and my mother and grandmother are a great help in raising funds for him. They adore him, since he is the youngest in my mother's family and quite the charmer."

"I don't think they're the only ones fond of your uncle," Bernice said.

"He always encouraged me to be myself and dream my dreams. You would like him, and I know he'd like you."

"More so than you will probably like my mother." Bernice turned her back toward Rasheen to have her apron untied. "In fact, I must confess that it was mother who forced me to make this call. She was unable to come herself due to another commitment, but she insisted I call in her place. Now that I've met you, I'm glad for her exigency."

Rasheen took the apron, along with her own and draped them across one of the desks. "I'll reserve judgment of your mother until tomorrow."

Bernice gave a relieved sigh. "Thank you for accepting. My mother would be most upset with me had you declined. As for myself, I will be happy to share your company."

*****

Rasheen turned into a circular drive and parked the buggy in front of a structure which resembled a southern plantation with its long gallery. Inside, she observed an

68

entrance hall large enough to serve as a small ballroom. She imagined ladies in elegant gowns with their trains trailing behind them as they descended the staircase; and she could almost hear waltz music floating through the rooms. The butler informed her that she was expected and ushered her into the parlor where Bernice was already waiting.

"Samuel, will you please let mother know that Mrs. Langston has arrived and we're in the parlor," Bernice said.

He bowed and disappeared from the room.

Rasheen only had a few seconds to let her gaze wonder around a room that was decorated as grand as those in the Langston home before an older woman dressed in a stylish brown striped dress glided into the parlor. Her soft white hair still had some traces of the same gold as Bernice's, but the similarities ended there. Unlike Bernice's delicate features, her mother's were full of sharp angles and her nasal voice grated rather than soothed.

"I do hope you'll allow us to host a formal luncheon for you so that you can meet some of the town's finer women," Bernice's mother said.

Rasheen clenched the folded hands in her lap. "I had hoped to escape formalities here in the county."

"My dear, you must let me give you a proper welcome. Just because we aren't in the city, doesn't mean we don't have the same standards for the members of Society," Mrs. Peterson insisted.

A few seconds later when her mother was occupied instructing the servants, Bernice leaned toward Rasheen and whispered, "Mother will want to show you off. Only the very snobbiest will be in attendance, and you'll find it a most enjoyable afternoon." She rolled her eyes. A behavior Rasheen wouldn't have expected from the reserved young Miss Peterson.

"I'm sure of it," Rasheen whispered back causing Bernice to choke back a giggle in response to the pained tone.

"What was that, dear?" Mrs. Peterson had completed her instructions and now turned her attention to the two young women.

Bernice coughed nervously. "We were just discussing Rasheen's new position, mother."

Mrs. Peterson gave a disapproving frown. "Mrs. Langston, I'm very happy that you're here with us, but it would be much better if it were under circumstances more becoming to your social standing. You should be seeking another husband. Young women such as you and my daughter need husbands to care for you."

"I think teaching is more productive way to spend my time, and I enjoy children." Rasheen tried to keep her voice from sounding defensive.

"It's a pity, Daniel dying so young and leaving no heirs. Now there is no one left to carry on the Langston name," Mrs. Peterson sighed.

"Mother! You have no right to speak of such personal matters."

Her mother continued undisturbed, "Don't be absurd, child. Pamela Langston was a friend from my girlhood days as was Lillian Hilliard and Ava Delacourte. I was sorry she didn't live to see her son marry. And then there was Jonathan's death. It broke the poor woman's heart. It was a tragedy, but then all things connected with that horrible war were, weren't they? At least she didn't live to bury her only remaining child. It would have been too much for her to bear."

Rasheen looked down at her gloved hands and fought hard to control the painful memories.

As if reading her thoughts, Bernice reached over, gave her a sympathetic pat on the shoulder, and said, "Might we speak of more pleasant matters with our guest?"

Mrs. Peterson waved the back of her hand. "The four of us planned that our children would marry one day, but then you came along and stole Daniel's heart and Bernice is being stubborn."

Samuel mercifully announced that luncheon was ready to be served in the dining room.

As she finished a bite of her crab cake, Mrs. Peterson continued the subject of young women and husbands. "It is my desire to see Bernice wed to Reginald Hilliard. Are you acquainted with the gentleman?"

Rasheen gave Bernice a sympathetic look. "Yes, I've met the gentleman," she said, purposely avoiding mentioning the fact that he was her traveling companion on the train ride to North County.

Bernice replied in exasperation. "Must we subject Rasheen to this argument?"

"I'm sure she would agree that Mr. Hilliard is a fine gentleman with a residence in the city and his country home here so that you would be able to spend time with your family. He would make a suitable match for any young woman."

Bernice set her fork down on the table with a loud thump. "I simply cannot tolerate any amount of time spent in that gentleman's presence."

"You must find a proper husband and take your place in society. If a man has a position, a good home and family name, then a woman may overlook tiny flaws in his character. Why can't you take your responsibilities more seriously?"

Rasheen coughed loudly as she placed her linen napkin over her mouth. "I'm sorry; I seem to have choked on a crumb." It would hardly help Bernice if she were to give her opinion of the esteemed Mr. Hilliard. She looked at the misery on her friend's face and wanted to tell Mrs. Peterson that Bernice had a responsibility to find her own happiness and not depend on a husband to care for her, but commented on the desert instead. "This cream cake is delicious."

"My cook studied under a French chef and makes

wonderful pastries and soups; but his entrees are excellent also." Mrs. Peterson daintily touched a linen napkin to the edge of her mouth wiping away a speck of cream.

Bernice mouthed a silent thank you to Rasheen, who then maneuvered the discussion to one of the Langston charitable events. Mrs. Peterson's face lit with anticipation. She was eager to hear about all the important people who had attended the gala affair. After they finished their meal, Bernice suggested she and Rasheen take a ride into town.

*****

Rasheen's first glimpse of the town was a pleasant surprise. Giant oak and maple trees shaded the cobblestone main street and inviting brick and wood buildings stood behind boardwalks.

They hitched the buggy to a post in front of the general store where an old man smoking a pipe occupied one of the two rocking chairs on the building's porch. A middle-aged man with a wide girth and smile to match jumped up from the other chair when the women approached.

"Mr. Becker, this is Mrs. Langston," Bernice said as they stopped before going into the store.

"Pleased to meet you, Mrs. Langston, and this here is my father," he said as the senior gentleman slowly rose from his chair and nodded at the two women.

He drew his bushy white brows together and scrutinized Rasheen for a few seconds. "You'd be staying at the Reilly place, right? You're the new teacher at Sara's Glen."

"You are right on both counts." She gave him a sincere smile.

"Wasn't sure about you, but you'll do. Well, welcome then, and if there's anything you need, just let my son know. If he doesn't have it in stock, he'll get it for you." Mr. Becker's father dropped back into his rocking chair and puffed the smoke from his pipe.

Inside the store, Rasheen had no doubt of the man's reassurance. Sturdy wooden shelves were filled with shoes, yard goods, farm implements, kitchen apparatuses, buttons, thread, and much more.

When they left the general store, they visited a bakery, and then passed the leather and harness shop, a boarding house, and a hotel with a café. Rasheen was curious about the boarding house since she didn't think there would be a need for such a place in addition to the hotel.

"Oh, but North County is a growing community. We have an iron works, stone quarry, mill, and we are only a short ride from Towson, so many of the people who have business there will stay at the boarding house since it is less expensive, but the café and hotel do a good business because of the train station. A lot of workers stay at the boarding house because of the housing construction along York Road and the surrounding area. The area has become a popular place for building summer cottages."

"Do I note a sense of pride in that little speech?" Rasheen asked.

"Maybe, just a little, but let's see the rest and you can judge for yourself." Bernice took her arm and led her on down the walkway. "Congratulations on winning over the senior Mr. Becker. He may be a little gruff, but he is well respected in North County and a good word from him carries a great deal of weight."

Rasheen shrugged. "I liked him."

"More importantly, he liked you." Bernice squeezed her arm.

They visited a few more shops before they passed the feed store and blacksmith's shop on the outskirts of town.

"This has been quite a tour. I've really enjoyed myself, but it's getting late, and I need to get home before supper. I wouldn't want to worry Martha."

As they started to walk towards their buggy, Rasheen caught a movement from the corner of her eye and looked over just in time to see a man shove a young boy to the ground. He raised his hand as if to strike the child when he struggled to stand, but upon realizing he was being watched, stopped, and pulled the youth to his feet instead.

She thought surely it must have been an accident and that she was mistaken about the perceived strike, but knew it wasn't when she felt a tight grip on her arm and looked over at Bernice's shock-glazed face. Without a word, the two women walked toward the man and the boy. Rasheen recognized the vole-faced man as Reginald Hilliard's driver and the boy as the same one she had seen with him at the train station.

The man gave the boy a keep-your-mouth-shut look and pushed him toward a nearby wagon. He ignored the two women and quickly jumped into the wagon beside the boy and snarled, "Git this rig movin, and I'll be having no more of your sass."

Rasheen watched the back of the wagon as it rolled toward the other end of the street. They should have done something, but what? By the time they reached the pair, the wagon was on its way.

"Do you know anything about Mr. Hilliard's driver?" Bernice shook her head. "How do you know that was Mr. Hilliard's driver?"

Rasheen told her of the incident upon her arrival at the train station. "He knocked that boy to the ground, and I'm sure he was about to strike him had we not intervened." She felt her impotent clenched fists hang at her sides.

"If that is his son, there is nothing we can do, and if he isn't then what is the boy doing with him, and why hasn't he told his parents about his treatment?" Bernice asked.

"I doubt the boy would utter a complaint. He seems terrified of that man. I did ask Mr. Reilly to see what he could do to have the boy attend school." There was something about the boy that had drawn her attention from the first time she laid eyes on him.

"Perhaps you can learn more if he is one of your students."

"Let's hope we're mistaken in our assumptions." Rasheen looked at the small silver watch with its Celtic swirls that was pinned on her dress. It had been a present from her grandmother when she finished college. Granny would have boxed the man's ears and taken the boy home with her if she'd been here. Never mind that they might all go to jail because of her actions.

Bernice looked puzzled. "Why are you smiling?"

"Oh, I was just thinking of how Granny would have handled that bully. I wish I had her courage."

Bernice studied her for a moment. "I don't know your Granny, but I have a feeling you've probably got more of her courage than your think."

CHAPTER 9

"Doesn't Mrs. Langston know what time we eat dinner?" Connor gestured toward Rasheen's empty chair.

Martha set the last serving dish on the table. "She had luncheon with the Petersons and then she and Bernice were going into town so she said not to bother about dinner for her."

Connor rolled his eyes and muttered, "Already she's starting with the Beau Monde. I hope Mrs. Langston can manage to fit teaching into her busy social life."

Chin raised, arms crossed, Martha began her interrogation. "Just what is your problem with Rasheen? She's a lovely young woman, and from what I've seen in the last two days, she's very conscientious."

"Might I remind you, that I'm a grown man, and entitled to my own opinions?" Connor asked in an irritated tone trying to wiggle out of the guilt she heaped on him.

But Martha continued to pile it on. "Connor Reilly, just what has gotten into you?"

"Has Mrs. Langston complained to you about my treatment?" Perhaps he might get her off track by countering with a question of his own.

"I asked her about the dog and when she told me about him, I realized she was the woman you were ranting about when you returned from your last trip. Don't you think you should give her a chance to prove herself and not pass judgment in advance? This isn't like you."

"She's here, is she not?" The idea of having to defend himself in his own home was irritating.

"You're making a judgment based on a past experience, and that's not a fair standard to hold her to."

Martha couldn't read him quite as well as she thought. It wasn't just about Amelia any longer. In addition to Mrs. Langston's beauty, she displayed spirit and intelligence. He could feel the beginnings of an ill-advised attraction. To put an end to the conversation before Martha sensed there was more, he answered, "All right, I'll try and be more open-minded."

Martha reached over and cuffed him gently alongside the head. "That's more like you."

*****

After the afternoon's luncheon, Rasheen was certain about her decision to leave Baltimore. A comfortable feeling settled over her when she passed through the gates of Sara's Glen and drove to the carriage house entrance. That was until Connor Reilly came out of the building, and helped her down from the buggy, taking her hand in his, putting his other hand to her waist to make sure she didn't fall. If it had been anyone else, she would have thought it a rather ordinary thing, but not him. She felt his hands on her in a way that was far from ordinary. They were standing so close she could feel his breath as he spoke.

"Good evening, Mrs. Langston. You're a little late for dinner."

Though the question was innocent enough, it was his roguish smile and her realization that she didn't want to lose his touch that tied her tongue. She stepped away and tried to regain her composure. "I …um…had a late luncheon at the Petersons, and then went into town." Before she could think of anything further to say, a stable hand appeared and unhitched the horse. She spoke to the young man for a few seconds and then turned to walk up the path toward the house. Mr. Reilly fell in step beside her, walking in silence.

The impact of his gentle grip when he took her arm as they climbed the porch sent a tingle down her spine. Such acts, though innocent enough on his part, reminded her of the small intimacies of marriage and feelings better left unremembered. *That's* why her nerves always acted up so in his presence. *Rubbish!* The man was about as innocent as a fox in the hen house, and her attraction was stirred by more than just memories.

*****

Rasheen removed the cups from the cabinet, and filled them from the kettle on the stove while Martha set out plates and sliced some cake.

"Thought you'd be interested in knowing that Keller was successful in servicing Muirne." John stretched his legs out before him and tilted his chair. "I figure she's due around the middle of May."

Connor let out a loud whoop as he jumped up and slapped John on the back almost knocking him over. "You know what this means?"

John struggled to regain his balance. "That you'll finally have your grand champion and that I'd better be more careful in the future when I give you good news."

Connor grinned. "I'm going down to the stables."

"What about your cake?" Martha asked.

"I'll have some later." Connor picked up an apple from the bowl on the table, started toward the door and then stopped and took another apple. "One for me too," he said over his shoulder.

"I wonder if the horse will get any." Martha shook her head.

"Why is he so excited about a pregnant mare?" Rasheen asked.

"Sara's Glen is primarily a horse breeding farm with some farming to bring in extra income, but most of its income comes from the sale of work horses and a few thoroughbreds for racing. His dream is to have a champion. That mare is going to be treated better than some wives who are expecting. I can promise you that." Martha filled the sink with hot water from the stove, and plunged her hands into the soapy water. Rasheen grabbed a towel from the nearby hook, and began drying the dishes as Martha handed them over to her.

A short time later, Connor returned from his visit to the stable and sat down to eat the slice of cake Martha had left at his place. "I'll be out riding most of the day tomorrow. Would you make me some sandwiches for my lunch?"

Martha looked over her shoulder. "Why don't you take Rasheen along?"

Rasheen put the last dried plate in the cupboard and hung the wet dish towel on the hook. "I'm sure Mr. Reilly will have a lot of things to attend to. I'd only hinder his efforts." Though she warmed to the idea of a nice ride about the property, she wasn't sure a ride with Connor Reilly was prudent.

"Not at all, it would be a pleasure." It was almost as if he had read her thoughts and was deliberately tormenting her. "I made Martha a promise to make you feel at home, and what better way than for you to become more familiar with Sara's Glen?"

The next morning Rasheen pulled her blue serge riding habit out of the trunk, and found the old denim clothes her mother had sent along for her charges. In the activity of settling in, she had forgotten all about them. A mischievous thought entered her mind. Granny would say it was her bad angel whispering in her ear. She threw the riding habit on the bed and dressed in one of the denim outfits, and then surveyed her reflection in the walnut oval-framed mirror that stood in the room's corner. Satisfied with her appearance, she quickly tucked the snug-fitting shirt into the trousers and pushed the trouser ends into her riding boots. She braided her hair into one long plait that hung down her back, took a deep breath, and headed downstairs, hesitating on the top step. Perhaps she should go back and change into the riding habit. She took a step back and faced her room, but then did an abrupt turn and forced her feet to move down the steps, and was most satisfied with that decision when she saw Mr. Reilly's reaction to her outfit.

He gulped his coffee down, choking in the process, before standing when she walked into the room. Good. Let him be the one unnerved for once. Perhaps this would help him reconsider his opinion of her. How many wealthy female ejits did he know that dressed in denim?

Martha broke the stunned silence. "What a wonderful idea! You'll be more comfortable in that attire. Why if I were twenty years younger, I would follow your example."

John slanted his wife a surprised glance. "Have you lost your senses?"

"Somehow, I can't envision you dressed in men's clothing, just doesn't seem proper." Connor Reilly gave a wry grin, all traces of his surprised look gone.

Rasheen folded her arms before her and looked Connor Reilly right in the eye. "Contrary to what you may think, I like to be practical. My Uncle Martin and his wife have a farm, and I spent many summers there helping with the chores. They have a friend from out West who stayed with them, and she dressed in men's work clothes when helping with the stock. No one seemed to mind. They were grateful for an extra pair of hands. What covered the the rest of the body was of little importance."

Mr. Reilly gave her a slow appraisal. "Don't know about propriety, but you certainly fill out…."

Martha pushed him back into his chair and gave him a threatening look. "Sit down and eat your breakfast before it gets cold."

Rasheen sat at the table and ate quickly in order to

catch up, since Mr. Reilly was already half finished his meal. Though it would have insulted most women that he and John had not waited for the ladies to be seated, she understood that they had probably been up hours and already attended to chores and were hungry. She liked the fact that Society's stringent rules didn't apply to this household.

Finn jumped up from his spot next to the stove when he realized something was happening, and plodded over to Connor. He patted the dog's head, and said, "Would you like to do some exploring today, lad?"

"Do you think he can keep up with the horses?" Rasheen asked.

"He'll probably go a little ways with us and then come back. I hope the sidesaddle we have is the right size for you, we only have the one."

"If it doesn't, I'm dressed to ride astride. I've done it before."

He ran his fingers through his hair bunching it in his fist at the top of his head. "Why am I not surprised at that? What about your reputation should someone see us?"

She was enjoying his discomfort. "I doubt that anyone from Baltimore will be on your property, and it really doesn't concern me."

He shrugged as he grabbed his slouch hat off the hook by the door. "All right then, but you need something to cover your head. The afternoon sun will be hot in the open fields. Do you have something, or would you prefer one of my hats to go with the rest of your attire?" He half-circled her like a wolf stalking its prey. The look he gave her wasn't one of censure like the ones she had received from Daniel so often in the past, but it made her just as uncomfortable.

Heat crept up her neck and into her cheeks. She turned her face away from him, grabbed one of the hats from the peg near the door, and tucked her braid under it.

"There, now if we come upon anyone in the distance, they will think I am one of the men."

"Not very likely," Connor muttered under his breath as he opened the door for her and then led her out to the stable yard where two horses were saddled and waiting.

Think you can handle her?" He asked as they approached a large chestnut mare that raised its head in curiosity.

"I should be all right." It had been awhile since she'd last ridden, but she had every confidence she could hold her own. She was looking forward to that glorious feeling of freedom that riding had always provided.

"What a beauty, you are," she said to the animal as she patted its neck. "What's her name?"

"Sassy."

"Sassy?"

"Don't be intimated by her name, she won't give you any trouble. "Sassy is a well behaved young lady." He stroked the horse's neck and then helped Rasheen mount, sending the now all too familiar tingle down her spine at his touch, even through her riding gloves.

"I'll trust your word." She adjusted herself in the saddle with no difficulty and fixed her feet in the stirrups.

"All right then?" He asked.

She nodded.

He mounted his own horse and rode slowly around the property near the house, making a pretense of pointing out various structures and their purpose. She suspected he was observing her to see if she could handle the horse, and since the animal was well behaved just as he said, she had no trouble at all. They passed the mule barn, granary, cow barn and back up to the north side of the house to the icehouse with its fieldstone walls and domed brick ceiling. He pointed toward the eastern perimeter of the property. "Over there is the smokehouse, some storage sheds, and outdoor privies."

They headed away from the structures and out over

the cut fields at a faster pace. Apparently, he was satisfied that she could handle her horse. When they came to an enclosed pasture, Connor held his hand up for her to wait, and then galloped on ahead. The horse leapt over the fence and landed gently. Thunder and grace. For a breathtaking moment, stallion and man appeared as one.

"Are you coming through?" Connor had ridden back to a nearby gate and opened it for her to come through. "Or did you plan to jump?"

Did he think she wasn't capable? She itched to show him, but such action would probably end up in broken bones for her. It had been too long since she had last ridden. She would be sore enough tomorrow; no sense in tempting fate.

"Not today." She gave what she hoped appeared to be a disinterested shrug as she rode through the opened gate.

They rode until they came to edge of the woods, entered, and followed along a well-worn path for a mile or so where they stopped at a stream to let the horses drink. He took some carrots from his shirt pocket and gave her one for the mare, before feeding his own horse. "I used to come here to fish a lot when I was a lad." He put his hand to his ear. "If you listen closely, you can hear the voices of the ancients beneath the stream, singing to its melody."

"Next you'll be telling me that the wood fairies come and dance along the stream's edge." She picked up a pebble and threw it into the clear water gurgling over flat gray stones.

"Well now, maybe we'll have to sneak up on them and then you'll be a believer, aye?"

She closed her eyes and breathed in the musty scent of wet leaves, and earth. "No need, I'm already a believer."

Stepping closer to the edge, she dipped her hand into the cold water. When she straightened again, she lost her footing on some damp moss and would have landed in an undignified position, had he not caught her arm. Sweet Saint Brigid the man rattled her right to her bones.

"Are you all right?" he asked, genuine concern creasing his brow. He was still holding her arm.

"Yes, just a bit clumsy." She wiggled her arm out of his hold.

He studied her closely for a minute and then pulled a leather-bound silver flask out of his saddle bag, removed the cap, filled it with some of the bottle's contents and handed it to her. She hesitantly took the cap and was surprised to find that it had no odor of spirits when she raised it to her lips to drink.

Featherlike laugh lines crinkled around his eyes, but his voice contained a hint of censure when he said, "You thought it was whiskey? Don't judge by appearances."

"Your own words, Mr. Reilly." She returned the flask and smiled sweetly. "I have no objection to a drink of whiskey now and again."

His eyes gave her a frank and admiring look. "Well, Mrs. Langston, you must admit your appearance is deceiving."

"Um, perhaps we had better go, if you're going to show me more of the property."

"As you wish madam." He made a flourish with his hat, his cheek dimpled by the now familiar mischievous smile, bowed low and then took her arm to lead her back to the horses.

They remounted and rode on along the stream's edge for a time before turning to go deeper into the woods. Eventually, they emerged from the trees and crested a hill where they overlooked amber and olive colored fields surrounded by woods of evergreens and deciduous trees.

"This is spectacular," she said as she marveled at the tree leaves shimmering in the sunlight. Though their coloring was the same, they were far more spectacular than any emeralds or diamonds.

He dismounted and helped her do the same. "I

thought you would enjoy the view. I could say that this is my favorite season, but then autumn comes with its shades of scarlet and gold, followed by winter's silver majesty, only to give way to spring when everything comes alive again. No matter the time of year, the view is wondrous."

She watched him as he stood silently and gazed out at the fields. "You have the Irishman's love of the land."

"Aye, it's a beautiful place; a gift beyond price."
"Words spoken from the lips of a farmer and not a lawyer," she said softly.

He turned to face her, his warm gaze gone; replaced by a glare reminiscent of a frozen pond – cold and unyielding. There was no dimple in his cheek now. The jaw was set in a hard line. "The words of a farmer are of no less value than those of a lawyer. Here at Sara's Glen, people are respected for their own worth, and appreciated for the work they perform."

"I did not, that is I meant…" Regaining her composure, she replied, "Not all are treated with respect, at least not ejit rich women Is that not correct?"

A shadow of annoyance crossed his face, yet he didn't mention Martha. "I don't believe I've shown you any disrespect." He leaned forward until he was only inches from her face.

Stiffening her spine and drawing herself up until she was almost standing on her toes, she said, "In spite of your word, you've already judged me without giving me the opportunity to prove myself." She fixed her gaze on him, defying him to disagree.

To her surprise, the beginning of a smile tipped the corners of his mouth. "Fair play to you. So there is still a bit of Scathack in you after all. Very well then, I'll withhold my judgment and my comments until the end of the school year, as promised."

"You remember Scathack?" She asked in disbelief. Yet the fact that he hadn't forgotten gave her a jolt of pure happiness.

"How could I not? Your confidence in your abilities was worthy of the name. I'm happy to see you haven't lost it. Do you remember the little gift I gave you?"

"Gae Blog? I still have it somewhere in my jewelry box." No need to mention that it was among her treasured possessions.

He gave her a pleased smile. "I made that for you because Scathack's spear had magical powers."

"I remember, and you said that someday when I was older I would have such power, only mine would be of speech and intellect."

"Was I wrong?"

She let out a sigh. "You weren't wrong, for all the good it did me. Not everyone thinks as you do."

For a moment he studied her intently. "I thought you said the opinions of others didn't matter to you."

"Not me."

"Who then?"

"It no longer matters."

Though she could see the concern in his gaze, she had no intention of sharing her unhappy memories. "Could we please alter the course of this conversation?"

He raised her hand to his lips. "I'll grant your request if you grant one for me. Since we were once friends, don't you think it's time we dispensed with the proprieties and called one another by our first names?"

She snatched her hand away. "Well, Connor it is then." Oh, this man was a devil to be sure. He could charm the birds off the bushes and the song from their throats. Her face felt warm. It must be the sun beating down, she thought. It couldn't be that she was blushing.

"All right, Rasheen, or perhaps I should say Scathack, shall we have our lunch now? I don't know about you, but I'm hungry." He tied the horses to a nearby tree and removed a small blanket from his saddle bag. She took it from him and spread it under a maple tree, while he retrieved their lunch from his bags and set it on the blanket. Once they were settled, she unwrapped the cloth-covered sandwiches and cookies.

He poured them each a drink from the small jug of lemonade and laughed when he handed her the cup. "Hope you aren't disappointed that it's only lemonade."

"What, a jug and no poteen?" She grinned.

"You know about Irish Moonshine? You didn't come by that knowledge from your Uncle Frank."

"My grandmother is from Ireland."

"What County?"

"Mayo."

"I was born in Kildare."

"Martha said you came to live with your aunt and uncle when your father died."

"They've been like parents to me. I don't have any memory of my mother as I was but a babe when she died, but I'm sure Martha already told you that."

Rasheen nodded. "She says your uncle bought this place to help you adjust to your new life."

"Only someone like my uncle could understand my love of horses and land. Those first few months I rode up here whenever I missed my father, and somehow I felt connected to him."

She thought of Daniel and how she wanted to escape his memory. Sara's Glen was helping her to do that, just as it had helped Connor remember. "There is something special about this place. I can see why you wouldn't want to live anywhere else."

"Uncle Patrick had hoped that I would go into politics, but my first love was always Sara's Glen. He said a man must make his own choices in life. My plan was to practice law and acquire enough wealth from my investments to enable me to purchase Sara's Glen from him, but he gave it to me. Can you imagine that? The man provided me with a loving family, educated me, and then gave me this beautiful land. He said it would have been left to me upon his death anyway, and he wanted to see me happy now."

"It's a blessing to have family to surround you when life changes," she said.

"Your family – Frank, they helped you through your grief when you lost your husband?"

"After Daniel's death, I had an emotional breakdown and returned home. If it hadn't been for my family's love and care, I may not have survived. I'm grateful, but I can't follow their wishes for my happiness. My mother would have me assisting her with her various charities with the hope of finding another husband. They mean well, but I don't want that."

He laughed. "Something I understand only too well, much to the dismay of my aunt and uncle."

Rasheen replied softly, "There is nothing wrong with marriage, unless it becomes difficult to separate the pain from the joy." She looked away from him and tried to push down the unhappy memories that were threatening to the surface.

He turned her to face him and said, "We all experience pain and loss." She didn't start when he tilted her chin to look up at the sky. "See how blue the sky is today? We may wish it could always be that way, but the darker skies help us appreciate the fair ones, and even the most furious storms have their majesty."

"I know you've experienced loss - your parents, your homeland, but you've never shared your life with someone as a spouse. There are many kinds of suffering, not all are caused by grief."

He bent his head forward and looked directly into her eyes, as if he were searching for something. His expression was thoughtful, contemplative, as if he were trying to reach a decision. She watched the play of emotions in his eyes.

Breaking the gaze, he leaned back on his elbows and studied a lone hawk soaring high above them in soundless flight. When the bird dipped behind the tree line and was out of sight, Connor finally spoke. "There was someone with whom I wanted to share my life, but she came from a very old and respected family. My blood is green; theirs is blue. The match would have been a disaster." He took a breath and looked up toward the sky as if searching for the hawk.

She noted that even though the statement had been matter of fact, there was a glint of pain in his eyes. It was a pain she was all too familiar with – rejection its name.

"If she loved you enough, none of that should have mattered." But it did matter. Acceptance didn't always come with love; at least it hadn't in her experience.

"She would have been unhappy living at Sara's Glen, and I would be unhappy elsewhere. In the end, we both would have been miserable." He gave a resigned shrug.

"If you try to be what you are not, everyone is unhappy," she said.

"So you understand?"

"A man makes his own choices in life, but a woman gives up that privilege when she marries."

"I would think in a happy marriage they make their choices together."

"In a happy marriage," she echoed.

Connor patted her shoulder. "We should start for home."

Neither of them spoke as they folded the blanket, packed it in the bags. In an attempt to lighten the mood, she said, "I'll race you back to the house."

"I'll give you a head start, but let me assure you, Scathack, you'll not win." They remounted their horses and true to his word, he gave her a good start.

The horses thundered over the fields. Connor beat her back, but she tried to argue that it was a tie. They were laughing when they brought the horses to a walk near the stables. "I'll take them in. You go on up to the house."

By the time she ascended the porch steps she was humming. It had been a lovely outing.

"I told you he could be a nice enough lad when he chooses." Martha rocked back and forth in the porch rocker, a satisfied smile on her face.

Caught by surprise, Rasheen stopped at the top of the steps. "It was nice to be out riding again. I'd forgotten how much I enjoy it."

"And the company?"

"You were right. Connor and I just got off to a bad start."

"Hmmmm. No more Mr. Reilly. Must've been a nice outing."

CHAPTER 10

"As she watched Bernice write the alphabet letters across the top of the blackboard, Rasheen decided that now might be the time to pose the question she had been considering. "Would you like to be my assistant? You needn't give me your answer right away. I'm sure you'll want to take time to think it through, but I would very much like to continue with…."Before she could finish her proposal, Bernice finished the sentence for her. "I would love to work with you."

Rasheen gave her an enthusiastic hug. "I was hoping you would agree. You've already been such a help. I don't want to ask Connor to pay your salary, so if you don't mind, I will pass mine along to you since I have no need of it. Though you probably get an allowance from your parents this will give you a bit of independence. Who knows it may be a whole new career for you."

Bernice stared down at the chalk that she rolled in her fingers. "Mother would never stand for me taking wages."

Rasheen understood, but wasn't going to let Bernice's subservience to her mother thwart her plan to help her friend find the courage to choose her own life's path. "You should have some money that is your own. You can tell your mother that I can't manage without you. There is no need for her to know about the salary. Just think how impressed she will be that you are indispensable to Mrs. Langston."

Bernice shook her head in disagreement. "You could manage very well on your own."

"Nonsense, I've come to depend on your help. Think of how much better it has made the children's learning experience to have two teachers," Rasheen insisted.

The hoped-for glint of independence gleamed in Bernice's eyes. "All right, we're agreed, and I promise to be an excellent assistant."

"Perhaps assistant was a poor choice of words; I think partner is more suitable. Truly, you've not only been helpful with the children, but you've made me feel more comfortable in my new role as teacher."

*****

Rasheen stood inside the school's doorway and swung the hand bell to call the children inside. Once everyone had settled in for the day, she passed out the *McGUFFEY'S ECLECTIC READERS* to the younger children sitting in the front of the room.

"Open your books to page sixteen. Agnes, would you please begin reading?"

The young girl stood, but remained silent and frozen to the spot next to her desk. "It's all right dear, take your time," Rasheen coached.

Finally, Agnes began to read. "Fa-fa-ther, Mo-mo-mo-mother, Sisssssster, Bro-o-o-ther, all dear, are ga-ga-thered near." As she struggled to finish the rest of the paragraph, one of the older boys in the back of the room mimicked her, producing snickers form some of others children around him. Jack Benson was seated next to the mimicker. He leaned over and whispered something, and the smirk-faced boy answered with a clenched fist displayed beneath the desk.

Rasheen stopped the snickers with what Bernice called "The Look." She would have missed the scene between the two boys had she not dropped her book mark and caught the movement from the corner of her eye when she bent to retrieve it.

From her position in the back of the room, Bernice raised a brow in unspoken question. Rasheen gave a silent nod that she had seen the exchange. She didn't want to address the problem until she had some time to consider how do handle it.

"Well done," she said to Agnes as the child finished reading her verse. "You may take your seat."

The day passed with no more incidents. After Rasheen dismissed the children, she and Bernice set about tidying the room. When she went to close the window near the play area, she saw Agnes sitting on a bench crying. There were a few boys and girls standing next to her. Rasheen stood on the side of the window, out of view, and listened.

"Wa-Wa-Wa-What's the ma-ma-matter, Agnes. Ca-Ca-Cat go-go-got your tongue?" One of the boys asked.

"Leave her alone. All of you get out of here." Jack stood in front of Agnes as if to shield her.

"What are you going to do about it?" The boy shoved Jack.

"I said leave her alone." Jack stood toe to toe with Luke Dancent, who was a good deal heavier and half a head taller.

"Make me." Luke shoved Jack again, this time knocking him to the ground.

A young girl pushed her way through the cluster of girls. "If you don't stop this instant, I'm going in and tell Mrs. Langston."

The children formed a circle in anticipation of a fist fight. The young girl turned and started toward the school house, but several of the boys blocked her way. "Mind your own business, Hildy," they shouted.

Both boys stood glaring at each other for a few seconds, each waiting for the other to make the first move. The bigger boy swung at Jack and hit him in the jaw. He staggered back, but before the bully could take another swing, Jack came at him like a swarm of angry wasps.

There was no doubt the bigger boy deserved to be taught a lesson, but Jack was going to be the one getting the worst of it if Rasheen didn't put a halt to things. She yelled out the window, "Jack Benson, you come in here this minute."

"Now you're going to get it," the bully taunted.

"And you, Luke Dancent, will stop bothering Agnes, or I'll have a word with your parents," Rasheen addressed the other boy. "Now go home the rest of you, right this minute." The children quickly dispersed, but Agnes remained on the bench, her sobbing now down to a few sniffles. Hildy sat next to her, wiping the smaller girl's eyes with a handkerchief she had pulled out of her dress pocket.

"Agnes, dear, you come inside also," Rasheen said.

Hildy walked up to the door with Agnes, and as she was about to turn and leave, Rasheen said, "Hildy, will you please come inside also?"

Once all three children were inside, she asked them to take seats in the front of the room. Leaning against the desk, she addressed Jack and Hildy, ignoring the fight that had just occurred. "It seems that Agnes has a problem with her speech. I would like the two of you to work together to help her. Would you be willing to do this?"

Jack looked confused, but agreed to help as did Hildy. Agnes shook her head forlornly. "M-m-m-mrs Lang-s-st-st-ston, I ca-ca-n't talk r-r-right and no one c-c-can fix it."

"You'll always have the problem, Agnes, but if you take your time and feel more confident, it will be better. There are exercises that you can do to help. We'll have Hildy and Jack work with you after school. Will you try?" She patted the little girl's shoulder.

"Y-y-yes ma'am."

"Is that agreeable to the two of you?"

"Yes ma'am," said Hildy.

"I'm not so sure about staying after," Jack said. "I have chores waiting for me when school's out." He was already looking at the door uneasily.

"Any help you can give will be appreciated." Rasheen wanted to address the matter further, but Jack pleaded to be dismissed, and remembering the incident in town, she sensed it would go hard on him were he to be late. "You may go now, but no more fighting. In the future, you will come to me if there's a problem. I'll be addressing the class about this matter making it clear that anyone who tries to settle things in fisticuffs will be spending time with me after school, so you needn't fear that the other boys will think you weak."

The much relieved boy bolted for the door.

"It was nice of you to take up for Agnes." Rasheen placed her arm about Hildy's shoulder and gave her a gentle squeeze.

"Th-th-ank you." Agnes smiled timidly at the other girl.

"Well, it wasn't very nice what they did to you. I'm sorry I couldn't stop them."

"I think after today things will improve. Now the two of you run along."

The girls walked from the room, arm in arm, but first stopped to bid farewell to Bernice who had silently sat in the back of the room. Once they had closed the door, she asked, "What are you going to do if Luke acts up again?"

"We'll watch him very closely in the next few days, and if he incites any more disturbances in our classroom, I'll make good on my threat to speak with his parents." Rasheen rested her chin on her fist as she sat at the desk. "Did you notice how concerned Jack was about getting home after school? I think there's more going on than just being late for chores."

******

The next few days, Rasheen tried to draw Jack out by praising him for lessons well done and seeking his assistance in things such as cleaning the blackboards, fetching water from the pump - any excuse she could invent.   He was always polite, but never revealed anything about his home life. She knew no more about him now than she did when he first entered her classroom.

On one occasion when he stayed after school to help with Agnes's exercises, Rasheen managed to get him to stay for a few minutes after the girls left using the excuse that she needed some wood from the pile in the back of the schoolhouse.   That was a lie because Connor's man would take care of it in the morning, but she needed an excuse to spend some time alone with Jack so she would have an opportunity to talk to him and try once more to learn something of his parents.

After the wood had been brought in she said, "If you get into trouble with your folks, I'll be happy to speak on your behalf."

"I don't have any folks. They're dead," Jack answered flatly.

That was a possibility she hadn't considered. "You're so young to have lost both parents. When did it happen?"

"My father died a few years ago. That's why we moved here. My mother worked for Mr. Hilliard as his housekeeper until her death last year."

"I'm sorry. It's hard to lose a loved one." She felt the pull of her own ever-present scar once again. Though her marriage hadn't been happy, she loved Daniel and missed him. How much more painful it must be to be an orphan. She wondered how a housekeeper would have had the means to provide for Jack's education. Hilliard didn't seem to be the type of employer who would worry over such a matter, so she ventured further into the boy's private life to ask about his previous schooling.

"I went to school when we lived in the city, but when my father died, we had no money, so my mother took a job with Mr. Hilliard. When we moved here she taught me. It was important to her that I keep up with my studies. I couldn't believe it when Mr. Hilliard said I would come to your school."

"Is Mr. Hilliard your guardian?"

"No ma'am. I don't think I have one, at least not officially. Mr. Chilcrit took me in to work with him when my mother died." Jack took a nervous step backward toward the door. "If I don't get my chores done because of school, he'll be upset with me."

"I won't keep you any longer." Rasheen hesitated a moment before deciding to make a leap of faith, then stood up and slowly and came around the desk to put her hand on his shoulder. "Jack, if you ever want someone to talk with, I'm a good listener."

He flinched at her touch.

"Oh dear, you've hurt yourself. Let me see if there are any bruises." Rasheen reached over to unbutton his shirt.

"No, it's fine, really," he said as jerked back turning his head away from her.

"If you've hurt yourself carrying the wood in, it's my responsibility to make sure you are all right. Come on, we'll go up to the house and put a little witch hazel on it. It won't hurt a strong lad such as you. As she was talking, she stepped closer and opened the shirt. What she saw horrified her. Angry red welts curled around the top of his shoulder. She was certain they continued down his back, but he jumped back once more putting distance between them, preventing her from further discovery.

"How did this happen?" She waited for his explanation, though she knew the answer.

"I, um, the rooster clawed me." His eyes darted in the direction of the door and his body tensed as if ready to sprint.

She shook her head. "No rooster did that to you." Chilcrit was responsible, she was sure of it.

"Yes, it did, Mrs. Langston, it---did, it did."

"A rooster got up on your shoulder and under your shirt like that. No, Jack, I don't think so. Those are strap marks. Who did this to you?" She asked, trying to keep her voice steady. "Was it Mr. Chilcrit?"

Jack hung his head and looked at his feet. He answered in barely a whisper.

"I can't tell you."

"Why?" She tried to keep her face expressionless, but could see her failure from the fear and shame in his eyes. Granny always said her face showed every emotion.

"Please....... It won't happen again. I'll be more careful next time."

Rasheen doubted the boy's assurances about a recurrence, but seeing his terror, she backed off. If she went to Connor about it, she had no doubt he would confront Chilcrit, and if the latter was Jack's guardian that would only make things worse for the boy. Besides, Connor was in Baltimore on business, and Jack hadn't identified who had beaten him. Though all indications pointed to Chilcrit, for all she knew it could be Hilliard. Experience had taught her that things weren't always as they seemed. She would have to wait until she could find out more about the boy's situation, and there was only one way of doing that. She grimaced at the thought of befriending Hilliard, but he was her only source of information other than Jack.

"All right, we'll put the matter aside for the present, but tell me why you're staying with Mr. Chilcrit. Are there no grandparents or aunts and uncles that might have taken you in?"

"No ma'am. I'm fortunate that Mr. Chilcrit agreed to let me work for him when my mother died. Otherwise, I'd be sent to live at the Almshouse. I shouldn't have come to school. He doesn't like me coming to school because it'll make me uppity."

He looked up at her with pleading eyes and his voice became agitated. "Mr. Chilcrit says I'm too old to go to an orphanage. Mrs. Langston, please don't say anything to anyone. I don't want to go to the Almshouse with all the crazy people. They'd do terrible things to me."

It would be pointless to try and convince him that Chilcrit had lied. She would have to let it rest for now. At least she could keep an eye on him this way and if she noticed any more abuse, she would do something. "All right, Jack, but will you come to me if you need help? We'll work something out so that you don't have to go away, I promise."

"Yes ma'am, I really have to be going now." He backed away, inching toward the door and freedom.

"I expect to see you in school tomorrow. If you don't attend, I shall have to notify Mr. Hilliard." She sensed the hopelessness and fear of the boy, and tried to reassure him. "It will be all right, Jack. You must trust me."

He looked at her with untrusting eyes. "Yes ma'am. Can I go now?"

She watched him walk down the steps, shoulders slumped, head bowed. Poor lad. Deceit, cruelty, and indifference were all he had known since his mother's death. Somehow she had to show him that she could be trusted.

CHAPTER 11

Connor checked the address on the letter he had received from Frank telling him that Kiernan McPhail was going to need legal assistance, folded the paper, and returned it to his pocket, as he continued down Carey Street. The rhythm of Mount Clare caught his attention so he stopped at the gate and waved to the guard posted by the front entrance with its *No Trespassers* sign. From his position, he could see the section of new roof going up over the area where McPhail's injury had occurred. His gaze then traveled to the open roundhouse where engines hissed, bells clanged, and wheels clacked over tracks as the metal giants were placed into position for maintenance.

He watched in fascination as an incoming engine moved into the roundhouse. Once it was positioned and locked onto the turntable's rails, men pushed the wooden handles on the table's ends to swing it around to be moved into an empty stall for repairs. Each man participated in the silent dance, the steps committed to memory from hours of repetition.

He lingered a few more seconds and then made his way to the end of the street and turned onto Lemmon Street where a young girl struggled to push the community water pump's handle up and down with both hands while holding the bucket in between her feet on the ground beneath the water's flow. Connor picked up the pail and handed it to her. "Here you go, lass, you hold 'er and I'll do the pushing." In a few minutes, the task was complete. The girl gave him a smile and curtseyed. She had the same rich sable colored hair as Rasheen, and the same smile, the one that started with a sparkle in her eyes, and then a full-fledged curving of the lips. "Let me carry that for you." He took the pail from her before she could protest.

She walked next to him in silence until they arrived at her house where she stopped and said, "I'll take the water now sir, and be thanking you for your kindness." The liquid in the pail splashed from side to side when she climbed the steps to her house, reaching right up to the rim and then falling back inside without spilling a drop. Just as she was about to close the door, Connor removed his hat and gave an exaggerated bow. Her laughter's melody would have cast a spell over the fairies, just like… There it was again. Even now when he was occupied with more important matters, Rasheen still crept into his mind. *Stop being an ejit and concentrate on the matter at hand.* He spun around and picked up his pace.

As he passed an ice wagon parked in front of the McPhail house, one of the horses left its calling card in a steamy plop on the cobbled street. Strong vapors rising from it stung his eyes, and the odor wafted into his nostrils. Similar mementos of earlier equine visits dotted the street. This wasn't the upper end of town, and the street cleaners took their good time getting the job done, if they bothered to arrive at all.

He climbed the two wooden steps and rapped on the door. A woman, who reminded Connor of a younger Martha, answered. "Father Hughes told us to be expecting ye today. Well now so, come in, come in."

Once he was inside the small parlor, a man a few years older than him struggled to rise out of a chair on the other side of the room. The poor soul was bent over like an old man.

Connor walked a few steps across the room. "Please, don't trouble yourself to be moving about." He shook Mr.

McPhail's hand and took a seat in the straight backed chair opposite him.

As soon as he was seated, Mrs. McPhail left the room. On the other side of the curtained archway, Connor could hear her getting the cups from the cupboard. He would be expected to have tea with them. No one ever left an Irish home without having some tea and a bit of food. To do so, would be an insult.

Kiernan McPhail studied him for a few seconds and then asked, "If ye don't mind me asking, how is it that a lawyer like yerself has work worn hands?"

Connor looked down at his hands. No one had ever mentioned their condition before. The men he worked with at Sara's Glen would not have cared, and he suspected that those he dealt with on a professional basis were less observant than McPhail.

"My father trained horses for a wealthy man in County Kildare, and I seem to have inherited that skill. Truth be told, I would spend all my time with the beasts, but I handle my uncle's legal affairs; and Father Hughes is a good friend, so from time to time he asks a favor of me."

"Aye, so that's the way of it. I'm to be a favor, am I now?"

Connor raised his hand, palm outward. "Please, don't take offense. You have a family to provide for. Father Hughes would not have asked me if he didn't think your case justified. I wouldn't be here if the company hadn't ceased paying you."

Kiernan McPhail frowned and anxiously rubbed his leg. "Aye, 'tis the way things stand at the present. We have some savings, but they're almost gone. Me wife takes in wash and does some sewing, but that won't be enough to pay the rent and buy food. I'll be finding something. There's no other choice."

"Your body needs time to heal before you think about taking on another job. Your family will be taken care of until the case is settled."

"We won't be taking charity, Mr. Reilly." McPhail gave him a piercing glare.

"It won't be charity. You can pay it back out of your settlement."

"What if there is none? Do ye really think we have a chance? The courts haven't been favorable to injured workers in the past."

"Don't believe everything you hear. There are more cases won than people realize. You just don't read about them in the papers. A lot depends on the circumstances involved in the injury. Look at the recent Turntable Cases." He couldn't believe people were daft enough to use the turntables as carousels, and then sue the railroad when they became injured. Many of them had been awarded settlements. In these cases, he felt the railroad wasn't responsible, not when the half-wits trespassed and misused the company's equipment. McPhail's case was another matter. "Tell me what happened on the day of your accident?"

Before McPhail had a chance to speak, his wife returned with tea and a tray of heavily buttered soda bread.

"This is grand." Connor said as he took a bite of the thick slice.

"I'm glad ye like it." Mrs. McPhail placed another slice on his plate before he could refuse, not that he would have done so. "Are ye taking Kiernan's case then?"

"I am indeed. He was just about to tell me about the events that took place on the day he was injured." Connor sat back in as a relaxed manner as he could manage in the small wooden chair.

McPhail winced, and let out a slow breath, as he reached for his cup on the small table next to his chair.

"Now ye see why we need the man's help? Look at ye, it will take months before yer back to yerself, if even then." Mrs. McPhail's concerned expression belied her harsh tone.

"Aye, 'tisn't as bad as at the start, but the pain knifes

me back when I move certain ways. The worst is the deadness in me leg. I'd be happier if I could feel something."

"Perhaps as more time passes, it'll improve." Connor tried to offer some encouragement before prodding the man. "You were going to tell me about your accident."

"The building where I worked is a busy, dirty structure, to be sure. Hazy smoke clouds yer vision and faint light filters through grimy windows. On a cold, wet day, ye won't find a more cheerless place. Steam and water spill onto the floor. Chills ye to the bone, it does." McPhail shivered. "Hammers pounding, engines popping off, and bells ringing – this is the racket that pesters yer ears all the day long. The air's thick with the smell of grease and sweat. Makes one miss working in the fields where the rain is soft and the air clean."

McPhail may have been adding more detail than necessary, but Connor didn't hurry him along. Instead, he gave a nod for he remembered what it was like to walk through a soft rain and feel the lush turf beneath his feet. Though it wasn't Ireland, there were still days like that to be had at Sara's Glen.

McPhail continued with no trace of bitterness in his voice. "Because I was a poor immigrant, no job was too hard. I wiped engines, turned tables, emptied cinders, and helped the machinists to lift and lug. Wasn't what I wanted, but it was good honest work. Eventually, I was promoted to mechanic."

He closed his eyes and paused as if trying to visualize something. "There was a hard rain all morning the day of the accident. I was worried about the roof with all that rain falling on it. You see, it needed repairs and the supervisor had put in a work order, but they hadn't got to it. The wind blew through and the water dripped on us. We're used to that because there's always some water coming in because of the holes in the roof for the engines' steam, but this was worse. Me face was so wet that I could scarce see me tools. When I wiped me eyes, I looked up at the roof just in time to see a big bulge directly over young Murphy. I shouted a warning, but there was too much noise. He didn't hear me so I ran to push 'em out of harm's way. A part of the roof fell right after I got to 'em. 'Twould've killed 'em for certain."

McPhail shook his head incredulously. "I thought I had cleared us both, but I didn't quite make it. Something hit me in the back. I'm not certain if 'twas a piece of machinery, or part of the roof. Murphy and I ended up under an engine, which most likely protected us and that's the truth of it. I was really afraid at first because I couldn't move. They took me to the City Dispensary and a Doctor Schmidt treated me. I think he's the reason I still have me leg. There was a nasty gash, but 'tis healed now."

Connor was pleased with this information. "Doctor Schmidt is a very fine doctor. You were lucky to have him treat you."

"Right ye are, right ye are. Ye know him then?"

"He's a good friend. Would you mind if I spoke with him about your case?"

"Ye can ask him anything ye like. Please give him me thanks once more."

"Be happy to do so. In the meantime, you're to rest and not worry. We're going to ask for a substantial settlement, and reinstatement of your employment. You may not be able to go back as a mechanic, but they should be able to provide you with something, perhaps a clerk or ticket master."

"Do ye really think the railroad will go for such a thing?"

"We won't know if we don't push them. Father Hughes thinks you could handle those types of jobs with the proper training. In fact, he was very impressed with some ideas you shared with him that might help relations between the workers and the railroad."

"I wrote 'em down and sent 'em to a Mr. Hilliard, but

he said I should stick to me own job, and leave such things to those in higher places."

With considerable effort, Connor refrained from any derogatory remarks regarding Hilliard. "Tell me about them."

"Well, ye see now, the railroad could start a program where there could be some kind of apprenticeship, and then a guaranteed job. This'd provide the company a new stock of men. Another thing would be to create a Hospital Fund where both the workers and the company contribute, instead of passing the hat among the workers every time there is an injury or death."

Connor fisted his hand at his side. "I think I know how to get around your Mr. Hilliard." It would be a pleasure to usurp Hilliard's so-called authority. The man wasn't held in as high esteem as he would have others believe, and the president of the railroad's son was a friend from Connor's college days.

McPhail looked hopeful. "I can write them again and send them to ye."

Mrs. McPhail went over to the small oblong table by the wall and pulled out two sheets of paper from under a book. "Here they be. Didn't seem right to throw 'em away, since Kiernan had taken the trouble to write 'em down and all."

Connor looked over the neatly written list. In addition to the things McPhail had mentioned, it presented a logical solution to many of the problems facing both the employees and the company. This man's ability was not being fully utilized working as a mechanic.

"I want you to concentrate on your recovery, and when you're well, we'll find something for you until we settle things with the railroad."

"Are ye offering me a job, then?"

"My uncle would be happy to have an employee like you, and you'll be able to provide for your family until we settle your case. You won't need that charity you were so riled about."

"Then I won't need to sue the railroad."

"You need to follow through on this course of action for the sake of the other workers, and for your own pain and suffering. This is the means to bring about change. The only way to get the public's sympathy is through the newspapers, and the papers will only be interested if there are more and more cases brought before the court."

"I'm afraid there'll be a lot of men seeking change in a different way if things don't improve. There are too many men injured on the job or worse," McPhail said.

"I know, but violence isn't the answer. We have to change the laws through the courts. Unfortunately, it's a slow process, but change will come."

"Let's hope it comes in time, before ejits like Naimh's brother stir the pot."

Mrs. McPhail gave her husband a disapproving nod. "We needn't be discussing family matters with Mr. Reilly."

"Darlin, e'll be finding out soon enough, so why not git it out in the open now? The man's involved in railroad matters and is bound to hear about yer brother. He may not be wanting to take our case after he hears about yer brother."

Mrs. McPhail gave a disgruntled humph.

"Is there something I need to know before we go to court?" Connor raised a brow in question.

"Me brother is a brakeman and has a bit of a problem with the drink. He hangs with a rough bunch, the lot of 'em good fer nothins. He thinks having ye represent Kiernan 'tis a waste of time."

She no sooner spoke the last words than the door banged open against the wall and a heavy, bearded man clomped into the room. He was fierce looking with unkempt flame locks flying in all directions.

Mrs. McPhail pointed at the titan in the doorway. "Mr. Reilly, me brother – Liam Kenney."

Connor stood and extended his hand, but the giant

glared at him, making no effort to take it. "'Tis the lawyer the priest sent? What 'er ye going to do for me sister and 'er man? Ye going to git 'em some money?" Kenny overwhelmed the air with his whiskey breath when he opened his mouth.

"I'm going to try and get them a decent settlement." Connor slowly dropped his hand to his side.

"Yeah, ye and the Road's going to be real generous with 'ol Kiernan here." The slurred words rang sarcastic. "I heard that ye really work for the railroad – not us working people." Liam shoved against Connor as he started toward the kitchen, pushing the curtains that divided the two rooms aside. He staggered over to the steps to the second floor and proceeded to crawl up them, banging loudly against the wall in the process.

Mrs. McPhail turned toward her brother and opened her mouth but Connor held up his hand to stop her before she spoke. He didn't want to be the cause of a disturbance in the family. Hopefully, Kenny would go to bed and sleep it off.

"Me brother 'twas always a heartache to me mam and da, but I promised to look after 'em when they died. I'll be keeping that promise, but I apologize for his rudeness."

Connor wished there was something he could do to help these people other than offering a job, and the hope of a settlement. He had a sinking feeling that Niamh McPhail's brother was more of a problem for them than her husband's injury.

"Don't concern yourself."

She grasped his hand with both of hers and held tight. "Thank ye for yer kindness, Mr. Reilly."

*****

Connor hurried up the wide stone steps of the brick building, and pushed open the door with the polished brass plaque noting the hospital's name and date of establishment. Once inside, he was greeted by a wizened old woman who sat behind a small desk at the front of a room lined with patient-filled beds. The long narrow room reminded him of a corridor. Quiet whispers, along with the occasional moan and the sound of someone snoring, filled the space.

"Yes sir, what is it ye be wantin?" she asked.

"I would like to see Doctor Schmidt, please." He reached in his pocket to retrieve a calling card.

Without taking it, she said, "Oh, I ain't seen 'em here today. Let me go ask Sister. Please wait 'er until I git back, right? The words were no sooner spoken than she disappeared behind a set of doors at the end of the room.

He surveyed his surroundings while he waited. Sunlight streamed through gleaming windows. The beds had fresh linens on them and the patients were scrubbed clean, probably a lot cleaner than most of them kept themselves when they were in good health. The cleanliness was the result of the efforts of the Sisters of Mercy who had come to help at the dispensary four years ago, and had made a vast improvement. According to Peter, they were firm, but sympathetic to the needs of the inmates, some of whom were permanent residents, since they had no home to return to after their recovery.

A few minutes later the old woman returned with an officious looking nun whose black wooden rosary beads hung straight from her waist and fell on the outside of her leg as she walked. At their bottom, a white ivory cross swung back and forth, like a clock's pendulum.

The nun inclined her head. "Good afternoon, sir, I'm Sister Imelda. May I assist you?"

Connor stood, holding his hat, not knowing whether to bow or shake her hand. He decided the former was the better choice. "Yes Sister, I have come to see Doctor Peter Schmidt."

"He is out of the building visiting a patient right now. Would you like to wait for his return, or shall I give him a message?"

"I didn't realize he went to patient's homes, but that

doesn't surprise me," Connor said.

"Doctor Schmidt is an exceptional doctor and a compassionate human being." Sister Imelda gave a hint of a smile.

Connor wrote a message on the back of the card he had been holding before handing it to the nun. "Will you see that he gets this?"

She took the card from him, wished him a good day, and left the room in a swish of long flowing white skirts and swaying beads.

He thanked the old woman for her assistance before leaving, and then settled himself in the carriage for the ride to his aunt and uncle's residence. It would be a few hours before Uncle Patrick returned home from the day's business so he would be able to do some work before dinner. There were papers that he needed to review for his uncle, and he wanted to start preparing for the McPhail case.

When he entered the sitting room, his Aunt Elaine gave him a pleased smile. "Did things go well today?"

"Yes ma'am, I stopped by the Dispensary and left a message for Peter to join us for dinner this evening. I promised to send your carriage to fetch him."

"It will be nice to see Peter; he works far too hard."

"His work is important."

"I know, but he needs to take care of his own health too you know. The boy needs to get out among people his own age more. When was the last time either of you attended a ball, the theater, or even a simple dinner party?" She let her needlework drop in her lap and frowned.

"Does it make you feel any better that he'll be joining us for dinner this evening? Now if you'll excuse me, I need to take care of some things. I'll be in the library for a few hours." Connor knew where this conversation was headed and he wanted to escape before his aunt started on him. He didn't want to get into *that* discussion.

******

A vigorous knock on the library door drew Connor's attention. "Come in," he snapped as he tossed the law book he had been reading onto the desk, and checked the clock. Had he really been at it for three hours?

Peter Schmidt walked into the room. "Elaine accuses me of working too hard, but maybe she should look at her other lad."

Connor grinned, his former annoyance at being disturbed now forgotten. He walked around the desk, grasped Peter's arm with one hand and shook his hand with the other. "I'm glad you could make it."

"You just want me here to protect you from her matrimonial hints."

"She does more than hint, and it isn't only me she wants to marry off, old friend."

"I think the two of us can handle her." Peter assured.

"Perhaps, but you're in more danger than me. Martha let it slip not so long ago that they have decided you need a wife to take care of you, and my aunt has decided to find one for you."

"And you?"

"They're a little more cautious with me. Martha thinks I'm still jaded in my opinion of woman because of Amelia."

"Are you?" Peter arched a tawny brow as if he were questioning a patient.

"Since when do you practice psychiatry?"

"Just asking as a concerned friend."

"Let's just drop it. There's something I wanted to seek your medical expertise on, but it'll have to wait until after dinner. I would imagine they're waiting for us." The two men went to the dining room where Patrick and Elaine waited for them.

*****

After desert and coffee, Elaine excused herself and left the men to their own conversation. Patrick poured whiskey into three small crystal tumblers. "We had hoped to see more of you now that you're living in the city, Peter."

"Unfortunately, I have very little free time. I'm hoping to find the time to take a small holiday and visit Sara's Glen."

"That's good. You need to think of something other than work. The two of you should be courting the young ladies. It's high time you found wives. I'm surprised Elaine hasn't brought the subject up yet."

Connor grimaced, "The evening is young."

All three laughed, but Patrick insisted, "I want to see babies before I'm too old to play with them."

Peter scowled and asked, "You wanted to talk to me about something, Connor?"

"So, that is the way of it then? I think I'll join your aunt in the parlor," Patrick downed the last of his drink and left the room, closing the door behind him.

Setting his empty glass on a nearby table, Connor said, "I understand you treated a railroad worker by the name of Kiernan McPhail."

"How do you know about that?" Peter asked.

"I'm representing him in a suit against the railroad. Frank Hughes asked me to take the case. Do you think he has any chance of recovering from his injuries?"

Peter rubbed his chin with the back of his knuckles as he spoke. "The leg will be weak, but he should regain feeling in it. He won't be able to return to the same type of work. It would be too much stress on his back."

"I'm going to threaten the company with a request for a jury trial and see what happens. A private investigator that I use from time to time is looking into the matter. He manages to find things that tend to get swept under the rug." Connor sat with his leg stretched out in front of him as he thought about the investigator. The fellow seemed to know everything about everyone in the city of Baltimore.

"I hope he finds what you need, but if you should go to

court, I'll make myself available." Peter stood and motioned toward the door. "We probably should join the elders in the other room. Are you ready for their prodding?"

"Between the two of us, we should be able to steer the conversation elsewhere," Connor said.

"Right; and we might have some of the fairies you used to tell me about when we were kids join us this evening."

*****

Connor looked at the familiar scene of his aunt and uncle, each in their favorite chair with only a table and lamp between them. He couldn't remember a time the two of them had ever been apart. Some day he hoped to have a marriage like theirs, but he would decide when the time was right and not be pushed into anything.

The younger men took their seats on the sofa just as they did whenever they were home. When they were boys, they spent their summers at Sara's Glen and their winters in the city residence while they attended school.

Puffs of smoke curled from Patrick's pipe in between his words. "Has Rasheen Langston settled in?"

"It's only been a month or so, but she seems to have adapted." An image of Rasheen clad in denim trousers and a snug fitting shirt danced before Connor and he fought to banish it from his thoughts.

"What's Mrs. Langston doing at Sara's Glen?" Peter asked.

"I hired her to teach the local children," Connor said.

Peter let out a low whistle. "How did you manage to get someone of her standing to teach?"

"Tch, tch, tch, if you came to visit us more, dear, you would know what's happening," Elaine scolded.

"Well, you would think Connor, or at least my parents, would write to me once in awhile."

"I'm sorry," Connor said in mock sincerity. "Sara's Glen now has a school on the premises for the children. At her uncle's request, I've hired Rasheen Langston."

"Umm and is that proper?

"She's a widow."

"But she isn't that old."

"She's not some silly young girl and need I remind you that your parents are there?"

"As I recall, Mrs. Langston is a very attractive woman." Peter's mouth curved into a mischievous smile.

Connor's frowned. "She is there to teach the children."

"Well, now, maybe I will just have to see for myself when I come to visit. Maybe it's time for me to enjoy some feminine companionship."

Connor knew Peter was tormenting him, but couldn't keep from falling for the bait. "You won't have time to distract my employee. I'll see that you are kept busy."

"I've been working far too hard lately. Maybe I should just spend my time resting at Sara's Glen." Peter gave him a smug wink. "You'll have a few weeks to spend with your new employee before my charming presence arrives."

"Actually, I won't be going home for awhile. I have several matters to clear up for Uncle Patrick," Connor said.

"Good, then we will be evenly matched for Mrs. Langston's affections."

"I'm serious about this. She was hired to teach. I do not want her distracted from her duties."

"It seems to me you're a bit sensitive about the matter."

The older couple exchanged knowing glances and Patrick said, "You two lads still act like you did when you were youths. Can't say as I like the arguing, but it's good to see you together."

"I'm only having some sport," Peter said.

Though Connor knew Peter had no intention of pursing Mrs. Langston romantically, the conversation had left him uncomfortable for reasons he couldn't explain.

"I am going to bed and I don't want to hear any loud

voices down here." Elaine kissed both young men and then walked over to Patrick and was about to kiss him also, but he took her hand instead and led her from the room. She stopped at the doorway, "Peter, if you wish to spend the night, your room is prepared."

"Thanks. I'll make use of it, but I'll be leaving early in the morning before you come downstairs so I probably won't see you."

"Take care then, and come have dinner with us more often. I want to see you again before we go to Sara's Glen for the Christmas holidays."

On her way out of the room, Elaine looked back at the two young men and said, "Wouldn't it be wonderful if we had children in the house to enjoy the holidays?"

CHAPTER 12

Peter ran his hand along the mare's side. "So, you think Muirne here is going to present you with a champion."

"Ireland is known for producing some of the finest race horses in the world, and we brought the sire over from Smythe Manor, in Country Kildare, so we should get a prize foal with both strength and heart from the match," Connor said.

"I think you might just be right, and Murine seems to be fine, but my expertise runs more in human pregnancies."

"Remember the first time your father let us watch a foaling?"

Peter nodded. "He was as excited as we were."

"I still feel like that every time I witness one. It is a miracle, that's for certain." Connor scratched behind the horse's twitching ears.

"Each creature struggles to come into this world and then to survive." Peter stared at the mare, a melancholy frown shadowing his face. "I've seen it in my work with the poor wretches at the dispensary. The tenacity of the spirit is indestructible, no matter the ills of the body."

"Speaking of bodily ills, I received some good news from my investigator regarding Kiernan McPhail's case. He located a letter from the superintendent denying the request for repairs to the building's roof. They knew that roof needed to be repaired all along. Someone's cutting expenses at the workers' peril."

Peter raised one brow in a questioning slant. "I'm sure you didn't receive the letter courtesy of the railroad."

"The investigator I hired is very good." Connor made no attempt to conceal the craftiness he was presently feeling, and let the smug smile present itself.

Peter patted Muirne on the muzzle one last time before the two men walked out of the paddock and latched the gate. "Will you be able to use it against them?"

Connor rested his back against the fence rail. "I certainly intend to try. They showed me a document stating that the roof had been scheduled for repairs the week after the injury; the assumption being that the accident occurred before they could make the necessary restoration. The letter proves they lied. I'm bringing suit against the company. Of course, they'll counter that they're not responsible for employee negligence."

Peter leaned on the rail, looking back at the mare. "The newspaper carried an article yesterday about the fierce competition among the railroads. Quite a few companies have closed. The working man loses all the way around. If the railroad goes under, he has no job. If they continue to cut rates, they make up the difference by paying lower wages until he can't afford to feed his family."

"If the parties involved aren't able to come to some kind of an agreement, it'll end as these matters have in the past. We'll be seeing violence and bloodshed in the streets of Baltimore." There was more than a hint of concern in Connor's voice.

The sound of female laughter interrupted their conversation. One of the ladies straddled her horse with her blue serge riding habit hiked up around the tops of her riding boots.

Before the two riders were within earshot Connor leaned over and whispered, "Guess which one is Rasheen Langston?"

Peter shook his head in disbelief. "That's Daniel Langston's widow? Good Lord Almighty!"

Connor slapped Peter on the back. "She's a little different than most of our acquaintances. I'm surprised you could be shocked so easily."

Peter hissed back, "You don't have to look so pleased with yourself."

"Oh, but I do." Connor remembered the tormenting he had taken from Peter at Elaine and Patrick's with regard to Mrs. Langston, and felt extremely pleased with himself. In fact, he would have enjoyed pursuing the conversation, but the ladies had reached them and were about to dismount. He reached up and put his hands about Rasheen's waist to help her down. She smelled of fresh lemons, not the usual flowery scents that women wore. A fresh glass of lemonade that soothed a dry throat and pleased the taste buds came to mind.

"I trust you had a pleasant ride." He made no attempt to release her once her feet were on the ground.

She blushed as she wiggled free from his embrace. "Yes, it was …ah… very nice." She started to step away, but the hem of her skirt had caught on the saddle, revealing her calves. It refused to budge when she tugged it.

"Allow me." Connor reached around her.

"I can get it." She gave a hard yank and not only did she fail to dislodge the skirt, but the horse took a step back pulling her with it. Connor somehow managed to keep them both afoot.

"Hold still before you get hurt." He lifted the saddle and moved the piece where the skirt was caught. Reluctantly, he let it fall in place.

"Oh yeah, pigs are flying," he muttered to himself.

"What?"

"Nothing."

"Did you say something about pigs?"

"It had nothing to do with you." It had everything to

do with her.

He turned his attention to Bernice, but Peter had already helped her dismount and was standing next to her. Bernice wore a moss green riding habit. Her blond hair was curled and tied back with a matching ribbon. Tiny ringlets framed her face, giving her the appearance of a woodland fairy princess. Connor suspected that Rasheen had been responsible for the new hairstyle.

Peter was chatting with Bernice as if they were long lost friends.

Connor approached them with Rasheen and said, "I see you've no need for an introduction to Miss Peterson, and I believe you already know Mrs. Langston."

Rasheen extended her hand to Peter. "Rasheen will do fine and I'm sure Miss Peterson would prefer you address her by her given name, isn't that right, Bernice?"

"Of course," Bernice agreed.

Before they could continue their conversation, the stable hand appeared and removed the saddles from the horses, hoisted them over the fence top, and came back for the animals. The others stepped away from the horses and Peter extended his arm to Bernice as they began to walk towards the house with Connor and Rasheen following.

When they reached the house, Rasheen and Bernice left the two men sitting on the porch.

"The gossips' tongues would start wagging, if they ever saw the way your teacher chooses to ride," Peter said.

Connor leaned his chair back and propped his feet up on the porch rail. "We only have the one sidesaddle, and Rasheen is accustomed to riding astride. It seems she spent summers on an uncle's farm where things were done differently than here in the civilized world, but I'll make sure we order a proper saddle for her since the ladies enjoy riding."

"If I had not seen it with my own eyes, I would swear you were pranking me. She's nothing like I expected, even

Bernice Peterson seems different than I remember her. I always thought her rather a prim little church mouse." Peter looked back toward the stables as if watching the women riding in once more.

"It appears to me that you took notice of the timid little creature."

Peter rolled his eyes at Connor's comment. "The lady has a keen intellect and was able to converse about my profession without resorting to twittering like most females. Apparently she has studied herbal cures and is interested in medicine."

Before Connor could continue his tormenting, Martha called the two men in from the porch. "I thought we would make it a special dinner and use the dining room, since we have Bernice and Peter with us this evening." A linen cloth covered the table, which was set with fine rose patterned china and Waterford Crystal in honor of the occasion.

Connor took a large platter from her and placed it in the center of the table. "Makes no difference if we eat in the kitchen on plain crockery, or in fancy surroundings, your cooking is grand."

"Stop with the blarney." Martha placed the last serving bowl on the table and directed each person to sit in a particular place. Connor was at the head of the table with Rasheen and Bernice on either side of him. Peter was seated next to Bernice, and Martha next to Rasheen. John sat at the opposite end of the table.

"Why didn't you have Elsie serve dinner tonight since we have a guest?" Connor asked. They only asked Mr. Johnson's daughter, Elsie, to help with the serving if they were entertaining guests other than family, which was rare. "Bernice has spent enough time here over the last weeks that she's family," Martha said.

If Bernice wasn't a guest, then why were they eating in the dining room and why the special linens and dishes? Connor kept the question to himself, while he watched

Martha as she clucked over Peter and Bernice. He could just imagine the conversation she would be having with his aunt when they were together the next time. They would be planning Peter's nuptials. In fact, he'd be willing to place a wager that a letter would be sent to his aunt in the next week regarding the matter.

Peter seemed blissfully unaware of his mother's matchmaking. Connor had never seen him behave in such a manner. Peter had his share of flirtations from the ladies, and he may have enjoyed some dalliances, but he guarded his heart from any serious attachment. Death had robbed him of love when he was young, and the physician had not been able to heal himself from the grief. But this evening his eyes rarely left Bernice. Was this the start of a serious romance, Connor wondered, or just a close friendship?

After dinner, Martha insisted that the young people take a walk around the autumn garden. Connor plucked the seed head from a withered plant, "No blossoms other than the mums, but the nip in the air is pleasant enough."

They stopped at the rose garden and sat on a bench to linger for a bit. The shrubs had a few brown leaves that would soon fall, leaving only the canes to withstand the harsher weather to come. One of the bushes held a solitary garnet colored bud. It would never open because it was hardened from the chilly evenings. Bernice looked around and said, "Even with the plants and flowers preparing for their winter sleep, this is still a lovely spot. It's no surprise that Rasheen is happy living here at Sara's Glen."

Connor felt an unexpected relief at that revelation. "The place does grow on you."

"I'm thinking of starting a practice in North County," Peter said staring out over the garden.

A stunned silence hovered in the air for a few seconds before Connor let out a loud whoop, "Why didn't you say something during dinner?"

"The thought has been rattling around my head for some time now."

"Well, it's the best news I've heard since John told me about Muirne. A champion horse, and my best friend come home; now I ask you, what more could a man desire?"

"I'm happy that you hold me in the same regard as your prized mare, but I think I would enjoy the companionship of these lovely ladies more so than myself or a horse." Peter inclined his head toward Bernice and Rasheen, but his gaze rested on the former.

Connor ignored the remark. "It'll be good to have you here again."

"I haven't decided for certain yet."

"What made you consider returning to North County?" Bernice asked.

"When I finished my medical training, I began doing clinical work at the City Dispensary. To look at the place now, it's difficult to believe that it was once a boarding school for the daughters of prominent families. Now it's a hospital for the poor and indigent. Most of my patients are already half dead of some fatal disease by the time I tend them. Then there are the maimed railroad and factory workers. In spite of the misery I'm forced to witness each day, I would still be able to sleep in the evening, were it not for the memories of the children. I'm tired of seeing young lives destroyed before they've even begun."

Connor noticed the weariness in Peter's eyes that hadn't been there during dinner. He understood where it came from only too well.

Bernice wrinkled her forehead and looked at Peter intently. "I don't understand."

"What Peter is saying is that there are many children maimed in the canneries and factories. Children who should be in school, but have to work because their parents need the money to help feed and shelter the family," Rasheen said.

"How is that you know so much? Most young women in your circumstances aren't concerned over such matters." Peter gave her an astonished look.

"I believe you know my uncle, Father Hughes."

"He's a good man. Pity there aren't a hundred more like him," Peter said.

"Many of the children of which you speak belong to his parish. He has shared the stories about how they work as long as twelve to fourteen hours, little ones so small that they have to stand on boxes."

"It's one thing to know of their plight, but quite another to face a six-year-old child who has lost fingers because he was careless with a knife due to the lack of rest." Peter let out a weary breath.

Bernice patted his hand, "How difficult it must be for you."

Peter squeezed her arm with his free hand, his eyes resting on her in a grateful manner.

Perhaps Martha was right after all. Connor let the moment be for a short time and then inquired, "So what are your plans?"

"I have not decided for certain."

"Your mother would be happy to have her boy back home. I can't say it would hurt me any to have you back at Sara's Glen, either."

"I would only plan on staying with you until I can find a place of my own closer to town where I can have a surgery."

"If you won't live with us, would you consider the stone house? It's on the outskirts of the property closer to town, which would suit your purpose, and I would prefer that someone who appreciates it live there."

Connor went on to explain to the two women that the house was the original structure on the property where Sara and James Bartlett lived over one hundred years ago. "In fact, Sara's Glen got its name from Sara Bartlett.

Someone – he rolled his eyes toward Peter – once told me that the ghosts of James and Sara visit occasionally."

"You can mock me if you will, Connor Reilly, but I saw them there that day when we were hanging about the place. I can't help it if they've never shown themselves to you."

"What happened?" Rasheen's eyes sparkled with interest.

"Connor thought I was playing a prank, but I saw them. They kept me from going into a nearby shed. The next day, one of the farmhands shot a rabid raccoon that had made a home in it."

"Sure, and then you aren't afraid of ghosts, are you?" Connor shook himself in mock fear.

"It just shows they know someone of quality," Peter snorted. "I'm not afraid, and just to prove it, I'll take you up on the offer if I decide to set up practice in North County."

Connor slapped him on the back. "Looks like you just made the decision."

"No, I was baited into a decision." Peter shrugged his shoulders in mock resignation. "I said I would take you up on your offer if I return to North County. It may not be for a few more years yet, so please refrain from mentioning it to my parents. I still have obligations at the City Dispensary."

Loud barking and whinnying from a nearby paddock prevented further discussion of the matter. They looked toward the sound, but were unable to see since a thick row of pines hid the noisemaker. They walked to the other side of the trees to investigate.

"Finn, come here this minute," Rasheen yelled. A surrounding circle of horses prevented the dog from obeying her command.

The two men called off the horses. As soon as one of the beasts moved, the dog shot out of the enclosure to freedom. He ran up to Rasheen wagging his tail as if to say, "I showed them, you don't have to worry."

Peter rubbed Finn's head saying, "You were trying to be a bully, that doesn't work around here. They are bigger than you."

Rasheen dropped down on her knees and threw her arms around Finn, "You could have been hurt, silly dog."

Connor rubbed the muzzle of the nearest horse whose head was over the fence. "I think Finn's learned his lesson. He won't bother the horses again, will you lad?" The dog gave a soft woof from the security of Rasheen's arms.

CHAPTER 13

Soft light from the setting sun's rays suffused the earth as if some mythological giant held a lantern above the landscape. Connor lingered a few minutes longer to savor the moment before opening the stable door. Once inside, he waited for his eyes to adjust to the shadowy darkness. It would be completely dark in half an hour, but he'd be out by then. No need to bother with a lamp.

A storm blew through earlier so the horses were already inside, but he wanted to check on things one more time. It was more of a ritual than a precaution. Being in the stable alone with the horses in the early evening reminded him of times he had shared with his father. It was a pleasant memory, and a good way to end the day's work.

Muirne raised her head, and twitched her ears. "Aye, my darlin, how are you this fine evening?" He murmured as he scratched gently between her eyes. "There now, how about a treat?"

He held an apple in the palm of his hand for her. She finished it in a few bites and then shoved his arm with her nose trying to get to the remaining one hidden in his pocket.

"Oh, so you want another?" He stood sideways so she could reach inside his pocket and retrieve the second apple. Once she had it out, he held his palm beneath it so as to catch any pieces that might fall. She chomped a few times, swallowed, and nibbled the few pieces that had landed in his hand. Then she nuzzled his shoulder for more. "That's all for tonight, lass."

He patted the horse on the neck one last time and was about to leave because it was becoming dark outside, when a muffled sound came from somewhere back in the stable. He cocked his head to one side in an effort to listen more closely. There was no sound other than the horses letting out snorts or whinnies. But it wasn't his imagination; he had heard something. Breath stilled, ears tuned for the sound, he paused to listen once more.

Sniff, sniff, ahhhhaaaa, then a long catch of breath. Connor took the lantern off the hook near Murine's stall, lit it, and edged his way toward the source of the noise until he rounded the corner to one of the empty stalls. When he held up the light he saw a young boy, curled in a ball, head resting on his chest. The child raised his head and stared over his knee tops, a look of terror in his eyes. Connor moved a few paces into the stall, but stopped and dropped the lantern to his side when the boy pulled himself into a tighter knot

From the little he could see without the direct light, it appeared that the lad's face was swollen and one eye blackened. Connor suspected there had been a contest of fisticuffs and this one had lost. "It's all right, lad, I won't harm you. What happened?" Mutely, the boy shook his head back and forth.

Connor approached slowly and offered his hand to the boy.

The youth wrapped his arms about himself even tighter, pressing his back against the rough planks of the stall's wall. This action caused him to raise his head and revealed more of his face. Realization hit Connor like a sucker punch to the stomach when he recognized the boy as the same one who had been with Hilliard's driver at the train station the day Rasheen had arrived.

He wasn't sure how to handle the boy. When the silence continued, he thought perhaps he might seek help from Rasheen or Peter, but he was afraid to leave for fear the boy might try to run if he were able.

Not quite sure what to say, he proceeded cautiously. "Are you one of Mrs. Langston's students?"

The mention of Mrs. Langston brought a flood of words. "Please, sir, don't tell Mrs. Langston. She doesn't understand. If I can just hide here for awhile, I'll be all right. I'll not be a bother to you. I can clean the stable for you tomorrow, if you'll only let me stay here tonight." He spoke rapidly. "I'll do a good job. Please, just don't tell her I'm here."

"No harm will come to you. Please let me help." Connor was afraid to touch him for fear of frightening him or disturbing his injuries. "Can you walk?" The boy nodded and stood up, unsteady on his feet, and by the way he was holding his arm, Connor suspected it might be broken. "What is your name, lad?"

"Jack," the boy whispered.

"All right then, Jack, will you come with me up to the house? We'll get you fixed up." The boy's head shot up and Connor could see the anxiety in his expression. "It's all right, son. No one will hurt you."

"Is Mrs. Langston there?"

"Mrs. Langston would never harm you."

The boy tried to jump up, but fell backwards. "Please, she's going to cause trouble. She won't mean to, but that's what will happen if she finds out he beat me again. He'll send me there. Please, don't let her know."

"Mrs. Langston works for me and if I tell her not to say anything, she won't. Where is it you don't want to go?"

The boy said nothing but shook his head.

"Jack, please come with me. All we're going to do is help you feel better, and then we can talk about what's bothering you." Connor spoke in the same tone he used when trying to calm a skittish horse.

Though wary, the youth finally obeyed. Connor held

the light in one hand while extending the other to Jack to help him rise, but the boy didn't take it. Somehow he managed to get himself upright and shuffle out of the stable into the darkness toward the direction of the light shining from the kitchen window. Connor kept close to the boy's side. He didn't want to take a chance the boy might try and run, though he doubted that would be possible. Silently, they climbed the porch steps.

"Jack, what happened?" Rasheen dropped her dishtowel and ran over to him. He winced when she touched his arm.

The boy gave Connor a pleadingly look, but before he could reassure him again, Peter came out of the library and asked, "What have we here?"

Connor took him aside and spoke in a low voice, "The lad was hiding in the stable. He's been badly beaten, and I think his arm may be broken. Be careful how you handle him; he doesn't trust adults and probably for good reason."

Peter gave an unspoken nod before requesting Martha to get his medical bag from his room and Rasheen to get a pan of hot water along with some soap.

Jack began begging them not to take him to the doctor's. "If they find out, they'll send me to that place."

Rasheen looked over Jack's head and spoke to Connor. "Mr. Hilliard's stable hand, Ronald Chilcret, told him that they'll send him to the Almshouse."

Connor felt his jaw tighten the way it always did when he was angry, but forced himself to remain steady as he spoke quietly to Jack. "Let's just get you fixed up for now and not worry about the rest of it. It just so happens that my friend here is a doctor."

Peter knelt down in front of the boy's chair. "I promise that no one is going to send you anywhere, but I would like to help you if you will let me."

Jack nodded apprehensively as Peter pulled out a listening contrivance to check his breathing. Next, he went to work cleaning the split lip and bruises with warm water and soap. When that task was completed, he asked, "May I take a look at your arm?"

Jack gingerly lifted his arm and presented it. Peter moved the arm in different positions, asking if the boy felt any pain. Jack winced during one of the movements, but sat stone faced through the remainder of the examination.

"I don't think the arm's broken, but we'll put it in a sling for now and I want you to keep it that way for a few days."

"I can't keep a sling on. How will I get my chores done? I have to go back tomorrow. You don't understand... Mr. Chil..." The boy bit his lower lip realizing he had given away the name of his abuser.

The two men spoke in unison. "You won't be going back with Mr. Chilcrit."

"Please, I have no place to go other than with him. I don't want to go to the Almshouse."

Connor knelt on one knee in front of the seated boy, but refrained from touching him. "Jack, no one is going to send you anywhere. You'll stay here at Sara's Glen with us, and are not to worry. We'll sort it all out tomorrow."

Martha fixed some hot cider and spice cake for Jack and offered the others the same.

Connor winked at Jack. "Martha makes the best cakes and pies in the world. When you're finished eating, she'll show you to one of the guest rooms. Looks like you could do with a good night's rest."

"I really need to get back." Jack fidgeted in his chair, not rising.

"You're never going back there with that horrible man." Rasheen shook her head as she choked out the words.

"Mrs. Langston, please..."

Connor shook his head. "Mrs. Langston's right, you won't be returning to Mr. Chilcrit, nor will you be going to the Almshouse. You have my word on it and I always keep my promises. Now rest easy, lad."

Martha held out her hand for Jack. "I've known him since he wasn't much older than you are, and that's the truth about him keeping his promises." Jack took the offered hand and walked up the stairs with her.

Connor asked Rasheen and Peter to step out on the porch with him. Once outside, he asked, "How badly was he injured?"

"Nothing seems to be broken. He was lucky this time, but he may not be so fortunate if there were another," Peter said.

"There won't be another. I suspect Chilcrit has been beating on the lad for some time," Connor said.

"What do you know about Chilcrit?" Peter asked.

"Nothing, other than that he works for Hilliard."

"Do you think Hilliard's aware of what's been happening?"

"I would hope not. Reg Hilliard is an ejit, but I don't think he would approve of such treatment as the lad has received at Chilcrit's hands."

"What are you planning to do?"

"I have to find some more information about the boy."

Rasheen twisted the end of her shawl, "What if that monster is his guardian?"

"Tomorrow, I'm going to pay a visit to Hilliard's place, and inform the two of them that Chilcrit is not to come near the boy again. If he trespasses on my property, I'll have him shot. Then I'm going to make a trip to the Towson Court House to file legal papers for guardianship of the boy. Since there aren't any relatives that we know of, I don't foresee any difficulties, but I'll still have someone investigate the matter." He inclined his head toward Peter. "I also have a doctor as a witness as to the extent of the lad's injuries."

Peter rubbed the knuckles of his right hand with its neighbor. "That doctor would like to go along on your visit to Hilliard and have a word with his employee."

"As tempting as it would be for both of us to beat him within an inch of his life, I don't think that's a good idea."

"If you change your mind, I'm ready."

Connor slapped Peter's shoulder. "Your hands are better suited for healing."

"When they went back inside, Martha had settled Jack in for the night. Connor sat down with her, and explained his intentions regarding Jack. "This will be extra work for you, but it can't be helped."

"I'm not worried about a little extra work. I'm more concerned about you. The boy's had a difficult time of it. There's a great deal more than just physical healing to be done. You have no idea how far the heart wounds go."

"Mother's right, there's no telling what Chilcrit's treatment has done to the boy," Peter said.

"He needs someone to look out for him. Are not each of us deserving of care and love one from the other? He's had precious little of that, and it is time he had his fair share. My father once told me that when it's all said and done, I'll have to ask myself if I lived my life in truth. I asked him what he meant and he said I would recognize the different truths in my life when I faced them. The truth of this matter is that Jack needs someone to look out for him."

"More than pictures on holy cards," Rasheen whispered.

"Holy cards?" Connor asked.

"I was just thinking about a conversation I had with my mother before I left home."

"And what did it have to do with holy card pictures?"

"My mother wasn't very fond of Finn, and I reminded her that God's countenance is often revealed in unexpected places – not just on holy card pictures. She has a lot of holy cards and says the prayers on the back of them faithfully."

"You compared a dog to God, oh Sweet Jaysus!" Connor couldn't stop laughing.

"Well, yes, and Uncle Frank agreed with me." Rasheen raised her chin and placed her arms in front of her.

"Oh, he would, now, he would," Connor said in between snorts.

*****

Long after everyone had gone to bed, Connor lay awake staring at the ceiling. He wanted to go over to Hilliard's and drag Chilcrit out of his bed and pound him into the ground. Maybe that would help relieve the anger he was feeling over the man's cruelty, but common sense prevailed. He got dressed and went downstairs to work it off doing work on some paper work instead.

Just as he settled into his desk chair, the sound of someone crying on the porch filtered through the closed library window. When he opened the door to the porch, he found Rasheen slumped in the porch swing, mindless of the cool night air. He reached inside and took his work coat from the peg near the door and silently draped it over her shoulders. She continued to sob.

He spoke softly as he placed his hand on her shoulder and gently rubbed. "There's nothing you could have done to prevent this. You can't blame yourself."

"He pleaded with me to let the matter go when I saw strap marks on him. I agreed, thinking it better to win his confidence; and that maybe it wasn't as bad as I thought. My wrong judgment could have gotten him killed. Had I brought the matter to you, he wouldn't be here now. That makes me as guilty as his tormenter."

The harvest moon gave her tear-streaked face a soft glow. He brushed the tears from her cheeks with his thumbs, and then tilted her face so he could look into her eyes.

"What would you have done? Jack's fear hid the truth. He's still afraid, and it's going to take time to gain his trust.

Don't blame yourself for the past. Now is what matters."

The woman was like no other he had ever known. She had been a self-assured burr on his arse in the beginning, but now she was every bit as vulnerable as the boy sleeping upstairs. He offered her his hand. "Come inside and get some sleep."

She took his hand and let him lead her inside to the bottom of the stairs where she hesitated for a moment and gave him a look filled with tenderness and compassion. "Martha's right, you're a good man, Connor Reilly." Then she patted his arm affectionately and turned away.

"Goodnight Rasheen," he whispered behind her as she climbed the stairs.

CHAPTER 14

Connor leaned against the fence and took the crisp autumn air into his lungs. "It looks to be a nice day."

"Are you referring to the weather or Thunderbolt's time?" John asked referring to one of the horses that had just completed its morning workout.

"Both. He has the intelligence, speed, and heart of a winner, no doubt as to that." Connor continued to discuss Thunderbolt's chances in the race they planned to enter him in at the end of the month and failed to pay attention to the horse that trotted up to the fence's edge. Before he realized what was happening, the horse leaned his head over the top rail and nipped his shoulder. He whirled away, cursing vehemently in Gaelic. "That is the last time! Bloody beast! You're going to find yourself living in the city, hitched to a hack."

John laughed and took a step away from the fence out of the animal's reach. "Do you really think anyone else would want him? Remember last spring? Martha has not forgiven him for that little piece of work."

Connor chuckled at the memory of Martha waving her broom at the horse's rump in an attempt to chase him from her kitchen garden. "At least he stays away from the house when he escapes now. I think he's afraid of her."

They stood away from the fence studying the horse, a large black colt. Midnight ran along the fence line at breakneck speed, stopped suddenly, whirled around and then trotted back to them, snorted and put his head down to chomp calmly on the grass on his side of the fence. Though the animal had provoked him, Connor knew he would never make good on his threat. "He is a beautiful animal."

"The lad seems to have befriended him. I saw him sitting on the fence petting him, and the horse stood perfectly still, no mischief at all. Maybe Midnight needs more attention, perhaps someone to take him out for a ride regularly." John took a step towards the fence and reached up to rub the back of Midnight's ear. "I was thinking the lad could do it."

Connor surveyed the horse with mistrust. "Do you really think that is a good idea? Midnight can be ornery, and Jack's still unsure of himself. He might feel protected from Chilcrit now, but he still doesn't trust us. He barely speaks, and his fear of making a wrong move is evident to anyone he comes in contact with. You know as well as I do that if he were to show any sign of that uncertainty to the horse, it could be dangerous."

"For some reason, he doesn't seem to fear the animal. You're the best trainer in the country, and you trained the horse. He can behave when he chooses to do so. At least give the idea some consideration."

The men returned to their chores and the day turned out to be as fine as the morning had promised. As he worked, Connor's mind turned to other things, not the least of which was Rasheen. Wasn't it enough that the woman had invaded his home? Must she also occupy his thoughts when he had other things to attend? It would seem so, for in truth, he had come to welcome the intrusions.

It was late afternoon when John came into the field where Connor was working with some of his men mending fences. Such acts earned the respect of his workers, and he valued their good opinion above that of the circle to which he was privilege.

"Come with me, you have to see this for yourself," John said.

He left the remainder of the task to the two other men, and went with John. They watched from a short distance as Jack leaned over the top rail of the fence feeding an apple to Midnight. John raised a questioning eyebrow.

"Feeding the beast is not the same as riding him."

"Midnight trusts him. You don't see him nipping at Jack, do you?"

Connor rubbed his shoulder where the horse had nipped him earlier, but John was right. The horse stood calm and was on his best behavior as he took the apple from Jack. He even twitched his ears forward in a friendly gesture.

"I'm going to put my concerns aside, but I hope we don't have cause to regret this."

"He seems to like you. How would you like to take him out for ride?" Connor asked over Jack's shoulder.

Jack reeled around to face them. "I helped Mr. Johnson, and Martha didn't need me to do anything and all my school work is done and…"

Connor placed his hand on Jack's shoulder. "It's all right, lad. Now about that ride."

Jack quickly moved out from under Connor's hand and looked at the horse wistfully. "I don't know how to ride."

Connor looked to John and raised an eyebrow. He really had misgivings now. John nodded reassuringly.

"I can teach you, if you like. Would you like to begin now?" Connor tried to make the question sound more confident than he felt.

"Really?" Jack asked with just a hint of enthusiasm.

"Really." Connor grinned and winked at the surprised boy.

John went to get the necessary tack and the lesson began.

"All right, now take the reins in your left hand and grab the base of Midnight's mane. Good, good, now put your left foot in the stirrup, parallel to his side. You don't want to poke his belly." Connor took a deep breath, and held the lead rope tightly. Visions of Jack poking Midnight and the horse taking off dragging the boy played in his mind, but Jack did exactly as he was told.

"You're doing fine, lad. Now, grab the back of the saddle with your right hand. Good, now balance on your left foot and bounce off the right one and swing it over the horse. Put your right foot in the other stirrup and take up the slack in the reins." Jack followed each step carefully, but on the second bounce when he hadn't gotten quite high enough, John gave him an extra boost.

"There you go, now you're ready to ride," John said as he stepped back.

Jack's forehead wrinkled in concentration.

"It's a lot to remember, but soon it'll come easy enough, and you won't have to think on it," John said.

Connor leaned back against the fence, "Look at him up there, 'tis like he was born to it. Now, make Midnight walk about a bit."

"How do I make him move?"

"First, you ask him nicely with a slight touch of your leg." Connor walked next to the horse and bent Jack's knee slightly, being careful not to let it touch the horse. "Put just a little pressure into it."

Jack did so, but Midnight ignored the prod and continued to munch grass. The boy sat rigid in the saddle.

"Use more pressure and pull the reins so that he can't get to the grass," Connor coached.

"What if he runs?"

Connor spoke quietly to John, "I was afraid this would happen."

John ignored him and coached the boy. "Connor has a lead rope attached to him. He won't let anything like that happen. You have to let him know that you're in charge. You're the master- not him."

Jack tugged on the reins gently. When the horse did

not respond, he pulled harder.

Connor, ready to grab the reins if necessary, held his breath and hoped that the horse behaved. As if reading his mind, Midnight started to walk slowly. "Well done. You can let up on the pressure now that he did what you want."

They let Jack walk Midnight around the paddock for a while and then showed him how to dismount and tend to the horse's needs. As they walked back to the house for supper, Connor said, "We'll continue your lessons tomorrow after school."

"Yes sir." The tone was a little more animated than usual.

During the next few days, the lessons continued with Jack making rapid progress, only once putting the reins in the wrong hand while beginning to mount. "No, lad, use the other hand." The boy flinched when Connor reached over to help him, and then sat still as a rabbit about to become a fox's dinner while the reins were placed in the correct hand.

On their walk back to the house after the day's lesson, Connor put his arm around Jack's shoulder and the boy, although startled, allowed it to remain. "My father was a horse trainer. You would have liked him; he had the gift of understanding horses the same as you. I hope someday you and I will be as close as he and I were."

Connor stopped walking and looked down at the boy. "Jack, I'll never strike you. If you make a mistake, then you learn, and we try to fix the problem. That goes not just for the riding lessons, but for anything that happens. I know it will take time, but I hope you'll come to trust me."

"I'm sorry, Mr. Reilly, I know you're different than….."

"Yes, I am. And one more thing - I'd appreciate it if you'd start calling me Connor. You're not one of the hired workers. You're family now."

*****

A few days later after they had finished the lesson and

Jack dismounted, Midnight made a deliberate attempt to step on Connor's foot. "I don't think so, boyo." He stepped back from the horse.

Jack backed away. "Oh no, you don't. Try it and you won't be getting any treats today." The horse looked at him, snorted and moved closer, but then thought better of it.

"Well done, lad, you've shown him that you're not his pawn."

Jack's eyes widened in astonishment. "I did. I really did, didn't I? I'm the boss, not him," he said in barely a whisper and then louder, "I'm the boss."

Connor placed his hand on the boy's shoulder and squeezed gently. "That you did, that you did indeed. In fact, I think you're ready to do some real riding. Tomorrow we'll go for an early morning ride out to the woods and back. Would you like that?"

"Yes sir." Jack bounced back on his heels and then back again.

A few more weeks and he would be letting out rebel yells when he was excited. Connor could almost hear Martha telling him to stop acting like a heathen, in the same indulgent voice she had used with Peter and him. The memory made him smile.

"I'll speak to Mrs. Langston, just in case we don't get back before school starts."

Jack gave an uneasy glance toward the school. "You think she'll mind?"

"I think she'll be happy that you've made such rapid progress." Connor gave him a wink. "Just leave her to me."

*****

After Jack had gone to bed, Connor told Rasheen about his plans for the next day and asked her if she had any objections. Her response was just as he had expected.

"Jack's doing well enough in his studies that he can take the entire day off if you like. Mind you, don't make a habit of it, but this is a special occasion. Teaching Jack to ride has increased his self-confidence. He's even starting to make friends at school, and is behaving more like a boy his age. When he spoke about Tommy Jones's stomach ailments at the dinner table and Martha had to shush him, I remembered some of our dinner conversations at home. My mother often had to silence my brothers from tales of disgusting occurrences that they found fascinating."

"I think he will be all right. I can't take credit for the riding lessons though, John saw him with Midnight and suggested them. I didn't think it was a good idea at the time, but John's instincts proved to be right."

"You saved him in so many ways." She placed her hand lightly on his arm and smiled. It was a simple gesture meant to be friendly, but being the focus of that feminine smile, the subject of that touch undid him. He wanted to take her hand and put it in his, to bring it up to his cheek, to kiss those smiling lips until she was as breathless as he himself felt at this moment.

Instead, he gave himself a mental scolding and patted the hand that was still resting on his arm. "Well now, I'd better get some rest if Jack and I are to have an early start," he said seeking an escape.

*****

Peter tossed the letter he had just read onto the desk. "What did Rasheen have to say about this?" He asked Connor.

"I haven't shown it to her yet. She blames herself for the treatment Jack received from Chilcrit. How's she going to feel when she finds out about this?" Connor bent down to grab a piece of wood from the stack next to the fireplace and threw it on the fire. He straightened and stood staring into the flames.

"That responsibility lies with Chilcrit and Langston, not her."

Their conversation was interrupted when the library door opened and Rasheen stepped inside. "I just wanted to retrieve the book I left here earlier." She started toward a chair near the window where a book rested on its arm, but stopped half way across the room. Frowning at the two men, she asked, "What's the matter with the two of you?"

"Perhaps it would be best if Connor spoke to you alone. I was just leaving anyway. I've some matters that need my attention." Peter rose from his seat, and crossed the room to the door. He gave Connor a nod and then closed the door behind him as he exited.

Rasheen stared after him in astonishment before looking to Connor for an explanation.

He motioned for here to sit in Peter's vacant chair. "I have some news regarding Jack."

She ignored the gesture as her gaze settled on the letter in his hand. "You don't look as if it is anything good."

Connor sat with the paper in one hand, and rubbed the side of his neck with the other. He looked down at the words on the piece of paper, no longer needing to read them since they were committed to his memory.

Dear Mr. Brinkers,

As per our discussion, in the matter of one Constance Trevelyn Benson, please try to locate mother and son. I trust you to use the utmost discretion in order to avoid any scandal should the boy be entitled to my support. My family's good name must be protected.
Daniel Langston.

After several moments of silence, he handed her the letter. Still not bothering to sit, she scoured its contents. When she finished reading, she looked up from the letter. "Daniel has some connection to Jack?"

"I checked into Jack's mother's background. Constance Trevelyn was the only child of a very wealthy man. She was orphaned as a child and since there were no family members to care for her, she became the ward of her father's business partner, a certain Mr. Benson and his wife. Apparently, Mr. Benson mishandled Constance's finances badly." Connor crossed his arms and sat back in the chair before continuing his story. He was careful not to let his own distasteful feelings towards Benson and Langston be revealed.

"When Constance found herself in such unfortunate circumstances as to be unmarried and with child, Benson, who was then a widower, married her. Jack was born six months after the wedding. A few years later, Mr. Benson died leaving Constance and the child with no income, since he had squandered her inheritance and ruined the business."

"How did you come by all of this information?"

"When I gave the information that we had to Mr. Brinkers to see if Jack had any living relatives, he remembered that your husband had hired him to try and find Constance. He wasn't successful because he was looking in the city among the wrong class. We still haven't figured out how she ended up here, but at least we know Jack has no living relatives other than you."

"Two years I lived with the man and he had no trust or faith in my ability to understand. We could have provided Jack with a loving home, but Daniel was more concerned with his precious family name than his own son's life."

"Is it possible that Daniel wasn't the father? Did he have any brothers? A cousin who may be the father?"

"When we married, Daniel was the only living member of his family. His brother was killed in the war and his father had been dead for years. For a long time it was just he and his mother."

"Do you think his mother knew about Jack?"

"I wouldn't know. She died before I met Daniel."

Rasheen threw her hands over her face and sobbed through them. "Will it ever end?"

Connor reached across the space between them, took the paper and handed her his handkerchief. "Will what ever end?"

"The everlasting pain!" She cried into the handkerchief as she blew her nose loudly. "Am I ever going to be able to put the past to rest?"

He stood, took her hands and helped her from the chair. "Well, he did try and do the honorable thing."

"Of course he did, after all, he was a Langston." Sarcasm rang in her voice. She fisted the handkerchief in her hand, stood up and rocked back on her heels. Her eyes were still haunted with an inner pain, but she spoke with resignation. "I'll agree to your guardianship of Jack, but when he's older, he must be told of his true parentage. I'll see that you are refunded for any expenditure as he is heir to the Langston fortune."

"I have agreed to care for the lad, and I will bear the expenses so encountered. We don't even know for sure if he is entitled to a portion of the Langston inheritance, so we'll need to handle that matter discreetly. Mr. Brinkers will continue the investigation. As far as Jack is concerned, let's follow through as originally planned. I think we can both agree that the boy needs some stability in his life at the present time."

She nodded and went to hand him his handkerchief, but then quickly pulled her hand back, an apologetic smile on her lips.

He looked at the crumbled piece of wet cloth and laughed. "That's okay, why don't you just keep it."

CHAPTER 15

Jack stuffed a heavily laden forkful of cake into his mouth. "You make the best chocolate cakes imf the wurlfd."

"Don't talk with your mouth full, young man." Martha said.

Connor eased into the chair at the head of the table where Martha had just placed his lunch. "I'll have some cake too, that is if the lad here hasn't finished it all." He reached over and pinched off a piece of Jack's cake, popping it into his mouth before taking a bite of his own sandwich.

"Hey," Jack protested.

"All right, if that is the way you choose to be. Deny a man a bit of nourishment, would you then?" Connor held his hand up and heaved a mock sigh.

"I'm planning on catching the morning train to Baltimore the day after tomorrow, if that is all right with you," Rasheen said as she took a seat at the table. "I want to get home a few days before Thanksgiving so I can have some time to visit with my family."

"I can travel with you as your escort if you like, or perhaps you would prefer Reg Hilliard's company? I understand he's spending the holiday with his cousin in the city, and I'm sure he would be more than happy to accompany you." Conner knew Rasheen wouldn't want to be trapped with Reg Hilliard again, but he couldn't resist a little devilment.

"Mr. Hilliard is an egotistical twit."

Stunned, Connor chocked back the coffee that filled his mouth and was about to spray forth. "Since you have such strong opinions where Reg is concerned, Jack and I will be your escorts."

"Not that I need an escort, but I would appreciate sharing your company on the train ride home. Why aren't you spending the holiday here at Sara's Glen?"

"My aunt and I have an agreement. I go to the city for Thanksgiving and they come here for Christmas. Martha has her family here for Thanksgiving. Her son, Johnny, and his wife, Violet, come and spend a few days with their children. Martha gets to spend time with her grandchildren. Then there's Peter this year, and what about Fred and Jeanette?"

Martha explained to Rasheen. "Fred is my second son. He and Jeanette were married last year. They'll be coming down from Frederick County and spending the night too. I'll have all my children home for the holiday."

"You never told me you had grandchildren," Rasheen said in surprise.

"I have two grandsons whom I love dearly, but I wish one of these boys would give me a girl. I was so happy when the two older ones gave me daughter-in-laws, but a little granddaughter would be nice."

At that particular moment, Peter strolled into the room. Connor glanced over his shoulder and said to Martha, "Well now, and maybe your youngest son will grant your wish."

"What wish might that be?" Peter asked as he reached for the slice of cake Martha was about to give Connor.

She swatted his hand and set the plate on the table next to Connor. "I swear one would think I'd never taught anyone any manners in this house."

Peter slid into the chair next to Connor. "Is that the wish? Manners? I assure you, mother, I have sterling manners in public."

"Not manners, grandchildren." Connor moved his cake away from Peter's reach.

"What about them?"

"Martha wants a granddaughter."

"Don't you think it would be better if one of my "married" brothers gives her one?"

Connor shrugged.

Bored with the grown-up's conversation, Jack went to the door and held it open for Finn. The dog wagged his tail as he went through the open door quickly followed by Jack.

Martha looked up from the table. "Don't let the door…"

Slam!

*****

Rasheen stood on the porch and hugged Martha amid a multitude of rapid last minute instructions.

"Connor, don't forget to give that package to Elaine and tell her to make sure to let me know which day they're to arrive for Christmas. Give them both my love. Jack, you mind your manners with Patrick and Elaine. Oh, what am I saying, you are such a good boy. Not at all like Connor and Peter when they were your age. Rasheen, you have a nice visit with your family."

Bags balanced under his arms and held securely in his hands, Connor looked over his shoulder from the bottom of the steps. "I was an innocent. Peter was a bad influence, but I managed to redeem him. Look how well he turned out?"

Martha paid no attention and was still talking when John finally kissed her and pushed her into the house. "If we don't leave now, they're going to miss their train." He ushered the remaining three into the carriage. Finn stood alongside the vehicle waiting. "No, boy, you stay here. I'll be back in a bit. Be good and take care of my Martha." He slapped the reins and they were on their way.

When they got to the station, Reg Hilliard was climbing out of his carriage and spotted them as soon as they pulled up. He waved wildly looking like someone having a convulsion.

"Bloody hell and demons," Connor muttered under his breath.

He looked over to see Rasheen bite her lower lip in a vain attempt to keep from laughing.

"And what does Martha say about cursing?" she asked.

"Martha isn't the one who's going to have to deal with him, now is she?" Connor whispered. Before he could hurry Rasheen and Jack in the opposite direction of Hilliard, his attention was drawn to Ronald Chilcrit, who glared at them as he unloaded Hilliard's baggage from the carriage.

Connor looked over at Jack to make sure he was all right. The boy kept his eyes to the ground and stood close. Placing a protective arm around his shoulder, Connor drew him to the rear of their vehicle, out of Chilcrit's view, while he helped John with their own bags. Rasheen followed and positioned herself near Jack as if she sensed the tension caused by Chilcrit's presence.

Chilcrit ignored them and went about his business, but no such luck with Hilliard. He came around to the back of the carriage before the bags were unloaded, preventing any escape. "What a happy circumstance to have a charming companion on the ride to Baltimore. I didn't realize you would be taking this train, Mrs. Langston. I don't see your private car." Hilliard craned his neck looking at the line of cars waiting to be boarded.

Rasheen forced a smile. "I only used it last time so Finn could travel with me. Since he'll be staying at home this time, there was no need for such luxury. The railroad has adequate accommodations and I see no reason not to patronize them." Featherlike laugh lines crinkled around her eyes and a look of pure devilment crossed over her face. "Oh silly me. Here I am telling a man of your importance about the fine service offered by your very own company."

That's my girl. Connor would have given her a salute had his arms not been full.

"Of course, of course, but I hope you will do me the honor of being your escort."

"That is most kind, but Mr. Reilly and Jack are traveling with me today." She gave Connor a grateful smile.

"Then at least allow me the pleasure of sharing the ride with you." Before she could answer, Hilliard took her arm and led her to the waiting train and seated himself next to her, leaving Jack and Connor to take the facing seat. Her annoyance at the arrangement was evident in the look she shot Connor. He wasn't feeling too pleased himself at the moment, but at least he felt some satisfaction in the fact that she had referred to Sara's Glen as home and the way she had handled Hilliard's expectations of a ride in the Langston car. Sad thing was that her witty sarcasm was wasted on the ejit, him being too thick headed to realize he had been insulted.

When half way through their journey, a babe in the next seat started to cry, Hilliard sniffed haughtily. "Children should be left at home with their nannies."

The young mother attempting to quiet the infant gave them an apologetic nod.

Connor was about to make a smart reply to Hilliard when he noticed Rasheen's expression of bored politeness change. Her eyes, which had just seconds ago been glazed over, sparked, and then her brows rose and her head tilted to the side ever so slightly. No sense in him interfering. He'd just sit back and enjoy the fireworks which he knew would be splendid.

Instead of the verbal bashing he had expected, she smiled sweetly at the young mother. "Not everyone has a nanny, Mr. Hilliard. Please excuse me?" When Hilliard didn't budge, she repeated her request. "Mr. Hilliard, I need to leave my seat."

Once he had risen and stepped out into the aisle, she left her seat and walked over to the woman with the fussy babe. The bedraggled mother gave her a grateful smile when she took the babe and asked if she might take it back to her seat. Hilliard gave her an annoyed look as he stepped out into the aisle once again for her to reseat herself along with the baby.

The infant continued to wail. She tried to quiet it for what seemed a long while. Hilliard fidgeted in his seat frowning. Connor continued to carry on a conversation with Jack, all the while watching and trying not to grin, but he couldn't resist the temptation to give Rasheen a wink.

To his surprise, she returned it, and then rocked back and forth with the infant, as she sang a lullaby. After awhile, the little one went off to sleep and she returned it to a grateful mother, forcing Hilliard to move to the aisle two more times.

"Where did you learn that song?" Connor asked after she had settled herself. "It is an old Irish tune."

"It's one of Granny's favorites."

*****

Hilliard tried to draw Rasheen into conversation and when that failed, proceeded to go on about his relatives in Baltimore. She nodded from time to time giving the illusion that she was paying attention, but she was thinking of her upcoming visit with her family. Suddenly the train slowed and then stopped, jarring her out of her thoughts. They were still several miles from Baltimore and nowhere near a depot. "Why are we stopping?" She asked.

"I'll go check with the conductor." Connor got up and started toward the back of the car. She arose to follow with Jack, but he told them to stay in their seats until he found out what was happening.

"Tsk, Tsk," said Hilliard, "I'll make sure to bring this delay up to the station master. After all, there is a schedule to be kept."

Rasheen remained silent. She hoped to discourage further conversation by not saying anything; so much for that dream. Mr. Hilliard had all the perception of a marble table top.

"Did I mention the fact that the president of the railroad and I are very close friends?" "Why just..." He droned on and on until Connor finally returned.

"There's Mr. Reilly," she almost shouted in relief.

"What happened?" She and Jack asked in unison.

Connor dropped down into the seat next to Jack. "The engineer thought he saw a lantern signaling danger ahead. When the crew went up and down the tracks to check, they didn't find anything. Guess Logan's ghost has taken to walking the tracks during the day."

"Who's Logan?" Jack sat in his seat like a spring about to uncoil.

"Oh, please, do tell us about Mr. Logan." Rasheen was pleased to note the spasm of annoyance that crossed Mr. Hilliard's face as a result of her request.

Connor must have noted it also because he gave her a wicked grin. "Well, now, you see, Robby Logan was a brakeman on this train a few years back. He slipped between the cars one icy night when he was walking on the overhead running boards. He fell to the track and the wheels passed over his body injuring him so seriously that he died in a few hours. Train crews on this track see his lantern from time to time, when they pass the spot where his death occurred. This is the first time anyone has seen it during the day. I guess he's just reminding us to pray for his departed soul." He crossed himself as he said this. "No sense in taking any chances."

"Come, come, you will frighten Mrs. Langston with such nonsense. The stop was an excuse for the crew to slack off the job, and nothing more. I'll see that they are reprimanded when I get back to my office." Hilliard puffed out his chest.

Connor's grin disappeared, the line of his mouth now firm, jaw set in a rigid line. "It caused the engineer and the fireman a great deal more work to get the stream up and the engine moving again. I doubt that the engineer would have stopped the train had he not thought there might be danger ahead. As for slacking, these men earn their pay by hard labor, long hours, blood, and broken bodies. They give their all, sometimes even their lives."

"We really mustn't discuss such matters in front of a lady such as Mrs. Langston. I'm certain we are distressing her," Hilliard said.

Rasheen was aware of the controlled manner in which Connor had just spoken and gave him a knowing look. "On the contrary, the distress is to the men and their families."

"Nonetheless, I prefer to change the subject to something more pleasant." Hilliard started into a monolog of his connections in Baltimore and Washington. When the train pulled into Camden Station and the bell clanged, he was still talking. As soon as it was safe to stand, Rasheen sprung out of her seat, not waiting for him to step out in the aisle. She scooted past him in an unladylike manner and scurried down the aisle before anyone could take her arm.

She was still walking at a brisk pace when Connor came alongside her. "My dear Mrs. Langston, why didn't you wait for young Jack or me to escort you from the train?" She looked over to where Hilliard was giving orders to a porter and they both laughed.

"That man is insufferable. If he is on the same train as we are when we return, I shall change my departure date. I swear it."

"If we have to hire a carriage to drive us all the way from Baltimore back to Sara's Glen, and it takes hours longer, we will do so rather than suffer another journey with Reg Hilliard. Depend on it."

*****

152

It had been over three months since Rasheen departed the city, and yet as they rode through the streets on the way to her family's home, she found that she didn't miss it. She was looking forward to her visit, but she was content with her life in the country.

She hoped to stay at Sara's Glen as long as possible to be near Jack; to be part of his life. Whatever Daniel's past mistakes had been, he had given her the boy and she loved him as her own.

Both she and Connor had agreed that it would be best not to mention any of Jack's history to her family. They would simply say Connor was his guardian, which at the present was the truth.

When they pulled up in front of her home, Connor helped her out of the carriage. Jack bounded from the vehicle in a burst of energy. He started to run toward the steps and then stopped and walked back to where the driver was unloading Rasheen's bags and took one of them. When the driver and Jack were out of hearing range, she asked Connor, "What really happened when the train stopped?"

"You don't believe in ghosts?" Amusement flickered in his eyes.

"Perhaps, but I don't think Mr. Logan visited us today."

"You are much too perceptive."

"I'm just curious or do you agree with Mr. Hilliard's opinion that I'm incapable of handling any worthwhile knowledge?"

"Scathack, you've just thrown a mortal blow." He grabbed his chest in mock pain.

"Connor?"

His expression grew serious. "Part of my story was true. There *was* someone with a lantern giving them the danger signal. When they stopped, the man ran into the woods and they weren't able to catch him."

"But why?"

"A brakeman was killed last week up in Martinsburg. It was an accident that could have been avoided had the company used the new Westinghouse Brakes, but they aren't using them on the freight trains because of the cost."

"But we were on a passenger train."

"They're trying to make a point by slowing down the passenger trains since they have the new brakes. The crew has to stop when they see the lantern because they never know for sure if the signal is legitimate or not."

"It wasn't that much of an inconvenience, but I imagine if they do this enough, it will cost the railroad."

"That's their intention. Sorry about the ghost story, but I needed to do something to distract Hilliard. Hopefully, he will be so annoyed at me, he'll not make good on his threat to complain about the stop."

"I enjoyed the story, and it was fun irritating that pompous jackass."

A muscle quivered in his jaw, then the dimple showed and finally the laughter came. "What was it you said about Martha and swearing?"

*****

"Miss Rasheen, it's so good to have you home. Your Granny's waiting for you." Mary took their wraps and led them to the parlor.

Rasheen hurried across the carpet in a swish of skirts and kissed her grandmother.

Granny touched her face and said, "You look well, child. The teaching, you like it then?"

"I do, very much. And Granny, you would love Sara's Glen. It's similar to Uncle Martin's farm, but on a much grander scale and…" She stopped in her description when she realized that Jack and Connor were standing at the room's entrance politely waiting to be introduced.

Rasheen made the introductions and Granny bade everyone to take a seat. "I'm sorry my daughter, isn't at home. I know she would have liked to have been here to greet Mr. Reilly and young Jack, here. She won't return until dinner, but you're welcome to stay until then."

"I appreciate the offer, Mrs. Hughes, but my aunt and uncle are expecting us."

"Only strangers refer to me as Mrs. Hughes and you, lad, don't fall into that group of people."

He raised an eyebrow. "All right, Granny, but I don't believe we've ever met. I would have remembered such a remarkable lady."

"Did you kiss the blarney stone before you left Ireland?"

"Would you doubt my word? I tell you I'd remember such a charming lady as you if we'd met." He flashed a roguish smile.

Rasheen could have sworn he was flirting with her grandmother.

"I can see why my granddaughter likes living at Sara's Glen," Granny chuckled.

"Where have you met Connor before?" Rasheen asked.

"Well now, you see, we haven't actually met. Your mother and I were attending a luncheon hosted by his aunt. I happened to notice a hand sneaking around the door frame and reaching for the finger sandwiches resting on a nearby buffet. It made its mark several times before the tray of refreshments was offered to the guests. I know all about growing lads' hunger, so I kept silent. Soon, the rest of the body attached to that arm crept past the door. It belonged to a handsome young man."

"I thank you for not getting me into trouble with my aunt." His eyes twinkled as he took her hand in his and kissed it.

"Oh, I doubt that could ever happen. She adores you. I knew it was you soon as I saw you; knew it from her description."

"The adoration is mutual, I assure you."

"Will you at least have some tea before leaving us and

perhaps some sandwiches?" Granny rang for Mary before giving him an opportunity to reply.

"You might as well give in. You are not leaving this house without eating something," Rasheen laughed.

Connor glanced at the rose patterned china clock that rested on the mantle. "I think we have time for a little something."

Mary wheeled in a cart filled with tea for the adults, milk for Jack, and sandwiches and cookies. Rasheen sipped her tea and nibbled an oatmeal cookie, while Jack and Connor devoured the sandwiches. She breathed in the spice scent of the cookie. "Lot's of cinnamon. Granny made the cookies."

"I did, and the bread too." Her grandmother said as she passed the plate to Jack for the third time.

"My grandmother takes over the kitchen for baking purposes, but leaves the cook to prepare meals," Rasheen said.

"No insult intended to your cook, but I doubt she could measure up to these cookies." Connor held up one of the cookies as if it were the winning cup in a horse race.

Granny beamed. "Any time you're in the city, please call, and I'll be happy to see that you have all the brown bread and cookies you wish."

"Be careful, Granny, you haven't seen how much these two can eat," Rasheen said.

After they had finished eating, Connor stood, "We must be going, but I thank you for your hospitality. I'll send word when I've made the arrangements for our return to Sara's Glen." He bowed to both women and motioned to Jack to do the same. Jack did so awkwardly and then looked longingly at the remaining cookies.

"A growing lad may need some nourishment on the ride home. Would you like me to have Mary wrap them up for you to take along?" Granny asked.

Rasheen shook her head, "Yes, it will probably take them all of half an hour to reach their destination."

"He could most likely survive the journey without perishing from starvation, but I'm sure he'd like more cookies. And perhaps he might share his bounty with a fellow passenger." Connor raised an inquiring brow at Jack.

The boy grinned, "Yes sir."

"He's a growing boy and a fine one at that. Come over here and give me a hug before you leave, young Jackie boy." Granny held her arms open and Jack walked over and bent down so she could embrace him. Rasheen was surprised at his response considering he had just met her grandmother. There was no stiffness in his movement, but then Granny had a way of making everyone feel as if she were their own grandmother.

*****

Once inside the carriage, Connor reached out to Jack for a cookie. The boy eagerly opened the package and the two munched the sweets. In between bites Jack said, "I like Granny. She's nice just like Miss Rasheen."

"You'll feel the same about Aunt Elaine and Uncle Patrick."

The boy was quiet for a few minutes and then shyly asked, "Are they like you?"

Connor ruffled his hair. "You'll like them fine. They're a lot like Martha and John."

Jack looked at Connor as if to speak but then stayed silent. He crumpled the empty cookie wrapper, opened it and then crumpled it again.

"What is it Jack? Is something troubling you?"

Jack hesitated for a moment and then asked, "How did you come to live with your aunt and uncle? You said your father was a horse trainer. What happened to him?" Jack looked down at the wrinkled wrapping in his lap, as if he were afraid to meet Connor's eyes for fear he had asked something wrong.

"It's all right. I don't mind talking about it. You see, when I was a little older than you are now, my father died and I was an orphan with no family in Ireland. He had arranged for me to come and live with his brother in the event that something happened to him, since my mother had died long before him."

The boy sat quietly, contemplating the information. Connor watched him realizing that he was comparing their situations.

"Were you afraid? I mean, were you afraid of your uncle?"

"Are you afraid of me?"

"I was at first, but I'm not now."

"At first I was afraid of what life with my aunt and uncle would be like. I was sad at leaving my country, and yet excited to be coming here. It was an adventure. I traveled across the ocean on a big ship. When it docked, my uncle was right there waiting. I look exactly like my father so he recognized me immediately. As soon as I stepped onto the pier, he caught me up in an embrace. My aunt was standing behind him and then she did her share of the same. If you don't know by now, lad, the Irish are a great race for hugging."

Connor looked into Jack's questioning eyes. "No, I wasn't afraid of my uncle. He's a good man. He'll love you the same as he does me, because we're family now." He put his arm around the boy and drew him against his side.

CHAPTER 16

Farewell shouts echoed back through the room as eager children scampered out the door at the end of the day. When it was finally quiet, Rasheen sat at the desk and rubbed her temples.

Bernice studied her with a concerned expression. "Do you have a headache?"

"It must be all the excitement of the Christmas holidays. I used to get them quite often, but I haven't had one since my arrival at Sara's Glen."

"Here, let me fix you some tea." Bernice retrieved two cups and saucers from the top of the bookcase, placed them on the ledge near the window, and poured them each a cup of tea from the kettle resting on the stove that heated the schoolroom.

Rasheen plucked a twiggy piece of greenery from her cup and eyed it suspiciously. "I've gotten used to drinking my tea with no cream while teaching, but what is this floating in my cup?"

"It's dried rosemary from the vase on the windowsill. Don't worry; I dipped it in a saucer of hot water to remove any dust before placing it in your tea. See, I still have the water in my saucer. It will help cure your headache. And you can put some dried lavender in a warm bath this evening to further alleviate your pain if it hasn't subsided. Martha has some in the kitchen pantry."

"Where did you learn all this?" Rasheen asked in amazement.

"When I was away at school, there was a woman who worked in the kitchen and she often made remedies for the girls. I used to go and sit with her whenever I could and write them down."

Rasheen nodded, not surprised that Bernice would find such a thing interesting. "My aunt uses herbal medicines. Her mother was a member of the Ute tribe. I remember one summer when we were visiting my uncle's farm, one of my brothers got an earache, and she gave him relief almost at once by using a compress soaked in a feverfew solution. Then she made him eat raw garlic to get rid of the infection. He was strong-smelling for almost a week and the other children made him keep his distance."

As they set about preparing to close the schoolroom for the next few weeks, Bernice said, "I'm going to miss you while you're home with your family."

Rasheen couldn't bear the thought of Bernice trapped in the Peterson home during the coming weeks. "Then why not come and spend some time with us? My family will love you."

"I dread being with mother and having no excuse for escape. She means well, but her constant harping about my station in life and responsibility to marry suitably is wearisome," Bernice said as she placed a book in the bookcase. "My sister will be home for a few days, but she'll be going to visit some friends from school right after Christmas and will be away for New Year's Eve. It would be nice to get away and visit the city for the holiday, but I wouldn't want to impose on your visit with your family."

"Nonsense, you'll come spend New Year's with my family. Tell your mother I'm going to take you to some of the events I'm required to attend as a representative of the Langston family. I'm sure you won't get any argument, especially if she thinks there would be desirable matches available."

Bernice looked at her anxiously. "You wouldn't do that to me, would you?"

"Silly girl, I've no intention of wasting my time with my family like that." Rasheen smiled to herself, knowing at least she had escaped that much of her past. No more endless boring one-sided conversations where she had to smile and keep her opinions to herself.

Bernice rested her chin on her forefinger. "I won't mention anything about any social obligations unless mother becomes difficult."

"Why my dear Miss Peterson, I do believe I'm corrupting you," Rasheen exclaimed in mock horror.

"Saving would be a more accurate description." Bernice laughed.

Rasheen took their coats off the pegs in the back of the room. "Better bundle up, it's getting colder. Will you come up to the house and visit with Martha for a bit?"

"Maybe I could spare a few minutes, just to wish her a Merry Christmas. I can't stay very long though. Mother's not happy with me these days. She doesn't think I should be working with you in the school and resents the time I spend here. She heard me mention that Peter might return to practice medicine here to my father, and I think she fears her plans for a proper marriage would be disrupted if I spend more time here at Sara's Glen."

Rasheen buttoned the last button on her coat with a flourish. "And would those fears be justified?"

"I have only been in his company when he visited in the fall, and he gave no indication of any interest other than our conversations on herbal cures."

Rasheen looked into Bernice's troubled eyes. "He may not know his own feelings. From the little time I've spent with him, I've found him to be a very serious man. I suppose that comes from the profession he has chosen. He did seem to smile a lot more when in your company."

"You aren't going to play matchmaker, are you?" Bernice asked anxiously.

"Not me. Trust your own judgment. Now, I must go pack my things. Connor is taking me to the station tomorrow morning, and I want to make sure I'm ready to leave on time."

*****

Patrick and Elaine Reilly had arrived for the Christmas holiday, bringing with them a flurry of activity. Connor, Peter, who had arrived the day before, and John unloaded the carriage while Elaine issued instructions. "The parcels wrapped in brown paper go to the kitchen. The trunk goes to our room, and the red box goes into the parlor. Connor, be careful with that, it contains things that are fragile." Elaine stepped back when the two younger women walked from the rear of the carriage.

"Rasheen, it is good to see you again. I was so happy to learn from Father Hughes that you had taken the teaching position here at Sara's Glen." She took Rasheen's hands in her own. "And who is this lovely young woman?" She inclined her head towards Bernice.

"You probably don't remember me, Mrs. Reilly, but I attended a garden party you gave here at Sara's Glen several years ago," Bernice said.

Elaine studied Bernice for a few seconds. "Bernice Peterson? Is that really you? My goodness, child, you've grown to a beautiful young woman." Elaine hooked arms with them as they moved toward the steps. "Come inside before the two of you catch cold. I think we have everything unloaded."

An older man with silver streaked black hair as thick as Connor's and features much the same, came alongside them and kissed Elaine's forehead. "Dear heart, I think you brought half of our belongings."

"Don't exaggerate, Patrick. These things are needed for our stay here, and I had to bring the gifts. We are spending Christmas at Sara's Glen with our lad after all." As they entered the parlor, she directed Bernice and Rasheen to take a seat on the sofa and then sat in a velvet rose button back chair that was one of a matched set beside the fire place.

Connor entered the room behind them. "And your lad is very happy that you'll be with him."

"Where else would we be on Christmas, dear boy?" Elaine asked.

"Yes, family should be together on Christmas and speaking of families, I'm Uncle Patrick." Patrick addressed the latter to Rasheen and Bernice.

"All right, Mr. Ril...., I mean Uncle Patrick," Rasheen answered. Bernice shook her head in agreement.

"And you may as well address my wife as Aunt Elaine, or she'll be upset with me."

Elaine nodded. "Yes, yes, after all, Rasheen's no stranger to us. Bernice spends considerable time here too, from what I have been told, so she must also be included in our little family."

*****

"So how do you find your position here at Sara's Glen?" Patrick asked Rasheen.

"I enjoy teaching more than I ever thought possible."

"I gather that Connor has changed his opinion of your qualifications, you being a female and him wanting a Jesuit and all that." Patrick gave her a wry grin.

Connor gave Rasheen a look of approval. "She has proven a most capable teacher."

"I'm so relieved that I measured up to your expectations." Rasheen raised her chin.

"Given your background, my reservations were justified, but I was wrong and am not too proud to admit it." Mischievous eyes caught and held hers, while he disarmed her with an irresistibly devastating smile.

Rasheen wondered if he had inkling as to how he set her pulses racing when he smiled like that.

She thought she saw Aunt Elaine raise her eyebrow at Martha. She was sure about it when the latter shrugged. While she was wondering what the unspoken words might be, Patrick surprised her with an unexpected invitation.

"I understand you'll be in the city with your family.

You must come to our New Year's ball."

Rasheen gave him an apologetic smile. "I'd be delighted to come, but Bernice is going to be my guest for the New Year, and I couldn't abandon her."

"Then the invitation is extended to her as well," Elaine said.

Rasheen was enjoying the Reilly's company here at Sara's Glen, but a ball would be overwhelming. "That's most gracious of you, but I'm not sure I'm ready to attend large social gatherings yet."

"It won't be that large, and you can stand on the outskirts of the room and listen to me poke fun at some of Baltimore's finest citizens," Connor said, and then leaned over and whispered, "And you can keep me from being bored out of my senses."

"We would be honored to have your family and Father Hughes as our guests also," Elaine added.

"I'm sure they would enjoy attending, but..." She might as well be a bird in a snare. What between Connor's pleading and Elaine's insistence.

"Good, then it's settled. I'll see that an invitation is sent to your parents as soon as we return."

"Wonder if Scathack or the Ice Queen will show up at the ball?" Connor mused half to himself.

"Ice Queen?" Everyone looked in their direction as Rasheen's voice rose an octave.

Connor gave her an apologetic shrug. "That's what I called you before you came to Sara's Glen. Whenever I saw you at any of the Beau Monde's gatherings, you seemed to be frozen."

"So now it is Ice Queen and Ejit Blueblood." She lowered her voice and sought to control the anger that was building up inside her.

"Easy, Scathack, that was before I got to know you. I was wrong." Connor gave her a contrite smile.

"You *were* wrong." Rasheen felt her color rising.

Elaine ignored the two of them and looked at Peter. "I expect you to be there also, young man. Connor will be more comfortable with you along, but the two of you are not to do anything to spoil my party."

"I'll be there, and I'll try to make him behave." Peter's expression was one of an angelic innocence.

Connor rolled his eyes. "That's like the devil trying to get me into heaven."

*****

Connor felt as peaceful in the small country church as he did sitting by the stream or walking his land. The building's lofty spire, illuminated by the moonlight, looked like an unadorned Christmas tree in a sky full of twinkling stars. Oil lamps and candles lit the inside of the church making the colors in the stained-glass windows appear as shimmering gems. The original building had been a dilapidated wooden structure. His uncle had supplied money for the new stone building when they started spending their summers at Sara's Glen. It became nicknamed the 'little cathedral' though it held only 300 people.

The parishioners were mostly farmers who worked hard to earn a living, loved their families, and helped their neighbor as the need arose. Gratitude enveloped him, for not everyone was as fortunate as those around him. He thought of all the working men and their families and prayed that the depression would soon end. He also prayed for the upper classes, that they would be more compassionate to the needs of their fellow man. He had the vantage point of having lived in both worlds and understood much.

Then the one thought that he had been trying to suppress by the others surfaced. It was just like Rasheen to burst into his thoughts rather than quietly creep into them. It had been so quiet at Sara's Glen since she and Jack had left to spend the holidays with her family. He hadn't realized how much he missed the way she came down the stairs in the morning, eyes sparkling, eager to start each day, or the intelligent discussions they had regarding his work for the railroad workers, and of her work with her students, or her interest in the farm and the horses. She made a room more cheerful with her presence.

In the next pew, a mother tried to restrain her toddler. The child had one leg over the back of the seat, when his father scooped him up amidst a loud squeal. After some whispering, more than likely about what would happen if Santa found out he was misbehaving in church, the child settled down. The mother kissed both her husband and child.

Connor felt a longing deep within him - felt an emptiness he hadn't felt since his father's death.

*****

In the city, Rasheen and Jack sat with her family in the second pew of the church, just behind the row of nuns. Jack's posture was like a young soldier. She suspected it was more out of fear of the nuns than the strangeness of the new suit he wore. After all, nuns were a new experience for him. Uncle Frank was at the pulpit giving his Christmas sermon, and life was peaceful and happy for this one night as far as Rasheen was concerned. After all, she was with her family and now she had Jack.

A question entered her consciousness like the first rain drop that falls into a barrel disturbing the calm surface. Something was missing. No, not something – someone. Connor had become her most trusted confident along with Bernice. She enjoyed sharing all the important things and the not so important things at Sara's Glen with him. Over the last few months, she had witnessed his kindness and come to admire his integrity.

And since she was in church, she might as well be honest and admit that it didn't hurt that he was the most handsome man she'd ever known. Not that she was interested in that sort of thing anymore, but it didn't hurt to appreciate what God created and God did a fine job when he put Connor Reilly together. She loosened the top buttons of her fur cape for it had suddenly gotten very warm, and she felt her face flush.

Did Connor miss Jack and her? She had taken Jack with her to spend Christmas with her family so that Frank could evaluate where he was in his studies to see if he was ready for Loyola the following year. Don't be silly, she admonished herself. Still, the thought lingered throughout the rest of the service.

At the end of the mass, they moved toward the back of the church with the departing congregation. When she reached the doors of the church, she grabbed Jack's arm and held him alongside her while she fumbled through her purse for some coins to drop into the metal box attached to the wall next to the church door.

Once the family was settled in the carriage and on their way home, Jack asked, "Why did you put money in that little box when you had already put money in the collection basket? Didn't you put enough in the basket?"

Rasheen laughed. "The money that was put in the collection basket is for the church upkeep and various other expenses, but the money that I put in the poor box goes for the care and needs of those less fortunate in the area. Granny says that if you put a few coins in the poor box every time you leave the church, you'll never be without coins in your own pocket."

"Aye, 'tis an old Irish custom," Granny nodded.
"The Irish sure do have a lot of customs and stories. I wish I was Irish," Jack sighed.

"Your guardian is Irish, now isn't that so? That makes you part Irish, doesn't it now?" Granny put her arm around Jack and drew him close.

"You really think so?"

"Aye, and would I have said it, if I did not?" Granny said.

"Aye," Jack gave a forceful nod.

CHAPTER 17

"So Bernice, Rasheen tells me you are assisting her with the school," Father Frank said.

"She is a treasure, not only as my helper, but as my friend." Rasheen gave Bernice a warm smile. She couldn't believe the transformation that had taken place once she and Mary took Bernice in hand. They had selected a robin's egg blue satin gown which brought out the color of her eyes. Mary had done her hair in the new Grecian style with ringlets dripping over a black velvet band.

"Good, good, and tell me how things are going with Connor. He hasn't asked for a replacement, so I assume you two have declared a truce. Have you dazzled him with your teaching skills yet?"

Rasheen hadn't seen her uncle during her Thanksgiving visit as he had been away on retreat. In her letters, she didn't mention Connor, only her students and life in general at Sara's Glen.

"He seems satisfied. As you said, he has not requested a replacement." She was not about to go into detail about her friendship with Connor Reilly.

"Well, his uncle was obviously charmed by you lovely ladies, and from what he told me, he isn't the only one looking forward to your attendance this evening." Frank winked.

Rasheen ignored his teasing and busied herself smoothing her skirt so her uncle wouldn't see her face and detect the excitement she was beginning to feel at the prospect of seeing Connor. "It was very nice of Uncle Patrick and Aunt Elaine to invite us to the ball. I'm looking forward to seeing them again."

Frank bent his head slightly. "Oh, aunt and uncle is it now?

"Uncle Patrick insisted we call them aunt and uncle. It was an easy request to grant since they are wonderful people. Their affection for Connor is obvious even to the most casual observer."

"There's more to those two than their love of Connor." Uncle Frank was in the mood to tell a story. She could tell by the way he stretched his legs out as far as they would go without crowding the other passengers. He let out a sigh and raised his brow as if asking if she was interested.

"And you are about to tell us, right?" It would take no further coaching on her part.

"Patrick and Elaine Reilly are two people that were going to be together no matter the hindrances, and hindrances there were, not the least of which was her father. She came from one of the wealthiest and oldest families in the city, and her father had definite plans when it came to his daughter's matrimonial prospects. He denied Patrick's request for her hand in marriage. It made no difference that Patrick had made his fortune and was wealthier than Elaine's family at that time. They ended up marrying without his consent, and he was so enraged that he disowned her. I tried to reason with him to reconcile with her, but the old man all but had me thrown out of his home. It was a terrible time for Elaine and Patrick."

Rasheen remembered the tender displays of Connor's aunt and uncle at Sara's Glen. "One can see how much in love they are, even after all these years. It took courage on her part to defy her father's wishes. I guess she thought he would come round eventually. Did he?"

"Her parents had four children, two died as infants. Only Elaine and her brother survived to adulthood, but he was killed in a riding accident. It was after his funeral that her father finally accepted the marriage. His wife had died some years before and Elaine was all he had left."

"Uncle Frank, I like a story with a happy ending."

"So do I," he patted her hand and added, "especially for those dearest to me."

As they passed a street lamp, the light shone into the carriage and reflected from his eyes. Her uncle's eyes had always reminded her of a rich green forest. They provided her with the same peaceful reassurance she found in a walk through the woods.

*****

After the carriage stopped, her father took her mother's arm and asked, "Frank, will you escort the younger ladies inside?"

Frank held his arms so Bernice and Rasheen could rest their hand on his forearm as they proceeded up the outside stairs of the Reilly residence. "How often does a priest have an opportunity to have a beautiful young lady on each arm? It will be my pleasure."

"Let's just hope there aren't some old gossips here this evening that will be carrying tales back to the bishop," Rasheen said.

Bernice laughed, "Stop teasing your uncle."

Frank sighed, "She has no respect for the clerical collar, I'm afraid."

Rasheen squeezed his arm and said, "Perhaps not the collar, but certainly the man."

Frank sighed, "Then if my teasing is over, may we proceed inside and enjoy the evening?"

After the maid took their wraps, they made their way through the guests to Patrick and Elaine and exchanged the usual pleasantries before Elaine turned her attention to Bernice. "I believe there is someone here this evening that will be happy you have arrived." Just as she finished the sentence, Peter left a group of men he had been speaking with and strode toward them.

"They make a handsome couple. I think they are well suited," Elaine said as they watched the couple glide away in a waltz.

"I agree, but one dance does not a couple make, and her mother has other plans for Bernice."

"Parents are not always right in their judgment of what is in the best interest of their child."

Patrick took his wife's gloved hand and kissed it. "Perhaps not always, dear heart, but sometimes they have good intentions."

"I think...." Rasheen's sentence was interrupted by a low whistle from behind her.

"Connor, will you please mind your manners?" His aunt smacked him on the arm with her fan.

"Sorry, aunt, but you must admit she is a most attractive woman." He lowered his voice and then his gaze. "It's a good thing you don't dress like that at Sara's Glen. It's enough to stop a poor man's heart."

Rasheen managed a retort. "You aren't a poor man and... um .... you look very nice too." That was an understatement. Connor Reilly dressed in work clothes was enough to set a woman's heart aflutter, but in evening attire, the man was beyond handsome. The contrast of the black formal coat and crisp white shirt made his hair look like polished ebony, which in turn made his dark blue eyes almost the color of midnight. Those eyes searched her face, making her feel as if he had reached into her thoughts. She felt the blush start at her cheeks and go right down to the tips of her toes.

Uncle Patrick gave his nephew a mock frown. "Well now that you've upset your aunt, the only way to redeem yourself is to ask the young lady to dance."

"I was just getting around to that. Would you do me the honor of sharing the next dance with me?" He gave her a roguish smile as he bowed.

"I was not planning on dancing this evening." She couldn't dance, not with all the people here who were Langston acquaintances. Surely tongues would wag. It was too soon for her to be doing such things.

As if reading her thoughts, Elaine looked around the

room and said, "Forget them, go enjoy yourself. If anyone dares to say anything, I will set them straight."

"It has been a very long time since I danced." She and Daniel rarely danced when they attended such events, because there was always someone wishing to speak to him.

"My dear lady, it's like riding a horse, one never forgets. You certainly did not." Connor didn't give her an opportunity to protest, but took her elbow and led her onto the dance floor.

"I have no dance card," she protested.

"I have always thought they were a stupid convention," he said as he placed one hand on her shoulder and the other about her waist. Her heart thumped so hard, she swore she heard it pounding in her ears, almost drowning out the waltz music that the orchestra was playing. She tried to focus as he drew her in a graceful circle in time to the music. One, two, three, --- one, two, three, ---she mentally tried to count, but still managed to miss a step and trod on his foot.

Before she could say she was sorry, he squeezed her waist reassuringly and gave her a wink and a reassuring smile. "You're doing just fine."

That was the smile she liked the best, the one that made a person feel no matter what was happening about them, it was all right. All uncertainty gone now, she glided with him about the room, feeling like a young girl at her first ball.

"Thank you for taking pity on me. I would have had to accept my aunt's displeasure for my whistle, and she would have given me no peace. But I make no apology for showing my appreciation of your beauty. Every man in the place is envious of me at this moment, just look around and you can read their faces."

"I think Martha's right about you and the blarney." If anyone was jealous, Rasheen thought, it was the young women. "I'm sure you will be saying such things to all your partners this evening."

His face grew serious. "I do not intend to dance with anyone else."

"You know very well that isn't appropriate. I've already broken several rules of propriety by attending this ball and then dancing too soon after Daniel's death," Rasheen said in a concerned voice.

"Sweet Jaysus, the man's been dead for over a year and half."

"Mind your words. Even if enough time had elapsed from his death, it still wouldn't be appropriate for us to dance exclusively with each other." Emotions conflicted within her. It wasn't propriety she was concerned with so much as the fact that she was beginning to feel so comfortable with his nearness.

He frowned as he followed her gaze to a corner where three or four ladies were huddled together, glaring in their direction. "You're probably right. My aunt can have an acid tongue when someone dares to criticize those for whom she has developed a fondness, but eventually you would have to face them without her protection."

The last strain of music drifted through the room as he finished his sentence. "Are you sure you don't want to become a hermit at Sara's Glen, and then we could dance the night away?"

"I think it would be best if you turned some of your attention toward your other guests." She took his arm and followed him off the floor where they joined Bernice and Peter who were standing near one of the velvet draped window alcoves.

Peter handed Bernice a small cup that he had just filled with punch from the cut crystal bowl across the room and then said to Connor, "Hilliard is over in the corner talking to the son of the railroad's president, no doubt filling him with nonsense regarding the workers. We need to become part of the conversation so the young man doesn't receive a lot of false information. The poor devils have enough difficulties in their lives right now without having to deal with an idiot like Hilliard trying to advance his position at their expense."

Rasheen shuddered. "I detest that man."

"Perhaps you should join us. You seem to have a way of handling Reg." Connor raised an eyebrow in invitation.

"You can be sure that Mr. Hilliard would not want to expose tender creatures such as Bernice and me to any conversation that might pertain to real life circumstances, since our delicate ears are only fit for dribble."

"My dear Scathack, I would hate to be the unfortunate individual who came up against such a tender creature as you in a battle of wits." Connor shuddered.

She slanted him a sly smile, her eyes sparkling. "Aye, Mr. Reilly, me Granny always says ye don't let yer opponent know yer strength. 'Tis a great strategy, no?"

Her shook his head and said, "I'm happy ye and me be friends then, lass."

"Then, if you delicate creatures will excuse us," Peter said as he gave Connor a shove in Hilliard's direction.

*****

"I'm not familiar with this pattern," Rasheen said as she and Bernice watched the intricate steps of a quadrille. She studied the dancers trying to make sense of the pattern and counts before the conductor called them, but was distracted when a sparkle of light caught her eye. It came from a diamond necklace worn by a waspish shaped blond dressed in a silver gown with amethyst colored stripes adorning the puffed train. The music stopped and the young woman's eyes met hers.

"Blast it." Rasheen gave an exasperated sigh. "Amelia Delacourte is coming in our direction."

"Mr. Astor is her escort this evening. No doubt she wants to make sure I take that information back to my mother," Bernice said.

"Not one of the Astors?" Rasheen asked in disbelief.

"A cousin, but she'll make sure everyone in attendance is introduced to him before the evening is over. No doubt she won't mention his first name or the fact that he is only related distantly." Bernice had barely whispered the last words before Amelia and her escort stood before them.

Amelia inclined her head toward Bernice and Rasheen. "Good evening Mrs. Langston, Miss Peterson, may I present Mr. Astor." Bernice and Rasheen exchanged pleasantries with Mr. Astor, and then Amelia dismissed him to get her a glass of punch.

"Mrs. Langston, how nice to see you out of mourning. It seems rather difficult to believe that two years passed since our dear Daniel left us."

"It hasn't been two years." Rasheen recognized the accusation and she should have ignored it, but she couldn't. She fisted the burgundy velvet of her gown in her gloved hands and then released it. Mary had suggested she wear it, and the simple truth was that it hadn't taken one ounce of persuasion.

"Dear me, I must apologize for my thoughtlessness." The woman fluttered her fan before a pale face with skin stretched taut over lightly rouged cheekbones. "How brave of you to dress in such a gown so soon. But then if you had gone into Half Mourning, you would be wearing such dull colors and you certainly wouldn't want to be attending balls. I know I could never do such a thing, and Daniel's mother wouldn't have set foot in a ball room in such a short time after her husband's death."

"I'm afraid I never quite managed to live up to Mrs. Langston's image." Rasheen felt the portrait's disapproving gray eyes on her, and searched the room as if it were hanging somewhere on one of the walls. All the past uncertainties swarmed around her as if she were standing in the middle of the Langston parlor instead of the Reilly ballroom.

"There are few of us that could." Amelia Delacourte

raised her chin, giving Rasheen a cool stare. "I was fortunate to have her as my godmother. She had great hopes for me, but unfortunately never lived to see them fulfilled."

A sharp pain in her lower lip made Rasheen realize just how hard she was struggling to keep from speaking her mind. She released the soft flesh from her teeth, sure that she must have drawn blood. Enough.

"Yes, I'm afraid I came along and disrupted the great Mrs. Langston's plans, but be assured, I paid for that mistake. No one wishes that her desires had been met more than I do. You would have been far more amenable to being molded to her image. In fact, there would be little molding to be done at all." Rasheen swept her eyes over Amelia, until they rested on the other's cool gray ones and realized just how accurate her statement was.

"Rasheen need not live under anyone's shadow. She is an inspiration to us all, especially her students." Bernice placed her punch cup on the tray of passing servant and placed herself between Amelia and Rasheen.

Amelia gave them a sardonic smile. "I forgot about your little adventure. I can see why you would want to live at Sara's Glen. Mr. Reilly is a handsome man, and most charming when he chooses to be so. I'm sure that must make your duties rather pleasant. The two of you appeared to be enjoying yourselves when you were dancing, but I think it my duty to advise you that your familiarity with one another seemed rather inappropriate given your position."

Rasheen kept her voice calm despite her shaking insides. "My position is no concern of yours. As to Mr. Reilly, you are mistaken."

Bernice threaded her arm around Rasheen in a protective manner. "You've managed to twist the truth beyond recognition," she said to Amelia.

"I was merely trying to remind you of your duty as Daniel's widow, but it would seem that you aren't interested in my help."

Before Rasheen could reply, Mr. Astor returned with Amelia's punch.

Amelia snapped her fan shut and took a sip of the punch before giving the cup to a passing servant. She then took Mr. Astor's arm and directed him toward a group of people across the room.

"That wretched woman wouldn't help a drowning kitten. The only thing she wanted to do was ruin your evening." Bernice's eyes shone fierce like a lioness protecting her cubs.

Rasheen let out a long breath. "She caught me by surprise. I tried to keep my tongue in check, but I've failed once again. The last thing I want to do is cause any scandal for the Reilly's."

"She was so vicious." Bernice shook her head incredulously.

"I don't want you to become subject for the gossips on my account; speaking of which, I see Mrs. Dunmore and her daughters heading in our direction." Rasheen squared her shoulders in preparation for the next attack.

Bernice gave her a push towards the pillared archway. "Go find a quiet room for yourself. I'll field the old hen and her chicks."

*****

Connor gently pushed the library door closed and stepped inside. Flickering light from the gas lamps washed across Rasheen's face as she stood before the mantle, staring up at the picture of the Reilly Coat of arms. For a long moment he stood quietly watching her, and tried to decide if she were a queen, a fairy, a waif, or a warrior; and finally reached the conclusion that she was all of them.

"I had the painting done for my uncle as a Christmas gift a few years back." He looked up at the ornately carved rich dark wood frame with its less than attractive subject matter. In the center of the shield there was a right hand cut off at the wrist dripping blood. At this moment, he felt as if he might like to be the cause of Amelia's bloodshed, if she were a man he would have beaten her to a bloody pulp for her vicious attack on Rasheen, even though he suspected Shathack was more than capable of defending herself.

"Fortitudine Et Prodentia. The English translation is By Fortitude and Prudence. Would you like me to explain the depictions?" He was standing beside her now.

She didn't turn to face him, merely shrugged in answer to his comment.

"Vert or green depicts hope, joy and loyalty in love. Yellow symbolizes generosity and elevation of the mind. The blood represents the Royal tribes of Ireland. Antiquity and strength are signified by the oak tree and the lions, except that they also show kingship, majesty, and courage. When I first came to live with him, Uncle Patrick bragged that our family came from royalty. I asked him how come my father ended up tending someone else's horses, and his answer was that we lost the battle."

He turned her towards him. "It seems we just lost another one. Bernice told me what happened with Amelia. I'm sorry I wasn't there to protect you."

"It wasn't your fault, and it isn't anyone's place to protect me. I brought it on myself by my actions, and I don't really care what the likes of her have to say. It's just that I lost control of my tongue, and I'm afraid I've become an embarrassment to your aunt. Causing embarrassment to those close to me seems to be my worst flaw. I'm sure the gossips are using me for tonight's amusement. Not only am I dressed inappropriately for my station in life, I danced and I left the room unescorted."

"I doubt that my aunt would disapprove of your behavior. On the contrary, it's Amelia she would chastise if given opportunity. And if anyone dares to speak ill of you in her presence, the party will really get lively."

She shook her head. "None of this would have

happened if I'd just stayed home."

"And denied me the pleasure of dancing with you?" The memory of her in his arms as they swirled around the ballroom made him wish they could have spent the entire evening that way.

She turned back towards the picture, changing the subject. "What about the snake entwined around the oak? I would think that it would denote evil and you certainly wouldn't want that to be representative of your family."

Reluctantly he continued his explanation. "Aye, now the serpent also portrays wisdom and health, and we Reilly's are a healthy lot to be sure."

"And are you wise, too?"

"Most of the time, I like to think so."

She turned her head from the Coat of Arms and looked at him for a long moment   "But not all of the time?"

"I was foolish in my earlier judgment of you." He motioned toward the sofa. "Come and sit." She stood mute, but he recognized the apprehension in her eyes.

"Please?" He kept his voice gentle as he took her by the arm and coached her to take a seat. "I think I should explain something. Amelia and I have a history. I met her in Boston when I was attending law school and she was there visiting friends. I thought she was in love with me, and perhaps she was; but our expectations of married life were not in harmony. She wanted to be a member of High Society and all I ever wanted was to develop Sara's Glen into a successful horse breeding farm. I finally realized that a union between us would be disastrous and broke it off. After an acrimonious parting, she returned home and sent me a letter saying that she was the one who had made a mistake by taking up with the likes of me. Her parents had a more suitable match planned for her."

Rasheen's brows drew together in an agonized expression. "The suitable match was Daniel. I came along and ruined everyone's plans. It's no wonder she hates me."

Connor absently stroked the top of her gloved hand. A simple act, completely inappropriate and yet it seemed so natural.

He let out a long breath. "I tried to avoid Amelia this evening, but she sought me out and engaged me in a lengthy one-sided conversation. Of course I was distracted, along with every other male in the room, when you arrived. I should have realized she would make trouble when she made a malicious remark about your gown, but I simply excused myself and dashed over to your side. I should have waited until I had the opportunity to escape her without drawing attention to you, but I wanted to get to you before you were surrounded by hordes of admirers. She was jealous of you, and with good reason. My lack of attention toward her only inflamed that jealousy."

"But that's ridiculous; I'm merely your friend. Perhaps she has had a change of heart about Sara's Glen and marriage to you."

True, she was his friend, but he doubted she realized just how precious that friendship had become to him. "I don't think Amelia has a heart."

He stood and helped her do the same, but before they left the room he hesitantly asked, "What do you want from life, Rasheen?"

"I'm happy with my life at Sara's Glen. I haven't thought beyond that." She took his arm to lead him out of the room before he could pursue the subject further.

CHAPTER 18

Jack stood at the library window watching the silent flurries fall onto the winter landscape. "How deep do you think it will be when it stops?"

"It's still coming down hard and fast with no signs of slowing down. I would say it will go into the early evening or longer." Connor looked up from the book he was reading and smiled at the boy. "Hanging around that window isn't going to influence its duration. Don't you have lessons to work on?"

"Have you completed the extra work I gave you?" Rasheen asked.

"Yes ma'am, would you like to see it now?"

"I'll check the arithmetic, but let Connor go over your Latin. He's the scholar in that subject. I didn't have the advantage of a Jesuit Instructor."

"Fortunate for you;" Connor replied wryly. "My teacher was a tyrant."

"The tyrant of which you speak happens to be my uncle."

"He may have been a doting uncle, but he was a demanding teacher."

She gave him a pointed look. "Would you have had it any other way?"

"No, I suppose not." He set his book on the small table next to his chair and turned his attention to Jack. "Come over here lad, and let me see what you've done."

Jack retrieved his work from the floor near the hearth where he had been working and handed each adult a handful of pages before scuttling over to the window again. "I hope Midnight is all right. He must hate being cooped up inside all day. Do you think I should go out to the stable and check on him?"

Connor held Jack's paper in one hand and beckoned with his other. "I think you need to read this sentence again."

Jack came to stand next to the chair and read, "Rei nulli prodest mora nisi iracundiae."

Connor nodded his approval. "Your pronunciation is perfect, but would you translate it again for me?"

"Anger is the one thing made better by delay."

"Then why did you write that anger is not made better by delay?" Connor shook his head in disbelief.

Jack leaned a hip against Connors chair and looked down at his shoes. "Guess I was thinking about something else."

"Snow, perhaps?" Connor playfully slapped the pages along the side of Jack's shoulder. Jack stood rigid, his face ashen.

Connor turned toward him. "I was only teasing. You know that, right?"

Jack took a deep breath and let it out. "I just forget sometimes. I'm sorry."

"You've nothing to be sorry for, lad." Connor put his hand behind the boy and gently rubbed his back in a reassuring manner.

Rasheen held out the papers she had just checked for Jack. "These are correct; well done." She had marveled at Jack's intelligence from the fist time he picked up a book in her classroom. The fact that she believed he was her stepson only increased her pride in his accomplishments. Daniel was to thank for that and yet he had not even known his son, or seemed to have had any inclination of doing so. Connor had become Jack's protector without a moment's hesitation. But then Connor didn't have a family name with all its ghosts dominating his life.

Before she could dwell on the matter any further, Martha appeared at the open doorway with a plate filled with ginger cookies and said, "Thought you might like a little afternoon snack." Before she could set the plate down, Jack grabbed two cookies and shoved half a cookie in his mouth. Martha lowered her chin and raised her eyebrows. "Mind your manners, boy."

Jack gave a sheepish grin and started to put one of the cookies back.

Martha raised the plate out of his reach. "Don't bother now. I came in here to ask you to get some more wood for the stove. There's plenty under the tarp on the porch, but put a coat on before you go out there. I don't want you getting sick. When you're finished, there are more cookies and some milk on the table waiting for you."

"Are we finished with the Latin?" Jack asked Connor.

Connor looked to Rasheen and when she nodded, he gave the boy permission to leave and then took Martha's arm and led her out of the room. He closed the door leaving Rasheen alone and curious as to the whispered conversation being held in the hallway.

When he returned, he replied to her unspoken inquiry. "Just a little surprise I've arranged for when it stops snowing."

"And what might that be?"

"If I told you, it wouldn't be a surprise, now would it?" He grinned, winking at her as he spoke.

At dinner, Rasheen and Jack tried wrangling information about the surprise from Martha and John, but the older couple gave no clues. John glanced toward the window as he finished his coffee. "Looks like it's slowing down so I guess you'll get your answer soon enough."

A little while later Jack pressed his face against the window pane and then turned back toward Connor and pleaded, "It stopped snowing. Can I go check on Midnight now?"

"Mr. Johnson took care of the horses, and I think it's time for the surprise. Martha, will you please help Rasheen get ready while I take care of the lad here?"

"Help me to do what?" Rasheen asked looking between Martha and Connor. "Before I submit myself to anything, I'd like to know just what's going on."

"Just this once," Connor said coming to stand before her, "will you just go along with something without arguing?"

"Come along dear," Martha said as she took Rasheen's arm and pulled her toward the hall, "I can assure you that you'll enjoy this surprise." Once in the hall, Martha leaned towards her, "You have your reasons for getting prickly when being ordered about and told nothing, but in this instance you have no need to worry. Your independence won't be compromised. Sometimes it's good to let someone else take charge. Not always, mind you, but sometimes."

She left Rasheen in her room, disappeared into one of the unoccupied bedrooms, and returned with a set of young men's woolen underwear. "Put these on and wear a heavy skirt over them. They were Connor's when he was a few years older than our Jack is now. You'll be good and warm in them. It's too bad you gave those denim trousers away. They would have come in handy this evening."

Rasheen quickly dressed with Martha's assistance. "So we're going for a sleigh ride."

"You'll find out soon enough. Have patience for pity's sake. Now let's go see if the boys are ready."

Jack and Connor were standing at the kitchen door waiting when they came downstairs. A blast of cold air rushed in when John opened the door. "Mr. Johnson has made a nice fire for you."

"Very well, then, let us be off." Connor stepped aside to let Rasheen and Jack out the door.

It was early evening, the last bit of light yielded to the darkness, as they trudged through the deep snow to the carriage house. She thought that surely someone should have brought the sleigh around to the porch for them. "Why haven't the horses been hitched to the sleigh yet?"

"We won't need any horses for tonight's amusement." Connor handed her the lantern as they entered the dark building and she held it high to illuminate the gloomy interior. When they reached the back wall, she understood his meaning. Hanging there in the quivering shadows created by the lantern light were four wooden sleds. Connor gave Jack and her each a sled, and then took one down for himself leaving one lone sled behind. Looking at it nostalgically, he spoke as if remembering long ago winters. "John made these for his boys. Peter brought them along when they moved to Sara's Glen, and we made good use of them during the winter vacations from school."

******

Dark pine branches sagged under the weight of crystal icicles and more than ten inches of new fallen snow. As they trudged through the unsullied white blanket toward their destination, Rasheen took a deep breath, filling her lungs with the chilly air that nipped her skin and produced a tingling sensation. It was marvelous to feel so alive.

When they reached the top of the hill, several youngsters waved and shouted out and then jumped on sleds to zoom down the slope. A deserted fire blazed nearby, its warmth and light ignored by the energetic sliders.

Jack watched his friends hesitantly and then asked Connor, "Can I ride with you a few times before I try it by myself?"

Connor put his arm around the boy. "Have you

never gone sledding?"

"No Sir."

"Why don't the three of us go down together and then if you like, you can try it by yourself? Is that all right with you, or would you prefer to go alone?" He asked Rasheen.

"Since I've never done this before either, I think riding together would be best."

Connor shook his head. "Neither of you has ever gone sledding? What deprived lives you have led. We will soon change that." He motioned for Jack to sit in the front of the sled and then for Rasheen to take her place behind Jack. Then he pushed the sled and ran alongside until they started to glide down the hill. When he jumped onto the sled and put his arms around her, pulling her against his chest, she felt a familiar sensation that was both exciting and disconcerting. There was no time to dwell on it because she had to hold tightly to Jack as they sped down the steep hill.

Their ride ended when the sled reached the flat part of the field. Jack jumped up, but Rasheen could not follow him. She twisted her head around towards Connor, brushing her cheek against his lips in the process and quickly turned away again. "Um, you can let go now."

Though only seconds elapsed, it felt an eternity before he jumped off the sled and stood next to her extending his hand with a perceptive smile on his face. She avoided looking at him as she accepted his assistance. The three of them climbed the hill in silence, except for when Jack's friends whizzed by and he called out to them.

After they reached the crest, Jack asked, "Can I try it by myself now?"

"If you like," Connor answered.

"Do you want to go alone or with me again?" He asked Rasheen.

She walked over to the fire. "I think I'll stand here for a bit and watch the two of you."

Connor and Jack each pushed off and zoomed down the hill. She stood by the fire thinking of the feel of his arms about her, the solidness of his body behind her, his warm breath against her cheek, the way he had held her longer than was acceptable and the way she had enjoyed his hands about her waist. Suddenly she was aware that his old clothing was next to her skin in a most intimate manner.

Jack and Connor went down the hill several more times until the latter finally came back to her and said, "You can't just stand by the fire all night, you must have a few slides at least."

"I think I'm ready now." She took the sled and positioned it at the top of the hill, adjusting her skirts so they were pulled up under her legs so as not to drag.

Connor checked to see that she had positioned herself properly on the sled, and then sent her on her way. Crisp, heady air hit her face, stealing her breath and scorching her eyes, as she whizzed downward. Flying through the night without a care, as if nothing could catch her was a glorious feeling. She quickly strode up the hill when the ride was over so that she could do it again. The speed was heady and she went down the hill several times until she finally had to stop for a few minutes to get warm.

Connor was already by the fire when she placed her sled out of the way and walked over to the log where he sat. She dropped down next to him holding her gloved hands near the flames to warm her cold fingers. Muffs and mittens were much better at keeping fingers warm, she thought, and made a mental note to purchase some mittens the next time she was in town. Mrs. Daniel Langston would never have been allowed to make such a purchase because mittens were unacceptable; but the school teacher, Rasheen Langston, was free to buy and wear whatever she pleased.

"I'm not sure if their energy keeps them warm or just keeps them going so that they don't notice the cold," she remarked as they watched the action going on around them.

"I would guess it's the energy." Connor waved to Jack as he started down the hill. All of the boy's previous apprehension gone, he raced with his friends.

"Are you rested enough to ride with me again? It's more fun with someone else along." Connor stood and extended his hand to her.

She recognized the seductive power in that intense cobalt gaze, and decided that having his body that close to hers again would not be a wise choice. Taking his hand, she said, "I have a better idea. Why don't we race one another?"

"You'll lose. I have more experience."

"Stuff and nonsense. Unlike horseback riding, it doesn't take skill to hurl down a slope."

"All right, then, shall we?" He took her arm and led her to the sleds.

By now, the children had realized what was happening. "Race, race, race," they chanted gathering at the starting point.

Several of the boys gave her a push and she was off with Connor trailing, but soon overtaking her. They were speeding down the hill tied neck and neck when her sled hit an obstacle, perhaps an old tree stump or large rock, covered by the snow. The abrupt cease of motion threw her off the sled and rolling down the hill for several yards until she finally landed in a small snowdrift. She lay there for a few seconds wondering if anything was broken, and then proceeded to wiggle her fingers and toes. Next she moved her arms and legs by making an angel in the snow. Everything seemed to be working fine.

When she finally tried to sit up, she was prevented from doing so by the anxious man leaning over her. "Rasheen, Rasheen, are you all right?"

Anger, displeasure, desire, all these things she had seen in a man's face before, but never had she seen fear like that which was staring down at her now. Somehow it unnerved her even more than his nearness.

"I'm fine." She made an awkward attempt to push herself over on one side to escape.

"Are you sure?" He held onto her arm preventing her from rising.

"Yes."

"Are you certain?"

"Do you think I'm some frail creature?" Her indignant breath came out in steamy cloud.

"Don't be silly, woman, I just want to make sure you're all right."

"Perhaps this will reassure you, if you won't take my word." Laughing, she picked up a fistful of snow and smashed it in her unsuspecting target's face.

"Bloody…" Connor yelled as he jumped back giving her a chance to scramble to her feet. She watched his surprised expression change to mirth right before she turned to run in the opposite direction as fast as she could.

"Prepare for battle, Scathack" he yelled after her.

The young people divided themselves between the two adults. Jack stood uncertain for a moment, but then apparently decided his loyalties were with Connor.

Snowballs hurtled through the air for several minutes with Connor's side gaining ground, and Rasheen's retreating until there was no hope for them to win the battle.

"We're beaten," she called out.

After the surrender, he grabbed her with one hand, and held a fistful of snow menacingly near her face with the other.

"Mercy, Mercy," she cried as she ducked her head away from the snow and buried her face in his chest while her entire body shook with laughter.

"How much mercy did you show me?" He pulled her face away from his chest and brought the cold powdery fluff within an inch of its mark, then let the snow drop from his hand and leaned closer. His expression stilled and grew serious. Their surroundings faded into the background. Her heart jolted as he gazed down at her before bringing his lips a mere whisper from hers. Their breath intermingled and went up in a cloud between them in a ghostly mist.

But the spell was broken when a barrage of snowballs pelted them. The children who had been on the winning side of the battle were having none of this nonsense. If their leader couldn't manage to give the defeated a proper punishment, then they would see to the matter.

Mr. Johnson came just in time to save the defenseless couple. He retrieved his own brood and told the other children their parents wanted them to come home.

"You saved us from a real pummeling." Connor brushed the powder from one of the snowballs that had made its mark from his coat sleeve.

"Happy to be of service. Do you want me to put the fire out or are you staying a bit longer?"

Jack gave Connor a pleading look.

Connor waved Mr. Johnson away. "I'll take care of it."

Then he smiled indulgently at Jack. "You may take a few more coasts down the hill, and then we have to be leaving."

Wasting no time, Jack took a running start and jumped on his sled.

"I don't remember when I've had so much fun," Rasheen said.

"It was a pleasure for me to watch you and Jack enjoying yourselves."

Mercifully, he didn't mention what had almost happened between them after the snowball fight. Following his lead, she continued, "I'm glad you invited me to come along."

"Oh, I needed some adult companionship, and you're much prettier than John, especially when you smile." His devilish eyes swept over her face. "I like to make people smile, especially beautiful women."

She simply had to gain control of herself. Even though it was innocent flirting, the man had her pulses pounding. She turned towards the fire, and placed her hands in front of it to warm them, though at the moment they were every bit as warm as the rest of her person. It was as if the sun were dancing within her center casting warm rays outward, and then back inside to course though her body, awakening sensations within her, sensations best left buried like autumn seeds in the snow-covered ground.

Behind her, Connor called out to Jack, "Make this your last slide."

She turned and watched Jack's descent down the hill. "You've done well by him. I think he has succeeded in putting the past behind him in such a short time because of your efforts."

"I want him to be a boy, to enjoy what's left of his youth. He'll have all the responsibilities that accompany adulthood soon enough. It would be nice if he can remember these good times and keep a little of the boy in him."

"Well, you've certainly kept a little of the boy in you," She teased, trying to keep the mood light.

"Now you sound just like Martha."

"That is the highest compliment you could pay me."

"It is at that." Connor threw snow on the fire after Jack returned from his ride. "That's enough for tonight lad; we have to be getting home. Martha and John will be worried about us."

"Yes sir. Thanks for taking me. It was fun." The boy set his sled in the snow next to the pile of smoldering wood that had been a circle of dancing flames moments before.

"It was fun. Makes me sorry I'll be busy getting ready for my trip and won't be able to join you tomorrow."

Rasheen found herself both disappointed and relieved

that he would be away for awhile. "When are you leaving for the city?"

"Day after tomorrow. My uncle's building a new warehouse and wants me to check out the site I might as well meet the builder and go over the plans and contracts while I'm there and save him the trouble of sending them to Sara's Glen. Hopefully, I can wrap it up in a week or two." He picked up the rope to her sled and walked over to retrieve his own.

Scattered patches of silver glittered in the moonlight as if the fairies had sprinkled their magic dust. The only sound as they walked home was the snow's crust crunching beneath their feet.

*****

Rasheen lay in bed and stared up at the starlit sky through the tangled branches of the tree outside her window. Sleep refused to come, despite her tiredness from the evening's sledding. She licked her lips remembering how close Connor had come to kissing her. Her stomach tightened in a hard ball. Was it relief or regret? Why did this have to happen now when everything was going so well between them? It couldn't happen. She wouldn't allow it.

She got up from the bed, walked over to her dresser and picked up the small hand carved spear, a replica of Gae Blog, the famous one belonging to the goddess Scathack. When she had told Connor she still possessed it, she didn't tell him how much it meant to her. It hadn't been gold or studded with emeralds as the one in the legend, but she had been thrilled to receive it because he had made it himself.

It had been her secret treasure, for she dreamed one day he would fall in love with her. Such dreams were crushed during a visit to his aunt's when she learned that he had met someone in Boston and an engagement announcement was soon expected. The announcement never came, but by the time he returned to Baltimore,

Daniel had come into her life.

But now here was Connor Reilly muddling her senses like she was a silly schoolgirl again, only she was no longer a schoolgirl with romantic dreams. Now she was a grown woman who wanted control over her own life. She turned the carving over in her hand and squeezed it hard before returning it to the dresser.

*****

Connor sat in his chair watching the log burn until the flames engulfed it and reduced it to red hot coals. Swirling the whiskey's amber liquid in his glass, he studied it as if it were a crystal ball that could give him answers to unasked questions. Never in his life had he known such fear as when Rasheen spilled off her sled. He felt certain his heart had ceased to function when he jumped off his own sled and ran to her. Though her reaction to his concern had shocked him at first, an overwhelming sense of relief followed.

He would have felt the same had it been Jack, but there was more to this thing with Rasheen. Sure there was the physical attraction, but he had been able to keep that in check because of their friendship and the nature of their relationship, but that attraction and friendship had deepened into something more on his part during the last few months. The realization had hit him like a hard packed snowball when she looked up at him begging for mercy. Sweet Jaysus, he had almost kissed her, right there with all the children present. If they hadn't intervened, she would have returned the kiss. He saw his own passion reflected in those dark eyes, his own hunger. Yet, she said nothing when they were alone, leaving him no choice but to let the matter drop.

Thoughts of her played in his mind like a dream --- the reserved woman always standing quietly next to Langston, the widow clutching a black-edged handkerchief as she stood next to her husband's grave. Somehow this woman seemed lifeless, not at all like the Rasheen he knew, the one who had a bit of a temper, who spoke her mind freely, and wasn't afraid of letting her intelligence show. It was as if she had become a completely different person both before and after Langston's death. Though she had never told him anything of her marriage, he had the impression that she hadn't been happy or maybe he had misunderstood. Maybe she was still mourning Langston and that's why she had made her position on emotional entanglements quite clear.

"I heard you got a snoot full of snow." John said from the library doorway.

"But in the end I held my own. Care to join me?" Connor raised his glass in question.

"I think I'm going to turn in. Martha should have the bed nice and warm by now. She'll fuss at me when I get in and put my cold feet up against her." He chuckled as he left the room.

Connor thought about his own cold bed and decided to throw another log on the fire. Taking the quilt from the bottom of the sofa, he wrapped himself in it and sat in his chair once more, and stared at the flames as they danced around its edges before shooting up like a gold spear. A jolt ran though his heart as if it had been run through with a sword. He rubbed his chest and felt only the steady beat of his heart.

CHAPTER 19

Everyone wanted to be outside, including the teacher. Rasheen walked around the room, stopping at a child's desk here or there to help them with their work, and fought to keep from walking to a nearby open window. An unseasonably warm March breeze flowed through the classroom fluttering the curtains.

Connor had left earlier in the week to go to Baltimore to meet with Ben Latrobe, the railroad's representative in the McPhail case. He confided to her that he suspected Latrobe was requesting a meeting to offer a better settlement in order to avoid a court case. Connor was no more anxious to drag the matter into the courtroom than the railroad. She was eager to learn the results of his meeting.

In an effort to push aside internal and external distractions, she forced herself to concentrate on the student she was helping. As was her practice, she periodically looked up to survey the room to make sure no one was misbehaving. She noticed Hildy's empty seat and shot a questioning look to Bernice. From the back of the room where she was working with some of the children, Bernice nodded an affirmation that she had given Hildy permission to leave. After a few minutes had passed and the girl didn't return, Rasheen walked back to Bernice and whispered, "Hildy's been outside for a long time now, is she feeling ill?"

"I don't know. She looked rather pale to me and she seems to have a stomach ache."

"I'd better go check on her." Rasheen slipped out the back door and walked a few feet around the side of the building to the privy.

"Hildy, are you all right?" She asked.

Silence.

She pounded on the door. "Hildy, please answer."

"I'm here," the young girl answered in a muffled voice.

"Are you all right?"

"I…I don't know."

"Open the door, dear. You're beginning to worry me."

An ashen Hildy came out of the small edifice. "Mrs. Langston, my dress is ruined," she said turning her back to Rasheen, revealing a large red spot. "I've been afflicted with Love's Wound." She clutched her midsection and fainted.

Rasheen reached out to catch her, but they slid slowly onto the ground together. With Hildy resting in her lap, she patted the young girl's hand and said, "Hildy, open your eyes. Please open your eyes, Hildy."

The young girl's eyes fluttered open, but she made no attempt to move. Rasheen struggled to slide Hildy off her lap and into a sitting position with her back propped up against the privy wall.

"Now you just rest here for a few moments while I let Miss Peterson know what's happening, and then we're going to let Mrs. Schmidt take care of you."

"Oh no, please don't tell anyone." Hildy clutched Rasheen's arm.

"I'll make sure no one else hears me."

Rasheen gently peeled Hildy's fingers from around her forearm and gave her a reassuring smile. From the open door, she motioned for Bernice to step outside.

Keeping her voice low, she said, "Hildy has started

her monthly flow, or has been afflicted with Love's Wound in her words. I'm going to take her up to the house and have Martha attend to her."

On their walk to the house, Hildy was afraid someone would see her dress. Rasheen assured her no one was about, but just the same she placed her shawl about the girl to alleviate her concerns.

"What have we here?" Martha asked when they came through the kitchen door.

"Hildy needs some assistance. It would seem she was surprised by an unexpected visitor this morning." Rasheen inclined her head toward the back of the girl's dress.

"My stomach hurts, Mrs. Langston." Hildy started to cry.

Martha wiped her hands on her apron. "You poor child. I'll fix you some nice hot tea, and while I'm doing that, Mrs. Langston can take you upstairs and help you change." Hildy's blush matched the shade of crimson coloring the back of her dress.

Martha gave her a sympathetic look. "Don't worry, I'll rinse out your things and we'll hang them outside in the sun. With this breeze, they'll dry before your friends finish school. No one will know."

Hildy looked out the window in the direction of the school house. "What if they don't dry in time?"

"They will, but if it will make you feel better, we'll hang them over the rail in the back so no one would see them if they came by."

"Thank you." Hildy let out a relieved sigh.

Rasheen took Hildy upstairs and had her change out of the soiled clothing. Then she handed her a clean small square towel. "Use this to keep your clothes from getting stained again." She showed her how to fold the towel and secure it inside the fresh under clothing which she had retrieved from another drawer. Next she went to the wardrobe and picked out a house wrapper. "This will do while you wait for your things to dry."

Hildy was still upset though she had stopped crying. "My life is over. I won't be able to do anything now that I am a woman."

"Rubbish. I think you have a few years to go before you are a woman."

"*The Purity Manual* says that when a young lady endures Love's Wound, she is afflicted for 20 days of the month. Surely, I don't have to explain such a thing to you. I have become a frail creature. It is the curse of our gender." She flung the back of her hand to her forehead in a sweeping motion and dropped back onto the bed.

Rasheen stifled the urge to laugh and managed a more serious tone. "As long as women subscribe to such foolishness, we'll never be free of all the restraints placed upon us. As for your monthly flow, for a day or so you may suffer some discomfort, but hot tea helps, and Mrs. Schmidt adds a liberal amount of honey which makes it more of a treat than a cure. If that doesn't do the trick, Miss Peterson can recommend some herbs that will alleviate your pain."

Hildy sat up and moved to the edge of the bed, rolling up the cuffs of the slightly oversized house wrapper, scrutinizing Rasheen as she gathered the soiled clothes. "You're different than most of the ladies I know."

"I guess in some ways it would seem so, but is that really such a bad thing? I manage to survive my monthly flow and don't waste the better part of a month worrying with it. Would you believe me, if I told you that I'm in the same circumstance as you are at the present time?"

The young girl's eyes widened in astonishment. "No ma'am"

"It is my second day and I feel just fine. It is a bit of an inconvenience to keep my clothes clean, but other than that, I don't even realize it's here each month, or worry about when it is arriving." Rasheen stroked the girl's hair reassuringly. "Now I have to get back to the classroom.

"Let's take these things downstairs to rinse out." She

gathered Hildy's soiled clothing in one arm and took the young girl by the arm with the other. "I'm going to leave you in Mrs. Schmidt's care for the remainder of the school day."

*****

When she returned, she reassured the children that Hildy would be all right and told them that they would be dismissing an hour earlier than normal. The remainder of the day went by quickly and she let the children go early as promised. After the last child had left, Bernice asked, "Why the early dismissal?"

"I need to run some errands in town."

How do you think Hildy's faring?" Bernice asked.

"Martha probably spoiled her all afternoon. I imagine it'll be hard to get her back to school tomorrow. She seems to think she'll be incapacitated for the next week or so."

Bernice bent down to retrieve a book that had fallen from one of the desks. "Hildy tends to be a bit melodramatic. I hope you enlightened her about the matter."

"I did my best. I told her that if young women continue to believe such foolishness, they'll never be free of the restraints placed upon them. Our gender will be cast as delicate china dolls - forever to be put on a shelf for display. I suppose some enjoy such treatment."

Bernice gave an unladylike snort. "I find it very difficult to picture us as china dolls."

"Not us, we're unbreakable." Rasheen took her friend's hand and raised their arms in the air in a triumphant gesture.

"Would you like to ride into town with me?" Bernice gathered her shawl and reticule.

"I thought I would take the buggy and follow you." Rasheen picked up a small rag and began wiping chalk from her hands. "I want to buy paper, pencils, and a few fountain pens for the children."

"It's wouldn't be a bother for me to take you."

"Then you would have to drive me home again and it would be getting late. But we can drop your vehicle at your house on the way, and you could come help me select my things, if you have the time."

They took Bernice's buggy home and stopped to visit Mrs. Peterson for a short time. Rasheen noticed that the older woman seemed distant toward her. While on the way to town, she remarked about the cool reception to Bernice.

"Because of our friendship, I spend more time at Sara's Glen. She feels it is distracting me from the more important matter of securing a suitable husband."

Rasheen shook her head and said through clenched teeth, "As if that were your crowning achievement."

"You obviously do not think such a thing, but what was being married like?" Bernice asked.

Rasheen felt a sense of long forgotten melancholy. "Let me answer that question with a story I once read. It was about a man who had a lovely garden, but seldom took the time to sit in it, since he was busy with many things. One day he decided to entertain his guests in the garden. As they sat beneath a large tree, a bird came and rested on one of the branches. The bird's gold feathers contrasted vividly with the deep jade leaves of the tree, but what caught everyone's attention was the song coming from its tiny throat. The man began to go to the garden every day after that and waited for the bird to come sit on the branch and sing for him."

"He decided to capture her so that he could protect her from any harm and have her at his disposal whenever he wished. The little bird was caught and placed in a large ornate gage. She was given the best seed and fruits, but her color turned dull mustard and she ceased to sing for the man during the day. Only during the night would the man be awakened by the sad chirping of the little bird as she sang a bittersweet song. For in her dreams she was free and soared to the heights."

"The man became unhappy because she failed to bring him the joy he had experienced in the garden. If he would only have allowed her to be free, she would have rested happily on his shoulder and sung the melody that was hidden deep within her soul." Rasheen let out a mournful sigh.

"Oh, you poor dear, it must have been horrible." Bernice took Rasheen's hand. "Mother says the physical intimacies of marriage are a distasteful duty."

"That was the soaring part. All else was duty, but the physical intimacy was pleasure. It was the only time I felt Daniel was pleased with me."

"I don't believe Connor would try and cage you," Bernice blurted out.

"Where in heaven's name does that have to do with our conversation?" Rasheen asked, caught off guard.

"You once told me that I should live my life on my terms. That was good advice, but more than that, you've been supportive and helped me to follow it. Now I'm going to be bold and suggest something to you. Connor is a good man. I think he has feelings for you that exceed friendship, and I also think you have the same feelings toward him."

"You're mistaken. Connor and I are fine with our friendship as it is." Rasheen struggled to hide the annoyance creeping into her voice. Memories of their sledding experience from the previous month gave credence to Bernice's words.

"I only wish your happiness. Don't you think it's time to let the past rest?"

"I am happy. Now shall we get to the store? I want to be home before dark." Rasheen looked up at the sky and noticed that the sun was no longer shining. "It appears as if we're going to have a late afternoon storm. We had better hurry."

Bernice sighed, but said no more.

A short time later they were walking in front of the blacksmith shop in earnest conversation when Rasheen tripped. Bernice grabbed her arm and prevented her from taking a nasty spill, but the bags she carried emptied their contents all over the walkway.

Ronald Chilcrit rose from the bench where he was sitting and before which Rasheen had just tripped. He took her by the arm, squeezing tightly. "Ought to be more careful, Mz. Langston. People 'at don't watch their step git hurt." The air around him reeked of whiskey.

"I doubt it's my step I need to watch." Rasheen fought the fear welling up in her chest and forced herself up to her full five feet and two inches.

"Jackie became mine when 'is ma died. She thought she was too good for ol Ronald, but in the end I got the kid. We was doin jus fine until you come along - you and 'at Irish trash 'at thinks 'is better 'en me. You stol what was mine."

"Jack isn't a piece of property, Mr. Chilcrit." She tried to break free, but he tightened the hold. "Let go of me."

"I think you had better do as the lady said." Mr. Webber, the smithy, had his meaty hand on Chilcrit's shoulder.

Chilcrit released Rasheen, as he glared at Bernice who had run inside to the blacksmith shop to get help. "The lady made a mistake. I was just trying to help."

"She doesn't appear to need it." Mr. Webber shoved Chilcrit back onto the bench and retrieved the spilled purchases.

While he was out of earshot, Chilcrit whispered to Rasheen, "It ain't over yet. Ya hear me. It ain't over."

Alarm and anger rippled along her spine, but she kept her eyes fixed on the ones that blazed murderously at her. "Do not threaten me."

Bernice turned her toward their buggy, forcing her to break the deadlock. "It's getting late. We really need to be getting home."

Mr. Webber handed the last package up to Bernice, once they were safely inside. "You ladies be careful. Chilcrit's a mean one when he's been drinking."

"Thanks to you, I don't think he'll be bothering us anymore today." Rasheen picked up the reins and looked back to see Chilcrit glaring at them.

As they pulled away, Bernice clutched her bag tightly. "Perhaps you should stay with me tonight."

"I am not afraid of that man. He only picks on defenseless boys." Rasheen tried to make her voice sound brave.

Bernice nervously glanced back toward Chilcrit, "All the same, what if he follows you?"

"I will be fine. Anyway, look at that sky, we're going to have a storm, and I want to get home before it starts."

"All the more reason for you to stay with me," Bernice persisted.

Rasheen pulled the vehicle around the circular drive to the Peterson's front door. "Martha would be worried if I didn't come home."

Bernice persisted. "We could send someone with word that you're staying with me."

"By the time they went to Sara's Glena and returned, they would be caught in the storm." Rasheen held the reins in one hand and placed her free arm about Bernice's shoulder giving her a reassuring hug. "Stop worrying, and let me get home before the storm hits."

*****

Rolling thunder and flashes of light caught Rasheen's attention as she slapped the reins, urging the horse to go faster. Just as she reached the halfway point to home, the wind kicked up and the temperature dropped. This was followed by a torrential downpour. As the storm worsened, the horse's ears twitched and he began to sidestep.

She managed to keep him under control until a bolt

of lightning struck a nearby tree with a deafening boom and crackle; splitting it down the middle amid smoke and sparks. The frightened horse let out a primal scream, reared up as if kicking at some invisible demon, came down hard, and then reared again. She pulled tight on the reins trying to keep control, and succeeded in doing so until another loud clap of thunder boomed and the animal bolted sending them into a ditch.

Once it was over, the horse calmed and stood placidly as rain poured off its back. After she regained her own composure, she got out and surveyed the damage. There was no hope for it; she would have to walk home.

She unhitched the horse, pulled her shawl over her bonnet in an attempt to save it from being ruined, and started down the road. Riding bareback would be faster, but there was no guarantee that the horse wouldn't rear again.

Rain pelted her back like ice shards, as the storm's fury engulfed her. Visions of the angry man she had left behind flashed in her mind. Such thoughts were foolish she told herself, but instinct pushed her to abandon the road and walk across the fields. He wouldn't come looking for her off the road, if indeed her fears were valid, which they were not, she tried to reassure herself. Besides, cutting through the fields would be faster. Wet gloves clung to her fingers making it hard to bend them and hold onto the reins. Tightly holding the reins with one hand, she used her other to peel off its glove and then repeated the process in reverse. She shoved the soaked gloves in her coat pocket and trudged ahead.

Dripping clumps of hair fell into her face and eyes, making it even more difficult to watch her steps. It was hard to manage the horse and hold the shawl in place over her already drenched bonnet, so she gave up altogether and yanked it off her head. The wind caught it, tossed it up, and swirled it around, causing it to look like an angry bird flying against the storm. In a few seconds it was caught in a clump of trees on the other side of the field.

Progress was slow and becoming more miserable as she stumbled over the deep furrows in the field. With hands growing numb from the cold rain, she held tight to the leather connecting her to the horse. Just when she thought things couldn't be worse, there was an earth shattering boom, then a crackle and sizzle as a jagged lightning bolt sped across the sky. The horse shied and tossed its head from side to side in large sweeps. He reared up screaming and then ran off. The leather straps ran through her hands leaving burns in their place.

She stood in the torrential rain and stomped her foot in the mud shouting after the animal, "Stupid beast will be home before me." Angry streaks of light hurtled across the dark sky, as she turned about trying to decide which way was the right direction. Suddenly she was not certain of anything.

Ahead of her, she saw a man's figure lit by the next lightning strike. Despite the drenched clothes clinging to her skin, she felt the small hairs on the back of her neck bristle. Fear paralyzed her as she remembered Chilcrit's threats. The man ahead beckoned her to come forward, but she stood frozen to the earth. How had he gotten so far ahead of her? She turned her back to him to run in the opposite direction, only to discover another man riding toward her. The only thing preventing him from barreling down upon her was the difficulty he had controlling his horse in the storm. Chilcrit's parting words raged through the storm, "It ain't over yet."

Panic constricted her chest as the acid taste of fear welled in her throat. She swung around to see the first man waving her towards him. Terror as sharp as the driving rain struck her. She turned, looked at the man pursuing her and then turned back to the man ahead. Another bolt of lightning spread across the blackened sky, snaking overhead and fanning out like a spider's web, illuminating the field and the man before her. It was then that she saw his tricorn hat. His unbuttoned waistcoat blew behind him in the wind of the storm. He waved for her to follow again, and this time she put her head down and ran in his direction.

There was another crack and the loud whinny of a horse accompanied by the scream of a man. Glancing over her shoulder, she saw that the man on the horse no longer pursued her.

Her guide led the way until she came over the rise of the final field before the house, and then he disappeared. She could see the lights inside and ran toward them, her breath coming in labored gasps. "Thank you James," she yelled over her shoulder to the empty field behind her as she raced up the house's steps toward warmth and shelter.

When she finally reached the door, it flung open and Martha exclaimed, "Lord have mercy! Get inside." The older woman looked her over as she stepped past and into the house. "We were frightened out of our wits when the horse showed up without you. John has gone looking for you."

As the warmth of the house hit her, Rasheen's frozen body reacted with a deep shiver. "I ran into a ditch and bent a wheel. I was walking the horse home when lightning struck and he took off."

Martha closed the door and turning back to her, plucked the sodden shawl from her shoulders and held it between thumb and forefinger as it dripped onto the floor. "Where is John? Didn't you see him on your way?" Though her voice remained steady a hint of worry flickered in her eyes.

"I didn't take the road. I thought the fields would be faster." Rasheen pushed the long wet strands of hair from her face.

Martha let out a breath. "For all the good it did you," she said as she headed toward the linen closet under the stairs. She returned with several towels and handed them to her. "Get upstairs and into some dry clothes before you get sick."

*****

Rasheen winced and looked down at her hands as she took the cup of tea Martha handed her. "I figured I could handle the horse better without my gloves."

"Never mind, we're prepared for such things around here. Even when the men wear gloves, someone always ends up with blisters." Martha went to the closet in the hallway and returned with some balm and bandage materials.

A short while later they heard the thumping of boots out on the porch. "That would be John returning," Martha said as she rose to open the door.

"What are you doing home, now?" She asked in a surprised voice.

"Thanks for the enthusiastic greeting." Connor, drenched from head to toe, stood at the threshold. "I finished early and got the last train. There was no one around to bring me home so I walked." He turned back to Martha after closing the door and hanging his hat and coat on the nearby pegs. "Could I possibly get something to eat? I'm starving."

She sighed and shook her head. "Get into some dry clothes, and I'll have something ready for you when you come downstairs. If this house isn't filled with sick people tomorrow, it will be God's own miracle. Now get going before you drip all over my floor."

By the time Connor was eating his meal, John had returned.

"Thank goodness you haven't any wet things to worry with," Martha said as she helped him out of his rubber coat and hung Connor's wet clothes on the drying rack near the stove. "There's no more room."

Connor looked over at Rasheen's wet clothes hanging next to his. "What were you doing out in weather like this?"

She shrugged and said, "I went into town and got

207

caught in the storm, and ended up on foot."

She told him about the accident, but didn't mention the incident in town or being chased by Chilcrit and rescued by James. "I'm sorry about the wheel, Connor."

He looked down at her bandaged hands and frowned. "That's not important."

John lit his pipe, took a long drag and blew out a curl of smoke. "When I came to the abandoned buggy, I figured you cut across the fields. Chilcrit was walking through the field towards the road, mumbling something about a ghost. He was pretty shook up. His horse must have thrown him."

Rasheen shivered and wrapped her arms about her, even though she was now warm and dry.

The movement hadn't gone undetected by Connor. "You should have stayed with Bernice. No telling what might have happened to you out there wandering around in the storm."

She was about to give him a flip reply, but saw real concern in his eyes. In addition, he looked weary from his wet walk home so she simply nodded an assent. She wanted to reassure him that there was no need for him to worry, but how could she do so when she didn't feel as secure as she had before the storm?

"Almost forgot," John handed her the bag containing her supplies for the children, "Found these in the buggy, and thought you'd want them."

Those around the table fell silent, seemingly lost in their own thoughts. For a few minutes the only sound in the kitchen was that of Martha filling a large copper kettle in the sink.

Jack, who had been sitting in the corner reading, looked at the bag quizzically. "Did you buy any candy?"

"I bought you a peppermint stick, but I got something even better – paper and copy books. I even got a few ink pens, but you children will have to share them. The cost was too dear."

"Don't worry about the expense. I told you to charge anything you need for the school to my account," Connor said.

"I paid for them with my own funds. I didn't think it fair that you should bear the expense," Rasheen said to Connor with a measure of satisfaction.

"I'll see that you're reimbursed."

She couldn't let it go. "It is no hardship to me. I wanted to do it."

"The school is my responsibility." His eyes held hers and she saw something in them, but couldn't quite read the mood, but one thing was sure, it would be of no use to argue with him.

"Very well," she replied curtly and then rummaged through the bag until she found Jack's treat. Finn padded over and put his head in her lap looking mournfully upset that she had forgotten him. She reached over to Connor's plate and took a small piece of bread for the dog. "There, lad, is that better?"

"Don't you know it's dangerous to do that?"

"What?"

"Come between a man and his food." There was a hint of a smile on his face now.

"Would you deny the poor beast a bite to eat?" Rasheen asked.

Connor glanced over at the dog that had gone back to his spot near the stove. "He doesn't look like he's starving to me."

*****

After Jack had gone to bed, John told them that he suspected Chilcrit had intended to harm Rasheen. "It wouldn't make sense for him to take the field. Hilliard's property was closer by way of the main road."

"I want you to take one of my men with you when you so into town in the future," Connor said.

Rasheen noted the note of concern in his voice, but she did not want to become a prisoner of her own fears.

"That will be an inconvenience to them and a bother to me. I can't spend my time worrying about the likes of Ronald Chilcrit."

"Your safety is my responsibility. I don't want you to leave here without an escort. Is that understood?" His mouth was set in a determined line and she realized further argument would be futile. It didn't help matters to know that he was right.

"Fine," she snapped.

Martha filled the cups with more hot tea. "I think we need a change of subject. Tell us about your trip to Baltimore."

"I met with Latrobe. We haven't reached an agreement yet, but we're close enough that we can avoid a court case. The sums are fair, but I'd like to see if we can't work something out for Kiernan McPhail's re-employment. There are jobs that he could perform for the company provided his back heals. I don't know if he wants to go back to the railroad, since his employment with my uncle is working well, but I want him to have the option of making his own choice."

"From what you told me, it was the company's responsibility and if the man can work, then they should take him back. I know they have no legal obligation, but what about a moral one?" Rasheen asked.

"That's the way I see it, but I'm not sure most folks would agree. Latrobe's taking my suggestion to his superiors, and he'll contact me for another meeting after their discussion."

"Were you able to visit with Patrick and Elaine?" Martha asked.

"They were in town for a short time, while I was there and then had to go to Annapolis. I think the governor has something in mind for Uncle Patrick."

"That would be wonderful for him," Rasheen said.

"No doubt about his fondness for the political world. Though I would see him happy, I don't want him taken away from his business interests for any length of time. If such were the case, it would mean more time away from Sara's Glen for me." Connor tipped his chair back and placed his hands behind his head. "As it was this time, I spent most of my time in Baltimore taking care of things for my uncle and only a short time on the McPhail business."

"Now that our evening's adventure is over and everyone is safe and sound, I think I'm going to bid you all good night." John rose from his chair and knocked the ashes from his pipe into a can near the stove.

"I think I'm going to try and get some sleep too. It was a trying afternoon," Rasheen pushed her chair in close to the table and removed the cups and saucers, placing them in the sink to be washed in the morning.

Martha looked over at Connor and said, "I think we could all do with a good night's rest."

He nodded agreement but stopped her from turning down the lamps. "I'll take care of them later. I'm going to soak in a hot bath before retiring."

*****

As Connor ran the water, he was thankful for the cistern on the roof. He had seen such a device at the Ridgely Estate and learned everything he could about its operation. Anything that would improve the quality of life at Sara's Glen interested him. Now if only he could find a way to bring hot water into the tub so that they didn't have to carry the kettles from the stove. Lowering his body into the tub, he thought on that matter. That would be his next challenge – hot water for the bath.

He stretched his arms over the rim of the claw foot tub, resting his neck and shoulders on its back. Every muscle in his body ached with the tension of the news he had received earlier. John was right; there was no reason for Chilcrit to have been in that field. If he had a grudge, it should be with him, not Rasheen. A chill ran though him despite the steam rising from the water surrounding his body.

Rasheen and Jack must be kept safe. Jack would be easy enough to keep out of harm's way, but it wouldn't be fair to restrict her to Sara's Glen, and though she hadn't given him much of an argument, he knew she wouldn't want to bother the men. Still, in the future she would not leave Sara's Glen without an escort whether she liked it or not. In fact, he would be more than happy to be that escort.

Escorting her about town wouldn't be a difficult task at all. In fact the thought was a rather pleasant one. From here his thoughts took a lecherous detour and he allowed them to travel the path for quite some time before drawing himself back.

Thoughts of his trip in town pushed the more pleasant ones of Rasheen aside. Kiernan McPhail had given him bad news during their meeting. The situation between the railroad and its workers had worsened over the last months, and he was concerned for men like McPhail.

Once more, he found himself smiling at the memory of Rasheen. When they discussed the McPhail case, her dark eyes sparkled, as she provided intelligent input. Most young women would have changed the subject; even his aunt didn't like such discussions. Martha was the only woman he knew who seemed interested in those types of matters - until Rasheen. If only she weren't so stubborn. His eyes closed and his thoughts once more wandered down the lecherous path he had enjoyed previously.

Some time later, he jumped out of the now cold water and reached for a towel, dried himself off and then realized he had forgotten his robe. Not wanting to bother with getting dressed in his discarded clothing, he wrapped the towel low on his waist and headed for his room.

*****

Rasheen closed her eyes and drifted off, but disturbing images of Chilcrit overtook her slumber. She woke with a start, her heart hammering and felt as if someone had placed an anvil on her chest. *Breathe, that's it, slow deep breaths.* Once more she closed her eyes, but sleep wouldn't come. She lit the oil lamp by her bed and discovered that the only book in her room was the one she had just finished. It would be futile to try and sleep when she was this restless. She picked up the lamp and headed for the library, then thought better of it, since she didn't want to disturb anyone. Besides, she was quite capable of finding her way in the dark.

Halfway down the hallway, she froze. Before her appeared an apparition of a man naked save for the white drape about his waist, and even that hung dangerously low.

"Good heaven's you scared me," she squeaked.

"I didn't expect anyone to be awake." Connor grabbed the towel holding it tighter about his hips.

"I can see that." Her lips twitched from an effort not to smile. It wasn't often one caught him off guard. She would have enjoyed the moment save for the fact that she couldn't keep her eyes from straying from his face. The storm had passed and moonlight streaming through the window at the end of the hallway washed over him, emphasizing a body that could have been the model for any of the Greek gods depicted in the marble sculptures in the museums she had visited. At least, what she could see of him looked like them, and there was very little left to imagine.

She felt her cheeks flush with heat and forced her gaze back to his face. His eyes were not those of a cold marble statue, no they were very much alive – eyes that could flash dark with anger or twinkle in mischief. They were doing neither at the moment. There was something else in them now, a sensuality that beckoned to her. His rugged handsome features captivated her once again as they always did, but in his present state of undress, there was so much more to admire, and she couldn't seem to avert her eyes.

Connor leaned against the wall and loosened his hold on the towel. If it dropped any lower, she wouldn't have to imagine his naked form. "What were you doing roaming about in the dark?"

The carnal undertones in the question didn't escape her. "I couldn't sleep and thought to get a book from the library to read for awhile." If she had a lick of sense, she would retreat back to her room, but Dear God in Heaven, she really didn't want to.

Man and woman stood neither giving quarter – seductive cobalt eyes locked with wild earthen brown - each daring the other to make a move.

Standing there in such an intimate manner, she fought the urge to touch his clean damp skin. He was a Celtic god who had cast a spell over her, freezing her in time and space.

The pit of her stomach tingled when his gaze left her face and moved slowly over her body. Aware that she had neglected to put on a robe and the cotton gown she wore clung to her curves, she sensed a threat unlike the one she had experienced earlier in the storm. An evening of passion wasn't worth the price she would end up paying.

She glanced downward where the now bulging towel covered just below his taunt mid-section. "Oh, um....." Suddenly, she didn't feel so defiant. "Maybe it would be best if I just went back to bed."

As she turned and fled back down the hall, a low deep voice roughened by frustration followed her. "It would have been better had you remained there in the first place."

With one hand safely on her bedroom doorknob, she looked over her shoulder at him and hissed, "I'm not the one roaming about without the benefit of clothing."

He shot back in her direction, "Perhaps you should go look in your mirror."

With a sharp gasp, she scooted into her bedroom and closed the door. She let herself fall backward onto the bed and stared at the dancing shadows on the ceiling. Damn the man!

*****

Damn the woman! Connor pulled the covers over him, turned on his side and gave his pillow a frustrated punch. Not being satisfied with that, he gave it a few more before finally throwing it across the room.

"Stupid ejit," he mumbled to his reflection in the dresser's mirror as he passed it to retrieve his pillow. He slammed his head into the pillow and then tossed from side to side.

It was becoming more and more difficult to keep his passion in check. Strange, he had had jolts of desire before, but now that his feelings for her were deeper; his physical needs were more pressing. The fact was undeniable, he wanted to make love to her and encountering her in such a state of undress had almost cost him his restraint. If he had gathered her up into his arms and carried her to his bed, she wouldn't have protested. She wanted him as much as he wanted her. Of that much, he was certain. He could still feel those dark eyes appraising his body, like soft velvet caressing his flesh.

He deliberately put away the fantasy. Sweet Jaysus, give him the fortitude to resist the temptation named Rasheen.

CHAPTER 20

"It's too beautiful a spring day to be inside." Rasheen said as she closed the last window of the school room.

"You'll get no argument from me," Bernice said.

"Why don't you come up to visit Martha? I'm sure she can spare some time to sit on the porch with us." Rasheen breathed in the fragrance from the lilac bush growing next to the school steps as she broke off a few nice sized branches of the lavender colored blooms to make a bouquet for Martha.

Bernice smiled. "I always enjoy spending time with Martha."

"Shall we go?" Bernice linked their arms together and pulled Rasheen towards the house in a playful fashion, as if they were two schoolgirls.

Martha waved to them from the porch as they came up the walkway. "Is school over so soon?"

Rasheen dropped into the swing and motioned for Bernice to do the same. "We dismissed the children early. Can you spare some time to sit a spell?"

"I always enjoy spending time with my girls," Martha propped the broom she had been using to sweep the porch against the railing and sat in one of the rocking chairs.

The three women enjoyed each other's company as they spent the next hour talking about the school and the latest news from town. They were in the midst of a story about one of the students and an unfortunate frog, when Connor bounded up the stairs of the porch. "Good afternoon, ladies. I passed some happy children on my way in from town."

"We dismissed a little earlier today since the teachers are suffering from a terrible case of spring fever." Rasheen swept the back of her hand over her forehead in a dramatic gesture.

"Seems to be a lot of that going around. I'm feeling rather peculiar myself." Connor gave her a roguish wink that made her blush despite her laughter.

"What are you smiling about? Have you been afflicted with the malady too?" Connor asked Martha.

Mercifully, Martha made no comment on the wink or blush. "I'm afraid not. I was just thinking about the new kittens you told me about this morning. Why don't you take the girls to the barn to see them?"

Bernice rose from the swing. "Perhaps I can see them tomorrow. It's about the time school would normally let out and I promised mother I wouldn't be late today. She's having a dinner party this evening and wants to make sure I have time to listen to all of her instructions as to which suitable gentlemen I am to speak to and what I'm to say."

Rasheen and Martha gave her commiserating looks, but refrained from comment.

Conner straightened from the porch railing, thoughtfully rubbing the back of his hand over the dark shadow on his chin. "Well, now, why don't we ask my stable hand to hitch your horse to the buggy, and while he's doing that, we can make a quick visit to see the kittens?"

Bernice's face lit with pleasure. "I would enjoy seeing them, but it'll have to be a short visit."

"No longer than it will take for him to get your vehicle ready." Connor held his hand over his heart. "I promise."

"Will you stop at the springhouse and bring me some cream for butter churning?" Martha asked.

"Yes ma'am. Now ladies, shall we?" He offered an arm to Bernice and then to Rasheen.

*****

"It's only me, Ginger," Connor whispered as he crouched down and inched closer to the mother cat. "I've brought my friends to see your new kittens." She greeted him with a litany of hisses from where she guarded her offspring near the corner of the barn, but quieted after he presented her with a gift of table scraps. When he reached over to pet one of the three kittens lying in the straw behind her, she stopped eating and hissed at him again, this time revealing a set of small fangs.

"Connor, do be careful." Bernice clutched Rasheen's arm.

He turned his head away from the cat toward the two women. "I thought she might let us handle them, but she isn't ready yet. At least she had the good sense to come back here where it is safe, but I'm worried about what to do with them when they start moving about. I don't want to risk one of the larger animals crushing them underfoot." He frowned as he straightened and looked about the building.

Rasheen bit back a smile. If need be, he would empty the barn of all its other creatures to ensure the safety of the tiny kittens.

Bernice asked with concern, "If they aren't handled soon, won't they become feral?"

"They're only a few days old, and Ginger's just being a protective mom. Before she had the kittens, she was very friendly. She would often rub against my leg purring for attention when I was out here trying to get some work done. I don't know about the tomcat though. I haven't seen him around, so she must have gone to meet him somewhere secret. I suppose she knew we wouldn't approve." His gave the cat a disapproving glance.

"What do you propose to do about it, I mean since you're her guardian?" Rasheen folded her arms in front of her, and tried to force a serious expression on her face, but found it impossible with the laughter she was choking back.

"Well now," Connor began in a very serious tone, mimicking her posture, " I could make the father take responsibility and do the honorable thing, but it would be hard to identify him even if he were around, since the kittens are rust colored like their mum except for that one. He pointed to the runt of the litter. It was cold black with white paws. "There are a lot of black and white cats in the area, so who knows about the father. Besides, I would not want to give them away, unless it was to a friend." He raised a questioning brow at Bernice.

"Oh, I would love to have one, but I'm afraid my mother wouldn't allow it." Bernice looked tenderly at the kittens.

Connor shrugged and changed the subject, telling them how Ginger had come to live at Sara's Glen. "One of the workers gave her to me last year when she was barely a babe herself. We needed a barn cat to keep the rodent population under control, and she's done a good job." He paused as he watched the tiny newborns squirm and nuzzle their mother.

"When these little ones get older, I plan to keep one in the house to catch mice. The year before last, a mouse got into Martha's crock of fat. Of course she threw it out and started a new one, but it took me a week before I could eat anything fixed in the skillet." He ended with an exaggerated shudder.

"You went an entire week without anything from the skillet. How *ever* did you survive?" Rasheen slapped her hand over her mouth in disbelief.

"There's such a thing as roasted meat, you know, and bread and cake are filling." Rasheen watched Connor staring at the little cat as she gathered her youngsters to nurse. The protectiveness and tenderness in his expression made her heart ache with longing. The kittens mewed for a few seconds and then quieted once they were settled against their mother's belly to be fed. He took his gaze off the cat and back to her, catching her by surprise. She quickly turned from him, as if she had been caught seeing something she shouldn't have.

He surprised her further when he said, "Bernice, why don't you go ahead and select a kitten. He'll be the one we keep at the house and you can visit him."

Bernice clapped her hands together like a little girl receiving her first doll. "Oh, may I?"

"Certainly."

Rasheen caught his eye and gave him an approving nod. His eyes twinkled as he gave her a broad wink. She looked thoughtfully at the kittens. "Have you checked to see if they are males, I mean since you are referring to Bernice's pet as him?"

"Madam, they are all males." Connor cast a smug grin in her direction.

"All right then. So, which is to be the house cat, Bernice?" She asked.

Excitement had Bernice bouncing on the balls of her feet as she pointed to the black kitten who was also the smallest of the litter. "That one."

"What are you going to name him?" Rasheen asked.

"Since he has the white paws, let's call him Boots," Bernice said without hesitation.

"Then his name is Boots and Mr. Boots will be coming to live in the house with us as soon as he is old enough to leave his mum, and his brothers will take charge of the dairy barn." Connor said.

He took the girls each by the arm and led them outside. "I guess we better see if your buggy's ready. I don't' want you to doubt that I'm a man of my word."

They walked back to the stable where the worker was waiting for them with Bernice's buggy. Connor helped her into the vehicle, and she thanked him for the kitten once more before she left.

"That was very nice of you," Rasheen said.

He shrugged. "It made her happy, and was no trouble for me."

"Still, it was a nice gesture," she said as she turned to walk back to the house.

He took her arm and turned her about. "If you think so, why not do something nice for me?"

Panic gripped her from her toes to her scalp. They had managed to keep things normal between them since their unexpected late night encounter. What was he suggesting?

As if reading her mind, his mouth curved in a teasing smile. "Would you walk to the spring house with me? Though severely afflicted with spring fever, I promise to remain a gentleman."

Her composure regained once more, she gave him a smile. "Of course you will." Her arm relaxed under his hold. "Shall we?"

The cheerful sound of gurgling water greeted them when they reached the spring house. As they rounded the shaded side of the building and came into the late afternoon sunlit area, Connor stopped and held out his arm for her to stay behind him. She obliged; but poked her head around his body. A large black snake was curled next to the entrance.

"Damnation! We don't have all afternoon to wait for the thing to move." He glared at the snake which ignored them.

"It's only a black snake, they aren't poisonous, and just as useful as your little Ginger and her family when it comes to catching mice." She looked around to find something to chase the reptile, and found a small rock to throw against the wall.

Connor grabbed her raised arm. "Don't. You haven't any idea which direction it will take," he whispered.

"It's going to get as far away from us as possible. We don't have to worry."

But he didn't let go. As she lowered her arm to drop the rock, Finn came bounding around the other side of the springhouse, spotted the snake, and wanted to play. He ran over to it barking and romping back and forth. The serpent coiled as if it would strike.

"Finn, come here," Connor shouted. Rasheen realized that though the snake was not poisonous, it could still bite if provoked enough, and the dog was doing a fine job of it. Finn looked at the man, then the snake, barked a few more times, and backed off. The snake seized the opportunity to escape, but not before emitting a foul odor.

"Blasted beast!" Connor cursed in Gaelic as he escaped into the springhouse leaving Rasheen and the bewildered dog inhaling the nasty reminder of the snake's displeasure.

She let the rock drop from her fist, bent down and patted Finn on the head. "Aw, there's a lad and aren't you the brave one? Ugh! You're lucky that wasn't a skunk or you'd be wearing this stink instead of smelling it."

A few seconds later Connor emerged from the building holding the cream. "I would have taken care of the matter if Finn hadn't interfered."

Rasheen bit her lips in an attempt to hide her grin at this display of wounded male pride which was so unlike him. "Of course you would."

"You do not believe me?"

"You are being foolish."

"Oh, it's foolish I am, is it now?"

She could see that his temper was rising and decided that it might be prudent to end the discussion. "No, no, of course not."

He didn't say anymore, but started back toward the

222

house in silence, with her skedaddling to keep up with his rapid, long strides.

He opened the screen door with his free hand, waited for her to enter and then forcefully kicked it shut with the back of his heel before walking across the room to the table and slapping the cream down with a thud, causing it to splash over the sides. Without saying a word, he went into the library, and slammed that door too. Rasheen glanced at Martha and saw a reflection of her own bewilderment.

"What's the matter with him?" Martha went to the screen door and opened it for Finn who was sitting on the other side whimpering to get inside.

After Rasheen gave her an account of the afternoon's adventure, Martha shook her head. "Sometimes as much as I love my son, I could really throttle him. When they were young, Connor was forever pulling pranks on Peter because he was so quiet and serious. To get back at him one day, Peter pulled a prank of his own and told him that black snakes were poisonous, that if the reptile bit him, he would die. Connor had never seen a snake before since they have none in Ireland, so, of course, he believed Peter's word as the gospel's own truth. I don't think he ever quite got over that first impression of the creatures."

Rasheen gave Martha a sheepish grin and nodded in the direction of the library. "Guess Finn and I could have behaved better."

"Give him some time alone." Martha patted her shoulder. "He's not one to hold onto his pride long."

*****

Connor excused himself as soon as he finished eating dinner, and returned to the library, leaving the door open this time. Martha gave Rasheen a nod and whispered, "He's beginning to calm down. Let's go out on the porch and enjoy the remainder of the evening."

Jack sat on the bottom step throwing a ball for Finn who sometimes returned it, but often left it go. It took

Jack a few times before he realized what was happening and finally stopped fetching the ball for Finn. At which point Finn dutifully retrieved the ball and dropped it at his feet.

Martha sat forward in the rocking chair and peered over the porch rail toward the drive. "Looks like we have company." She frowned upon recognizing Mr. Hilliard's buggy. "I was looking forward to a quiet evening and now we'll have to endure that pompous fool. Good thing he is not dumb enough to bring Chilcrit on this property. The mood Connor was in earlier, he would have broken both their necks," she spoke softly as Hilliard ascended the porch stairs.

"Good evening ladies, Mr. Schmidt," Hilliard removed his hat and gave a slight bow.

"Evening, Mr. Hilliard," Martha and John said in unison.

Rasheen gave a slight nod of her head in acknowledgement.

"Is Mr. Reilly at home?"

"What can I do for you?" Connor leaned nonchalantly against the door frame.

His stance didn't fool Rasheen. The man was like a panther sizing up his prey, silent and deadly. Too bad Hilliard didn't have the sense to run.

"I'm taking over the Sherman case from Ben Latrobe. Shall we go somewhere we can speak in private?" Hilliard asked.

Connor kept his relaxed pose, but the air crackled with tension. "I have nothing to discuss with you unless the railroad is willing to reconsider their offer. The loss of a man's leg may not mean anything to them, but it means a great deal to him and to the family who depends on him."

Hilliard gave the women an apologetic frown. "I hardly think this is appropriate subject matter in the presence of ladies."

"Sorry. Rasheen, Martha, are you offended?"

Connor gave an exaggerated look of concern.

"Does being a woman excuse one from compassion and concern for a fellow human being's plight?" Rasheen asked.

"You are a tender hearted woman, Mrs. Langston, but surely you have no understanding of such matters. The man should have been more careful. The company can't be responsible for every worker that gets hurt," Hilliard said.

Rasheen wanted to slap that patient look of superiority from the simpleton's face, but kept her lips firmly pressed together, digging her fingernails into the palms of her hands.

"I have found no negligence on his part. He is entitled to compensation." Connor's voice was low, not a whisper, but a deep steady tone.

"Oh yes, definitely a panther," Rasheen thought. "A sleek cat who was about to take down his slow-witted, well-fleshed victim."

"They are entitled to nothing. The company paid him for his work, now he is useless. The railroad needs able bodies, not cripples. It is a business, not a charity." Hilliard puffed out his chest and raised his shoulders as if such an action would bring him up to Connor's height.

"A business is responsible for the safety of its workers," Connor's voice was even more controlled than before – a sign that he was finished toying with his prey.

"No, a business is responsible to make money for its investors. Perhaps you should review the laws regarding company liability for workers." Hilliard's voice hit a pitch at least two octaves higher.

"As a matter of fact, I've studied the laws, and interpret them differently than you have. It's time to let a judge decide which of us has the better understanding." Connor stood away from the doorframe, tension evident in the hard line of his jaw.

"You are no longer working in an Irish stable. Why

must you persist in representing the lower classes?" Hilliard's lips twisted in a sour smile as he wagged his finger at Connor. "Could it be that you've still not grown accustomed to your current station in life, even after all this time?"

What was wrong with the fool? Didn't he realize the man he was insulting could throttle him with the least bit of effort? How dare he speak to Connor in such a manner on his own property. Rasheen rose from her seat and stood before him. "Sir, Mr. Reilly would do better to walk with the lower classes, than to promenade in the filth of greed with the pigs who think themselves above an honest day's work." The words hung like icicles on an invisible line, surrounded by the frozen human forms around them.

Hilliard finally spoke after what seemed hours, though in reality was only a second or two. "I meant no offense, Mrs. Langston; I would just have Mr. Reilly remember that he is a member of the better class."

Had the man not a lick of sense? Did he not know when to be quiet? Her temper had been tested to its limits. She was about to reach for a nearby flower pot, when as if reading her thoughts, Connor quickly came alongside of her and stood close enough to pin her arm by her side with his body. She would have reached around him had she not been momentarily distracted by his nearness.

"Is there anything else you wish to discuss?" He asked Hilliard before she was able to gain control of her senses.

"Well yes, I was going to ... that is...never mind. Good evening." He made a hasty retreat, not bothering to cover his balding head with the hat clutched in his hand.

Rasheen pushed Connor away. "Of all the arrogance!" "That man should be forced to spend a week as a common laborer, and I would pay to be his boss." She paced back and forth across the porch continuing her rant as the other four stared in silence.

Finally, Martha got up and pulled Jack by the collar. "Come on, you need to get ready for bed now."

Jack whistled for Finn and the two of them went inside with Martha and John.

Connor leaned against the porch rail. "Hilliard thinks I'm less intelligent or capable than he or his peers because I avoid pretension and am comfortable in my life style. It works to my advantage most times because people like him underestimate me."

"I suppose so, but I would have liked to serve him his arrogance for dinner?" She fingered the flower pot.

"I suspect his reason for coming here this evening wasn't so much to discuss that case as it was to see you. That little discussion was just a ploy to impress you. I heard that there's to be a dinner party being given by one of the local society matrons and I'm certain he would have asked you to accompany him, had you not been so unfriendly to the poor gentleman." A wry glint appeared in the dark blue eyes that never left hers.

"Are you going to lecture me on conduct unbecoming a lady?" She tightened her fingers over the top of the flower container and met his surprised gaze. "Women are to sit meekly and never dare speak an opinion and Dear St. Brigit, do not ever let us show that we might not be afraid of something as simple as a snake."

He threw up his hands in surrender. "I cannot see you behaving in a meek manner. If the facts were made plain, I would think men might discover that women have worthy opinions. It's unfortunate that most females choose to hide their intelligence under a false demeanor, and obtain their desires through deceit. You could never do such a thing because you're true to yourself and those about you." His gaze traveled to her curled fingers. "You were going to aim that flower pot at his head, weren't you?"

"Tell me you weren't fighting the desire to destroy that arrogant little toad."

"What would I have accomplished? Perhaps I might have had some momentary satisfaction, but would that have helped my client?"

She removed her fingers from the flower pot, and leaned her forearms on the porch rail. Looking out over the fields, she said, "And if I had hit the man, it would have ruined everything."

"I would have cheered for you, but I'm afraid all of Baltimore would be talking about how the refined Mrs. Langston has become a savage since being in the employee of one Connor Reilly." He rocked back on his heels and laughed, eyes twinkling.

"Martha told me what happened with Peter and the snake when you were a boy."

"Now you know my Achilles Heel. Finn didn't help matters. Ejit mongrel."

CHAPTER 21

Rasheen pulled a petticoat from the bureau, stepped into it, and then went to the wardrobe to choose a skirt to go with the soft rose blouse she was wearing. She chose a plain black skirt, but frowned when she buttoned it and saw that it was a bit long. Not wanting to go to the bother of selecting another outfit, she decided to wear the skirt. She would just have to remember to hold it up when she walked, as she had when she dressed in high fashion with skirt trains dragging the floor. Thank heavens she had escaped all that and was able to dress more comfortably here at Sara's Glen.

She fastened her shoe buttons, tossed the button hook onto the top of the bureau, and started out of the room, only to stop short in the doorway when a strand of hair fell against her cheek. "Isn't this going to be a grand day?" she muttered as she back tracked to the dressing table and secured the strand with a hair pin. She gave herself a quick inspection in the mirrored armoire before leaving the room.

Finn came bounding down the hallway as if to greet her, but veered off towards Connor's room. She reached for his collar, but missed. "Come back here, you." He ignored her and pushed Connor's door open. Marching down the hall, she started to go in after him only to stand at the doorway in disbelief. He jumped up on the quilt-covered bed and rolled over, an invitation for her to scratch his belly. The rascal!

She went to within half a dozen paces of the bed before she was aware of someone watching her, and then heard a man's voice, soft and husky. "And just what do we have here?"

Connor gave her a sidelong glance. He stood at his shaving stand, as he scraped away the last bit of the previous night's stubble. If he was disturbed by the dog on his bed, it wasn't evident in his relaxed manner.

She swallowed hard. "Finn... that is... he..." The words were there somewhere, but she couldn't seem to get them from her brain to her mouth. Connor made no comment, but instead, rinsed the blade, meticulously dried it, and put it in the wooden holder. And then just as carefully, rinsed the soap brush and laid it in the soap cup. It wasn't until he turned toward her as he dabbed the last bit of soap from his chin that she realized he was bare-chested, and made no effort to cover himself. "Um... I...didn't know you were... that is ...ah... I thought you would be downstairs already."

"And isn't it my good fortune that I am not? Having a beautiful woman in my bedroom is a rather pleasant way to start the morning." He gave her a salacious grin.

She averted her eyes, looked at the fireplace on the opposite wall, the windows that flanked it on either side, the carved walnut dresser, anywhere to avoid staring at him.

Devil take him. He was making her feel like a blushing virgin.

Carnal energy charged the atmosphere. Unsure of herself, she walked over to the bed where Finn rested. "I'll just get him out of your way." The dog dipped his head, as he ducked out of her grasp and jumped from the bed, making her lose her balance and topple onto the bed.

Face-down, sprawled on Connor's bed, she struggled to sit up only to have her loosely pinned hair fall about her shoulders. She raised herself so that she was able to sit back on her heels and felt around the top of the quilt for her pins and secured her hair as best she could. Once that was done, she tried to straighten her legs; but discovered that the toe of her shoe was caught in her petticoat. Making a hasty escape was impossible. She tried to free it without revealing her limbs, but was unable to do so. Now she sat in the middle of his bed, not quite knowing what to do so she stared at the bed's massive headboard and its ornate carving, trying to think of a graceful way out of her predicament. If it had been anyone else, she would have lifted the skirt, limbs be damned, but not here, and certainly not now.

"So you like my bed?" His voice was low and purposefully seductive, with just a hint of amusement. "I have to admit I've never had a woman fall into it in quite that manner before."

She swallowed hard, and almost chocked on the air pocket that was stuck in her throat. "I like the Rococo Style." Of all the stupid things to say, she chided herself. Here she was in the middle of his bed and she was discussing furniture styles. And just how many women had been in his bed? She was sure none had been in this particular bed. Martha would never stand for such a thing. But there were other beds.

He picked up the conversation as if it were the most natural thing in the world for her to be in such a state. "My aunt picked this because she thought it would be more masculine. Do you find it so?" His silky voice held a challenge.

Her gaze met his and her pulse skipped a beat. "I think it's pretty."

"Pretty?" He let out an exaggerated sigh. "That description does little for my virility." He walked across the room towards her with a mischievous grin.

She smelled the clean crisp scent of his shaving soap, as he leaned over and took her foot and turned it just enough to untangle the petticoat. "Such a dainty foot," he murmured as his cheek brushed against hers when he straightened. Her skin tingled from the contact, and she wanted desperately to reach up and stroke his freshly shaven face. Longing, fear and lust whirled inside her, and she wasn't sure she could stand much more.

Sparing her further torment, he retrieved his shirt from the chair next to the bed, and mercifully turned away from her when he loosed his trousers to tuck it in. Then he walked over to the shaving stand to get the wash bowl and towel. He threw the towel over his arm and held out his free hand to help her off the bed. "If there is nothing else, maybe we should go downstairs now."

Thankfully, her mind and body were finally moving together but a shiver still ran down her spine at his touch. She felt better once they reached the kitchen and saw Martha busy at the range making pancakes on a large griddle. John was finishing up the last of his breakfast and Jack had just started.

Grabbing two cups from the cupboard, Rasheen poured coffee from the pot on the stove for herself and Connor, and then took her seat.

Martha glanced over her shoulder at Connor. "You're a little late for breakfast this morning."

"I had a slight distraction while I was shaving." He waited until Rasheen had her cup to her lips and then gave her a wicked grin. "Rasheen likes my bed," he said to Martha's back.

Martha wheeled around from the range, spatula in hand, as if it were a weapon pointed at him. "What?"

Rasheen spilled coffee, splashing it across the table. "Finn ran into Connor's room and I went to get him. I wouldn't have gone in there if I'd known. You see...well my shoe got caught in my petticoat and I tripped and fell on the bed."

"Oh, I see." Martha's lips curved in a bemused smile. "I cannot see why you are still shaving in your room when we have a perfectly good wash room down here."

Connor shook his head. "We only have the one

water closet and everyone seems to need to use it in the morning. I have already spoken to someone about converting the dressing room that adjoins my room into a washroom."

"Elaine always thought that would make a nice nursery should you ever have any children," Martha said in an innocent voice as she grinned at Rasheen. Before she could say anything else, they were interrupted by a sharp knock at the back door. "Now who is that this early in the morning?" Martha left her spot by the range to answer the door and returned with a telegram.

Connor reached up to take it from her when she sat at the table, but she slapped his hand. "Not for you this time." Tears welled in her eyes as she read the piece of paper and a smile lit her face. "John, we have a new grandchild. It's a girl."

Rasheen jumped up and hugged her. "Oh Martha, I am so happy for you."

Connor reached across the table and shook John's hand. "Congratulations."

"Guess you'll want to take a trip to Frederick." He patted Martha's hand. "I'm sure they could use some help."

She took a long breath and said, "I really would like to see her, but what about you and Rasheen?"

"We'll manage just fine."

Rasheen let her arms drop from around Martha's neck. The last thing she needed was to be left alone in the house with Connor, even with Jack there. Martha gave her an understanding look. "It wouldn't be proper for the two of you to be here alone."

"What about me?" Jack asked.

"You are not an adult." Martha frowned.

"The three of us could do well enough, but let us keep Martha happy," Connor said to Jack and then to Martha, "If it will make you feel any better, I will get a telegraph out to Aunt Elaine and ask her and Uncle Patrick to stay with us until you return."

"That will be the only way we leave this house." Martha tucked the telegram in her apron pocket and went back to the stove. "A girl, finally," she sighed.

"You never told us the baby's name," Rasheen said.

"I never read that far." Martha fished the telegraph from her pocket. More tears. "They named her Martha Ann after both of her grandmothers."

*****

Happy that the day was ended, Rasheen walked up the hill to the house. The children were getting restless, but they still had another month of school before summer vacation. All she wanted to do right now was sit on the porch with a nice glass of lemonade, but Martha and John had left early in the morning and Elaine and Patrick were coming in on the afternoon train from Baltimore.

Connor had hired someone to do the cooking and house cleaning while Martha was away, but she couldn't start until tomorrow so Rasheen would have to see to dinner this evening. When she reached the house, Connor was sitting on the porch waiting for her. Blast it. She thought she would have at least an hour or two before they arrived.

"Where's Patrick and Elaine?" she asked.

"They are not coming." He gave her a sheepish grin. "My uncle was called to Annapolis on emergency business for the governor."

Rasheen felt her heart pounding against her chest. "Did you know this before Martha left?"

"Martha deserves to spend some time with her new grandchild, and she would never have gone otherwise. Besides, I promise to be a perfect gentleman." Connor placed his right hand over his heart.

"Of course you will." She walked past him to the door, but he sprang up and opened it before her hand even got to the knob.

"Can you fix something for dinner? I am starving,"

he said as he shut the door behind them.

She went to the row of hooks on the wall near the door and removed an apron. "I left Jack in the school yard with some of the other boys. Will you please get him? By the time the two of you wash up, I should have dinner on the table. Martha started a roast before she left this morning. All I have to do is slice some bread and fix the plates." If she could keep her mind and hands occupied, maybe she could hide the panic swirling around in her stomach.

On his way out the door, he said, "Mr. Johnson's daughter will be here in time to have breakfast ready tomorrow morning so you won't have to worry with that."

Fixing meals was the least of her worries, she thought as she stared out the window over the kitchen sink watching him walk down the porch steps.

*****

Rasheen adjusted the rumpled sheets and turned her body toward the open window, where a light evening breeze brought in the faint scent of roses, along with the songs of lovesick toads. Their music normally lulled her to sleep, but not tonight. Her restlessness was such that she would have thrown anything within reach at the noisy amphibians just to quiet them if she could throw something far enough to reach the pond. From the sounds outside, there would be hundreds of little toads hopping about this summer.

When she finally closed her eyes and drifted off to sleep, she dreamt of Connor. He was sleeping peacefully, but even in sleep there was a positively sensual smile on the man's lips. He woke and reached for her without speaking. Giving into her desires, she moved into his embrace. Every part of his body rippled with muscle from his chest and strong arms to his narrow waist.

She sat bolt upright and shook her head, her breath came in ragged gasps. Sweet St. Brigid, what in blazes was happening? She arose from the bed and stumbled over to the window for some air. In the moonlight she saw Connor walking to the stable on one of his many trips to check on Murnie now that her time was close.

After a long time passed and he didn't return, she decided to go see if everything was all right. Not wishing to make the same mistake as the evening of their encounter in the hallway, she put on her chenille robe before leaving the room, and then crept down the stairs. When she reached the kitchen door, she hesitated. Perhaps this wasn't such a wise choice given her current state of mind. But what if Murnie was giving birth, she reasoned with herself. He might need her help.

A pebble ground into the arch of her bare foot as she stepped off the porch, but the discomfort wasn't enough to make her go back inside and get her slippers. Moonlight lit the pathway to the stable save for a few long shadows here and there cast by the dogwood trees that graced the back lawn.

She stood silently in the stable's doorway for a few moments – listening and watching. A knot of tenderness pulled in her chest. Connor crouched beside Murine, and gently stroked her belly. The mare shifted uncomfortably.

"Easy darlin," he cooed softly, "you'll soon be rid of this discomfort." Reflected lamplight glimmered over his face, revealing a serious expression. Without looking in her direction he said, "Are you coming inside or just going to stand there?"

She wasn't surprised that he had known she was there all along. They had reached a point where each of them sensed when the other was near. After a moment's hesitation, she stepped closer. "How do you know I will not faint at the sight of blood?"

The seriousness left when he straightened and grinned at her. "For one thing, there's no blood at the moment; and for another, I cannot imagine you fainting at anything. You are far too sensible for such nonsense. Besides, if you weren't interested in seeing Murine give

birth why would you be out here at this time of the night?"
He slanted one dark brow.

She gazed at the mare's swollen belly, awed by the knowledge that there was a living creature on the inside ready to make its way into the world, yet feeling the same old regret that there would never be the flutter of new life in her own body. Determined to divert her joyless thoughts, she asked, "I thought you might need me to go for help if she was in labor."

"Unless there is a problem, I can handle things."

She dropped down into the straw, and rubbed her bruised feet, regretting not taking the time to put on slippers before leaving the house. When she noticed Connor watching her, she quickly covered her bare feet with the hem of her robe.

Without a word, he walked over to a bench against a nearby wall and retrieved something from beneath it. "They aren't your size, but they'll have to do for now." He tossed a pair of well worn work boots in front of her, and then dropped down beside her. Next he removed his own boots and tossed the socks to her. "These will help cushion your feet and keep them from blistering."

"I can't…"

"Don't argue." He knelt beside her and grabbed one of the socks from her lap yanking it over her foot.

When his fingers brushed her ankle, she quickly put the remaining sock on. "All right, all right, but I can manage without any help."

"As you wish, madam." He threw his hands up before shoving his bare feet back into his boots.

The boots he had given her were several sizes too large as were his socks. Served her right. She shouldn't be out here dressed in her night clothes; she chided herself as she leaned against the rough wooden stall and shivered from the night air. Though it was late spring the nights could be chilly on occasion and this was one such occasion.

"Here, wrap up in this." Connor placed one of the horse blankets around her shoulders. She turned and noticed that he wore no coat and his sleeves were rolled up. Though he didn't show it, she imagined he must be cold too.

"Why don't we share it?" She asked as she handed him one end of the blanket. "Have you lost your mind?" A little voice screamed from somewhere in the depths of her conscience.

"Be quiet," she mentally ordered.

He took the blanket and pulled it around him until he was snuggled in at her side with the corners of the blanket in front of them. Now she was beyond warm from the close physical contact with him. It felt as if her flesh was being incinerated. Where was her common sense tonight? A few minutes ago she was worried about him touching her feet and now here she was sitting alone with him in a most intimate manner.

He looked over at her and his smile, the one that showed the dimple in his cheek, completely destroyed any denial. "I read that in one of the Indian tribes if a squaw opens her blanket and invites a brave inside, she has taken a fancy to him. Have you taken a fancy to me?"

The truth was she had taken more than a fancy to him. He inhaled slowly, brought her hand to his mouth and kissed the back of her fingers as he let out his warm breath. She shivered deliciously. "Well?" Dark eyebrows raised inquiringly above eyes that caught and held hers as he brought his face closer until she could feel his breath against her cheek. In silent reply she trailed her fingers up to the ebony locks falling into his face and pushed them back. This was insane, what was she doing? She dropped her hands to her sides and looked down at the straw covered floor boards, anywhere but into those mesmerizing eyes brimming with both tenderness and passion.

Swallowing hard, she tried to remind herself why she

must leave. Staying here with him would only lead to things left best unexplored, but her brain stopped working when he took her in his arms and kissed her softly, running his hands up her back, through her hair; then back to cradle her face. "So beautiful," he whispered in between silky light touches of his lips on hers. She could feel his chest rise and fall against her own as she broke away from his kiss. "Connor ...I...."

"What would you have me do, Rasheen? If you want me to stop, then you'd better leave now."

She should leave, but she wouldn't. The hand that she had brought up to push him away rested over his heart, feeling its strong steady beat. His kiss danced over her lips sending heat and tremors traveling through her limbs. She felt a familiar ache flooding through her as she leaned into his tense body.

"You know what's going to happen if you stay," he murmured, desire flashing in his eyes as he searched her face.

What happened to the sensible woman she had become? Mixed feelings surged through her. The protests at the back of her throat remained silent. In desperation, she clung to him, her body swimming through a haze of sensations. His gentle touch contrasted with unyielding lips. She felt his passion there, just under the surface, barely contained. It was frightening and exhilarating. It was a mistake. She freed herself from his embrace and backed away.

"Bloody hell, Rasheen, I'm a man, not a damn eunuch. Get the hell out of here."

She turned away from him, and stumbled toward the barn door.

*****

Connor was absent from the breakfast table the next morning which meant Murine must have given birth some time during the night. Eager to see if the new foal had arrived, Jack gobbled his breakfast and asked for permission to stop at the barn before school. He caught up with her just as she reached the school steps and told her that the new foal was a male and his name was Rurac, the Irish word for champion. When the school day was over, he sped out the door and back to the new foal.

"Shall we go see the new arrival?" Bernice asked as they walked down the school steps.

"I don't think that would be wise right now. Connor and I had a disagreement." It was hardly a disagreement, but how could she possibly explain what was happening between them?

Bernice lowered her brows. "Would you like to talk about it?"

"It's nothing serious. We just need some time apart, that's all." Rasheen gave Bernice a gentle push in the barn's direction. "You go ahead and pay homage to the little prince. If anyone asks about me, just say I'll be down later."

Connor didn't come up for dinner. She fixed a plate of food for Jack to take to him after they had eaten, but that was over two hours ago. The girl Connor had hired to help with the household chores and cooking had left for the evening. The water was still in the dish pan, long since gone cold waiting for Connor's dish to be washed.

Evening's lonely shadows crept in through the windows, filling the room as they chased away the light. Rasheen took a match from the ones Martha kept on the shelf above the stove and lit the kitchen lamp. The flame shot up, settled and then shed its light throughout the room. How was she ever going to face Connor now? Everything in her life was a mess and it was her fault. As if in answer to her question, the door opened and Jack burst through. "Why didn't you come down to see Rurac?"

"I...."

Connor came in behind Jack and carefully closed the door. "I will make sure she sees him." He dropped the dish he had been holding into the water in the pan. "Go get washed up for bed so I can take a bath."

Jack disappeared into the bath room, only to reappear a few minutes later to have his face and hands checked by Rasheen. After receiving her approval, he bounded up the stairs with Finn on his heels. Connor followed them. He hadn't spoken one word to her.

Left alone, Rasheen felt the tears welling in her eyes, blinked them back and washed the last dish, dried it, and hung the towel on the rack to dry. She wasn't about to go upstairs and risk passing Connor on the steps when he returned for his bath. Pouring herself a cup of tea she really didn't want, she sat at the table and stared at the steam rising from the hot liquid.

A few moments later, Connor returned with a change of clothing and his shaving razor and soap. He set the razor on the table and threw the clothes over a chair. Then he took the large iron kettle near the stove and drained the reservoir of hot water into it. Wordlessly, he left the room. She heard the splash of water being dumped into the tub in the adjoining room before he returned with the empty kettle. Setting it back in its place next to the stove, he turned and looked at her for long moment before gathering up the razor and clothes.

The anger and frustration she had seen in his eyes last night were gone, replaced by a shimmer of weariness. Thick dark stubble shadowed his jaw. She reasoned that was why he was shaving in the washroom tonight – that and the fact that he would not be disturbed. His hair had bits of straw in it and his clothes were caked in dirt. He must have worked with the horses all day after tending to Murine and her foal. The unwelcome tension between them grew tighter until she had to look away. Quiet footsteps on the floor boards echoed back to her as he left the room. She wondered how they were ever going to get past last night, and knew they couldn't.

*****

Rasheen removed the pins from her hair and let it cascade down over her shoulders and back. She sat at the mirror, and picked up the silver-handled hairbrush. Its pattern cut into her palm when her grip tightened as she drug it through her thick tresses. Would Connor let her at least finish out the school year? There were only a few weeks left, surely they could manage to get through them as long as they had Martha and John around. But then she would have to leave. They would have to work something out regarding Jack, but there was no way she could stay here now.

Finn's wild barking interrupted her melancholy thoughts. She grabbed her robe followed the dog as he bolted down the stairs. Jack followed close behind. "Who's at the door? No one ever comes to the front door."

She didn't answer him, but opened the door to find Amelia Delacourte and Reginald Hilliard.

"Who's knocking on the door this time of the night?" Connor's voice sounded from the other side of the parlor. Rasheen turned around to see him now beside her dressed in only his trousers. His hair was wet and a towel was draped over his bare shoulder.

"Damnation! As if my life weren't already in the water closet," she muttered to herself.

Amelia's frank and admiring study of Connor's naked chest, before putting up a smoke screen of wide eyed innocence made Rasheen wish she hadn't opened the door so wide.

Amelia pushed her way inside past Rasheen, dragging her companion with her. "Just look at the boy there, a witness to their immorality," she said to Hilliard in a shocked tone as she waved her hand toward Jack.

Connor spoke to Jack in a quiet reassuring tone. "Go back to bed, lad. Everything is all right. This is just some silly grown-up stuff."

Once they heard the sound of Jack's bedroom door

closing, Connor let loose his anger. "What in the hell do the two of you mean by coming here upsetting my household?"

"My maid told us what was going on here. Even if the boy is a bastard, he deserves a better example than what the two of you are setting. You should never have removed him from my cousin's care." Amelia gave a nod in Hilliard's direction.

"First of all, the lad was not being cared for by your cousin, and just how does your maid know what goes on in this house?" Connor's voice remained calm, but Rasheen could tell he was practicing restraint. No doubt he would like to physically remove the two of them from the premises.

"She heard it from your new cook." Amelia answered smugly, as if she was well aware of his desires.

"Elsie would never gossip," Connor said.

"Oh, it was quite accidental. Your maid inquired about some kind of spice Mrs. Schmidt used and my maid asked her if she were training with Mrs. Schmidt. The stupid girl was caught off guard and let it slip that she was managing your household for the next two weeks while Mrs. Schmidt visited her family."

Rasheen wanted to put her fist in that venomous mouth to stop the flow of words, but Amelia's reference to Jack puzzled her. "Why are you calling Jack a bastard?

"I was the one who arranged for his mother to come work for my cousin."

Connor raised his brows. "And just why were you so caring about Jack and his mother?"

"It was the Langston name I was concerned with, not some common whore. My dear godmother confided in my mother what Jonathan had done."

Rasheen took in a deep breath. "Jonathan was Jack's father? Mrs. Langston knew about Jack?"

"After Jonathan was killed, that woman wrote to my dear godmother saying she was pregnant with his child,"

Amelia continued. "Of course my godmother would never acknowledge her claim and even if Jonathan had lived, she would never have accepted her as a daughter-in-law. After all, wealth isn't a substitute for good breeding."

"That still doesn't explain your involvement in all this after Connie's husband's death," Connor said.

"My dear godmother died right after Mr. Benson." Amelia gave an exaggerated sigh. "I was afraid Daniel might find that letter and feel responsible for his brother's sins. God knows he had enough dealing with his own mistake." She tossed her head at Rasheen. "Something had to be done to protect the Langston name, so I arranged for Reginald to hire the woman and get her out of the city. The conditions of her employment were that she was to tell no one about the circumstances of her bastard's birth. She was to leave no forwarding address or tell anyone where she was going."

Rasheen balled her fists at her sides. "You heartless bitch. Do you have any idea what that child suffered?"

Hilliard, who had been silent up to this point, must have realized trouble was brewing. He waved his hand in the air as if swishing a fly. "It's of little importance now. We're more concerned with the matter at hand."

By this time Connor had placed himself between Amelia and Rasheen. "And what might that matter be?" He asked.

"Well we can hardly have someone like this woman teaching the children of our community." He jabbed his finger in Rasheen's direction. "It's my duty as a leader of the community to see that she is removed at once. You'll have to find another teacher."

"Now why would I want to do a thing like that?" Connor asked.

"Because she obviously has no morals." Amelia's mouth twisted into a sneer.

Connor placed his arm around Rasheen's waist and pulled her to his side. "Be careful of the way you speak about my wife."

Rasheen was too stunned to move or even speak. Apparently he had caught Amelia off guard too as she stood with her mouth agape.

"And just when did this wedding take place?" Hilliard securitized Connor's features. "I don't remember seeing anything about it in the newspapers and something like Mrs. Langston remarrying would have merited considerable coverage in the society section of the Sun Paper."

"We eloped yesterday. Our families do not even know about the marriage. Now if you'll excuse us, we're very tired. I am sure you understand."

By this time Rasheen had regained her senses. "I do not need you to defend me. I…"

Her words were swallowed by Connor's lips pressed hard on her own and his arms wrapped firmly around her preventing any escape. The man was kissing her senseless. Through a haze she heard the sound of nervous coughing.

"Well then I guess we can leave now," Hilliard said as he backed out the door trying to pull Amelia with him.

Connor raised his face from hers, giving her an opportunity to set matters straight, and she would have done so, but his kiss had left her speechless and weak in the knees. She offered no resistance when he kept her firmly encircled with his arm about her waist.

"I believe the two of you owe my wife an apology." He spoke to the intruders in a voice that was soft as velvet, yet edged with steel.

"Of course, please accept my sincerest apology," Hilliard stuttered as he once more attempted to take Amelia's arm to lead her out the door.

Amelia glared at the two of them, ignored her cousin's extended arm, and said, "That was a disgusting display of affection."

Connor lowered his cheek until it was against Rasheen's and held her close, as if ready to repeat the aforementioned display. "That's odd. I found it rather enjoyable."

Amelia turned on her heel and stormed out the door. Hilliard scrambled after her leaving the door open behind him. After the carriage had rolled down the driveway and the lamps faded from view, Rasheen broke free from Connor's embrace and wheeled around to face him. "Have you gone insane?

He walked over to close the door and leaned up against it. "It was the best I could do under the circumstances."

"What do you mean the best you could do? Hilliard cannot make you dismiss me. It is your school on your property."

Connor folded his arms in front of himself. "The Delacourte's and Hilliard could make life very unpleasant for the children's parents."

"Most of the men work for you." Rasheen let out an impatient breath.

"That may be true, but they depend on the merchants in town for goods, and in case you are not aware, the Delacourte family owns the bank. But that is not my main concern."

Rasheen brought her fist to her heart as realization hit. "Jack."

He nodded. "Those two wouldn't give a care about his welfare, but they would be sure he was removed from my custody. Can you imagine what would happen if Chilcrit got his hands on him again?"

She shuddered inwardly at the thought. "What are we going to do?

Connor's eyes flashed and his head snapped to the side ever so slightly. "We are going to get married."

Surely he had taken leave of his senses. "That is ridiculous. We can't get married, and even if we did, you told them we were married yesterday. What if they check the records?"

"They will not be bothered. But it would take us a few

days to get a license and be married in Baltimore. I have a friend in Relay who can arrange it so we can get a license without waiting. We will leave tomorrow morning and be married by evening."

Her head was spinning, her world somersaulting out of its orbit. She had to find something to bring him to his senses. "What about the children and school?"

"Bernice can manage without you for one day. You can explain things to her tomorrow morning before we leave."

Rasheen felt as if she'd just been pushed off a cliff into a deep river and couldn't seem to end her downward plunge. Marriage wasn't in her plans, and certainly not under these circumstances.

As if reading her thoughts, he placed a finger beneath her chin and tilted it upwards. "We have no choice. This is the only way."

She gave a resigned shrug and turned to go upstairs. "Jack and I will be ready at the end of the school day tomorrow."

He reached out and took her hand pulling her back. "Elsie can stay here with Jack."

"Why can't Jack go with us?"

"Because we are going to be on our honeymoon."

She took a quick breath of utter astonishment. "Honeymoon?"

"We may not have a choice in this marriage, but we are damn well going to enjoy the pleasures of matrimony." His eyes caught and held hers waiting for an objection.

Last night's loneliness and confusion melded together in an upsurge of yearning until she was helpless to offer any.

He took her in his arms; his lips touched hers like a whisper sending shivers of desire racing through her. She ran her hands across his bare shoulders feeling the muscles tense and relax, and pulled him closer.

Letting out a groan, he pulled away and held her at

arm's length. "As difficult as this is for me to do, I'm afraid we'll have to wait until tomorrow evening to finish this. We would not want Jack to wake up and bring some truth to Amelia's accusations."

Blood surged from her heart, rushed to her brain and made her tremble. She took a deep breath to steady herself.

He gave her one of his devilish grins. "You need to get some rest. Tomorrow is going to be a busy day, and the evening promises to be even more exhausting."

CHAPTER 22

"What are you looking for?" Rasheen asked.

Connor looked up and down the aisle. "Not what – who." He scanned the passenger car once more. "There he is."

Much to her surprise, her uncle Frank strode toward them from further down the aisle. "Uncle Frank?"

"I telegraphed him last night and asked him to meet us in Relay. This train is the nearest connection from Baltimore."

Frank took the seat facing them. "You didn't tell me Rasheen would be joining us."

Rasheen turned toward Connor who was now seated snugly beside her. "Why did you have to involve my uncle in this affair?"

"Because he's going to perform the ceremony."

Two deep lines creased Frank's forehead as he silently scrutinized Rasheen and Connor. "I assume you have an explanation."

Connor leaned forward and spoke in a soft voice. "I'll explain everything when we get to Duncan's. I do not wish to discuss it here in case someone was to overhear what needs to be a private conversation."

Frank accepted Connor's answer and the rest of the trip was spent discussing Connor's involvement in the plight of the railroad workers or catching up on family news. For her part, Rasheen remained quiet unless brought into the conversation.

The train's wheels clacked over the tracks, bringing

her closer to yet another major life change. She might have taken control and stopped this insanity, but she kept silent and let herself be swept along in the Connor's whirlwind. Why had she allowed herself to fall in love with him?

When they reached Relay, Duncan Kissam was waiting for them on the platform. He didn't look the type of individual Connor would count among his close friends. Rasheen thought he appeared more aristocratic, like the type of gentlemen associated with Amelia Delacourte and Reginald Hilliard.

"Never thought I would see this day so soon. After your escape from Miss Delacourte, you swore you would stay a bachelor until you were at least in your forties," he said to Connor as they settled themselves in his carriage.

Noting the obvious distaste for Amelia in Mr. Kissam's voice, Rasheen decided she had made a hasty judgment.

Connor shrugged and said, "Circumstances don't always work out the way we plan."

"What do you think of all this, Father Hughes?" Duncan asked.

"I'm waiting for an explanation before I form an opinion." Frank's gaze turned toward Rasheen and Connor.

Connor told them of the visit from Amelia and Hilliard, mercifully leaving out the more embarrassing parts.

Rasheen learned that he had sent telegraphs to Duncan and Frank the night before. When she asked about the risk of trusting the telegraph operator, Connor told her that the man was the father of one of her students who had a stuttering problem, and as far as the man was concerned, Mrs. Langston was a saint for all that she had done to help his little Agnes.

"So, you can see he would not spread any gossip, and besides, all I said in Frank's message was to meet me in

Relay. I did not say you would be along or why I needed him. The wire was sent to Frank Hughes, not Father Hughes. I did ask Duncan to make the necessary arrangements for the special license, but that could have been for Mr. Hughes."

Frank shook his head. "As if I don't get into enough trouble with the church hierarchy on my own."

"Well, it's all worked out now, hasn't it?" Connor asked.

Rasheen wondered how he could say such a thing. Nothing would ever be the same once they were married. Her emotions whirled and skidded as she remembered how she had failed to live up to Daniel's expectations of a wife. And here she was about to make the same mistake after promising herself she would never marry again.

*****

Duncan's wife, Eleanor, ushered her guests into the parlor after they finished their lunch. "Of course, Duncan would like to offer you gentlemen cigars and brandy here in the dining room while we ladies are banished to the parlor, but we can dispense with the separation this afternoon. I'm sure Rasheen won't mind if you have your brandy in the parlor and you can have the cigars later."

"Connor does not smoke." Duncan said, and then inclined a questioning nod to Frank who also shook his head. "Well, then there is no problem, no problem at all."

Rasheen liked this young woman who had no problems dispensing with the dictates of proper social behavior. Eleanor had heavy strawberry blond hair piled atop her head. The color of her hair drew attention to her freckled face, but her blue eyes were the most striking thing about her appearance. More than a hint of mischief twinkled in those eyes. She looked over to Connor who was standing near a window swirling the brandy in his glass. "I always thought Amelia was the wrong girl for you. She's too spoiled and immature. We were both glad to hear that you broke the engagement."

Connor said nothing, but raised his glass in a silent salute.

"If you'd sent your wire a day later, you'd have missed us. We were to leave for Newport this morning," Duncan said.

"I can't see you mixing in with that crowd." Connor snorted.

"We go to some of the balls, but other than that, we spend our time walking the beach and sitting on the porch reading. My family has a modest cottage that was there long before the Bellevue crowd took over. It's a nice place to spend the summer," Eleanor said.

"I like to keep my wife happy," Duncan added. "You will understand what I mean soon enough."

Eleanor patted his hand, giving him an appreciative look. "My husband is a tolerant man."

Duncan placed a gentle kiss on her forehead.

Rasheen had never seen such a public display of affection. It warmed her heart and gave her hope. She was about to apologize for ruining their plans, when Eleanor said, "We would not have wanted to miss this wedding. I can tell you are going to make our Connor very happy, and I know he will make you happy. It is obvious that he adores you."

Rasheen felt a blush creep over her cheeks and looked over to see Connor gazing at her as if she were the only person in the room. *Maybe…*.

"I stopped by the clerk's office this morning to see about your marriage license before meeting you and didn't have time to wait for them to prepare it. It should be ready now." Duncan rose from his seat and motioned for Connor to follow him.

Rasheen's eyes also wandered the parlor noting the quiet-colored walls hung with pastoral paintings, the Dresden Clock resting on the mantle, and the hand carved rosewood side table upon which rested a Sevres bowl.

"This is a lovely room for a wedding."

Uncle Frank shook his head. "You have to be married in a church, if I'm to perform the ceremony."

"St. Augustine's is about a half mile away," Duncan said.

Frank put the palm of his hand to his forehead. "I know the pastor. He's a stickler for rules. He'll want to know why we aren't doing this in my parish."

"You'll think of something," Connor looked over his shoulder as he and Duncan left the room.

Once the two men were gone, Eleanor excused herself to check on her children who were in the nursery with their nanny.

"How many children have you?" Rasheen asked.

"We have two little boys. Phillip is almost a year old and little Duncan is three and a half. They should be taking their afternoon nap now, but after the wedding, I'm sure they would like to meet you. They enjoy meeting new people."

"I would like that very much." Rasheen said.

As Eleanor was leaving, Frank asked her to close the door. She gave a knowing smile and nodded.

Rasheen found herself under her uncle's intent gaze.

"Are you certain you want to proceed with this marriage?"

"I'm entering this marriage of my own free will."

"If you are doing this under duress, I cannot perform the marriage, not even for Jack's sake."

"I told you I'm fully aware of my actions."

"Then I have another question for you." He walked over to her chair knelt before her and took both her hands in his and gave them a gentle squeeze. "Do you love him?"

"I have been in love with Connor since I was a young girl. I have only just admitted it to myself."

"I thought as much, but wanted to hear it in your own words." He gave a relieved sigh.

She wrestled with her conscience. Should she voice

her doubts to Uncle Frank or keep silent? If he called a halt to this wedding, what would happen to Jack?

"Rasheen?" One copper silver-streaked eyebrow rose in a questioning slant. "Tell me what's troubling you."

Rasheen took a deep breath and let the words spill out. "I was forced on Connor as his teacher and now he is going to be stuck with me for life. He may be physically attracted to me now, but what happens when that attraction wanes?"

Her uncle chuckled. "No one ever forced Connor Reilly to do anything. Why do you think he sent for me? He knew I'd ask you if you were sure about this marriage. He wanted to make sure you had a way out." Uncle Frank stood and opened his arms. She rose from her chair and stepped into them. "This marriage will be different than your first. Connor will accept your independent spirit and intelligence. He will appreciate all the gifts you bring to his life." His words muffled into her hair as he rested his head on the top of hers and held her tightly like he did when she was a little girl needing assurance after one of her battles with her brothers and male cousins.

*****

St. Augustine's stood on a high hill above the small town of Ellicott Mills. The church rectory was connected to the church by a short pathway. Once they were all out of the carriage, Frank motioned for them to go inside the church while he took the path to the rectory. He returned a few minutes later with the church sacristan. "I'll just go put on the proper vestments and we can get on with the wedding." While he was talking to them, the sacristan disappeared behind the sacristy door. Frank leaned over the pew and lowered his voice. "Lucky for us, Fr. Albright has given permission for the ceremony to be performed in his church."

"What did you tell him?" Rasheen whispered.

"I told him that you didn't want any publicity due to the Langston name. He agreed without one single objection.   See, the Good Lord is in favor of this marriage." Uncle Frank waved his hand toward the altar. "Now let's see about getting the two of you married." With those words he disappeared behind the closed sacristy door.

Connor took her hand in his and raised it to his lips brushing a tender kiss on her gloved knuckles. The scent of candle wax and wood with faint traces of incense filled the air around them. They were familiar and pleasant scents to her, somehow giving her a sense of peace. Perhaps her uncle was right.

A few minutes later the door to the sacristy opened and her uncle came out with the sacristan. Rasheen and Connor stood before the altar with Duncan and Eleanor on either side. Uncle Frank proceeded with the wedding, but when it came to Rasheen's vows, she just couldn't go back on her promise to herself never to take another vow of obedience. Instead she said she would love, honor and respect Connor.   Her uncle repeated the words, love, honor and obey and she stuck to her original promise of love, honor and respect.

Connor gave her uncle one of his most masterful looks and said, "Respect will be far more desirable than obedience."   Mercifully, Uncle Frank went on with the wedding. She was a wife once more.   She didn't have time to process any of her emotions or thoughts, because when Connor kissed her, the world stopped.

*****

Finally, he was alone with his new wife, *his* wife. Well, almost alone if you didn't count the occasional couple strolling by them as they sat on a bench in the hotel's gardens. Connor felt the same surge of pride and possessiveness he had felt when he placed the ring on her finger. When he had pulled it out of his pocket during the wedding, she looked surprised and for a moment he was afraid she might not accept it, but she removed her glove and held out her hand. The ring slid on as if it had been made especially for her.

After the wedding, they had returned to Duncan's for the rest of the afternoon, played with the children, and then had an early dinner with the Kissams before leaving for the hotel. He didn't play with the children, but left that to the two women who got down on the floor, skirts about them while they tickled small bellies, and played with wooden trucks and blocks. Rasheen was having so much fun helping Phillip stay astride the rocking horse, that he thought he would never get her to leave. It was obvious she loved children, but he had known that from the times he had seen her interact with her students and the way she cared for Jack.

Now they were sitting on the bench, his arm about her, watching the sunset shedding a golden light on the various floral colors changing reds to scarlet, orange to flame, and blues to midnight. They lingered until the sun faded and darkness was about to descend. He planted a gentle kiss on her neck and took her hand. "There's a bucket of champagne waiting for us in the room."

With her free hand she reached up and touched his cheek. "There's something I have to tell you before we go inside."

He took her hands and kissed the gloved palms. "What is this all about? It is too late for you to have a change of heart."

"I need you to stop distracting me." She removed her hands and folded them tightly in her lap. "You may be the one having a change of heart once you hear what I have to say. I should have stopped this wedding. I have not been honest with you or myself because of my feelings for you."

Now she had his full attention.

"There are ways of preventing children." She blurted out the words.

The remark took him by surprise after seeing the way she had enjoyed herself with his friend's children earlier in the afternoon, but women died in childbirth, so he could understand her fear. "And you want me to use these means?"

"No."

"What do you want?"

"The reason that I do not have any children from my first marriage is not because we employed such means. We wanted children, but I could not conceive." Her voice was fragile and shaking. "If we consummate this marriage, then you will have no way out. As it stands now, we could stay married until Jack is safely in school in Baltimore and then you would be free to seek an annulment."

He heard the pain in her voice, saw it in her expression. "There's more to marriage than having children."

"Please....think... about what you are saying. Don't take this lightly. You may think it doesn't matter now, but later it will be different. You will come to resent me, just like Daniel did."

He put his hands on her shoulders and looked into her tormented dark eyes. "I know exactly what I am saying, and I know what I am doing. My aunt and uncle did not have any children, and look how happy they are. You are not some brood mare."

"Every man wants offspring to bear his name. You're uncle has you."

"I was fifteen when I came to live with them. Young children can be an inconvenience. They drain their parents' energy, energy that could be spent on more pleasurable pursuits. Think about it. This way we'll have more time to pursue one another's happiness and welfare. Here, let me demonstrate." He lowered his head and placed a kiss at the base of her neck and continued until he reached her lips. When he released her mouth, he looked into her eyes for a sign that he had convinced her. He had lied about babies being a bother, but if life with her meant no children, then so be it. He couldn't bring himself to even imagine what life without her would be now that he had her as his wife.

She took a deep breath and said, "But you said you wanted a family someday."

"And I have one with you and Jack." He resumed kissing her neck.

"Connor, please stop. Jack doesn't bear your name like you bear your uncle's."

He raised his head. "Are you sure you want me to stop?"

She frowned.

He gave a frustrated sigh. "Very well, then. Jack doesn't need my name. I still consider him my own, and that's all that matters, but if he is willing, we can give him my name."

"It isn't all that matters, not to me. I don't want to wake up one day and find that I'm a burden to you."

"Sweetheart, that will never happen. A pain in the arse maybe, but you will never be a burden. Look inside your wedding band. What does it say?"

"When did you even have time to purchase a ring, much less have it engraved?" She removed her glove and looked down at the wide silver band with its Celtic knot design encircling her finger and removed it. The inscription read – Love, Friendship, and Loyalty.

He took the ring from her and once more placed it on her finger. "All the children in the world won't make a happy marriage if these ingredients are lacking. Perhaps a man might be happier if his wife's affections aren't divided." She left her hand in his and rested her head on his shoulder. The sun was gone now, and the Viaduct Hotel, known for its beautiful night lights was aglow with Chinese lanterns. Even the garden was alight with fireflies.

Connor lifted her head and placed a soft kiss on her lips. "Now can we stop all this talk of children and get on with the business of wedded bliss, or am I going to have to haul you over my shoulder like a sack of potatoes?"

"You wouldn't dare," she said grabbing the edge of the bench with one hand.

"Do you really want to find out?" Raising an eyebrow in inquiry, he gave her a wicked grin.

She offered no further argument.

"Good." He stood and extended both his hands to help her from the bench.

*****

When Connor opened the door and stood aside for her to enter, she saw three silver vases filled with dozens of roses interspersed with baby's breath and green ferns. Their sweet spicy fragrance drifted through the air.

He moved to stand beside her, his hand still pressed firmly in the small of her back and pulled her a little closer. "If I cannot take you on a proper honeymoon, I figured the least I could do was make the room special for you."

"I have never had anyone order roses just for me." Not a white rose in the bunch, these roses were meant for her and her alone. She stood on her toes to reach up and kiss his check. "Red roses are my favorite."

"I heard you mention that to Martha once. According to the florist, red roses represent passion." Connor placed his hat on the rack in the corner of the room. Rasheen undid the pin in her hat and set it on a nearby dressing table, along with her gloves. Then she removed her jacket and hung it in the mahogany wardrobe. He did likewise with his jacket and then loosened his tie, removed it, and tossed it next to her hat.

"Would you like some champagne?" While walking over to the bucket where the champagne was chilling in ice, he unbuttoned the top buttons of his shirt exposing just enough of his chest to start that pulsing knot in her stomach again.

She nodded as she sat on the settee and smoothed her skirt. Once he handed her the champagne, he set his own glass on a nearby table and removed his shoes and socks, shoving the latter into the shoes and placing them under the settee. His gaze roved her body and lazily appraised her. "You're much too uncomfortable."

He crossed the room to the dressing table, retrieved the button hook, and knelt in front of her. Before she could protest, he unfastened the hooks on her shoes and removed them. Once he had them resting next to his own, he slowly ran his hands up one calve removed her garter and stocking and then the other, all the while fueling that knot in her stomach. When she was barefoot, he ran the palm of his hand over the heel and the then the arch of her foot, trailing his fingers over the top of her foot.

She surprised herself by letting out a sound like a purr. "Ummmm, I never thought that a mere foot could bring such pleasure."

"I have many pleasures in store for you this evening, wife."

*****

Lying at her side, he traced the curve of her cheek with a fingertip. At last he could give into all the things he had imagined. He was a starving man who had just had a feast set before him, and feast he did from her forehead all the way to her toes, until there was no part of her that he didn't know in the most intimate manner.

His last vestiges of restraint unraveled and disintegrated as she filled every one of his senses until there was nothing but her.

He gave her every part of his being and accepted the same from her until one spirit soared out of the mortal world into a magic realm, swirling in a rainbow of light, up into the heavens where it shattered and fell back to earth in a shimmering shower.

When he opened his eyes, she was looking up at him with tears in hers.

"I've never experienced anything so beautiful before," she said as she traced her finger along his cheek. "It was more than just physical pleasure."

He whispered softly in Gaelic, words of endearments

and placed a soft kiss on her lips as he stroked her hair and felt her chest rise and fall against his own in a comforting rhythm. Feeling a sweet release from the terrible need that had lived inside him for so long, the need he had kept in check until she was ready. He wondered how she could have ever been ready for what had just happened; how either of them could. He loved this woman with not just his body, but his very soul.

*****

When they arrived home from the train station, John and Martha were on the porch waiting for them. Connor had wired them about the marriage and they had hurried home.

"I should be upset with the two of you running off like that, but I'm too happy to scold. Martha motioned for Rasheen to sit in one of the rocking chairs. "Give me your hat and gloves. I'll put them on the side table and then get us some nice cold lemonade."

A few minutes later, she appeared with a tray laden with a pitcher and several glasses. She filled one of the glasses for Rasheen and one for herself, but left the others empty.

Rasheen twisted her head toward the door through which John and Connor had disappeared into the house. Martha shrugged and said, "They were holed up in the library by the time I got inside." Though Martha appeared unconcerned, Rasheen suspected something serious was being discussed. Her heart beat quicker despite the older woman's reassurance. "Something's happened." She jumped up out of the chair as a terrorizing thought hit her. "Jack, where's Jack?"

"Sit down and stop behaving like a hysterical female. Jack's out riding on Midnight." Martha inclined her head toward the back door. "Connor will tell us everything as soon as they finish."

Would he? Rasheen wondered. Or would he be like Daniel and keep things he considered too worrisome to himself? He had promised things would be different between them, but Daniel had changed once the marriage vows had been spoken. She gave herself a mental shake. Connor kept his promises, and Daniel had made no secret of his expectations of a wife. She was the one who had been foolish enough to think he would soften after they were wed. The sound of the two men returning drew her out of her unpleasant memories. Connor stood behind her chair and rubbed her shoulders. Looking up at him, she asked, "Is everything all right?"

He kissed the top of her head. "It will be." So he wasn't going to tell her what was going on. Maybe it was something with the railroad workers. They had heard rumors of a pending strike in Martinsburg, so maybe that was it. But he had always shared such information with her before. He was going to shut her out, just like Daniel. A lump formed in her throat as she tried to blink back the tears brimming beneath her eyelids. Connor came around and knelt in front of her and took her hands in his. "One of the men saw Chilcrit lurking around the school. He must have known we were gone and was after Jack."

Rasheen clutched his hands. "Jack's out on Midnight now."

"He has two of my men with him." Connor looked up at John. "I want all the men to carry weapons and if he shows his face around here again, they are to shoot to kill."

John nodded. "I already gave that order."

"Good."

Rasheen rested her head on the chair back. "Why did he wait until now?"

Connor stood up and pulled a chair next to hers and dropped into it. "Hilliard fired him for stealing. He is angry, and Jack has always been his whipping boy."

"I doubt that he's hanging around here. He won't be able to get a job, and I turned it into the Sheriff's office so they will be on the lookout for him too. The best they can do is charge him with trespassing," John rested his hip on the porch rail. "I don't think he wants another altercation with Finn."

"Finn went after him?" Rasheen asked.

"From what Mr. Johnson said, he probably would have stopped him too, if Chilcrit didn't have a stolen horse nearby. Finn held onto the devil's trouser leg until he jumped into the saddle, and the horse reared up forcing the dog to back off. It was a shame Finn didn't connect with him sooner. Then he could have sunk his teeth into some flesh."

Right on cue, Finn bounded around the corner and up the steps, tail wagging. Rasheen jumped out of her chair and threw her arms around him. "Good dog." Finn rolled on his back presenting her with his belly to rub.

"That's right, take advantage of the lady's sympathy you mutt," Connor teased.

Rasheen looked up at him over the dog's head. "Well, he is a hero."

"How am I supposed to compete with that?" Connor growled.

"You'll think of something."

"I'm sure I will." Connor leaned over in his chair and nibbled her ear.

Rasheen's cheeks flamed as she looked over at Martha and John. "Martha doesn't mind, do you?"

"Mind your manners, young man." Martha stood and took John's hand to encourage him to rise also. "Would you help me with the tray, dear?"

When they were alone with just the dog, Connor took Rasheen's hand and drew her away from Finn. "Let's go upstairs and see what I can think of to compete with this beast."

She put her arms about his waist, stood on her toes and kissed his cheek. "There's no competition. You were my hero when you came through that door and told me what was happening without keeping anything from me."

"You are far too easy to please lady. I can think of

other more pleasant things that would make you happy." He took her hand and led her inside. "Mr. and Mrs. Reilly will be retiring early this evening," he murmured.

CHAPTER 23

"What in the name of Sweet Jaysus is taking her so long?" Connor leaned against the scrolled trim of the parlor's archway and raised his voice loud enough to be heard throughout the entire house. "The guests of honor are going to be late."

"Mind your language young man." Martha swatted his arm as she passed by him on her way into the parlor from upstairs where she had been helping Rasheen dress. "She sent me down to keep you quiet. Your impatience will not hurry her along any faster. I know you hate these things, but Bernice is her friend, and she could not very well refuse her request to give a party in honor of your marriage."

"We have been married for almost two months now. Bernice would not have waited that long to throw this little soirée. I would wager the earnings from Rurac's first race on that." He stepped out into the hall and looked impatiently toward the stairs before returning to his chair. "This affair is for Mrs. Peterson's benefit."

"Do you really believe that?"

"I certainly do, and the only reason we are to endure it is that Bernice and Rasheen are appeasing her." Connor looked toward the doorway once more, hoping that Rasheen would be standing there. "This evening is more about making a match for Bernice. The ejit woman has her sights set on Reggie Hilliard as her future son-in-law."

"Bernice is such a sweet girl. I had hoped Peter might realize that fact, but he seems to be buried in his medical practice. I don't believe there is any hope for that boy." Martha clenched her hands in her lap. "How in the name of heaven could she wish that horrible bore on her child?"

"Well, she does, and there's nothing we can do to change her mind. Rasheen and I just need to get through this evening." He let out an exaggerated breath. "That is, if Rasheen ever makes an appearance." The sound of swishing satin and taffeta interrupted them as Rasheen came through the door. White satin rosebuds adorned her upswept mahogany hair and a diamond encrusted dog collar necklace encircled her throat. He let his gaze travel leisurely from the top of her head all the way down to her feet and back up to her smiling face, and noticed the absence of a blush. Instead, her eyes held his in a seductive gaze as she secured the loop at the bottom of the emerald gown's train to her wrist.

"Did I just hear someone mention Mr. Hilliard?"

"Forget him. You are the most beautiful woman I've ever seen."

Martha nodded. "I knew she was the one for you the moment I saw her in those denim trousers. You need someone to stand up to you." She rose and gave Rasheen a hug. "I believe Connor would like a moment with you before you leave. I'll be in the kitchen should you need me." She left the room closing the door behind her.

Rasheen gave him a puzzled look.

"I don't want to see you in Langston jewels. You are my wife now." Not giving her a chance to speak, he removed the dog collar necklace from her throat and tossed it on the side table next to a black lacquered box. Iridescent pearl trim shone in the light when he picked up the box and handed it to her. No words were spoken between them as she removed the strand of pearls and held it at arm's length. A diamond teardrop swung gently back and forth held securely by a tiny gold circle. She stared at it as if in a trance, her face troubled.

He gently kissed her cheek. "If it doesn't suit you, we can find something else." While it was true he didn't know her taste in jewelry, he couldn't imagine her not appreciating the gift.

"It's lovely. It's what it represents that bothers me."

"And what might that be?"

"Men give jewelry as a sign of their power and wealth, to show that a woman belongs to them. You just said I'm *your* wife now."

"It's true I want the world to know you're mine and have no more ties to the Langston name, but there are other reasons. For instance, Amelia and Hilliard will be there tonight, and we don't want to give them any reason to doubt our wedded bliss."

Her dark brows slanted in a frown. "I'd forgotten about them."

"There were other reasons I picked this particular necklace."

She fingered the necklace more warmly. "You've given me enough reasons. I like it much better than the other. In fact, it's something I would have chosen."

"I would have taken you to pick it out yourself had I not wanted it to be a surprise, but you still need to hear my other more selfish motive."

"You aren't selfish."

"Oh, but I am." He took the necklace from her placing it around her neck and fastening it. "While you're wearing this little present, think of intimacies to come such as this." He lifted the teardrop and ran his forefinger across the pulse of her throat where it had rested. "Or this." He kissed the same spot and felt her pulse race beneath his lips. His lips captured her lips in a thorough kiss, and her arms went round his neck.

"I'll have difficulty concentrating on anything else

while wearing this, now that you've filled me with such images," she whispered softly in his ear right before she placed a light kiss there and then followed it by more down the side of his neck.

"That was my intention, but I believe you just turned the tables. We'll continue this later," he said as he gently pushed her away.

"We shouldn't keep our hostess waiting, since we are the honored guests." She gave him her arm. "I believe I heard someone bellowing as much a short time ago."

"The things a man will endure for love," he sighed.

As they left the room, she smiled and whispered, "I'll make it up to you."

He bent down and returned her whisper. "I intend to hold you to that promise." He placed his arm securely around her as they walked out to the carriage.

The driver stood by the opened door and said, "Evening Mr.Reilly, Mrs.Reilly. Mr. Reilly, would you take offense if I were to say that your Mrs. is looking very lovely this evening?"

"You would have to be a blind man not to notice and a mute not to speak." Connor took Rasheen's hand and put his arm on the small of her back as he helped her into the vehicle.

The ride was pleasant, as there had been just enough rain the previous night so that no dust kicked up when the carriage wheels rolled over the surface and no puddles to splash up muddy water as they went bumping along. Connor's dulcet mood ended once they arrived at the Peterson mansion. Rasheen and he had discussed Mrs. Peterson's motives of using this gathering to promote an attachment between Bernice and Hilliard, but he hadn't told her of his other concern. Though he couldn't think of anything further Amelia could do to hurt Rasheen, he knew she would never give up her scheming.

When they reached the door to the Peterson mansion, the butler stepped aside for them to enter and then promptly escorted them to their hostess, who was standing in the drawing room near Bernice and Reg Hilliard. Mrs. Peterson held out her arms to Rasheen and kissed her on the cheek. "Here is the happy couple now. I was just saying how nice it is when young people find suitable partners."

Rasheen dug her fingers into Connor's forearm as a warning not to make any sarcastic remarks. Through clenched teeth, he grumbled, "You have a large debt to repay, my love."

Behind her fan, she whispered, "Behave yourself and the reward will be worth it."

He was about to tell her it was impossible to do so in her presence when Bernice's mother leaned over and whispered to them, "Oh, here comes our dear Amelia and her escort, Mr. Charles Linley Astor. He's a relative of *The* Mrs. Astor, you know."

Rasheen looked toward the entering couple. "I believe I met him at Uncle Patrick's Winter Ball."

The older woman gave a smug smile. "They're expected to announce their engagement very soon, a secret known by only her closest friends."

"Poor devil," Connor muttered under his breath. This gained him a warning tap from his wife's closed fan.

*****

Once everyone was assembled in the drawing room, Mrs. Peterson assigned dinner partners. Mr. Astor escorted Rasheen into dinner, and Connor had the misfortune of being Amelia's dinner partner. Just as Connor had predicted, poor Bernice was saddled with Hilliard.

Rasheen found Mr. Astor an amiable conversationalist and was actually enjoying herself until Amelia remarked on her necklace. "Was that my godmother's?" She asked with an innocent smile.

Rasheen looked across the table to where Amelia was seated next to Connor and remembered his promise of things to come later in the evening. "My husband presented me with this token of his affection just before we left our home this evening." She ran her fingers over the teardrop. Her eyes caught the wolfish smile he shot her across the table. "He wishes me to only wear gifts from him in the future. I suppose I'll have to donate the Langston jewels to charity. Since you seem to so fond of them, I'll make sure you know which charity will be auctioning them off." She couldn't resist throwing that little barb at Amelia.

Amelia directed her gaze to Rasheen's wedding ring. "One would have thought he would buy a proper wedding ring before any other jewelry."

Rasheen was startled for a moment and then remembered that her fingers were no longer covered by her gloves since she had buttoned them back after being seated for dinner. She looked down at her uncovered fingers and brought the one with her wedding ring closer to her. "This ring means more to me than any other he could possibly purchase, for it was his mother's."

Connor gave her an appreciative nod.

But Amelia wasn't finished. In a voice heavy with sarcasm, she said, "Well, I suppose it would have to do since Connor acted in such an impetuous manner and no doubt behaved as brutish as one of his stallions." From across the table her eyes clawed at Rasheen like talons. "You really should have insisted he wait until you could have had a proper wedding."

Rasheen felt her temper flare. Proper etiquette be damned. If Amelia wanted a cat fight, she was bloody well going to give her one. "Your choice of words is not far off the mark. The word impetuous comes from the Latin word impetus which means violent. Impetuousness is characterized by sudden and forceful energy or emotion, impulsiveness and passion."

"You are not going to bore us with a classroom lecture, are you?" Amelia smiled nastily. "I would think you could forget such drudgery for one night.

"I think you would find it very interesting to learn how a stallion services a mare," Rasheen continued in a cool voice. The guests sat in shocked silence as she continued, "My husband, of course, is not a violent man, but he is passionate, and I certainly find him a force of energy, not unlike his prized stallions There is a great deal of strength involved in horse breeding, and impetuousness on the stallion's part implies strength or potency. For instance, sometimes the mare needs to be forced into accepting the stallion. And men are the ones doing the forcing. I always thought men were the forceful ones in life, but I have found lately that a woman can be just as forceful, but in a different manner."

Rasheen stopped and looked directly at Amelia and spoke in the most innocent tone she could manage. "Oh dear me, you're probably wondering if the mare is hurt by the stallion. I can assure you precautions are taken to see that she isn't injured. The stallion's hooves are wrapped in heavy woolen material."

"This is hardly suitable dinner conversation," Amelia protested.

"You were the one who brought up the subject matter," Rasheen persisted.

"I've never...." Amelia fluttered her hand to her bosom.

"Seen such a magnificent spectacle? Then by all means let me continue," Rasheen took a sip of wine, just for a touch of suspense, and then went on. "Once he gets the scent and sight of the mare, the stallion can barely be restrained. He'll snort and toss his head so that you would swear he's going to break loose, but he doesn't. His handlers guide him to the rear of the mare and when the command is given, he is allowed to rear over her back. The primal cries and shrieks are enough to make you wonder if the mare is being tortured. I assure you, she isn't. Quite the opposite, actually. Though the stallion is

… shall we say… well endowed, the mare will allow him complete control until he gives his last gallant effort."

Rasheen gave a loud sigh and looked around the table. Several of the ladies looked on the verge of fainting, but the men looked as if they were disappointed that her description was completed. Amelia regained her voice and said, "Connor, I can't believe you allowed your wife to speak of such matters."

Connor's expression was unreadable. In his quiet voice, the one that was controlled and threatening, he said, "My wife is a brilliant teacher, but perhaps she should have been a bit more discreet in her subject matter. I'm sure she'll do so in the future. She seems to have forgotten herself in the excitement of the evening, is that not right, my dear?"

Rasheen gave a silent nod, all the while seething with anger. Once dinner was over, and they had left the dining room, Connor remained at her side solicitous throughout the rest of the evening. Somehow she managed to get through the evening with considerable effort by going through the familiar ritual of idle party chat that had been drilled into her during her marriage to Daniel.

*****

They had been in the carriage barely five minutes, and Connor knew he would never make it home without at least kissing his wife. He was thinking of the delights he had promised her earlier in the evening and considering how well she had handled Amelia this evening, she deserved a reward, and he was going to be more than happy to provide it. He leaned over and kissed her on the neck expecting her to respond by turning her head and kissing him in return, but was shocked at her reaction to his amorous attention.

"Is that all I am to you? " In the darkness, he couldn't read her face, but he heard the anger in her voice. "You humiliated me this evening." Rapidly he played the evening through in his mind. He'd been on his best behavior.

"And just how did I do that?"

"By insinuating you would monitor my choice of subject matter in the future."

He tried to take her arm, but she pulled away. "Your subject matter was a bit scandalous, but…."

"Allow me. My behavior was unsuitable for your wife. I embarrassed you, and in the future I must remember my place." Though the words were spoken in sarcasm, there was an underlying note of sadness. "The only thing that's changed is the name of the man I'm disgracing, it would seem." She scooted farther away from him until she was flat against the other side of the carriage.

An image of his wife wielding Gea Blog, as its sharp blade cut to the bone, his bone, played in his mind. She had struck a blow to his pride by comparing him to Langston. It wasn't his intention to detract from her story, but rather to keep Amelia from responding. He thought she had done a splendid job of quieting Amelia, and he was about to show her just how "inspiring" her description of horse breeding had been when she flew into her rage. Curse Langston, and curse his entire gender for their treatment of the perceived weaker gender. Weak gender? There was nothing weak about Rasheen. She had both declared war and defeated him instantaneously.

After two months of marriage to him and almost a year under his roof, she still didn't know him. That's what stung. That's what kept him from correcting her misunderstanding of his actions. Neither of them said another word the rest of the ride home. Once they were inside the house, she stormed up the stairs. He didn't go after her, but went to the library instead and poured himself a glass of whiskey. It was going to be a long night.

*****

Rasheen didn't have to open her eyes to know that Connor wasn't in bed, nor had he been there at all during the night. She rolled over and pulled his pillow to her.

273

She had spent the night tossing and turning, battling alternate feelings of anger and remorse. In the end, she had to admit he was justified in being upset with her. She had crossed the line of propriety in her battle with Amelia, but she was too stubborn to go to him.

The thin night gown she had worn last night was already wet from perspiration. It was going to be another hot and humid day. She sighed, and sat up dangling her feet over the edge of the bed, pulling the gown away from her body and trying to get some air between the damp fabric and her skin.

Sliding off the bed, she walked over to the window and peered out at the silver shadowed fields below. The ghostly appearance of a deer or fox emerged from the woods beyond and then glided once more into the protection of the morning mist. Her next expectation was to see winged fairies flying about in the silken threads as they returned to their abodes after a night of merriment. There was no sound, only the breathless silence that one experiences just before the beginning or end of life. She held the vision a few minutes longer before the stirrings of dawn slowly illuminated the landscape.

She turned from the window and set about getting dressed. More than anything she wanted Connor to come through the door, to put his arms around her, hold her close, and make her forget that last night ever happened. The pain grew with each heavy beat of her heart, and the tears crashed in waves deep inside her, and then surged to the surface. She was a fool to think she could make her own choices. Her heart made the choice and hadn't given so much as a second thought to her independence.

On her way downstairs, Connor passed her on the stairway, but didn't say a word. Not even Good Morning. Her arm ached to reach out to him, but pride held it close to her body. She heard his footsteps echo down the upstairs hall, as she continued downward.

When she went into the kitchen for breakfast, Martha

was busy at the stove turning pancakes. "I would ask if you had a nice evening, but from the looks of your husband this morning, it's not necessary. What happened?"

Rasheen dropped into her chair at the table. "I really would rather not discuss it."

Before Martha could inquire further, Connor came into the room. "What about breakfast?" Martha asked.

"Not hungry," he said as he headed out the back door, slamming it behind him.

*****

Martha plated the pancakes and brought them to the table along with another plate of bacon. "Guess it will just be you then." She poured herself a cup of coffee and sat across from Rasheen.

Rasheen made no attempt to fill the empty plate before her from the serving plates on the table. Her stomach lurched at the sight and smell of the food sitting in front of her. "I'm not very hungry this morning."

Martha sipped her coffee, but kept a steady gaze on Rasheen, waiting for her to speak.

"Jack will be down for breakfast," Rasheen said in an attempt to dodge Martha's questions.

Martha set her cup down and folded her arms across her chest, lowering her chin. "He was up hours ago and had breakfast with John. They're getting the morning chores done, and then John's taking him and some of his friends fishing over at the Gunpowder River. I already have a picnic lunch packed for them. Now are you going to tell me what happened between you and Connor?"

Despondent over the current situation with Connor, Rasheen decided to unburden herself to Martha. When she finished with her accounting of the previous night's events, Martha shook her head in disbelief. "One thing I know for certain is that Connor respects you and would never publicly humiliate you. You need to talk to him. Let him be for awhile, and then the two of you will straighten this out." She took Rasheen's empty plate and put a pancake and some bacon on it. "You cannot have a discussion with that boy without some sustenance."

Rasheen's stomach pitched once more. "I really can't eat anything right now. I am feeling a little queasy this morning."

Martha rose from her chair and took Rasheen's chin in her hand and looked into her eyes. "My goodness. No wonder you are so emotional. You're pregnant."

Rasheen shook her head impatiently. "That's impossible. I was married for two years and never got pregnant."

Martha went back to the stove and poured her some tea. "This might be better than coffee, and I think we have some soda crackers in the cupboard somewhere." She brought the tea over to Rasheen and then retrieved the crackers.

"I hate to disappoint you, but I really am not pregnant," Rasheen insisted. "If there was anything I could have done right for Daniel, it would have been to give him an heir. That was the one thing in our marriage we both wanted."

Martha poured herself another cup of coffee and sat down. "Since you seem to know a great deal about horse breeding, allow me to tell you a little story. We had a mare named Honeysuckle that Connor's uncle wanted to breed. They tried to impregnate her on four different occasions with various stallions and she never took. Patrick finally gave up on her. One day a stable hand told him that he thought Honeysuckle was pregnant. They had left her loose in the back pasture along with some of the other horses. Patrick said that wasn't possible; that she had failed with four different stallions. Sure enough, a few months later, Honeysuckle delivered a beautiful foal. It seems she just needed the right stallion. Trouble is, we never did know which one it was."

"Interesting story, but I'm not a brood mare,"

Rasheen sipped the tea slowly.

"Well, suppose we see what develops, *Honey*," Martha chuckled.

Rasheen needed a change of subject. "Do you have time to come down to the school with me? The new desk I ordered for Bernice came yesterday, and I want to see how it looks."

"I would like to see it. She's going to be so surprised. Are you going to show it to her now or wait?"

"Her mother has been keeping her busy with social obligations since Amelia Delacourte is here for the summer. I'll be glad when school starts, and we can get back to normal." Rasheen wondered if that was possible after last night's episode.

"And no doubt those obligations include Mr. Hilliard. I would imagine Bernice will be glad to escape to the schoolroom." Martha put the pancakes and bacon in the ice box and looked down at the water tray. "Speaking of things full of themselves, I'd better empty this before we leave, and get one of the men to bring up some more ice from the ice house."

*****

In her entire life she had never fainted. It had to be the heat. The last thing she remembered before coming to in one of the porch chairs was leaning against the kitchen garden fence and fighting for her breath, as the moisture-laden air filled her lungs and weighed them down.

One of the men carried her to the house, and he and Martha were standing over her, worried expressions on their faces. She assured them she was all right, and Martha dismissed the workman once she was certain Rasheen could stand on her own. Still she insisted that Rasheen take a cool bath, and got no argument. Just before Rasheen closed the door to the bathroom, Martha said, "I would feel better if Peter were here and could take a look at you."

Rasheen pulled the pins from her hair and set them

on the edge of the tub, shook out her hair, and then slid further down into the water until her entire head was submerged. It felt good to finally have the heat completely drawn from her body in the cool water. When the need for air forced her to resurface, she brought just her face out and leaned her head back so that it rested against the back of the tub.

Martha wasn't the only one who would feel better if Peter were there. Connor and she had been so busy enjoying married bliss as he liked to put it, she hadn't realized her monthly visitor hadn't arrived since they'd been married. She had always dreaded that monthly reminder of her failure as a wife when she was married to Daniel. And now she had never given it a second thought, just assumed it would arrive on schedule as always. The thought of being pregnant never entered her mind until Martha brought it up this morning. She needed a doctor to confirm Martha's suspicion that she was pregnant.

Babies are an inconvenience. That's what Connor said on their wedding day. How was he going to react to the news? She couldn't imagine him not wanting a child, no matter what he had said. It just didn't fit with the man she knew, any more than his chastisement of her last night. Maybe she didn't know him as well as she thought.

Deep joy mingled with apprehension as she ran her hand over her stomach and swore it felt swollen, more rounded. Probably just her imagination, she told herself.

She needed to tell Connor about her suspicions. But she couldn't. Doubts surfaced and swirled around her, like evil spirits. The best thing to do was to wait until she saw Peter. Until then, this was going to be her little secret.

*****

Connor hoisted his saddle off of its resting place, and stormed toward the open door. When he reached just outside the stable, a hand on his shoulder stopped him.

"Do you really think it's a good idea for you to ride right now?" asked John.

Connor wheeled about, stomped back inside, and threw the saddle down on the rack. Angry as he was, he knew John was right. Once in Ireland when he was a young boy, he had taken a horse out in a fit of temper and been thrown. He wasn't hurt, but he received a severe scolding from his father. "If you wish to break yer ejit neck, that's just grand, but don't be taking it out on the poor horse." His father's voice may have been stern, but his face told a different story. Connor had never forgotten that expression.

He gave a silent nod to John and walked away. As he reached the stable door, he felt Finn's cold nose brushing against his hand. "All right then, I'll tolerate your company, but no foolishness; do you hear me?" The dog barked and ran ahead.

Man and canine traipsed over the fields until they came to an uncut corn field and walked around it to the edge of the woods. As they approached, Connor could see the sun's light shining through in silver veiled shafts surrounded by dark shadows. He walked into the shadows and felt the coolness on his skin. Even his temper seemed to cool as he trod deeper into the forest.

When he came to the stream bank, he dropped to the ground and leaned against an oak tree. From his resting place he looked out over the rushing water as it made its journey over flat brown stones and sharp jagged protrusions of gray that glistened. The crystal liquid seemed to have an energy all its own. Resting his head against the tree, he closed his eyes, and absently petted Finn as he listened to the songs of ancient voices rising from deep within the flowing stream.

The intensity of his anger had died down some. When he ran the conversation with Rasheen from the previous night over in his mind, he could see where she would have drawn the wrong conclusion. He should have cleared it up, but he was too angry at being compared to Langston.

Love heals all wounds. The words came to him as clear as church bells on a spring breeze, yet there was no audible voice. The words came as if they had been his own thoughts. Finn let out a low growl, and Connor felt the fur beneath his hand rise. When he opened his eyes, he saw Sara Bartlett standing on the other side of the stream with a baby in her arms. James stood at her side with his arm around her. Connor blinked as they faded from view. Finn was up on his feet barking at the other side of the stream.

This wasn't the first time James had appeared to him, but he had never seen Sara or the baby before. Though he had never spoken of it to anyone, he had seen James from time to time when he made his evening visits to the stables. He had always thought the spirit protected Sara's Glen and its residents. Apparently, the whole family was becoming involved.

He gave Finn a pat on the head and left his resting place. "Come on, lad, we need to go home. I have to make things right with my wife."

*****

A soft rain danced on the rooftop, gently waking Rasheen from her sleep. She lay there for a few seconds listening and then decided she'd better check to see if she needed to close the window, though she was loath to do so since a nice breeze replaced the earlier heat. When she sat up, the towel she had wrapped around her head fell onto the pillow reminding her that she'd fallen asleep without brushing her hair. She shook out the tangled waves and swung her legs over the edge of the bed. Before she put her feet to the floor, she saw Connor sitting in the chair pulling his wet socks off. "The rain came suddenly. I was out walking. One minute the sun was shining and the next it was pouring." He looked up at her, and the yearning in his eyes echoed the same longing deep inside her.

"Connor….."

"Come here." He wore a weary expression, and there

was a pleading tone in his vice as he asked, "Please."

He didn't have to ask. She walked over to where he sat and stood mutely.

Her grabbed her hand and brought it to his lips as he pulled her onto his lap and stroked her hair. Instinct told her the gesture was meant to comfort and not patronize.

She whispered into his chest, "I don't want to be angry anymore."

"Nor do I, but we cannot just forget last night happened." He touched her lips with a gentle kiss.

She deepened the kiss and wanted more, but he gently broke away. "There will be plenty of time for reconciliation after we make things right between us."

"I thought that's what we were just doing."

"We can make love and ignore last night's hurt and everything will be fine for now, but the problem will still be there."

Rasheen felt the tears sting her eyes as she gulped for air in an attempt to remain calm. She didn't want a repeat of last night. The only remedy was to let him have his say. To her surprise, he took his thumbs and tenderly brushed the drops running down her cheeks.

"Sweetheart, don't cry. You were wrong about me wanting to lecture you, you know. I was about to say how funny it was to watch all the faces around the table, the women trying to look scandalized, but hanging onto your every word and the men looking so enthralled that I had a strong desire to disarrange a few aristocratic faces."

Her mind whirled in bewilderment. "Then why did you sound so angry? Why did you humiliate me?"

He gathered her closer against his chest. "Amelia would have torn you to shreds with her barbs, and since she's a woman, I could not take her outside and beat the nastiness out of her. I was frustrated and angry with her, not you."

She stirred uneasily in his lap. "If you really weren't angry with me, then why didn't you set me straight in the carriage last night instead of letting me rant like an irate fishwife?"

"I was about to show you how arousing your instruction had been when you...."

"Compared you to Daniel." She closed her eyes reliving the pain of that accusation. "I am so sorry," she barely whispered.

"I am not Langston; I would never destroy your spirit the way he did." His voice was firm, determined. For a long time they sat in silence except for the sound of their breathing against the backdrop of raindrops splashing on the roof. He took her face in his hands and his gaze softened. "I don't want you to change in any way."

"Someone like Amelia wouldn't have caused a scandal at the dinner table," she said.

"Ah, but who would want a hot house orchid? Such a flower may be beautiful, but it has no real fragrance, and once removed from its environment, it withers and dies. You, on the other hand, are the fairest of all the flowers in the garden." He traced her jaw with two fingers and moved on down her neck to the opening of her robe. "It's true. I see you as a wild rose with strength and substance to endure the elements, thorns that may be prickly, but beauty that blinds the eye and perfume that seduces the senses. And mine are being seduced in the most pleasing manner at the moment."

"Don't give me your blarney." She could barely get the words out through the delightful shivering he was sending through her. Why must the man be the stronger sex, while woman is branded the weaker? Even in the act of physical intimacy, a man becomes rigid and inflexible, while a woman must become soft and pliable." She got up and turned to walk towards the bed.

He pulled her back. "Perhaps, but you forget there are things that are soft that can capture and hold, and there is no escape."

"Name one."

"The mud in the fields after a few days of heavy rain will snag a wagon wheel, and the wagon is useless until the ground dries out."

She shook her head. "Mud? You are comparing me to mud?"

"There are others, but that is all I can think of at the moment. Soft pliant ground captures and holds. Escape is very difficult. In my case, I willingly summit to my captor."

*****

Connor looked up at the ceiling with his hands resting behind his head and whispered, "Sweet submission."

"I will never think of that word in the same way again," she said as she traced her fingers along his bottom lip.

"That was my intention."

"You were successful," she said as she left the bed and bent over to pick up her robe not bothering to put her arms through the sleeves, as she planned to dress and go downstairs. Connor came up behind her and placed his arms about her crossing his hands over her midriff. For a second it was if he knew about the possibility of a pregnancy, but that was ridiculous, she reminded herself.

"Amelia's little performance merely caused us an inconvenience, but there will be no more inconveniences when it comes to our matrimonial bliss." He pulled her close, his breath warm against her neck.

She leaned her head against his. "Do you really think we will go through life without another argument?"

"I certainly hope not. I suspect we'll have a good many arguments, but we will reconcile a lot faster as long as there are just the two of us involved."

Just the two of us, the words sent a chill to the pit of her stomach in spite of his warm hands resting there.

CHAPTER 24

The sound of carriage wheels as they clacked over cobblestones outside the bedroom window awakened Rasheen from her dreams. Lovely dreams they were, of a man who possessed grace and strength, intelligence and wit, and a lover's skills that might have been equal to those of Eros. She turned on her side and gently stroked Connor's cheek, and watched as a slight smile formed. His eyes opened slowly bestowing her with a lazy gaze full of seduction.

"Did I wake you?" she whispered.

"No, but since you have disturbed me, I think you should fulfill your promise."

"You just said you were not asleep, and I made no promises." Rasheen propped herself up with an elbow; her hair falling onto his chest.

"Sweet wife, allow me to show you what you have just done with a mere touch." He brought her down on top of him and caressed her back as he kissed her slowly.

"Ummm, but what about Elaine and Patrick? They will be waiting breakfast for us. If we were home, we would have been up hours ago."

"We are not home though, and I think my aunt and uncle still have morning dalliances. It seems to me that I recall the two of them coming downstairs for breakfast late a few times when I have stayed here."

"That doesn't surprise me, since Patrick is related to you. But we are guests and should not be disrupting the

284

household schedule."

He rolled her over, trapping her with an elbow on either side. "It's my home too, and now yours as well. My aunt and uncle are happy I've found such a desirable wife and would be very upset with me were I to neglect my husbandly duties." He looked down at her, brows arched mischievously above determined eyes.

She responded in between nibbles to his ear and neck. "That may be so, but it is getting late, and we are probably causing them an inconvenience."

"Might I remind you, love, that I am going to spend the day visiting my uncle's new warehouse and taking care of legal matters for him? Besides, we have not been married quite two months. I know my uncle. He would feel that something was wrong were we to come downstairs too early. Now shall we continue?"

*****

Much later, as they were descending the stairs, hand in hand, he whispered in her ear, "Perhaps we will have time for another dalliance before dinner."

She gave him a gentle poke in the ribs. "Behave yourself, or we will not be having anymore dalliances for awhile."

He put his arm about her waist and led her into the dining room. "Would you like to place a wager on that?"

Elaine looked up from her place at the table in the breakfast room. "Good morning, you two; we ate breakfast without you since we thought you would be tired from your trip, but I will have another cup of coffee with you. What are you wagering on?"

"My wife seems to think she could resist my methods of persuasion," Connor said.

Rasheen felt the warm blush washing over her face when Elaine gave them a bemused smile.

Thankfully she was spared further teasing when Henry, the Reilly butler, bought out a platter of toast, eggs, and bacon, whereby Connor proceeded to fill his plate.

Rasheen covered her cup with her hand before Henry could fill it with coffee. "I'll have tea."

"Since when are you drinking tea with breakfast?" Connor asked.

"I seem to be getting one of my headaches, and tea would be better," Rasheen lied as she took a piece of toast and buttered it lightly, adding a bit of Martha's strawberry preserves. She was no longer able to stomach coffee in the morning.

He gave her a concerned look. "You didn't mention anything about a headache earlier."

"I didn't have it earlier." She patted his hand reassuringly before she took a bite of the toast.

"Is that all you are having for breakfast?" Are you sure you are all right?" Connor asked.

Knowing that she was concealing something from him was almost more than she could bear. "I am just not that hungry right now. The headache is probably upsetting my stomach."

"Just the same, I think you should see Peter while we're in Baltimore. Would you prefer that I stay home with you?" Connor had gotten up from his chair and stood behind her rubbing the back of her neck.

"You go take care of your business so we can have some time with our families." She shrugged her shoulders up squeezing his hands affectionately as they rested on her shoulders. "I will see Peter later in the week." She didn't like deceiving Connor, but she wanted Peter to verify her pregnancy before she shared the news with her husband.

"Actually, you will see him this evening." Elaine took a sip of her coffee before setting the rose patterned china cup gently in its saucer. "Peter will be joining us for dinner. He's conducting a class on antisepsis at the University Hospital. It has something to do with that Doctor Lister in Glasgow that he met when they were both attending a conference in New York a few years back."

Connor resumed massaging Rasheen's shoulders. "Peter told me about his association with Lister. It appears Doctor Lister has done research on antisepsis with considerable success. Peter used the man's methods and was pleased with the results, but it took awhile to convince his colleagues. You know how closed minded the medical profession can be. Peter must be happy to know that so many lives will be saved once this method becomes common practice. Do you think he will have time to see Rasheen?"

"We will make sure he has time to examine her before dinner. I will send word for him to bring his medical bag," Elaine said.

"I'm really not feeling that bad, but if it will make the two of you feel better, I'll seek Peter's advice." Rasheen reached up to her shoulders and rested her hands over Connor's. She hoped he would react positive to the news once she confirmed it.

He leaned down and planted a kiss on her cheek. "It would certainly make me feel better."

"Are you ready?" Patrick asked from the doorway.

Connor gave her another kiss and then kissed his aunt. "We will see you two ladies this evening."

Patrick came into the room and gave each of the women a kiss before the two men departed for the day.

Rasheen waited until she heard the carriage drive away before asking, "I thought I might visit my mother and granny. Would you like to come with me? I know they would enjoy seeing you."

"I would enjoy that very much, but have you forgotten that I have guests coming for a luncheon this afternoon?" Elaine asked.

"Oh that's right I forgot," Rasheen lied. Elaine had mentioned it the previous evening. "Then I suppose it is just as well that I not be underfoot."

"Don't be silly, child. You would be one of the few individuals in attendance whose company I would actually enjoy. It will be a rather stuffy affair. I wish I could escape the thing myself, but duty prevails."

"Then you have no objections if I do not attend?"

"Of course not, but what about your headache? Perhaps you should lie down."

"I'm feeling better now. I probably just needed to eat something." Rasheen said.

"Connor and Patrick have taken the carriage." Elaine looked toward the window.

"I can hire a cab. It's not like it is that far. In fact, I could walk."

Elaine studied her for moment before saying, "If anything is amiss you know you can confide in me."

Rasheen rose from her chair and walked over to the older woman, kneeling at her side and taking her hands. "Everything is fine and I would confide in you if it were necessary. It has just been so long since I have seen my family, and I am going to have to smooth some ruffled feathers because of our elopement." How could she tell Elaine that she would not be confiding in her family or anyone else until she had an answer?

Elaine planted a kiss on her forehead. "I will send one of the servants to fetch you a cab and accompany you."

Rasheen planned on seeing Peter after visiting her family, and she did not want a servant tagging along. Whatever the verdict was, she needed time alone to sort things out. "You will need all your servants for your luncheon. I would feel guilty taking an extra pair of hands away from you."

Elaine looked through the doorway at the servants bustling up and down the hallway with flowers, china, and silver. "If you're sure you will be all right, it probably would be easier on the staff not to lose the help."

As she kissed Elaine on the cheek before going to the cab, Rasheen noticed a scuffle taking place across the street. She turned to see a blind beggar arguing with a police officer.

Elaine followed her gaze. "It would not do him any good even if they allowed him to stay here. The residents on this block have no use for the poor, unless it involves a society charitable event. They like their works of mercy recognized by their peers."

*****

Her anxiety and impatience grew as the cab rode down Charles Street on the way to her family's home. She would much rather have had her visit with Peter over with early in the day; but since he was off giving a lecture, that would have to wait until the afternoon. The cab's motion made her queasy, but she wasn't sure if it were the baby or her nerves. The baby – she placed her hand on her abdomen. "Please be there this afternoon, Peter," she whispered to the empty seat across from her.

She drew the shade back from the vehicle's window and looked out in an effort to distract her thoughts. Perhaps the city sites would do the trick. Maybe something had changed in the last year. A large pot of bright red geraniums on display in a florist window drew her attention. On impulse, she had the driver stop the cab. "I'll just be a minute," she said over her shoulder as he opened the shop door for her.

She purchased the geraniums and was about to pay for them when she spotted another pot with pink petunias spilling over its sides and purchased them as well. The shop owner carried the two pots out to the cab and handed them to the driver who placed them in the boot before returning to assist Rasheen into the vehicle.

"I would like to stop at New Cathedral Cemetery first," she said before he closed the door. She heard the low whistle he gave before jumping up into the driver's seat. She was taking him in the opposite direction of where they were headed originally. That would earn him and extra fare.

An hour later, they pulled up in front of the cemetery's Brobdingnagian iron gates which were swung open against their stone pillars. They rode through them and then followed the driveway for a short distance before stopping out of respect for a funeral that was in progress just ahead. From the cab's window, she could see four midnight horses, with their heads adorned in the customary black plumes. The animals stood as ghostly sentries before the hearse with only an occasional snort disturbing the quiet.

She watched and waited as the graveside service ended and the family members walked away. Other mourners followed at a discrete distance, and then stood by silently as the family entered their carriage and drew the curtains closed. The others entered their carriages, and the procession rolled out of the cemetery, leaving the empty hearse behind.

No longer still, the horses whinnied and pawed the ground, ready to move on. The driver gave a flick of the whip and the hearse jerked back and then forward. Reflected sunlight shot from its silver trim and momentarily blinded her as the hearse followed the same path as the other carriages. She closed her eyes against the sunlight and listened to the doleful rattle of the wheels rolling on the cobblestones as it echoed back into the cemetery's tranquil atmosphere. Once the hearse had slipped through the cemetery gates, her driver got down from his seat and asked her to direct him to the grave site.

This was her first visit to Daniel's grave since his funeral. There had been too much grief in the beginning, and when that finally subsided, only to be replaced by anger, she had left for Sara's Glen. She wasn't sure how she felt now, or why she had decided to make this visit. Perhaps it was an impulsive reaction to seeing the geraniums in the florist window. Poor Daniel. He had disapproved of such capricious actions. Surely he was looking down from heaven and frowning upon her.

Pots in hand, the driver followed as she led the way to the small fenced in area where the Langston graves were located. The sun shone between a jumble of billowing clouds, chasing shadows among the trees and headstones. Flowers perfumed the air with sickening sweetness as they wilted and faded upon the graves they blanketed.

She opened the gate to the family plot, and instructed the driver to place the flowers side by side near Daniel's grave marker.

"Will that be all, ma'am?" he asked.

"Yes, thank you."

He gave a slight bow and walked back to stand alongside the carriage with his hat held at his side.

Rasheen surveyed the Langston grave markers. There were the two small ones with the names of the sons, one for Daniel, and the other for Jonathan. The third larger ornate one was chiseled with the names of Pamela and Charles Langston, their parents.

She looked down at the two contrasting plants. Their colors clashed in disharmony. She stared for a long while, and then placed her hand on Daniel's headstone. "They just do not blend; do they?" she whispered as she touched his name with the tips of her fingers. "We tried to love each other in our own fashion as best as we were able." She knelt on the cool grass, and closed her eyes. "Now I may be carrying the child I always thought would bring happiness to our marriage, but Connor may not want it. The ironic thing is that he and I are in perfect harmony in all of the things that caused discord in our marriage."

A light tickling sensation distracted her. When she opened her eyes, she discovered a small butterfly on the fingers that rested atop Daniel's gravestone. Amazed, she studied it as it sat slowing fanning white wings tinged with just a hint of pale blue. It was the loveliest butterfly she'd ever seen. She tilted her head to the side as she watched it. In a few moments it took to the air again and flitted around the flowers resting on the grave. Then it perched on the top of Daniels grave marker for a few moments more before soaring heavenward.

She watched as it disappeared from sight. Without knowing why, she had an odd sensation that Daniel had just bestowed his blessings on her life and her happiness. It was a ridiculous notion, but still, it was there.

Reaching out, she again touched the letters carved into the granite. Then she removed the petunias, rose and took her leave. The two plants clashed, and Daniel's grave should have the ones he would have wanted. The driver came to help her with the petunias, but she motioned for him to stay put and walked around the nearby graves looking for one on which to place the pink flowers.

Rounded gravestones, crosses and statues, some as tall as a man, stood like silent sentinels before the remains resting beneath their shadows. From atop an obelisk, a raven gave a deep, throaty, kraa as it stepped from one foot to the other on the monument's carved drape. Finally, it ruffled its feathers and called out once more before flying off. When she reached the marker, she read its inscription –

> *The Banshee mournful wails.*
> *In the midst of the silent, lonely night*
> *Plaintive she sings the song of death*
> *Pay heed to the white lady of sorrow.*
> *It may be you she weeps for on the morrow.*

The words were from an old Irish ballad. She shuddered at the thought of the Irish death fairy, and made the sign of the cross. One could never be too cautious.

A nearby grave with a headstone in the shape of an angel caught her eye. She stopped and read the inscription, *"Emily Rose, our little angel watching over us from heaven."* The dates chiseled in the stone revealed that the little girl had died before her first birthday. Rasheen set the flowers next to the headstone on the child's grave. The thought of having such a precious life taken was unbearable, although she knew it happened frequently. In a protective gesture, she placed her hand over her abdomen and turned away to walk back to the carriage.

Distant church bells sounded the hour, making her realize it was time to move on. If she didn't hurry, she wouldn't have time to see Peter. She would have to make a short visit with her family before going to the Dispensary.

*****

"Mrs. Reilly, how nice to see you," Mary said as she ushered Rasheen inside.

"Mrs. Reilly?" Rasheen raised her brows.

Once she was inside, Mary said, "I just wanted to use your new name. I like it. Suits you, you know."

"At least one person is not upset with me for my hasty marriage," Rasheen laughed. "Where are mother and granny?"

"You just take yourself into the parlor, and I'll have them down in the shake of a feather duster."

Before Rasheen could say anything further, she was pushed into the parlor, and Mary disappeared. Not long after, her mother and grandmother rushed into the room. "Just look at her, she looks positively radiant," her mother said giving her an enthusiastic embrace.

"She looks different for certain," granny agreed. "It must be that new husband of hers."

Rasheen laughed. "Do I really look radiant?"

"Child, you are glowing like a firefly," Granny said. "Hmmm, perhaps it might be more than just that new husband. Is there anything you would like to share with us?"

"Such as?" Rasheen made an attempt to give the look she used when one of her students needed settling down.

Granny was not one of her students. "Am I going to be a great granny?"

Rasheen took a deep breath in a futile attempt to keep from blushing and pull off the half lie she was about to tell. "You know very well, that is impossible." First Martha, and now granny. Did she really look that different?

Granny's pale blue eyes studied her for a long moment before saying, "All in good time."

Mercifully, her mother came to the rescue. " I am happy for you, Rasheen. I think you and Connor will have a good life together."

Rasheen breathed a sigh of relief. Apparently there was to be no scolding about the elopement.

"A good looking man like that couldn't help but make her happy." A faint light twinkled in the depths of Granny's eyes. "Would you care to tell us about it?"

"You are impossible." Rasheen kissed her grandmother's cheek. "You should be ashamed of yourself to be hinting at such things."

Granny smiled sheepishly. "Connor 'tis a fine looking, strong young man now. What's the harm in sharing the details? We would keep them amongst ourselves."

Rasheen's mother waved her hand. "Enough! Stop teasing her."

Granny gave a wounded sigh, but the only response she got from the other two women was laughter.

"I almost forgot to tell you that Connor's Aunt Elaine sends her love. She would have come with me, but she had a luncheon scheduled, and she thought I might want to spend time with my family alone at first."

"Nonsense, she is family too now," Granny said.

"That's exactly what I told her," Rasheen said, and then told them about her visit to the cemetery. "The last time I was in a park alone, I picked up Finn and now I'm picking up butterflies. At least I didn't bring this one home." She squeezed her mother's hand.

"A butterfly would be easier to manage than that beast," her mother huffed.

Granny let out a loud breath. "Sweet Blessed Mother

Mary!"

"Oh, Granny, I thought you liked Finn."

"Tis not from Finn for which I am asking protection. Legend has it that the soul of the departed leaves in the form of a white butterfly."

"Well, I hope that Daniel's soul hasn't been earthbound all this time, but I did feel a sense of peace that I had never felt when Daniel and I were married, so perhaps there may be a grain of truth in your legend."

During lunch, Rasheen listened to all the news of the family since she had been away. They also discussed city events and the plight of Frank's parishioners. The railroad's Board of Directors had recently raised the investor's dividends by 10% and then cut the employee's salaries by 10% for anyone who made over a dollar per day. It was the second salary cut in less than a year.

"Things have gotten much worse," Rasheen said. "Connor is concerned there may be trouble."

"Men can no longer afford to buy bread to feed their families," Granny said.

"Perhaps Connor can work something out for the workers with the company. He has been successful in negotiating terms in the past. I doubt the company wants a strike. For all we know, he might be speaking with the railroad officials this very moment. He and Uncle Patrick were to spend the day in the city attending to business affairs."

Granny heaved a weary sigh. "For the sake of a great many families, I hope your husband can work a miracle."

"There is naught can be done about it now." Rasheen's mother rose from her seat and took her daughter's hand. "You look tired, dear. Get home and have a rest before dinner. We will have plenty of time for a longer visit then."

Holding her mother's hand, Rasheen rose from her chair. "I am a little weary."

"Well then, off with you." Her mother rang for

Mary.   Rasheen stood at the hall mirror and smoothed her bonnet's ribbons before securing it with a large pin, smiling to herself as she did so. That had gone much easier than she thought. Now she would have enough time to visit Peter and get back to Patrick and Elaine's without arising any suspicion.

"Make sure you get that rest before this evening." Her mother hugged her and then stepped back and gave her a maternal gaze.

Rasheen had a feeling both Granny and her mother knew her secret, but she wasn't ready to share it. "Don't worry about me, mother, I will be fine, but I promise to rest if it will make you feel better." *Just as soon as Peter verifies my secret.*

CHAPTER 25

"Congratulations. I would say you and Connor are going to be parents in early spring from the information you gave me." Peter sat on the other side of a scarred walnut desk, a wide smile on his face. "I'm glad you came to me. I don't get to give happy news often."

Rasheen sat mutely, not knowing what to say. It was no longer a secret. Someone else knew and that made it all the more real. Fear and joy filled her heart.

Peter's smile faded. "You do want this child?"

"I very much want this baby, but I'm not sure how Connor is going to feel about it." Her voice cracked as she told Peter what Connor had said on their wedding day about not wanting babies.

"You must have misunderstood him. He has always wanted children, lots of them. That was one of the reasons for the broken engagement with Amelia."

"He told me the reason he broke it off with her was that she would not be happy living at Sara's Glen. Why did he lie to me?" She felt the tears stinging her eyes as she tried to blink them back.

Peter came around and sat on the edge of the desk taking her hands in his. "It was not a lie. I happened to be at Sara's Glen when the final blow up came. It is the only time I have seen Connor drink to excess. His inebriated state is the reason I know the truth."

Rasheen shook her head. "I thought he was the most honest man I'd ever met until now."

Peter squeezed her hands. "The only reason he hasn't told you the truth is that he wanted to spare your feelings because he loves you. I have never seen him as happy as he is when he's with you."

"Why did he lie about the reason for the break up then?"

"I told you. He doesn't tell anyone the whole story where Amelia is concerned. He's too much of a gentleman for that."

"Well what is the whole story?"

Peter studied her for a long moment as if trying to decide if he would answer her question before finally speaking. "Connor had been in the city visiting Amelia, and they got into a discussion about their future. He made mention of the fact that he wanted children, and she told him that she didn't want them, but she understood his desire for an heir so if the first born was a male, she would be finished with childbearing. If it were a female, then she would have one more and no more. I cannot believe this, but he agreed to that and he even agreed to spend more time in the city than at Sara's Glen. She would have had him, had it not been for the next demand she made. She wanted a nanny to raise the children so as not to have them interfere with their lives. They would be traveling and entertaining; children would not fit into their lifestyle as she saw it. Any children they had would be left home for months at a time while they traveled abroad as is fashionable for members of her class. His children would grow up without any emotional connection to him."

"There wasn't even the remotest possibility that she would spend any time at Sara's Glen. If he wanted to come here with his horses for a few weeks each year, that would be fine, but they would live in the city. These were the things that opened his eyes to her true nature. He broke it off, came home to Sara's Glen, and shut himself in the library for several hours, until mother became quite upset and had me go in after him. I have never seen him like that before and hope never to again. It was then that he told me the story. I got him up to bed and the next morning, we both agreed that what he had told me would stay between us. The only reason I am sharing this with you now is to ease your mind, as I am sure he would want me to do under the circumstances."

Rasheen felt hope wedge its way into heart. She jumped up and hugged Peter. "You have just set my world aright."

"Enjoy it, because things will be different in a few months." The wide grin was back on Peter's face. "Go home and get some rest. I'm glad I'll be there this evening to share the occasion. Now maybe the elders will leave me alone since they are getting their wish for babies in the family."

Rasheen tilted her head to the side and studied him for a minute. Contrary to his words, he looked just a bit envious to her. "Peter, why don't you consider marriage? I know someone who would be…"

Peter got up from his chair and took her arm. "Now don't you start," he said as he walked her to the door of his office. Just as he opened the door to the corridor, they heard a loud clanging noise coming from outside the building.

"Something serious must be going on." He heaved a weary sigh. "Looks like I might not make dinner this evening."

When they stepped into the hospital corridor, the injured were already coming in. A policeman stopped Peter and explained that there was a riot in the city.

"Ma'am, I hope you weren't planning on going anywhere," the officer said as he noticed Rasheen standing next to Peter.

"I have a hack outside and am just going home. It's not that far."

The officer gestured toward the door. "If that was your hack out front, he had to move down to the end of the next block."

Peter looked up from the man on the stretcher whose head wound he had been checking. "You better stay here. Send word with your driver that you're with me so they know you're safe."

The officer shook his head in agreement. "I'll take your message to the driver for you so you don't have to leave the building."

Rasheen went back to Peter's office and scribbled a quick note to Elaine and Patrick, but when she came out the policeman was on the opposite corner helping bring in the injured. Not wanting to disturb him, she decided to walk down the block to where her hack had moved by herself, rationalizing that no one would bother her since everyone in the crowd outside the Dispensary was either injured themselves or carrying in the injured.

*****

Rasheen gave the driver her message, paid him and turned to head back to the hospital. An angry crowd was forming on the opposite corner of the hospital, and several policemen were trying to move them further down the block. She had only taken a few steps when she saw a figure coming away from the crowd toward her. As the distance between them shortened to about ten feet, she saw the dark round spectacles worn by the blind. His slouch hat was pulled low over his forehead until it touched the glasses; an unkempt beard covered his cheeks and chin. He carried a tin cup in one hand and a stick in the other, but he didn't seem to be using the stick to feel his way along the walkway.

A cold shiver ran up the back of her spine and she turned to stop the hack, but it was already down the street and about to turn the corner. The driver would never hear her if she tried to call him back. Besides, she reasoned, the man ahead was probably just trying to get away from the mob and not thinking to use his stick. Nonetheless, she edged toward the street trying to put more horizontal space between them as he grew closer. But when she moved, he moved in the same direction until he was by her side when it came time for them to pass. Recognition glimmered and shot through the back of her brain, refusing to come forward.

"Well, well, well, look who it is." He had stopped and now blocked her way.

Terror struck as his voice brought forth the elusive recognition. "Let me pass, or I'll call one of the officers." Rasheen tried to keep her voice from shaking as she addressed Ronald Chilcrit.

There was a large city block between her and safety. Even if she yelled no one would hear her in all the commotion. Her only hope was to try and run and get as close to the crowd as possible.

She started to bolt, but he grabbed her arm and spun her in the opposite direction. Before she could react further, she felt pressure in her side. When she looked down, she saw a large knife pressed against her.

"You and me is gonna take a nice walk. I want to show you where I have to live now, thanks to you and yer 'usband." Chilcrit was pushing her in the opposite direction of safety. "I lost my job with Hilliard, thanks to you."

Rasheen tried to speak calmly. "What are you talking about?"

The knife pushed harder. "Wid'out my helper, I couldn't keep up and Hilliard fired me." The knife pushed harder. "Been here in the city earning my way as a beggar. I suppose I should thank you. I makes more money than I ever did working for that penny pincher Hilliard, but I don't like begging. I swore I would come back and get even with you and that bastard yer married to, but you made it right easy by comin to me."

How could he have known they were coming to the city? They didn't even know themselves until the night before they left. She wanted to ask him, but the knife reminded her of the danger of provoking him.

As if reading her thoughts, he continued, "I was at the train station when you arrived. It was easy to find out where Reilly lived. I went there and waited for my chance."

"You were the blind man the policeman chased," she said remembering her conversation with Aunt Elaine.

He turned his head and spat on the curb. "Stupid copper did me a favor. I ordered a hack around the corner and sat in it to watch. You made the rest easy, except for following you all over town waiting for my chance. Now yer gonna pay for what you cost me."

She chocked back the reply she wanted to make and tried to make her tone meek. "Perhaps I could reason with Mr. Hilliard and get him to take you back."

"Too late for that now."

She saw a police wagon sitting down the block and hoped that meant the officers were nearby. But Chilcrit quickly pulled her into a nearby alley away from the street. She thought about trying to run, but couldn't risk it with the knife pressing so close. There was more at stake than just her life now. "Where are you taking me?" she asked.

He jerked her arm. "I told you. We're goin to my new home. Yer gonna come down a long way and not be so high and mighty. You need to be taught a lesson." His face was so close his glasses bumped against her cheek bone. She could smell the whiskey on his breath, the foul odor of his unwashed body and clothes, and desperately wanted to turn away, but she knew that would only provoke him so she unsuccessfully tried to will the wave of nausea that crashed inside her stomach. "I am going to be sick," she said just before she turned her head to the side and vomited, catching the edge of his tattered coat with the contents of her stomach as they spewed forth on the sidewalk.

*****

"Must be a bad fire," Connor mused to himself as he

gave his hat and coat to the Reilly butler, and closed the door on the shrill noise outside. All had been quiet at the warehouses, but there were more than the usual loiterers hanging about.

Another piercing sound much louder than the fire bells shook the house. "Good heavens, what is that?" Elaine's eyes grew wide as she lifted her cheek for her husband's kiss.

"Big Sam, the new alarm system the city installed last month. It's only to be used in a case of great emergency." Connor and his uncle exchanged uneasy looks. The news they had received at the warehouse earlier had not been good. All the freight trains leaving Martinsburg had been stopped by striking workers at Cumberland, and the crews taken from them. Governor Carroll had called out the state militia in response. Connor doubted that Baltimore would escape the mayhem which had begun its journey down the tracks. Though the heat and humidity of the last week had finally broken, the air was thick with tension. The men he had seen standing about earlier in the day were like fuses just waiting for a spark to set them off.

His hopes were dashed further when he heard a horse and cab pull up in front of the house, and pulled the window drape aside to look out. The driver jumped down and bounded up the stairs. Connor didn't wait for the butler to announce the caller, but followed close on his heels as he opened the door. Before the butler could speak to the visitor, the man looked at Connor and asked, "Are you Mr. Reilly?"

"Patrick or Connor?"

The man thrust a folded piece of paper at him. "This here's a message for Connor Reilly from Father Hughes."

Every muscle and nerve in his body tightened as he read the message. "Did Father Hughes already leave the rectory?"

"Yes, Sir. He said I was to take you directly to Camden Station."

Connor looked out the window at the waiting cab. "You go on out, I'll be along in a minute."

"I am afraid the strike has reached Baltimore. Frank wants me to meet him at Camden to see if we can prevent a riot, or at the very least, keep his parishioners out of it," he said to Patrick and Elaine, both of whom were standing in the doorway with worried expressions.

"I'll go along with you. I want to make sure the warehouses are secure," Patrick said.

Connor shook his head. "I'll see to them. It won't be out of the way. I hope Rasheen has the good sense to stay with her family, but she may have already left before this started. At any rate, I would feel better knowing you were here with Aunt Elaine and her in case things change."

****

Militia marching down Front Street blocked the carriage from reaching the warehouses. Connor opened the window and yelled, "Go around the block and take the next street." He would have to see to the warehouses later if he hoped to get to Camden before the militia. As they rode down the street, he could hear the mob's angry shouts just one street over. It sounded as if the crowd was in front of the militia. He rapped on the roof of the carriage for the driver to stop. "Stay here, I'm going to cut through the alley and see what is happening," he shouted as he jumped out of the vehicle.

He halted about a third of the way into the alley. Refuse and human waste were piled on the sides spilling over into the center making passage without wading through it nearly impossible. The stench was nauseating. Several rats scurried back and forth having their evening meal. One large one paused for a moment and stared at him with its beady red eyes, taking a stance as if ready to attack.

"Steady there vermin, I have no wish to do battle with you." He couldn't see anything at the other end of the alley opening onto Front Street, but could hear the commotion. The crowd must be further up the street. That would give him time to get to Camden Station before them. He ran back to the carriage and ordered the driver to move at breakneck speed.

When they arrived at the station, there was already a sizable mob there. The police were making an unsuccessful attempt to block the entrance from the shouting mob. One of the officers directed him to Frank, who was addressing the crowd from the top of a rail car. Connor climbed up onto the car next to him.

"You will accomplish nothing, here. Go home to your families," Frank shouted down to the crowd.

"Yer a priest, what do ye know of hard work?" Someone shouted back.

"Look, it be the lawyer, who sez he is going to help us." Connor recognized that voice. McPhail's brother-in-law, Liam Kenney, was inciting the mob.

"I have done well by your brother-in-law, have I not?" Connor yelled above the racket.

"Yeah, and how does that help the rest of us?"

"If you damage railroad property, no one will be able to help you. You will be arrested. Is that what you want?"

"We want to be treated like men and not beasts of burden," shouted someone in the crowd. "They cut our wages and gave themselves a raise; them in their fine houses and us not even able to feed our families. We only want what's fair."

"Listen to 'em. 'E's right. Make 'em pay," Liam Kenney screamed.

"I want every one of you to go home now." Frank commanded.

"Priest, ye got no authority here," someone retorted from the horde that was growing bigger as the businesses and factories shut down for the day. "Get back to yer church where ye belong."

"Listen to me, you will not only lose your jobs over this, but you could be hurt or maybe even worse. Think of your wives and children. You have every right to be angry over the way things have been handled, but this is not the way to settle it. Mr. Reilly is working to have the wage cut reversed, but you must let him work within the frame of the law."

Big Sam blared again drowning out any other sound and they quieted down some, but stood firm.

"If you do not go home now, I will see that you are excommunicated from the church." From the tone in his voice, Frank might as well have had the bishop's miter atop his head along with the staff in his hand.

Connor jerked his head away from the crowd. "You have no authority to do that." No one other than Frank could hear him above the noise.

At the last threat, several of the men in the crowd turned and walked away.

"They believed your bluff." Connor shook his head incredulously.

"It's not the excommunication they fear, but the wife's wrath when it comes time for her to go to Sunday mass alone," Frank said as more men began to follow those turning away.

Connor felt a little calmer as the mob thinned. Perhaps they might just get through the evening with no violence. Those hopes were dashed when he heard the noise of the militia and rioters from Front Street arriving. The remaining men in the yard joined forces with the Front Street crowd and bedlam broke out.

Kenney grabbed a kerosene barrel and rolled it toward a nearby wooden freight car that sat waiting for repairs. The barrel burst open upon contact with the car spilling its liquid contents against the car and the surrounding area.

Connor jumped down from the car where he had been standing and ran after Kenny who was trying to light a match. "Ejit," he yelled. "Think of the damage you'll cause."

"Look at the damage they did to me," Kenney cried as

he held up his two-fingered right hand. "Did they care when I lost me fingers trying to couple their cars? Would they care if I fell and broke all me bones? No, they would find another poor bastard to replace me and pay 'em even less."

Connor knocked the matches out of Kenny's hand before he could light them. The two men traded blows back and forth. Connor dodged Kenney's latest jab and hit him on the side of the face producing a crunching sound. He wasn't sure if it was Kenney's jaw or his own fisted fingers breaking. The man had a face like a stone wall.

Bricks, rocks, and debris thrown by the mob were flying all around them. Connor moved his head out of reach of the other man's fist, and was about to throw another punch when Kenny's right fist collided with his jaw. The giant blurred in front of him as he struggled to stay on his feet before falling face first into the dirt. When he lifted his head, he saw Kenney struggling with the matches trying to light them with the fingers of his uninjured hand while holding the box in his mangled fist.

A spark caught and the flame ran down the line of spilled liquid, up to the car engulfing it in flames. Kenney cried out in agony as flames caught his kerosene soaked cuffs and then shot up his trousers. Connor struggled to make his way toward the burning man shouting, "Drop and roll, for the love of Christ, man."

Kenny seemed not to hear and in his confusion ran into the glowing car disappearing in a wall of flames. Then there was no sound save that of the crackling wood as the fire devoured it.

*****

Chilcrit took the vomit soaked end of his coat and rubbed it in Rasheen's face. "Yer gonna pay for that too. By the time I finish wid you, you 'es gonna be screamin nice and loud."

Rasheen's heart pounded as fearful images swept

through her mind. Somehow she had to escape, but how? They were out of the alley now and on a back street she didn't recognize. They turned down another alley and came out on a side street across from the railroad yard. She could see the tracks ahead. Some were empty, but several had lines of cars with no engines.

Further up ahead she saw the crowd and heard the shouting. There was bedlam everywhere. If he took her through the crowd, she could get help. Those hopes were dashed when he suddenly turned to the right toward one of the tracks with the wooden cars.

The only people nearby were two men fighting near the cars. She reasoned that if he got close enough to the fight, perhaps she could create some kind of distraction to get him to move the knife away long enough for her to escape.

As they approached, one of the men in the fight broke off from the other and set a car on fire. Chilcrit let out an oath and drug her toward the burning car which apparently had been his home from his reaction. In his attempt to run and drag her, he loosened the pressure of the knife. She seized the opportunity to escape by turning and hitting him with her fist, pushing up as hard as she could under his nose - a trick she had learned from one of her older male cousins during a childhood visit to her uncle's farm. Then she lifted her skirts and took off in the direction of the man standing near the burning car, praying he would come to her aide.

Shock overtook her when she got close enough to recognize Connor.

*****

Connor turned his head and stumbled a safe distance away; his insides convulsed at the unfamiliar scent of burning flesh. Sweet putrid, streaky air punished his nostrils. He bent over taking deep breathes for the smell was so thick he could almost taste it. When he straightened, Rasheen was running toward him. "What in the hell…"

In the next second the air flooded out of his lungs when he saw Ronald Chilcrit waving a knife, close on her heels. She was close enough that he could have pulled her to safety when Chilcrit grabbed her by the hair, placed her in a chokehold and began to pull her toward the burning car shouting, "She's gonna burn. Yer gonna see what it's like to have something taken away from you."

Rasheen kicked back hard and hit her captor in the shin. He cursed as he released his hold to retrieve the knife which had fallen from his hand when he attempted to regain his balance. She ran toward Connor and reached him just ahead of Chilcrit.

Connor caught her arm and swung her behind him. Chilcrit's face twisted into an expression that left no doubt of his intention. He let out a primal scream, lifted the knife and lunged.

Connor pushed Rasheen to the ground, and knocked his opponent to the ground, but Chilcrit's knife was lodged in his left shoulder. Chilcrit was beneath him trying to reach for the knife. He tried to grab his opponent's arm, and felt the pain shoot through his shoulder. Chilcrit managed to roll them over so that he was on top and once more reached for the knife. That was the last thing Connor remembered before the gunshot followed by blinding pain, dizziness, and darkness.

CHAPTER 26

It was so hot. Had he gone to hell when he died? It couldn't be hell, there were no flames and someone was putting something cold on his head. He drifted off again before finally coming to in a haze. Peter stood over him doing something, but he couldn't tell what. Maybe Peter was praying for him. No, Frank was there doing that. The room was long and white and there were moaning sounds. Then it all disappeared in the fog that swirled around him faster and faster until he was sucked into its vortex, losing consciousness once more. When he finally emerged from the blackness, the whirling mist was gone and Rasheen was sitting next to him. He blinked a few times to make sure he was awake.

"Connor," she whispered.

The lips kissing his hand were warm and he wanted to pull her close and never let her go. He made an effort to sit up and do just that, only to feel the pain in his shoulder.

"Keep your head down. You received a nasty blow even for that hard noggin of yours." Peter came through the doorway and walked over to the bed. "I told her that there was no way I would let you leave us."

The sharp pain in Connor's shoulder at the sudden movement had distracted him from the pounding that he now felt in his head. He closed his eyes tightly for a moment and then asked, "Never mind my head, what's wrong with my shoulder?"

"Chilcrit planted a knife in it."

"I remember fighting with Kenney and then seeing Rasheen running toward me. Chilcrit was chasing her. I tried to protect her from him, but then there was a shot. Then I woke up here and thought I was dead.

Peter came next to the bed and put a thermometer in Connor's mouth.

"I …" Connor tried to talk around the glass stick in his mouth.

"Be quiet for a minute, please." Peter's tone was professional. After what seemed forever, he removed the irritating object. "There's no fever."

Connor gave an impatient outburst. "Why would there be a fever? I am not sick."

"You are not stupid either. You have heard me speak of infections caused by wounds enough times to make you aware of the danger. Now answer a few questions for me so I can assess your head injury."

"It hurts like hell."

Peter held up one finger. "How many?"

"One."

Peter held up three fingers.

"Now?

"Three."

"Do you know where you are?"

"In my room at my uncle's house."

"Do you remember coming to the hospital?"

"I came to and saw a long white room and heard moaning, but then passed out again. That must have been the hospital, but how did I get here?"

"They brought you to the hospital, and once I had your knife wound treated, we moved you here because we needed your hospital bed. Besides, you'll heal faster here and it will be easier on Rasheen."

Connor shuddered as his memory returned to the previous day. "Kenney burned to death. I tried to stop him from setting the car on fire. Pity his poor family."

Peter shook his head. "He has no family here except for his sister. As tragic as his death may be, it will lighten her burden from what I have heard of the man."

Connor tried to focus on Peter when he spoke, but his headache was such that he wasn't able to keep his eyes trained on Peter's face. He concentrated on looking up at the ceiling's wide expanse instead. "Perhaps, but don't you wonder what made him the way he was? His sister and her husband are good people."

Rasheen soaked a cloth in a bowl of lavender water that was sitting on the marble topped washstand, wrung it out and placed it gently on Connor's head.

Connor knitted his brows together as he attempted to revisit the past events. "What happened to Chilcrit?"

Out of the corner of his eye he caught Rasheen give Peter a look of inquiry. There was some kind of unspoken communication between them. Whatever had transpired had not pleased his wife. She gave a slight nod to Peter before answering, "Chilcrit was going to throw me into the burning car. I managed to escape him and run to you. You threw yourself at him. That's how you got the knife wound. Fortunately, one of the Guardsmen saw what was happening and shot him before he could do further damage."

"I thought I was the one shot." Connor made an effort to try and raise his voice above a whisper. Each word he spoke hammered his temples.

"Is Chilcrit dead?"

"Yes."

"But what was he doing in the city with that crowd? And why were you there?"

"Apparently, he had been living in the city since leaving Hilliard's. He blamed that on you along with Jack's loss," Peter said.

Connor shut his eyes tightly in a vain effort to relieve his pain and then opened them to try and focus on the faces around him once more. "And he thought he would get to me through Rasheen?"

"To his twisted mind it was justice."

Connor's eyes turned to Rasheen. "But how did he get you?"

Peter jumped in once more before Rasheen could speak. "He abducted her when she was returning to the hack she had hired to visit her family."

They weren't being truthful with him. Peter may have learned to wear a professional mask, but Rasheen could never hide her emotions. Something was bothering her. Maybe a change of subject would throw them off guard and he could revisit the topic later. "How long before I'm free of this cannon resting on my head?"

"It will take a few days, or longer. You were hit with something fairly large, perhaps a brick. That, added to the pummeling you took, didn't help matters. We are lucky your skull wasn't split wide open. Always did say you were thick headed. I want to keep a close eye on the shoulder wound. You are to stay here until the stitches come out so I can see that it doesn't become infected."

"And how long might that be?"

"As long as it takes."

Connor made a vain attempt to rise up on his good arm, only to fall back and feel the pain crash through his head and shoulder. Through gritted teeth he replied, "I cannot be lying about here. I need to get back to Sara's Glen."

"My father can take care of things until you have recovered. If that shoulder becomes septic, you could lose your arm." Peter measured out a potion. "Now take this and get some rest. It will help your headache."

Connor saw Rasheen give Peter a questioning look as he swallowed the liquid in the glass Peter handed him. "There is something you are not telling me. What is it?"

"Nothing that cannot wait until you get some rest." Peter turned to leave and motioned Rasheen to come with him.

Connor felt himself getting drowsy. "She can rest with me." The words were already getting difficult to form.

"Not until that arm heals." Peter ushered a reluctant Rasheen out the door.

The last thing Connor heard was her muffled voice on the other side of the door saying, "Why did you not want me to tell him?"

"Tell me what?" He croaked, before sleep blanketed the words.

*****

Connor awoke to see Frank sitting by his bed. "Where is my wife?"

"I sent her downstairs for a bit to get something to eat. She has not left your side since we brought you home." The same concern shone in Frank's eyes that had been in Rasheen's.

Striving for some levity, Connor said, "Well, at least you are not ready to say the prayers for the dead, so guess I'm in no danger." He forced himself into a sitting position. Frank grabbed the pillows and arranged them in a manner to support him. "What happened with your parishioners at Camden?" Connor winced as the pain shot through his shoulder from the movement.

"Do you remember that most of the local railroad men left when I threatened them with excommunication?"

Connor smiled as the memory came back. "I do remember that, yes."

"I think we saved their jobs and possibly their lives. It got really ugly. There were a lot of drunken men about in addition to the railroad workers; most of them unemployed factory workers feeding on the frenzy. They destroyed railroad cars, tore up track, and tried to break into the buildings. It took over 500 federal troops to restore peace."

"How many deaths and injuries were there?"

Frank shook his head. "I don't know how many injuries there were, but there were fourteen deaths at the last count. Most of them took place around Front Street when the Sixth Regiment was trying to get to the station."

"I heard the shots when I tried to cut through an alley to get to Front Street."

"It was better that you didn't get through. From the account I was given, the Militia marched through a hail storm of bricks, but still managed to keep calm. They might have made it to the station without incident, had it not been for some ejit from the crowd firing a shot that hit one of their comrades. The Guardsmen returned fire into the mob and that's when the riot broke out. Under the circumstances, the Guardsmen aren't to be blamed. It's lamentable that some of those killed were innocent bystanders."

Connor laid his head back on the pillow. "I understand the desperation of the men, but this is only going to hurt their case in the public's opinion."

Frank rubbed his hand across his brow thoughtfully. "When you recover, perhaps you can speak to the railroad management to see if the two sides can reach some sort of compromise."

"As soon as I can leave this bed, I will meet with the railroad president's son and see what the two of us can do. He seems to be more open minded than his father and the other older members of the Board. Perhaps Kiernan McPhail could speak for the workers. If we can get the company management to listen to his ideas, I think it would be of benefit to all parties."

Frank looked surprised. "It sounds as if you have given this considerable thought."

"Unfortunately, I was not able to act soon enough."

"It's going to take time, but at least it will be a start. Now, I'm going to leave you to get some rest before my niece chastises me. She has that terrible temper, don't you know?" Frank gave a mock shudder.

"Speaking of Rasheen, she seems to have something worrying her."

"She was concerned about you and seems a bit subdued, but that's understandable," Frank tried to assure him.

"There's something she's not sharing with me." Connor repositioned himself on the pillows. "She seems quieter. I thought she may have confided in you."

"She has been under a lot of strain these last few days worrying about you. It did not look like she was any less affectionate in her actions towards you just a few moments ago."

Connor knew Frank would not break a confidence. Rather, he would tell him to speak to his wife. "Perhaps you are right. Maybe my injury's making me see things that do not exist." Connor tried to feel reassured, but a nagging feeling tugged at his gut.

*****

After Frank had gone, Connor brooded until he had himself good and angry. He flung off the sheet that covered him and sat up, shoulder burning, head throbbing, and dizziness making the room sway. He waited a few seconds and then swung his feet over the edge of the bed, stood, and almost fell before steadying himself. Once he had accomplished that task, he felt for the bedside table and followed it, using it for support until he came to the windowsill. Luckily for him, his bed was near the window where a big overstuffed chair sat. He painfully dropped his body down into the chair and looked out the window to the small garden in the back of the house. Rasheen and his Aunt sat on the ornate iron bench beneath the great elm tree. They were joined by Frank for a few minutes and then Rasheen stood and walked toward the house. Most likely she would be joining him in a few minutes with his dinner. As hungry as he was, there would be no dinner until he got some answers.

Just as he predicted, she appeared with a tray which

she sat on the table. Surprise and displeasure shown in her eyes. "Peter does not want you out of bed yet."

"That is his problem. I am not a damn invalid and will not be treated as such."

She gave him an exaggerated smile. "I am happy you are feeling better darling, but please have a care for Peter's orders."

"Peter's orders can go to hell. I want to know why you were at Camden Station with Chilcrit. I am not convinced that Peter told the entire truth. Why did you have a need to visit your family when we were going to have dinner with them that very evening?"

Rasheen rubbed her forehead with her fingertips, hiding her eyes from him. Finally she knelt in front of him and took his hands in hers. It was then he could see the uncertainty in those dark pools pleading with him for something, but what?

"I did visit my family, but that was an excuse to get out of the house alone so I could visit Peter at the hospital."

Now it was beginning to make sense to him, but he was suddenly hit with a fear so cold, it felt as if a shard of ice were stuck in his heart. "What about...?"

Before he could finish the question, she put her finger to his lips. "I went to see Peter to have him confirm my pregnancy."

"Are you pregnant?" There was a note of anxiety in his voice. What if she weren't pregnant? What if it was something else; something that took life instead of giving it?

She gave him a puzzled look, and then looked away. When she turned toward him again, tears wet her eye lashes. "Peter told me you would be happy about the baby."

Now it was his turn to be puzzled. "Why would I not be?"

"Your inquiry is not that of a happy father to be."

"You and Peter were so secretive; I thought maybe something had gone wrong." He raised her hands kissing them before pulling her up onto his lap; ignoring the pain such an action cost him.

"Connor, watch out for your stitches," she protested as he lifted her arm and placed it around his neck.

Placing his good arm about her waist drawing her closer, he said, "I was wondering when you were going to get around to sharing the news with me."

She let out a long breath. "Then you are happy?"

"I am over the moon. How could you think otherwise?"

She proceeded to remind him of his remarks on their wedding day about babies being an inconvenience that distracted a woman's affections, distancing her from her husband.

Resting his hand on her abdomen, he said, "I had to find some way to reassure you that there were so many reasons I was marrying you and if we could not have children, we would be grateful for all the other good things in our lives. That was the only thing I could think of at the time. Would you have believed me, if I had told you how desperately I need you in my life? My body craves the physical intimacies we share as much as it does food or water or even the very air I breathe. You share my hopes and dreams for Sara's Glen and listen to my ideas about railroad reform for the workers. You make me laugh, and though I enjoy a good argument with you, the thought of making love to reconcile afterwards is downright blissful. I find happiness watching the joy on your face when you describe a good day with your students or when you reach a child that has been having difficulty learning. You are beautiful, intelligent, and generous in spirit, more than I could have ever hoped for in a wife or lover. Can you believe that now?"

She looked up at him smiling. "When did you know I was pregnant?"

"I should have realized it sooner, but I was so busy enjoying making love to you every night, it didn't occur to me until the day we had the argument and I stormed out of the house. Do you remember?"

She gently kissed his cheek. "I was miserable."

"I walked to the stream and it wasn't until James and Sara Bartlett and their baby appeared to me, that I realized you were pregnant."

"You saw James too?" she asked.

"I have seen him from time to time, but that was the first time the entire family has appeared. I reasoned that they were sending me a message and that's when I started to figure it out." He snapped his head to one side in a sudden motion of recognition, wrinkling his brow, and wincing at the pain shooting through his head from the sudden movement. "When did you see them?"

"I only saw James. He led me to safety during the storm when Ronald Chilcrit was chasing me last spring." She gently stroked his hand, the hand that now rested over their unborn child. "I suppose most people would not like having a resident ghost family, but I rather like the idea."

He laughed. "Here we are discussing our unborn child and you want to know the details of our ghostly protector's visits."

"Obviously, that ghost has something to do with it," she said.

"Love, I managed that on my own. Would you like me to remind you how this baby was conceived? "He began to unfasten the buttons in the back of her dress.

She playfully slapped his hand away. "You will have to restrain yourself until that shoulder is healed."

"Ah, but will you be able to wait that long?" He teased.

"I will just have to manage the sacrifice," she sighed.

Playing with the buttons, he said, "Are you sure?"

"Do not make this more difficult. I promise to make it up to you."

Before he could torment her further she asked, "Why

did you not confront me about the pregnancy the day you found out?"

"Given the circumstances of our marriage, I was afraid you might see it as another entrapment."

"And I thought the same about you. What a fine pair we are." She looked up at him and saw her own joy reflected in his eyes. "Uncle Frank once told me that eventually someone would come into my life to help me get beyond everything bad that came before – someone who would show me the rainbows created in my soul by all the tears shed in unhappiness."

ABOUT THE AUTHOR

Alice and her husband, Drew, live in Harford County, Maryland. She worked for several decades as an administrative assistant for various professionals including lawyers, engineers, educators and even the clergy. In between jobs, she received her AA degree with honors from Essex Community College where she took every writing class offered. She is a member of the Romance Writers of America.

When not writing, she enjoys reading historicals and biographies. She enjoys reading anything from the colonial period to the Gilded Age. Her other favorite pastime is baking, especially cookies.

She and her husband have traveled all over the United States, and parts of Canada and Ireland. Favorite places these days are Colonial Williamsburg, Seneca Lake in upstate New York, and Cape May, NJ.

Alice can be contacted at alicebonthron@gmail.com.

Made in the USA
Columbia, SC
02 April 2018